18

"'I DON'T THINK THAT LOOKS VERY MUCH LIKE IT'" [p. 18.

THE LANDLORD AT LION'S HEAD

BY

WILLIAM DEAN HOWELLS

ILLUSTRATED BY
W. T. SMEDLEY

DOVER PUBLICATIONS, INC.
NEW YORK

Published in Canada by General Publishing Company, Ltd., 30 Lesmill Road, Don Mills, Toronto, Ontario.

Published in the United Kingdom by Constable and Company, Ltd., 10 Orange Street, London WC2H 7EG.

This Dover edition, first published in 1983, is an unabridged republication of the work as first published in book form in America by Harper & Brothers, New York, 1897. *The Landlord at Lion's Head* was originally published serially in *Harper's Weekly* (July–December 1896).

Manufactured in the United States of America
Dover Publications, Inc., 180 Varick Street, New York, N.Y. 10014

Library of Congress Cataloging in Publication Data

Howells, William Dean, 1837–1920.
    The landlord at Lion's Head.

    I. Title.
PS2025.L3 1983   813'.4   82-17821
ISBN 0-486-24455-5

ILLUSTRATIONS

THE LANDLORD AT LION'S HEAD.

I.

IF you looked at the mountain from the west, the line of the summit was wandering and uncertain, like that of most mountain-tops; but seen from the east, the mass of granite showing above the dense forests of the lower slopes had the form of a sleeping lion. The flanks and haunches were vaguely distinguished from the mass; but the mighty head, resting with its tossed mane upon the vast paws stretched before it, was boldly sculptured against the sky. The likeness could not have been more perfect, when you had it in profile, if it had been a definite intention of art; and you could travel far north and far south before the illusion vanished. In winter the head was blotted by the snows; and sometimes the vagrant clouds caught upon it and deformed it, or hid it, at other seasons; but commonly, after the last snow went in the spring until the first snow came in the fall, the Lion's Head was a part of the landscape, as imperative and importunate as the Great Stone Face itself.

Long after other parts of the hill country were
opened to summer sojourn, the region of Lion's Head
remained almost primitively solitary and savage. A
stony mountain road followed the bed of the torrent
that brawled through the valley at its base, and at a
certain point a still rougher lane climbed from the
road along the side of the opposite height to a lonely
farm-house pushed back on a narrow shelf of land,
with a meagre acreage of field and pasture broken out
of the woods that clothed all the neighboring steeps.
The farm-house level commanded the best view of
Lion's Head, and the visitors always mounted to it,
whether they came on foot, or arrived on buckboards
or in buggies, or drove up in the Concord stages from
the farther and nearer hotels. The drivers of the
coaches rested their horses there, and watered them
from the spring that dripped into the green log at the
barn ; the passengers scattered about the door-yard to
look at the Lion's Head, to wonder at it and mock at
it, according to their several makes and moods. They
could scarcely have felt that they ever had a welcome
from the stalwart, handsome woman who sold them
milk, if they wanted it, and small cakes of maple sugar
if they were very strenuous for something else. The
ladies were not able to make much of her, from the
first ; but some of them asked her if it were not rather
lonely there, and she said that when you heard the cat-
amounts scream at night, and the bears growl in the
spring, it did seem lonesome. When one of them declared that if she should hear a catamount scream, or a
bear growl, she should die, the woman answered, Well,

she presumed we must all die some time. But the ladies were not sure of a covert slant in her words, for they were spoken with the same look she wore when she told them that the milk was five cents a glass, and the black maple sugar three cents a cake. She did not change when she owned upon their urgence that the gaunt man whom they glimpsed around the corners of the house was her husband, and the three lank boys with him were her sons; that the children whose faces watched them through the writhing window-panes were her two little girls; that the urchin who stood shyly twisted, all but his white head and sunburnt face, into her dress, and glanced at them with a mocking blue eye, was her youngest, and that he was three years old. With like coldness of voice and face, she assented to their conjecture that the space walled off in the farther corner of the orchard was the family burial-ground; and she said, with no more feeling that the ladies could see than she had shown concerning the other facts, that the graves they saw were those of her husband's family and of the children she had lost: there had been ten children, and she had lost four. She did not visibly shrink from the pursuit of the sympathy which expressed itself in curiosity as to the sicknesses they had died of; the ladies left her with the belief that they had met a character, and she remained with the conviction, briefly imparted to her husband, that they were tonguey.

The summer folks came more and more, every year, with little variance in the impression on either side. When they told her that her maple sugar would sell

better if the cake had an image of Lion's Head stamped
on it, she answered that she got enough of Lion's
Head without wanting to see it on all the sugar she
made. But the next year the cakes bore a rude effigy
of Lion's Head, and she said that one of her boys had
cut the stamp out with his knife; she now charged
five cents a cake for the sugar, but her manner remained the same. It did not change when the excur-
sionists drove away, and the deep silence native to the
place fell after their chatter. When a cock crew, or
a cow lowed, or a horse neighed, or one of the boys
shouted to the cattle, an echo retorted from the granite base of Lion's Head, and then she had all the noise
she wanted, or, at any rate, all the noise there was,
most of the time. Now and then a wagon passed on
the stony road by the brook in the valley, and sent
up its clatter to the farm-house on its high shelf, but
there was scarcely another break from the silence, except when the coaching parties came. The continuous
clash and rush of the brook was like a part of the
silence, as the red of the farm-house and the barn was
like a part of the green of the fields and woods all
round them: the black-green of pines and spruces, the
yellow-green of maples and birches, dense to the tops
of the dreary hills, and breaking like a baffled sea
around the Lion's Head.

The farmer stooped at his work, with a thin, inward-
curving chest, but his wife stood straight at hers; and
she had a massive beauty of figure, and a heavily
moulded regularity of feature that impressed such as
had eyes to see her grandeur among the summer folks.

She was forty when they began to come, and an ashen
gray was creeping over the reddish heaps of her hair,
like the pallor that overlies the crimson of the autumn-
nal oak. She showed her age earlier than most fair
people, but since her marriage at eighteen she had
lived long in the deaths of the children she had lost.
They were born with the taint of their father's family,
and they withered from their cradles. The youngest
boy alone, of all her brood, seemed to have inherited
her health and strength. The rest as they grew up
began to cough, as she had heard her husband's brothers and sisters cough, and then she waited in hapless
patience the fulfilment of their doom. The two little
girls whose faces the ladies of the first coaching party
saw at the farm-house windows had died away from
them; two of the lank boys had escaped, and in the
perpetual exile of California and Colorado had saved
themselves alive. Their father talked of going too,
but ten years later he still dragged himself spectrally
about the labors of the farm, with the same cough at
sixty which made his oldest son at twenty-nine look
scarcely younger than himself.

II.

ONE soft noon in the middle of August the farmer
came in from the corn-field that an early frost had
blighted, and told his wife that they must give it up.
He said, in his weak, hoarse voice, with the catarrhal
catching in it, that it was no use trying to make a living on the farm any longer. The oats had hardly
been worth cutting, and now the corn was gone, and
there was not hay enough without it to winter the
stock; if they got through themselves they would have
to live on potatoes. Have a vendue, and sell out
everything before the snow flew, and let the State take
the farm and get what it could for it, and turn over
the balance that was left after the taxes; the interest
of the savings-bank mortgage would soon eat that up.

The long, loose cough took him, and another cough
answered it like an echo from the barn, where his son
was giving the horses their feed. The mild, wan-eyed
young man came round the corner presently towards
the porch where his father and mother were sitting,
and at the same moment a boy came up the lane to
the other corner; there were sixteen years between the
ages of the brothers, who alone were left of the chil-

dren born into and borne out of the house. The young
man waited till they were within whispering distance
of each other, and then he gasped, "Where you
been?"

The boy answered, promptly, "None your business,"
and went up the steps before the young man, with a
lop-eared, liver-colored mongrel at his heels.   He
pulled off his ragged straw hat and flung it on the floor
of the porch.   "Dinner over?" he demanded.

His father made no answer; his mother looked at
the boy's hands and face, all of much the same earth-
ern cast, up to the eaves of his thatch of yellow hair,
and said, "You go and wash yourself."   At a certain
light in his mother's eye, which he caught as he passed
into the house, with his dog, the boy turned and cut
a defiant caper.   The oldest son sat down on the bench
beside his father, and they all looked in silence at the
mountain before them.   They heard the boy whistling
behind the house with sputtering and blubbering
noises, as if he were washing his face while he whistled;
and then they heard him singing, with a muffled
sound, and sharp breaks from the muffled sound, as if
he were singing into the towel; he shouted to his dog
and threatened him, and the scuffling of his feet came
to them through all, as if he were dancing.

"Been after them woodchucks, ag'in," his father
huskily suggested.

"I guess so," said the mother.   The brother did
not speak; he coughed vaguely, and let his head sink
forward.

The father began a statement of his affairs.

The mother said: "You don't want to go into that; we been all over it before. If it's come to the pinch, now, it's come. But you want to be sure."

The man did not answer directly. "If we could sell off now, and get out to where Jim is in Califorrny, and get a piece of land—" He stopped, as if confronted with some difficulty which he had met before, but had hoped he might not find in his way this time.

His wife laughed grimly. "I guess if the truth was known, we're too poor to get away."

"We're poor," he whispered back. He added, with a weak obstinacy, "I d' know as we're as poor as that comes to. The things would fetch something."

"Enough to get us out there, and then we should be on Jim's hands," said the woman.

"We should till spring, maybe. I d' know as I want to face another winter here, and I d' know as Jackson does."

The young man gasped back, courageously, "I guess I can get along here well enough."

"It's made Jim ten years younger. That's what he said," urged the father.

The mother smiled as grimly as she had laughed. "I don't believe it'll make you ten years richer, and that's what *you* want."

"I don't believe but what we should ha' done something with the place by spring. Or the State would," the father said, lifelessly.

The voice of the boy broke in upon them from behind. "Say, mother! A'n't you never goin' to have dinner?" He was standing in the doorway, with a startling cleanness of the hands and face, and a strange wet sleekness of the hair. His clothes were bedrabbled down the front with soap and water.

His mother rose and went towards him; his father and brother rose like apparitions, and slanted after her at one angle.

"Say!" the boy called again to his mother. "There comes a peddler." He pointed down the road at the figure of a man briskly ascending the lane towards the house, with a pack on his back, and some strange appendages dangling from it.

The woman did not look round; neither of the men looked round; they all kept on in-doors, and she said to the boy, as she passed him: "I got no time to waste on peddlers. You tell him we don't want anything."

The boy waited for the figure on the lane to approach. It was the figure of a young man, who slung his burden lightly from his shoulders when he arrived, and then stood looking at the boy, with his foot planted on the lowermost tread of the steps climbing from the ground to the porch.

III.

THE boy must have permitted these advances that he might inflict the greater disappointment when he spoke. "We don't want anything," he said, insolently. "Don't you?" the stranger returned. "*I* do. I want dinner. Go in and tell your mother, and then show me where I can wash my hands."

The bold ease of the stranger seemed to daunt the boy, and he stood irresolute. His dog came round the corner of the house at the first word of the parley, and while his master was making up his mind what to do, he smelled at the stranger's legs. "Well, you can't *have* any dinner," said the boy, tentatively. The dog raised the bristles on his neck, and showed his teeth with a snarl. The stranger promptly kicked him in the jaw, and the dog ran off, howling. "Come here, sir!" the boy called to him, but the dog vanished round the house with a fading yelp.

"Now, young man," said the stranger, "will you go and do as you're bid? I'm ready to pay for my dinner, and you can say so." The boy stared at him, slowly taking in the facts of his costume, with eyes that climbed from the heavy shoes up the legs of his

thick-ribbed stockings and his knickerbockers, past
the pleats and belt of his Norfolk jacket, to the red
neckcloth tied under the loose collar of his flannel
outing-shirt, and so by his face, with its soft young
beard, and its quiet eyes, to the top of his braidless,
bandless slouch hat of soft felt. It was one of the
earliest costumes of the kind that had shown itself in
the hill country, and it was altogether new to the boy.
"Come," said the wearer of it, "don't stand on the
order of your going, but go at once," and he sat down
on the steps with his back to the boy, who heard these
strange terms of command with a face of vague envy.

The noonday sunshine lay in a thin silvery glister
on the slopes of the mountain before them, and in the
brilliant light the colossal forms of the Lion's Head
were prismatically outlined against the speckless sky.
Through the silvery veil there burnt here and there on
the densely wooded acclivities the crimson torch of
a maple, kindled before its time, but everywhere else
there was the unbroken green of the forest, subdued
to one tone of gray. The boy heard the stranger fetch
his breath deeply, and then expel it in a long sigh,
before he could bring himself to obey an order that
seemed to leave him without the choice of disobedi-
ence. He came back, and found the stranger as he
had left him. "Come on, if you want your dinner,"
he said; and the stranger rose and looked at him.

"What's your name?" he asked.

"Thomas Jefferson Durgin."

"Well, Thomas Jefferson Durgin, will you show me
the way to the pump, and bring a towel along?"

" Want to wash ? "

" I haven't changed my mind."

"Come along, then."   The boy made a movement
as if to lead the way in-doors; the stranger arrested
him.

"Here! Take hold of this, and put it out of the
rush of travel, somewhere."   He lifted his burden
from where he had dropped it in the road, and swung
it towards the boy, who ran down the steps and embraced it.   As he carried it towards a corner of the
porch, he felt of the various shapes and materials in it.

Then he said "Come on!" again, and went before
the guest through the dim hall running midway of
the house to the door at the rear.   He left him on a
narrow space of stone flagging there, and ran with a
tin basin to the spring at the barn, and brought it
back to him full of the cold water.

"Towel," he said, pulling at the family roller inside
the little porch at the door; and he watched the
stranger wash his hands and face, and then search for
a fresh place on the towel.

Before the stranger had finished, the father and the
elder brother came out, and after an ineffectual attempt
to salute him, slanted away to the barn together. The
woman, in-doors, was more successful, when he found
her in the dining-room, where the boy showed him.
The table was set for him alone, and it affected him
as if the family had been hurried away from it that
he might have it to himself.   Everything was very
simple; the iron forks had two prongs; the knives
bone handles; the dull glass was pressed; the heavy

plates and cups were white, but so was the cloth, and all were clean. The woman brought in a good boiled dinner of corned beef, potatoes, turnips, and carrots, from the kitchen, and a teapot, and said something about having kept them hot on the stove for him; she brought him a plate of biscuit fresh from the oven; then she said to the boy, "You come out and have your dinner with me, Jeff," and left the guest to make his meal unmolested.

The room was square, with two north windows that looked down the lane he had climbed to the house. An open door led into the kitchen in an ell, and a closed door opposite probably gave access to a parlor or a ground-floor chamber. The windows were darkened down to the lower sash by green paper shades; the walls were papered in a pattern of brown roses; over the chimney hung a large picture, a life-size pencil-drawing of two little girls, one slightly older and slightly larger than the other, each with round eyes and precise ringlets, and with her hand clasped in the other's hand.

The guest seemed helpless to take his gaze from it, and he sat fallen back in his chair at it, when the woman came in with a pie.

"Thank you, I believe I don't want any dessert," he said. "The fact is, the dinner was so good that I haven't left any room for pie. Are those your children?"

"Yes," said the woman, looking up at the picture with the pie in her hand. "They're the last two I lost."

" Oh, excuse me ! " the guest began.

" It's the way they appear in the spirit life. It's a spirit picture."

" Oh ! I thought there was something strange about it."

" Well, it's a good deal like the photograph we had taken about a year before they died. It's a good likeness. They say they don't change a great deal, at first."

She seemed to refer the point to him for his judgment; but he answered wide of it:

" I came up here to paint your mountain, if you don't mind, Mrs. Durgin —Lion's Head, I mean."

" Oh, yes. Well, I don't know as we could stop you, if you wanted to take it away." A spare glimmer lighted up her face.

The painter rejoined in kind. " The town might have something to say, I suppose."

" Not if you was to leave a good piece of intervale in place of it. We've got mountains to spare."

" Well, then, that's arranged. What about a week's board ? "

" I guess you can stay, if you're satisfied."

" I'll be satisfied if I can stay. How much do you want ? "

The woman looked down, probably with an inward anxiety between the fear of asking too much and the folly of asking too little. She said, tentatively, " Some of the folks that come over from the hotels say they pay as much as twenty dollars a week."

" But you don't expect hotel prices ? "

"I don't know as I do. We've never had anybody before."

The stranger relaxed the frown he had put on at the greed of her suggestion; it might have come from ignorance or mere innocence. "I'm in the habit of paying five dollars for farm board, where I stay several weeks. What do you say to seven for a single week?"

"I guess that'll do," said the woman, and she went out with the pie, which she had kept in her hand.

IV.

THE painter went round to the front of the house and walked up and down before it for different points of view. He ran down the lane some way, and then came back, and climbed to the sloping field behind the barn, where he could look at Lion's Head over the roof of the house. He tried an open space in the orchard, where he backed against the wall enclosing the little burial-ground. He looked round at it without seeming to see it, and then went back to the level where the house stood. "This is the place," he said to himself. But the boy, who had been lurking after him, with the dog lurking at his own heels in turn, took the words as a proffer of conversation.

"I thought you'd come to it," he sneered.

"Did you?" asked the painter, with a smile for the unsatisfied grudge in the boy's tone. "Why didn't you tell me sooner?"

The boy looked down, and apparently made up his mind to wait until something sufficiently severe should come to him for a retort. "Want I should help you get your things?" he asked, presently.

"Why, yes," said the painter, with a glance of surprise. "I shall be much obliged for a lift." He started towards the porch where his burden lay, and the boy ran before him. They jointly separated the knapsack from the things tied to it, and the painter let the boy carry the easel and camp-stool which developed themselves from their folds and hinges, and brought the colors and canvas himself to the spot he had chosen. The boy looked at the tag on the easel after it was placed, and read the name on it—Jere Westover. "That's a funny name."

"I'm glad it amuses you," said the owner of it.

Again the boy cast down his eyes discomfited, and seemed again resolving silently to bide his time and watch for another chance.

Westover forgot him in the fidget he fell into, trying this and that effect, with his head slanted one way, and then slanted the other, his hand held up to shut out the mountain below the granite mass of Lion's Head, and then changed to cut off the sky above; and then both hands lifted in parallel to confine the picture. He made some tentative scrawls on his canvas in charcoal, and he wasted so much time that the light on the mountain-side began to take the rich tone of the afternoon deepening to evening. A soft flush stole into it; the sun dipped behind the top south of the mountain, and Lion's Head stood out against the intense clearness of the west, which began to be flushed with exquisite suggestions of violet and crimson.

"Good Lord!" said Westover; and he flew at his colors and began to paint. He had got his canvas into such a state that he alone could have found it

much more intelligible than his palette, when he heard
the boy saying, over his shoulder, " I don't think that
looks very much like it." He had last been aware of
the boy sitting at the grassy edge of the lane, tossing
small bits of earth and pebble across to his dog, which
sat at the other edge, and snapped at them. Then he
lost consciousness of him. He answered, dreamily,
while he found a tint he was trying for with his brush,
" Perhaps you don't know." He was so sure of his
effect that the popular censure speaking in the boy's
opinion only made him happier in it.

" I know what I see," said the boy.

" I doubt it," said Westover, and then he lost consciousness of him again. He was rapt deep and far
into the joy of his work, and had no thought but for
that, and for the dim question whether it would be
such another day to-morrow, with that light again on
Lion's Head, when he was at last sensible of a noise
that he felt he must have been hearing some time
without noting it. It was a lamentable sound of
screaming, as of some one in mortal terror, mixed
with wild entreaties. " Oh, don't, Jeff! Oh, don't,
don't, don't! Oh, please! Oh, do let us be! Oh,
Jeff, don't! "

Westover looked round bewildered, and not able,
amid the clamor of the echoes, to make out where the
cries came from. Then, down at the point where the
lane joined the road to the southward, and the road
lost itself in the shadow of a woodland, he saw the
boy leaping back and forth across the track, with his
dog beside him; he was shouting and his dog barking

furiously; those screams and entreaties came from
within the shadow. Westover plunged down the lane
headlong, with a speed that gathered at each bound,
and that almost flung him on his face when he reached
the level where the boy and the dog were dancing
back and forth across the road. Then he saw, crouching in the edge of the wood, a little girl, who was
uttering the appeals he had heard, and clinging to
her, with a face of frantic terror, a child of five or six
years; his cries had grown hoarse, and had a hard,
mechanical action as they followed one another. They
were really in no danger, for the boy held his dog
tight by his collar, and was merely delighting himself
with their terror. The painter hurled himself upon
him, and with a quick grip upon his collar, gave him
half a dozen flat-handed blows wherever he could plant
them, and then flung him reeling away.

"You infernal little ruffian!" he roared at him; and
the sound of his voice was enough for the dog; he
began to scale the hill-side towards the house without
a moment's stay.

The children still crouched together, and Westover
could hardly make them understand that they were in
his keeping when he bent over them, and bade them
not be frightened. The little girl set about wiping
the child's eyes on her apron in a motherly fashion;
her own were dry enough, and Westover fancied there
was more of fury than of fright in her face. She
seemed lost to any sense of his presence, and kept on
talking fiercely to herself, while she put the little boy
in order, like an indignant woman. "Great, mean,

ugly thing! I'll tell the teacher on him, that's what
I will, as soon as ever school begins. I'll see if he
can come round with that dog of his scaring folks!
I wouldn't 'a' been a bit afraid if it hadn't 'a' been for
Franky. Don't cry any more, Franky! Don't you
see they're gone? I presume he thinks it smart to
scare a little boy and a girl. If I was a boy, once, I'd
show him."

She made no sign of gratitude to Westover: as far
as any recognition from her was concerned, his inter-
vention was something as impersonal as if it had been
a thunder-bolt falling upon her enemies from the sky.

"Where do you live?" he asked. "I'll go home
with you, if you'll tell me where you live."

She looked up at him in a daze, and Westover heard
the Durgin boy saying, "She lives right there in that
little wood-colored house at the other end of the lane.
There ain't no call to go home with her."

Westover turned, and saw the boy kneeling at the
edge of a clump of bushes, where he must have struck;
he was rubbing with a tuft of grass at the dirt ground
into the knees of his trousers.

The little girl turned hawkishly upon him. "Not
for anything *you* can do, Jeff Durgin!"

The boy did not answer.

"There!" she said, giving a final pull and twitch
to the dress of her brother, and taking him by the
hand tenderly. "Now, come right along, Franky."

"Let me have your other hand," said Westover, and
with the little boy between them they set off towards
the point where the lane joined the road on the north-

ward. They had to pass the bushes where Jeff Durgin was crouching, and the little girl turned and made a face at him. " Oh, oh! I don't think I should have done that!" said Westover.

" I don't care!" said the little girl. But she said, in explanation and partial excuse: " He tries to scare *all* the girls. I'll let him know' t he can't scare *me*."

Westover looked up towards the Durgin house with a return of interest in the canvas he had left in the lane on the easel. Nothing had happened to it. At the door of the barn he saw the farmer and his eldest son, slanting forward and staring down the hill at the point he had come from. Mrs. Durgin was looking out from the shelter of the porch, and she turned and went in with Jeff's dog at her skirts when Westover came in sight with the children.

V.

WESTOVER had his tea with the family, but nothing was said or done to show that any of them resented or even knew of what had happened to the boy from him. Jeff himself seemed to have no grudge. He went out with Westover, when the meal was ended, and sat on the steps of the porch with him, watching the painter watch the light darken on the lonely heights and in the lonely depths around. Westover smoked a pipe, and the fire gleamed and smouldered in it regularly with his breathing; the boy, on a lower step, pulled at the long ears of his dog, and gazed up at him.

They were both silent till the painter asked, " What do you do here, when you're not trying to scare little children to death?"

The boy hung his head, and said, with the effect of excusing a long arrears of uselessness, " I'm goin' to school as soon as it commences."

" There's one branch of your education that I should like to undertake, if I ever saw you at a thing like that again. Don't you feel ashamed of yourself?"

The boy pulled so hard at the dog's ear that the dog gave a faint yelp of protest.

"They might 'a' seen that I had him by the collar. I wa'n't a-goin' to let go."

"Well, the next time I have *you* by the collar, *I* won't let go, either," said the painter; but he felt an inadequacy in his threat, and he imagined a superfluity, and he made some haste to ask, "Who are they?"

"Whitwell is their name. They live in that little house where you took them. Their father's got a piece of land on Lion's Head that he's clearin' off for the timber. Their mother's dead, and Cynthy keeps house. She's always makin' up names and faces," added the boy. "She thinks herself awful smart. That Franky's a perfect cry-baby."

"Well, upon my word! You *are* a little ruffian," said Westover, and he knocked the ashes out of his pipe. "The next time you meet that poor little creature, you tell her that I think you're about the shabbiest chap I know, and that I hope the teacher will begin where I left off with you, and not leave blackguard enough in you to—"

He stopped for want of a fitting figure, and the boy said, "I guess the teacher won't touch me."

Westover rose, and the boy flung his dog away from him with his foot. "Want I should show you where to sleep?"

"Yes," said Westover, and the boy hulked in before him, vanishing into the dark of the interior, and presently appeared with a lighted hand-lamp. He led the way up-stairs to a front room looking down upon the porch roof, and over towards Lion's Head, which Westover could see dimly outlined against the night sky, when he lifted the edge of the paper shade and peered out.

The room was neat, with greater comfort in its appointments than he hoped for. He tried the bed, and found it hard, but of straw, and not the feathers he had dreaded; while the boy looked into the water-pitcher, to see if it was full, and then went out without any form of good-night.

Westover would have expected to wash in a tin basin at the back door, and wipe on the family towel, but all the means of toilet, such as they were, he found at hand here, and a surprise which he had felt at a certain touch in the cooking renewed itself at the intelligent arrangements for his comfort. A secondary quilt was laid across the foot of his bed; his window-shade was pulled down, and though the window was shut, and the air stuffy within, there was a sense of cleanliness in everything which was not at variance with the closeness.

The bed felt fresh when he got into it, and the sweet breath of the mountains came in so cold through the sash he had lifted that he was glad to pull the secondary quilt up over him. He heard the clock tick in some room below; from another quarter came the muffled sound of coughing; but otherwise the world was intensely still, and he slept deep and long.

VI.

THE men folks had finished their breakfast and gone
to their farm-work hours before Westover came down
to his breakfast, but the boy seemed to be of as much
early leisure as himself, and was lounging on the
threshold of the back door, with his dog in waiting
upon him. He gave the effect of yesterday's cleanliness freshened up with more recent soap and water.
At the moment Westover caught sight of him, he
heard his mother calling to him from the kitchen,
" Well, now, come in and get your breakfast, Jeff,"
and the boy called to Westover, in turn, " I'll tell
her you're here," as he rose and came in-doors. " I
guess she's got your breakfast for you."

Mrs. Durgin brought the breakfast almost as soon
as Westover had found his way to the table, and she
lingered as if for some expression of his opinion upon
it. The biscuit and the butter were very good, and
he said so; the eggs were fresh, and the hash from
yesterday's corned beef could not have been better,
and he praised them; but he was silent about the
coffee.

" It a'n't very good," she suggested.

"Why, I'm used to making my own coffee; I lived
so long in a country where it's nearly the whole of
breakfast that I got into the habit of it, and I always
carry my little machine with me; but I don't like to
bring it out, unless—"

"Unless you can't stand the other folks's," said
the woman, with a humorous gleam. "Well, you
needn't mind me. I want you should have good coffee, and I guess I a'n't too old to learn, if you want
to show me. Our folks don't care for it much; they
like tea; and I kind of got out of the way of it. But
at home we had to have it." She explained, to his
inquiring glance. "My father kept the tavern on the
old road to St. Albans, on the other side of Lion's
Head. That's where I always lived, till I married
here."

"Oh," said Westover, and he felt that she had
proudly wished to account for a quality which she
hoped he had noticed in her cooking. He thought
she might be going to tell him something more of herself, but she only said, "Well, any time you want to
show me your way of makin' coffee," and went out of
the room.

That evening, which was the close of another flaw-
less day, he sat again watching the light outside, when
he saw her come into the hallway with a large shade-
lamp in her hand. She stopped at the door of a room
he had not seen yet, and looked out at him to ask,
"Won't you come in and set in the parlor, if you
want to?"

He found her there when he came in, and her two

sons with her; the younger was sleepily putting away some school-books, and the elder seemed to have been helping him with his lessons.

"He's got to begin school next week," she said to Westover; and at the preparations the other now began to make with a piece of paper and a planchette which he had on the table before him, she asked, in the half-mocking, half-deprecating way which seemed characteristic of her, "You believe any in that?"

"I don't know that I've ever seen it work," said the painter.

"Well, sometimes it *won't* work," she returned, altogether mockingly now, and sat holding her shapely hands, which were neither so large nor so rough as they might have been, across her middle, and watching her son while the machine pushed about under his palm, and he bent his wan eyes upon one of the oval-framed photographs on the wall, as if rapt in a supernal vision. The boy stared drowsily at the planchette, jerking this way and that, and making abrupt starts and stops. At last the young man lifted his palm from it, and put it aside to study the hieroglyphics it had left on the paper.

"What's it say?" asked his mother.

The young man whispered, "I can't seem to make out very clear. I guess I got to take a little time to it," he added, leaning back wearily in his chair. "Ever seen much of the manifestations?" he gasped at Westover.

"Never any, before," said the painter, with a leniency for the invalid which he did not feel for his belief.

The young man tried for his voice, and found enough of it to say: "There's a trance medium over at the Huddle. Her control says' t I can develop into a writin' medium." He seemed to refer the fact as a sort of question to Westover, who could think of nothing to say but that it must be very interesting to feel that one had such a power.

"I guess he don't know he's got it yet," his mother interposed. "And planchette don't seem to know either."

"We ha'n't given it a fair trial yet," said the young man, impartially, almost impassively.

"Wouldn't you like to see it do some of your sums, Jeff?" said the mother to the drowsy boy, blinking in a corner. "You better go to bed."

The elder brother rose. "I guess I'll go too."

The father had not joined their circle in the parlor, now breaking up by common consent.

Mrs. Durgin took up her lamp again, and looked round on the appointments of the room, as if she wished Westover to note them too: the drab wall-paper, the stiff chairs, the long, hard sofa in hair-cloth, the high bureau of mahogany veneer.

"You can come in here and set, or lay down, when-ever you feel like. it," she said. "We use it more than folks generally, I presume; we got in the habit, havin' it open for funerals."

VII.

Four or five days of perfect weather followed one another, and Westover worked hard at his picture in the late afternoon light he had chosen for it. In the morning he tramped through the woods and climbed the hills with Jeff Durgin, who seemed never to do anything about the farm, and had a leisure unbroken by anything except a rare call from his mother to help her in the house. He built the kitchen fire, and got the wood for it; he picked the belated pease and the early beans in the garden, and shelled them; on the Monday when the school opened he did a share of the family wash, which seemed to have been begun before daylight, and Westover saw him hanging out the clothes before he started off with his books. He suffered no apparent loss of self-respect in these employments, and while he still had his days free he put himself at Westover's disposal with an effect of unimpaired equality. He had expected evidently that Westover would want to fish or shoot, or at least join him in the hunt for woodchucks, which he still carried on with abated zeal for lack of his company when the painter sat down to sketch certain bits that struck him. When he found that Westover cared for nothing in the way of sport, as people commonly understand it, he did not openly contemn him. He helped him get the flowers he studied, and he learned to know true mushrooms from him, though he did not follow his teaching in eating the toadstools, as his mother called them, when they brought them home to be cooked.

If it could not be said that he shared the affection which began to grow up in Westover from their companionship, there could be no doubt of the interest he took in him, though it often seemed the same critical curiosity which appeared in the eye of his dog when it dwelt upon the painter. Fox had divined in his way that Westover was not only not to be molested, but was to be respectfully tolerated, yet no gleam of kindness ever lighted up his face at sight of the painter; he never wagged his tail in recognition of him; he simply recognized him, and no more, and he remained passive under Westover's advances, which he had the effect of covertly referring to Jeff, when the boy was by, for his approval or disapproval; when he was not by, the dog's manner implied a reservation of opinion until the facts could be submitted to his master.

On the Saturday morning which was the last they were to have together, the three comrades had strayed from the vague wood road along one of the unexpected levels on the mountain slopes, and had come to a standstill in a place which the boy pretended not to know his way out of. Westover doubted him, for he had found that Jeff liked to give himself credit for

"A LANK FIGURE OF A MAN AT THE FOOT OF A POPLAR-TREE"

woodcraft by discovering an escape from the depths
of trackless wildernesses.

"I guess you know where we are," he suggested.

"No, honestly," said the boy; but he grinned, and
Westover still doubted him.

"Hark! What's that?" he said, hushing further
speech from him with a motion of his hand. It was
the sound of an axe.

"Oh, *I* know where we are!" said Jeff. "It's that
Canuck chopping in Whitwell's clearing. Come
along!"

He led the way briskly down the mountain-side
now, stopping from time to time, and verifying his
course by the sound of the axe. This came and went,
and by-and-by it ceased altogether, and Jeff crept forward with a real or feigned uncertainty. Suddenly
he stopped. A voice called, "Heigh, there!" and
the boy turned and fled, crashing through the underbrush at a tangent, with his dog at his heels.

Westover looked after them, and then came forward. A lank figure of a man at the foot of a poplar,
which he had begun to fell, stood waiting him, one
hand on his axe-helve and the other on his hip. There
was the scent of freshly smitten bark and sap-wood in
the air; the ground was paved with broad, clean chips.

"Good-morning," said Westover.

"*How* are you?" returned the other, without moving
or making any sign of welcome for a moment. But
then he lifted his axe, and struck it into the carf on
the tree, and came to meet Westover.

As he advanced he held out his hand. "Oh,

you're the one that stopped that fellow that day when
he was tryin' to scare my children.   Well, I *thought*
I should run across you, some time." He shook hands
with Westover, in token of the gratitude which did
not express itself in words.   "How *are* you?   Treat
you pretty well up at the Durgins'?   *I* guess so.   The
old woman knows how to cook, anyway.   Jackson's
about the best o' the lot *above* ground, though I don't
know as I know very much against the old man, either.
But that boy, I declare I 'most feel like takin' the
top of his head off when he gets at his tricks.   Set
down."

Whitwell, as Westover divined the man to be, took
a seat himself on a high stump, which suited his
length of leg, and courteously waved Westover to a
place on the log in front of him.   A long ragged beard
of brown, with lines of gray in it, hung from his chin,
and mounted well up on his thin cheeks toward his
friendly eyes.   His mustache lay sunken on his lip,
which had fallen in with the loss of his upper teeth.
From the lower jaw a few incisors showed at this slant
and that as he talked.

"Well, well!" he said, with the air of wishing the
talk to go on, but without having anything immediately to offer himself.

Westover said, "Thank you," as he dropped on the
log, and Whitwell added, relentingly, "I don't suppose
a fellow's so much to blame, if he's got the devil in
him, as what the devil is."

He referred the point with a twinkle of his eyes to
Westover, who said: "It's always a question, of

course, whether it's the devil. It may be original sin
with the fellow himself."

"Well, that's something so," said Whitwell, with
pleasure in the distinction rather than assent. "But
I guess it ain't *original* sin in the boy. Got it from
his gran'father pootty straight, I should say, and maybe the old *man* had it second-hand. Ha'd to say just
where so much cussedness gits statted."

"His father's father?" asked Westover, willing to
humor Whitwell's evident wish to philosophize the
Durgins' history.

"Mother's. He kept the old tavern stand on the
west side of Lion's Head, on the St. Albans Road, and
I guess he kept a pootty good house in the old times
when the stages stopped with him. Ever noticed how
a man on the mean side in politics always knows how
to keep a hotel? Well, it's something curious. If
there was ever a mean side to any question, old Mason
was on it. My folks used to live around there, and I
can remember when I was a boy hangin' around the
bar-room nights hearin' him argue that colored folks
had no souls; and along about the time the fugitive
slave law was passed, the folks pootty near run him
out o' town for puttin' the United States Marshal on
the scent of a fellow that was breakin' for Canada.
Well, it was just so when the war come. It was known
for a fact that he was in with them Secesh devils up
over the line that was plannin' a raid into Vermont in
'63. He'd got pootty low down by that time; railroads
took off all the travel; tavern 'd got to be a regular
doggery; old man *always* drank some, I guess. That

was a good while after his girl had married Durgin. He was dead against it, and it broke him up consid'able when she would *have* him. Well, cne night, the old stand burnt up and him in it, and neither of 'em insured!"

Whitwell laughed with a pleasure in his satire which gave the monuments in his lower jaw a rather sinister action. But as if he felt a rebuke in Westover's silence, he added: "There ain't anything against Mis' Durgin. She's done her part, and she's had more than her share of hard knocks. If she was tough, to sta't with, she's had blows enough to meller her. But that's the way I account for the boy. I s'pose I'd oughtn't to feel the way I do about him, but he's such a pest to the whole neighborhood that he'd have the most pop'la' fune'l— Well, I guess I've said enough. I'm much obliged to *you*, though, Mr.—"

"Westover," the painter suggested. "But the boy isn't so bad, all the time."

"*Couldn't* be!" said Whitwell, with a cackle of humorous enjoyment. "He has his spells of bein' decent, and he's pootty smart, too. But when the other spell ketches him, it's like as if the devil got a hold of him, as I said in the first *place*. I lost my wife, here, two-three years along back, and that little girl you see him tormentin', she's a regular little mother to her brother; and whenever Jeff Durgin sees her with him, seems as if the Old Scratch got into him. Well, I'm glad I didn't come across him, that day. How you gittin' along with Lion's Head? *Sets* quiet enough for you!" Whitwell rose from the stump, and brushed the clinging chips from his thighs. "Folks trouble you any, lookin' on?"

"Not yet," said Westover.

"Well, there ain't a great many *to*," said Whitwell, going back to his axe. "I should like to see you workin' some day. Do' know as I ever saw an attist *at* it."

"I should like to have you," said Westover. "Any time."

"All right." Whitwell pulled his axe out of the carf, and struck it in again with a force that made a wide, square chip leap out. He looked over his shoulder at Westover, who was moving away. "Say! Stop in, some time you're passin'. I live in that wood-colored house at the foot of the Durgins' lane."

VIII.

In a little sunken place, behind a rock, some rods away, Westover found Jeff lurking with his dog, both silent and motionless. "Hello!" he said, inquiringly.

"Come back to show you the way," said the boy. "Thought you couldn't find it alone."

"Oh! why didn't you say you'd wait?" The boy grinned. "I shouldn't think a fellow like you would want to be afraid of any man, even for the fun of scaring a little girl." Jeff stopped grinning, and looked interested, as if this was a view of the case that had not occurred to him. "But perhaps you like to be afraid."

"I don't know as I do," said the boy, and Westover left him to the question a great part of the way home. He did not express any regret, or promise any reparation. But a few days after that, when he had begun to convoy parties of children up to see Westover at work, in the late afternoon, on their way home from school, and to show the painter off to them as a sort of family property, he once brought the young Whitwells. He seemed on perfect terms with them now, and when the crowd of larger children hindered

the little boy's view of the picture, Jeff, in his quality
of host, lifted him under his arms and held him up so
that he could look as long as he liked.

The girl seemed ashamed of the good understanding, before Westover. Jeff offered to make a place
for her among the other children who had looked long
enough, but she pulled the front of her bonnet across
her face and said that she did not want to look, and
caught her brother by the hand and ran away with
him. Westover thought this charming somehow; he
liked the intense shyness which the child's intense
passion had hidden from him before.

Jeff acted as host to the neighbors who came to
inspect the picture, and they all came, within a circuit
of several miles around, and gave him their opinions
freely, or scantily, according to their several tempera-
ments. They were mainly favorable, though there was
some frank criticism, too, spoken over the painter's
shoulder as openly as if he were not by. There was
no question but of likeness; all finer facts were far
from them; they wished to see how good a portrait
Westover had made, and some of them consoled him
with the suggestion that the likeness would come out
more when the picture got dry.

Whitwell when he came attempted a larger view of
the artist's work, but apparently more out of kindness
for him than admiration of the picture. He said he
presumed you could not always get a thing like that
just right, the first time, and that you had to keep
trying till you did get it; but it paid in the end. Jeff
had stolen down from the house with his dog, drawn

by the fascination which one we have injured always has for us; when Whitwell suddenly turned upon him, and asked, jocularly, "What do you think, Jeff?" the boy could only kick his dog, and drive it home, as a means of hiding his feelings.

He brought the teacher to see the picture, the last Friday before the painter went away. She was a cold-looking, austere girl, pretty enough, with eyes that wandered away from the young man, although Jeff used all his arts to make her feel at home in his presence. She pretended to have merely stopped on her way up to see Mrs. Durgin, and she did not venture any comment on the painting; but when Westover asked something about her school, she answered him promptly enough, as to the number and ages and sexes of the school-children. He ventured so far toward a joke with her as to ask if she had much trouble with such a tough subject as Jeff, and she said he could be good enough when he had a mind. If he could get over his teasing, she said, with the air of reading him a lecture, she would not have anything to complain of; and Jeff looked ashamed, but rather of the praise than the blame. His humiliation seemed complete when she said, finally, "He's a good scholar."

On the Tuesday following, Westover meant to go. It was the end of his third week, and it had brought him into September. The weather since he had begun to paint Lion's Head was perfect for his work; but with the long drought it had grown very warm. Many trees now had flamed into crimson on the hill slopes; the yellowing corn in the fields gave out a thin, dry sound as the delicate wind stirred the blades; but only the sounds and sights were autumnal. The heat was oppressive at mid-day, and at night the cold had lost its edge. There was no dew, and Mrs. Durgin sat out with Westover on the porch while he smoked a final pipe there. She had come to join him for some fixed purpose apparently, and she called to her boy, "You go to bed, Jeff," as if she wished to be alone with Westover; the men folks were already in bed; he could hear them cough, now and then.

"Mr. Westover," the woman began, even as she swept her skirts forward before she sat down, "I want to ask you whether you would let that picture of yours go on part board? I'll give you back just as much as you say of this money."

He looked round and saw that she had in the hand dropped in her lap the bills he had given her after supper.

"Why, I couldn't, very well, Mrs. Durgin," he began.

"I presume you'll think I'm foolish," she pursued. "But I do want that picture; I don't know when I've ever wanted a thing more. It's just like Lion's Head, the way I've seen it, day in and day out, every summer since I come here thirty-five years ago; it's beautiful!"

"Mrs. Durgin," said Westover, "you gratify me more than I can tell you. I wish—I wish I could let you have the picture. I—I don't know what to say—"

"Why *don't* you let me have it then? If we ever had to go away from here—if anything happened to us—it's the one thing I should want to keep and take with me. There! That's the way I feel about it. I can't explain; but I do *wish* you'd let me have it."

Some emotion which did not utter itself in the desire she expressed made her voice shake in the words. She held out the bank-notes to him, and they rustled with the tremor of her hand.

"Mrs. Durgin, I suppose I shall have to be frank with you, and you mustn't feel hurt. I have to live by my work, and I have to get as much as I can for it—"

"That's what I *say*. I don't want to beat you down on it. I'll give you whatever you think is right. It's my money, and my husband feels just as I do about it," she urged.

"You don't quite understand," he said gently. "I expect to have an exhibition of my pictures in Boston this fall, and I hope to get two or three hundred dollars for Lion's Head."

"I've been a *proper* fool!" cried the woman, and she drew in a long breath.

"Oh, don't mind," he begged. "It's all right. I've never had any offer for a picture that I'd rather take than yours. I know the thing can't be altogether bad after what you've said. And I'll tell you what! I'll have it photographed when I get to Boston, and I'll send you a photograph of it."

"How much will that be?" Mrs. Durgin asked, as if taught caution by her offer for the painting.

"Nothing. And if you'll accept it, and hang it up here somewhere, I shall be very glad."

"Thank you," said Mrs. Durgin, and the meekness, the wounded pride, he fancied in her, touched him.

He did not know at first how to break the silence which she let follow upon her words. At last he said : "You spoke, just now, about taking it with you. Of course you don't think of leaving Lion's Head!"

She did not answer for so long a time that he thought she had not perhaps heard him, or heeded what he said, but she answered, finally : "We did think of it. The day you come we had about made up our minds to leave."

"Oh!"

"But I've been thinkin' of something since you've been here that I don't know but you'll say is about as wild as wantin' to buy a three-hundred-dollar picture with a week's board." She gave a short self-scornful laugh; but it was a laugh, and it relieved the tension.

"It may not be worth any more," he said, glad of the relief.

"Oh, I guess it is," she rejoined, and then she waited for him to prompt her.

"Well?"

"Well, it's this; and I *wanted* to ask you, anyway. You think there'd be any chance of my gettin' summer folks to come here and board, if I was to put an advertisement in a Boston paper? I know it's a lonesome place, and there ain't what you may call attractions. But the folks from the hotels, sometimes, when they ride over in a stage to see the view, praise up the scenery, and I guess it *is* sightly. I know that well enough; and I ain't afraid but what I can do for boarders as well as some, if not better. What do you think?"

"I think that's a capital idea, Mrs. Durgin."

"It's that, or go," she said. "There ain't a livin'
for us on the farm any more, and we got to do some-
thin'. If there was anything else I *could* do! But
I've thought it out, and *thought* it out, and I guess
there ain't anything I can do but take boarders—if I
can get them."

"I should think you'd find it rather pleasant on
some accounts. Your boarders would be company for
you," said Westover.

"We're company enough for ourselves," said Mrs.
Durgin. "I ain't ever been lonesome here, from the
first minute. I guess I had company enough when I
was a girl to last me—the sort that hotel folks are. I
presume Mr. Whitwell spoke to you about my father?"

"Yes; he did, Mrs. Durgin."

"I don't presume he said anything that wa'n't true.
It's all right. But I know how my mother used to
slave, and how I used to slave myself; and I always
said I'd rather do anything than wait on boarders;
and now I guess I got to come to it. The sight of
summer folks makes me sick! I guess I could 'a' had
'em long ago, if I'd wanted to. There! I've said
enough." She rose, with a sudden lift of her powerful frame, and stood a moment as if expecting Westover to say something.

He said, "Well, when you've made your mind up,
send your advertisement to me, and I'll attend to it
for you."

"And you won't forget about the picture?"

"No. I won't forget that."

The next morning he made ready for an early start, and in his preparations he had the zealous and even affectionate help of Jeff Durgin. The boy seemed to wish him to carry away the best impression of him, or at least to make him forget all that had been sinister or unpleasant in his behavior. They had been good comrades since the first evil day; they had become good friends even; and Westover was touched by the boy's devotion at parting. He helped the painter get his pack together in good shape, and he took pride in strapping it on Westover's shoulders, adjusting and readjusting it with care, and fastening it so that all should be safe and snug. He lingered about at the risk of being late for school, as if to see the last of the painter, and he waved his hat to him when Westover looked back at the house from half down the lane. Then he vanished, and Westover went slowly on till he reached that corner of the orchard where the slanting gravestones of the family burial-ground showed above the low wall. There, suddenly, a storm burst upon him. The air rained apples, that struck him on the head, the back, the side, and pelted in violent succession on his knapsack and canvases, camp-stool and easel. He seemed assailed by four or five skilful marksmen, whose missiles all told.

When he could lift his face to look round, he heard a shrill, accusing voice, "Oh, Jeff *Durgin!*" and he saw another storm of apples fly through the air toward the little Whitwell girl, who dodged and ran along the road below, and escaped in the direction of the school-house. Then the boy's face showed itself over

the top of one of the gravestones, all agrin with joy.
He waited and watched Westover keep slowly on, as
if nothing had happened, and presently he let some
apples fall from his hands, and walked slowly back to
the house, with his dog at his heels.

When Westover reached the level of the road, and
the shelter of the woods near Whitwell's house, he
unstrapped his load to see how much harm had been
done to his picture.   He found it unhurt, and before
he had got the burden back again, he saw Jeff Durgin
leaping along the road toward the school-house, whirl-
ing his satchel of books about his head, and shouting
gayly to the girl, now hidden by the bushes at the
other end of the lane, "Cynthy! Oh, Cynthy! Wait
for me! I want to tell you something."

IX.

WESTOVER received next spring the copy for an advertisement from Mrs. Durgin, which she asked to have him put in some paper for her. She said that her son Jackson had written it out, and Westover found it so well written that he had scarcely to change the wording. It offered the best of farm-board, with plenty of milk and eggs, berries and fruit, for five dollars a week at Lion's Head Farm, and it claimed for the farm the merit of the finest view of the celebrated Lion's Head Mountain. It was signed, as her letter was signed, "Mrs. J. M. Durgin," with her post-office address, and it gave Westover as a reference.

The letter was in the same handwriting as the advertisement, which he took to be that of Jackson Durgin. It inclosed a dollar note to pay for three insertions of the advertisement in the *Evening Transcript*, and it ended, almost casually: "I do not know as you have heard that my husband, James Monroe Durgin, passed to spirit life this spring. My son will help me to run the house."

This death could not move Westover more than it

had apparently moved the widow. During the three weeks he had passed under his roof, he had scarcely exchanged three words with James Monroe Durgin, who remained to him an impression of large, round, dull blue eyes, a stubbly upper lip, and cheeks and chin tagged with coarse hay-colored beard. The impression was so largely the impression that he had kept of the dull blue eyes and the gaunt, slanted figure of Andrew Jackson Durgin that he could not be very distinct in his sense of which was now the presence, and which the absence. He remembered with an effort that the son's beard was straw-colored, but he had to make no effort to recall the robust effect of Mrs. Durgin and her youngest son. He wondered now, as he had often wondered before, whether she knew of the final violence which had avenged the boy for the prolonged strain of repression Jeff had inflicted upon himself during Westover's stay at the farm. After several impulses to go back and beat him, to follow him to school and expose him to the teacher, to write to his mother and tell her of his misbehavior, Westover had decided to do nothing. As he had come off unhurt in person and property, he could afford to be more generously amused than if he had suffered damage in either. The more he thought of the incident, the more he was disposed to be lenient with the boy, whom he was aware of having baffled and subdued by his superior wit and virtue in perhaps intolerable measure. He could not quite make out that it was an act of bad faith; there was no reason to think that the good-natured things the fellow had done, the constant little

offices of zeal and friendliness, were less sincere than
this violent outbreak.

The letter from Lion's Head Farm brought back
his three weeks there very vividly, and made Westover
wish he was going there for the summer.   But he was
going over to France for an indefinite period of work
in the only air where he believed modern men were
doing good things in the right way.   He had had a
sale, in the winter, and he had sold pictures enough
to provide the means for this sojourn abroad; though
his Lion's Head Mountain had not brought the two
hundred and fifty or three hundred dollars he had
hoped for.   It brought only a hundred and sixty; but
the time had almost come already when Westover
thought it brought too much.   Now, the letter from
Mrs. Durgin reminded him that he had never sent her
the photograph of the picture which he had promised
her.   He encased the photograph at once, and wrote
to her with many avowals of contrition for his neglect,
and strong regret that he was not soon to see the
original of the painting again.   He paid a decent reverence to the bereavement she had suffered, and he
sent his regards to all, especially his comrade Jeff,
whom he advised to keep out of the apple-orchard.

Five years later Westover came home in the first
week of a gasping August, whose hot breath thickened
round the Cunarder before she got half-way up the
harbor.   He waited only to see his pictures through
the custom-house, and then he left for the mountains.
The mountains meant Lion's Head for him, and eight
hours after he was dismounting from the train at a

station on the road which had been pushed through
on a new line within four miles of the farm. It was
called Lion's Head House, now, as he read on the side
of the mountain-wagon which he saw waiting at the
platform, and he knew at a glance that it was Jeff
Durgin who was coming forward to meet him and take
his hand-bag.

The boy had been the prophecy of the man in even
a disappointing degree. Westover had fancied him
growing up to the height of his father and brother, but
Jeff Durgin's stalwart frame was notable for strength
rather than height. He could not have been taller
than his mother, whose stature was above the stand-
ard of her sex, but he was massive without being bulky.
His chest was deep, his square shoulders broad, his
powerful legs bore him with a backward bulge of the
calves that showed through his shapely trousers; he
caught up the trunks and threw them into the baggage wagon with a swelling of the muscles on his short
thick arms which pulled his coat sleeves from his
heavy wrists and broad, short hands.

He had given one of these to Westover to shake
when they met, but with something conditional in his
welcome, and with a look which was not so much fur-
tive as latent. The thatch of yellow hair he used to
wear was now cropped close to his skull, which was a
sort of dun-color; and it had some drops of sweat
along the lighter edge where his hat had shaded his
forehead. He put his hat on the seat between himself and Westover, and drove away from the station
bareheaded, to cool himself after his bout with the

baggage, which was following more slowly in its wagon. There was a good deal of it, and there were half a dozen people, women of course, going to Lion's Head House. Westover climbed to the place beside Jeff to let them have the other two seats to themselves, and to have a chance of talking; but the ladies had to be quieted in their several anxieties concerning their baggage, and the letters and telegrams they had sent about their rooms, before they settled down to an exchange of apprehensions among themselves, and left Jeff Durgin free to listen to Westover.

"I don't know but *I* ought to have telegraphed you that I was coming," Westover said, "but I couldn't realize that you were doing things on the hotel scale. Perhaps you won't have room for me?"

"Guess we can put you up," said Jeff.

"No chance of getting my old room, I suppose?"

"I shouldn't wonder. If there's any one in it, I guess mother could change 'em."

"Is that so?" asked Westover, with a liking for being liked, which his tone expressed. "How is your mother?"

Jeff seemed to think a moment before he answered:

"Just exactly the same!"

"A little older?"

"Not as I can see."

"Does she hate keeping a hotel as badly as she expected?"

"That's what she says," answered Jeff, with a twinkle. All the time, while he was talking with Westover, he was breaking out to his horses, which he governed with his voice, trotting them up hill and down, and walking them on the short, infrequent levels, in the mountain fashion.

Westover almost feared to ask, "And how is Jackson?"

"First rate. That is, for him. He's as well as ever he was, I guess, and he don't appear a day older. *You've* changed some," said Jeff, with a look round at Westover.

"Yes; I'm twenty-nine, now, and I wear a heavier beard." Westover noticed that Jeff was clean shaved of any sign of an approaching beard, and artistically he rejoiced in the fellow's young, manly beauty, which was very regular and sculpturesque. "You're about eighteen?"

"Nearer nineteen."

"Is Jackson as much interested in the other world as he used to be?"

"Spirits?"

"Yes."

"I guess he keeps it up with Mr. Whitwell. He don't say much about it at home. He keeps all the books, and helps mother run the house. She couldn't very well get along without him."

"And where do you come in?"

"Well, I look after the transportation," said Jeff, with a nod toward his horses. "When I'm at home, that is. I've been at the Academy in Lovewell the last three winters, and that means a good piece of the summer too, first and last. But I guess I'll let mother talk to you about that."

" All right," said Westover.   " What I don't know
about education isn't worth knowing."

Jeff laughed, and said to the off horse, which seemed
to know that he was meant, " Get up, there ! "

" And Cynthia ?   Is Cynthia at home ? " Westover
asked.

" Yes.   They're all down in the little wood-colored
house, yet. Cynthia teaches winters, and summers she
helps mother.   She has charge of the dining-room."

" Does Franky cry as much aa ever ? "

" No.   Frank's a fine boy.   He's in the house too.
Kind of bell-boy."

" And you haven't worked Mr. Whitwell in, anywhere ? "

" Well, he talks to the ladies, and takes parties of
'em mountain-climbing. I guess we couldn't get along
without Mr. Whitwell.   He talks religion to 'em."
He cast a mocking glance at Westover over his shoulder. " Women seem to like religion, whether they
belong to church or not."

Westover laughed, and asked, " And Fox ?   How's
Fox ? "

" Well," said Jeff, " we had to give Fox away.   He
was always cross with the boarders' children.   My
brother was on from Colorado, and he took Fox back
with him."

" I didn't suppose," said Westover, " that I should
have been sorry to miss Fox. But I guess I shall be."

Jeff seemed to enjoy the implication of his words.
" He wasn't a bad dog.   He was stupid."

When they arrived at the foot of the lane, mounting

to the farm, Westover saw what changes had been
made in the house. There were large additions, taste-
less and characterless, but giving the rooms that were
needed.   There was a vulgar modernity in the new
parts, expressed with a final intensity in the four-light
windows, which are esteemed the last word of domes-
tic architecture in the country.   Jeff said nothing as
they approached the house, but Westover said, " Well,
you've certainly prospered. You're quite magnificent."

They reached the old level in front of the house,
artificially widened out of his remembrance, with a
white flag-pole planted at its edge, and he looked up
at the front of the house, which was unchanged, except that it had been built a story higher back of the
old front, and discovered the window of his old room.
He could hardly wait to get his greetings over with
Mrs. Durgin and Jackson, who both showed a decorous
pleasure and surprise at his coming, before he asked,
" And *could* you let me have my own room, Mrs. Durgin ? "

" Why, yes," she said.   " If you don't want something a little nicer."

" I don't believe you've got anything nicer," Westover said.

" All right, if you think so," she retorted.   " You
can have the old room, anyway."

X.

WESTOVER could not have said he felt very much
at home on his first sojourn at the farm, or that he
had cared greatly for the Durgins. But now he felt
very much at home, and as if he were in the hands of
friends.

It was toward the close of the afternoon that he
arrived, and he went in promptly to the meal that was
served shortly after. He found that the farm-house
had not evolved so far in the direction of a hotel as
to have reached the stage of a late dinner. It was tea
that he sat down to, but when he asked if there were
not something hot, after listening to a catalogue of the
cold meats, the spectacled waitress behind his chair
demanded, with the air of putting him on his honor,
" You among those that came this afternoon? "

Westover claimed to be of the new arrivals.

" Well, then, *you* can have steak or chops, and
baked potatoes."

He found the steak excellent, though succinct, and
he looked round in the distinction it conferred upon
him, on the older guests, who were served with cold
ham, tongue, and corned beef. He had expected to

be appointed his place by Cynthia Whitwell, but Jeff
came to the dining-room with him, and showed him
to the table he occupied, with an effect of doing him
special credit.

From his impressions of the berries, the cream, the
toast, and the tea, as well as the steak, he decided
that on the gastronomic side there could be no question
but the Durgins knew how to keep a hotel; and his
further acquaintance with the house and its appointments confirmed him in his belief.   All was very
simple, but sufficient; and no guest could have truthfully claimed that he was stinted in towels, in water,
in lamp-light, in the quantity or quality of bedding, in
hooks for clothes, or wardrobe or bureau room.   Westover made Mrs. Durgin his sincere compliments on her
success as they sat in the old parlor, which she had
kept for herself much in its former state, and she
accepted them with simple satisfaction.

"But I don't know as I should ever had the courage to try it, if it hadn't been for you happening along
just when you did," she said.

"Then I'm the founder of your fortunes?"

"If you want to call them fortunes.   We don't
complain.   It's been a fight, but I guess we've got the
best of it.   The house is full, and we're turnin' folks
away.   I guess they can't say that at the big hotels
they used to drive over from to see Lion's Head at
the farm."   She gave a low, comfortable chuckle, and
told Westover of the struggle they had made.   It was
an interesting story and pathetic, like all stories of
human endeavor: the efforts of the most selfish ambi-

tion have something of this interest; and the struggle
of the Durgins had the grace of the wish to keep their
home.

"And is Jeff as well satisfied as the rest?" Westover asked, after other talk and comment on the facts.

"Too much so," said Mrs. Durgin. "I should like
to talk with you about Jeff, Mr. Westover; you and
him was always such friends."

"Yes," said Westover; "I shall be glad if I can be
of use to you."

"Why, it's just this. I don't see why Jeff shouldn't
do something besides keep a hotel."

Westover's eyes wandered to the photograph of his
painting of Lion's Head which hung over the mantel-
piece, in what he felt to be the place of the greatest
honor in the whole house, and a sudden fear came
upon him that perhaps Jeff had developed an artistic
talent in the belief of his family. But he waited silently to hear.

"We did think that before we got through the improvements last spring a year ago we should have to
get the savings-bank to put a mortgage on the place;
but we had just enough to start the season with, and
we thought we would try to pull through. We had a
splendid season, and made money, and this year we're
doin' so well that I ain't afraid for the future any
more, and I want to give Jeff a chance in the world.
I want he should go to college."

Westover felt all the boldness of the aspiration, but
it was at least not in the direction of art. "Wouldn't
you rather miss him in the management?"

"We should, some. But he would be here the best part of the summer, in his vacations, and Jackson and I are full able to run the house without him."

"Jackson seems very well," said Westover, evasively.

"He's *better*. He's only thirty-four years old. His father lived to be sixty, and he had the same *kind*. Jeff tell you he had been at Lovewell Academy?"

"Yes; he did."

"He done well, there. All his teachers that he ever had," Mrs. Durgin went on, with the mother-pride that soon makes itself tiresome to the listener, "said Jeff done well at school when he had a mind to, and at the Academy he studied real hard. I guess," said Mrs. Durgin, with her chuckle, "that he thought that was goin' to be the end of it. One thing, he had to keep up with Cynthy, and that put him on his pride. You seen Cynthy yet?"

"No. Jeff told me she was in charge of the dining-room."

"I guess *I'm* in charge of the whole house," said Mrs. Durgin. "Cynthy's the housekeeper, though. She's a fine girl, and a smart girl," said Mrs. Durgin, with a visible relenting from some grudge, "and she'll do well wherever you put her. She went to the Academy the first two winters Jeff did. We've about scooped in the whole Whitwell family. Franky's here, and his father's—well, his father's kind of philosopher to the lady boarders." Mrs. Durgin laughed, and Westover laughed with her. "Yes, I want Jeff should go to college, and I want he should be a lawyer."

Westover did not find that he had anything useful to say to this; so he said, "I've no doubt it's better than being a painter."

"I'm not so sure; three hundred dollars for a little thing like that." She indicated the photograph of his Lion's Head, and she was evidently so proud of it that he reserved for the moment the truth as to the price he had got for the painting. "I *was* surprised when you sent me a photograph full as big. I don't let every one in here, but a good many of the ladies are artists themselves—amatures, I guess,—and first and last they all want to see it. I guess they'll all want to see *you*, Mr. Westover. They'll be *wild*, as they call it, when they know you're in the house. Yes, I mean Jeff shall go to college."

"Bowdoin, or—Dartmouth?" Westover suggested.

"Well, I guess you'll think I'm about as forth-putting as I was when I wanted you to give me a three-hundred-dollar picture for a week's board."

"I only got a hundred and sixty, Mrs. Durgin," said Westover conscientiously.

"Well, it's a shame. Any rate, three hundred's the price to all *my* boarders. My, if I've told that story once, I guess I've told it fifty times!"

Mrs. Durgin laughed at herself jollily, and Westover noted how prosperity had changed her. It had freed her tongue, it had brightened her humor, it had cheered her heart; she had put on flesh, and her stalwart frame was now a far greater bulk than he remembered.

"Well, there!" she said. "The long and the short of it is, I want Jeff should go to Harvard."

He commanded himself to say, " I don't see why he shouldn't."

Mrs. Durgin called out, " Come in, Jackson," and Westover looked round and saw the elder son like a gaunt shadow in the doorway. " I've just got where I've told Mr. Westover where I want Jeff should go. It don't seem to have ca'd him off his feet, any, either."

" I presume," said Jackson, coming in, and sitting lankly down in the feather-cushioned rocking-chair which his mother pushed towards him with her foot, " that the expense would be more at Harvard than it would at the other colleges."

" If you want the best, you got to pay for it," said Mrs. Durgin.

" I suppose it would cost more," Westover answered Jackson's conjecture. " I really don't know much about it. One hears tremendous stories at Boston of the rate of living among the swell students in Cambridge. People talk of five thousand a year, and that sort of thing." Mrs. Durgin shut her lips, after catching her breath. " But I fancy that it's largely talk. I have a friend whose son went through Harvard for a thousand a year, and I know that many fellows do it for much less."

" I guess we can manage to let Jeff have a thousand a year," said Mrs. Durgin, proudly, " and not scrimp very much, either."

She looked at her elder son, who said: " I don't believe but what we could. It's more of a question with me what sort of influence Jeff would come under there. I think he's pretty much spoilt here ! "

"Now, Jackson!" said his mother.

"I've heard," said Westover, "that Harvard takes
the nonsense out of a man. I can't enter into what
you say, and it isn't my affair; but in regard to influence at Harvard, it depends upon the set Jeff is thrown
with, or throws himself with. So, at least, I infer
from what I've heard my friend say of his son there.
There are hard-working sets, loafing sets, and fast
sets; and I suppose it isn't different at Harvard in
such matters from other colleges."

Mrs. Durgin looked a little grave. "Of course,"
she said, "we don't know anybody at Cambridge, except some ladies that boarded with us one summer, and
I shouldn't want to ask any favor of them. The trouble would be to get Jeff started right."

Westover surmised a good many things, but in the
absence of any confidences from the Durgins he could
not tell just how much Jackson meant in saying that
Jeff was pretty much spoiled, or how little. At first,
from Mrs. Durgin's prompt protest, he fancied that
Jackson meant that the boy had been over-indulged
by his mother. "I understand," he said, in default
of something else to say, "that the requirements at
Harvard are pretty severe."

"He's passed his preliminary examinations," said
Jackson, with a touch of hauteur, "and I guess he
can enter this fall, if we should so decide. He'll have
some conditions, prob'ly, but none but what he can
work off, I guess."

"Then, if you wish to have him go to college, by
all means let him go to Harvard, I should say. It's

our great university, and our oldest.   I'm not a college man myself; but if I were, I should wish to have
been a Harvard man.   If Jeff has any nonsense in
him, it will take it out; and I don't believe there's
anything in Harvard, as Harvard, to make him worse."

"That's what we both think," said Jackson.

" I've heard," Westover continued, and he rose and
stood while he spoke, " that Harvard's like the world.
A man gets on there on the same terms that he gets
on in the world.   He has to be a man, and he'd better be a gentleman."

Mrs. Durgin still looked serious.   " Have you come
back to Boston for good, now?   Do you expect to be
there right along?"

" I've taken a studio there.   Yes, I expect to be in
Boston, now.   I've taken to teaching, and I fancy I
can make a living.   If Jeff comes to Cambridge, and
I can be of any use—"

" We should be ever so much obliged to you," said
his mother, with an air of great relief.

" Not at all.   I shall be very glad.   Your mountain
air is drugging me, Mrs. Durgin.   I shall have to say
good-night, or I shall tumble asleep before I get up-
stairs.   Oh, I can find the way, I guess; this part of
the house seems the same."   He got away from them,
and with the lamp that Jackson gave him found his
way to his room.   A few moments later some one
knocked at his door, and a boy stood there with a
pitcher.   " Some ice-water, Mr. Westover?"

" Why, is that you, Franky?   I'm glad to see you
again.   How are you?"

"HE SAW THE GIRL IN THE MORNING"

"I'm pretty well," said the boy, shyly. He was a very handsome little fellow of distinctly dignified presence, and Westover was aware at once that here was not a subject for patronage. "Is there anything else you want, Mr. Westover? Matches, or soap, or anything?" He put the pitcher down and gave a keen glance round the room.

"No, everything seems to be here, Frank," said Westover.

"Well, good-night," said the boy, and he slipped out, quietly closing the door after him.

Westover pushed up his window, and looked at Lion's Head in the moonlight. It slumbered as if with the sleep of centuries, austere, august. The moon-rays seemed to break and splinter on the outline of the lion-shape, and left all the mighty mass black below.

In the old porch under his window Westover heard whispering. Then "You behave yourself, Jeff Durgin!" came in a voice which could be no other than Cynthia Whitwell's, and Jeff Durgin's laugh followed.

He saw the girl in the morning. She met him at the door of the dining-room, and he easily found in her shy, proud manner, and her pure, cold beauty, the temperament and physiognomy of the child he remembered. She was tall and slim, and she held herself straight without stiffness; her face was fine, with a straight nose, and a decided chin, and a mouth of the same sweetness which looked from her still gray eyes; her hair, of the average brown, had a rough effect of being quickly tossed into form, which pleased him; as

she slipped down the room before him to place him
at table he saw that she was, as it were, involuntarily,
unwillingly graceful. She made him think of a wild
sweetbrier, of a hermit-thrush, but if there were this
sort of poetic suggestion in Cynthia's looks, her acts
were of plain and honest prose, such as giving Westover the pleasantest place and the most intelligent
waitress in the room.

He would have liked to keep her in talk a moment,
but she made businesslike dispatch of all his allusions
to the past, and got herself quickly away. Afterwards
she came back to him, with the effect of having forced
herself to come, and the color deepened in her cheeks
while she stayed.

She seemed glad of his being there, but helpless
against the instincts or traditions that forbade her to
show her pleasure in his presence. Her reticence became almost snubbing in its strictness when he asked
her about her school-teaching in the winter; but he
found that she taught at the little school-house at the
foot of the hill, and lived at home with her father.

"And have you any bad boys that frighten little
girls, in your school?" he asked, jocosely.

"I don't know as I have," she said, with a consciousness that flamed into her cheeks.

"Perhaps the boys have reformed," Westover suggested.

"I presume," she said, stiffly, "that there's room
for improvement in every one," and then, as if she
were afraid he might take this personally, she looked
unhappy, and tried to speak of other things. She

asked him if he did not see a great many changes at Lion's Head; he answered gravely that he wished he could have found it just as he left it, and then she must have thought she had gone wrong again, for she left him in an embarrassment that was pathetic, but which was charming.

XI.

AFTER breakfast Westover walked out and saw
Whitwell standing on the grass in front of the house,
beside the flag-staff. He suffered Westover to make
the first advances towards the renewal of their acquaintance, but when he was sure of his friendly intention he responded with a cordial openness which the
painter had fancied wanting in his children. Whitwell
had not changed much. The most noticeable difference
was the compact phalanx of new teeth which had re-
placed the staggering veterans of former days, and
which displayed themselves in his smile of relenting.
There was some novelty of effect also in an arrange-
ment of things in his hat-band. At first Westover
thought they were fish-hooks and artificial flies, such
as the guides wear in the Adirondacks to advertise
their calling about the hotel offices and the piazzas.
But another glance showed him that they were sprays
and wild flowers of various sorts, with gay mosses and
fungi and some stems of Indian-pipe.

Whitwell seemed pleased that these things should
have caught Westover's eye. He said, almost imme-

diately, "Lookin' at my almanac? This is one of our
field-days; we have 'em once a week; and I like to let
the ladies see beforehand what nature's got on the bill
for 'em, in the woods and pastur's."

"It's a good idea," said Westover, "and it's fresh
and picturesque." Whitwell laughed for pleasure.
"They told me what a consolation you were to the
ladies, with your walks and talks."

"Well, I try to give 'em something to think about,"
said Whitwell.

"But why do you confine your ministrations to one
sex?"

"I don't, on purpose. But it's the only sex here,
three-fourths of the time. Even the children are mostly
all girls. When the husbands come up Saturday nights,
they don't want to go on a tramp Sundays. They
want to lay off and rest. That's about how it is.
Well, you see some changes about Lion's Head, I
presume?" he asked, with what seemed an impersonal
pleasure in them.

"I should rather have found the old farm. But I
must say I'm glad to find such a good hotel."

"Jeff and his mother made their brags to you?"
said Whitwell, with a kind of amiable scorn. "I guess
if it wa'n't for Cynthy she wouldn't know where she
was standin', half the time. It don't matter where
Jeff stands, I guess. Jackson's the best o' the lot,
now the old man's gone." There was no one by at
the moment to hear these injuries except Westover,
but Whitwell called them out with a frankness which
was perhaps more carefully adapted to the situation

than it seemed.   Westover made no attempt to parry
them formally; but he offered some generalities in
extenuation of the unworthiness of the Durgins, which
Whitwell did not altogether refuse.

"Oh, it's all right.   Old woman talk to you about
Jeff's going to college?   I thought so.   Wants to
make another Dan'el Webster of him.   Guess she can's
far forth as Dan'el's graduatin' went."   Westover
tried to remember how this had been with the states-
man, but could not.   Whitwell added with intensify-
ing irony of look and tone: "Guess the second Dan'el
won't have a chance to tear his degree up; guess he
wouldn't ever b'en ready to try for it if it had de-
pended on *him*.   They don't keep any record at Harvard, do they, of the way fellows are prepared for their
preliminary examinations?"

"I don't quite know what you mean," said Westover.

"Oh, nothin'.   You get a chance some time to ask
Jeff who done most of his studyin' for him at the
Academy."

This hint was not so darkling but Westover could
understand that Whitwell attributed Jeff's scholarship
to the help of Cynthia, but he would not press him to
an open assertion of the fact.   There was something
painful in it to him; it had the pathos which perhaps
most of the success in the world would reveal if we
could penetrate its outside.

He was silent, and Whitwell left the point.   "Well,"
he concluded, "what's goin' on in them old European
countries?"

"Oh, the old thing," said Westover. "But I can't speak for any except France, very well."

"What's their republic like, over there? Ours? See anything of it, how it works?"

"Well, you know," said Westover, "I was working so hard myself all the time—"

"Good!" Whitwell slapped his leg. Westover saw that he had on long india-rubber boots, which came up to his knees, and he gave a wayward thought to the misery they would be on an August day to another man; but Whitwell was probably insensible to any discomfort from them. "When a man's mindin' his own business any government's good, I guess. But I should like to prowl round some them places where they had the worst scenes of the Revolution. Ever been in the Place de la Concorde?" Whitwell gave it the full English pronunciation.

"I passed through it nearly every day."

"I want to know! And that column that they pulled down in the Commune that had that little Boney on it: see that?"

"In the Place Vendôme?"

"Yes, Plass Vonndome."

"Oh, yes. You wouldn't know it had ever been down."

"Nor the things it stood for?"

"As to that, I can't be so sure."

"Well, it's funny," said the philosopher, "how the world seems to always come out at the same hole it went in at!" He paused, with his mouth open, as if to let the notion have full effect with Westover.

The painter said, "And you're still in the old place, Mr. Whitwell?"

"Yes, I like my own house. They've wanted me to come up here often enough, but I'm satisfied where I am. It's quiet down there, and when I get through for the day I can read. And I like to keep my family together. Cynthy and Frank always sleep at home, and Jombateeste eats with me. You remember Jombateeste?"

Westover had to say that he did not.

"Well, I don't know as you *did* see him, much. He was that Canuck I had helpin' me clear that piece over on Lion's Head for the pulp-mill; pulp-mill went all to thunder, and I never got a cent. And sometimes Jackson comes down with his plantchette and we have a good time."

"Jackson still believes in the manifestations?"

"Yes. But he's never developed much himself. He can't seem to do much without the plantchette. We've had up some them old philosophers lately. We've had up Socrates."

"Is that so? It must be very interesting."

Whitwell did not answer, and Westover saw his eye wander. He looked round. Several ladies were coming across the grass towards him from the hotel, lifting their skirts and tiptoeing through the dew. They called to him, "Good-morning, Mr. Whitwell!" and "Are you going up Lion's Head to-day?" and "Don't you think it will rain?"

"Guess not," said Whitwell, with a fatherly urbanity and an air of amusement at the anxieties of the

" 'ACQUAINTED WITH MR. WESTOVER, THE ARTIST?' "

sex, which seemed habitual to him.   He waited tranquilly for them to come up, and then asked with a
wave of his hand towards Westover, "Acquainted
with Mr. Westover, the artist?"   He named each of
them, and it would have been no great vanity in Westover to think they had made their little movement
across the grass quite as much in the hope of an introduction to him as in the wish to consult Whitwell
about his plans.

The painter found himself the centre of an agreeable excitement with all the ladies in the house.   For
this it was perhaps sufficient to be a man.   To be rea-
sonably young and decently good-looking, to be an
artist, and an artist not unknown, were advantages
which had the splendor of superfluity.

He liked finding himself in the simple and innocent
American circumstance again, and he was not sorry to
be confronted at once with one of the most characteristic aspects of our summer.   He could read in the
present development of Lion's Head House all the
history of its evolution from the first conception of
farm-board, which sufficed the earliest comers, to its
growth in the comforts and conveniences which more
fastidious tastes and larger purses demanded.   Before
this point was reached, the boarders would be of a
good and wholesome sort, but they would be people
of no social advantages, and not of much cultivation,
though they might be intelligent; they would certainly
not be fashionable; five dollars a week implied all
that, except in the case of some wandering artist or
the family of some poor young professor.   But when

the farm became a boarding-house and called itself a
hotel, as at present with Lion's Head House, and people paid ten dollars a week, or twelve for transients, a
moment of its character was reached which could not
be surpassed when its prosperity became greater, and
its inmates more pretentious.   In fact, the people who
can afford to pay ten dollars a week for summer board
and not much more, are often the best of the American
people, or at least of the New England people.   They
mav not know it, and those who are richer may not
imagine it.   They are apt to be middle-aged maiden
ladies from university towns, living upon carefully
guarded investments; young married ladies with a
scant child or two, and needing rest and change of
air; college professors with nothing but their modest
salaries; literary men or women in the beginning of
their tempered success; clergymen and their wives
away from their churches in the larger country towns
or the smaller suburbs of the cities; here and there an
agreeable bachelor in middle life, fond of literature
and nature; hosts of young and pretty girls with distinct tastes in art, and devoted to the clever young
painter who leads them to the sources of inspiration
in the fields and woods.   Such people are refined, hu-
mane, appreciative, sympathetic; and Westover, fresh
from the life abroad where life is seldom so free as
ours without some stain, was glad to find himself in
the midst of this unrestraint, which was so sweet and
pure.   He had seen enough of rich people to know
that riches seldom bought the highest qualities, even
among his fellow-countrymen who suppose that riches

can do everything, and the first aspects of society at
Lion's Head seemed to him Arcadian.   There really
proved to be a shepherd or two among all that troop
of shepherdesses, old and young; though it was in the
middle of the week, remote alike from the Saturday
of arrivals and the Monday of departures.   To be sure
there was none quite so young as himself, except Jeff
Durgin, who was officially exterior to the social life.

The painter who gave lessons to the ladies was already a man of forty, and he was strongly dragoned
round by a wife almost as old, who had taken great
pains to secure him for herself, and who worked him
to far greater advantage in his profession than he could
possibly have worked himself; she got him orders;
sold his pictures, even in Boston, where they never buy
American pictures; found him pupils, and kept the
boldest of these from flirting with him.   Westover,
who was so newly from Paris, was able to console him
with talk of the salons and ateliers, which he had not
heard from so directly in ten years.   After the first
inevitable moment of jealousy, his wife forgave Westover when she found that he did not want pupils, and
she took a leading part in the movement to have him
read Browning at a picnic, organized by the ladies
shortly after he came.

XII.

THE picnic was held in Whitwell's Clearing, on the side of Lion's Head, where the moss, almost as white as snow, lay like belated drifts among the tall, thin grass which overran the space opened by the axe, and crept to the verge of the low pines growing in the shelter of the loftier woods. It was the end of one of Whitwell's "Tramps Home to Nature," as he called his walks and talks with the ladies, and on this day Westover's fellow-painter had added to his lessons in wood-lore the claims of art, intending that his class should make studies of various bits in the clearing, and should try to catch something of its peculiar charm. He asked Westover what he thought of the notion, and Westover gave it his approval, which became enthusiastic when he saw the place. He found in it the melancholy grace, the poignant sentiment of ruin which expresses itself in some measure wherever man has invaded nature, and then left his conquest to her again. In Whitwell's Clearing the effect was intensified by the approach on the fading wood road, which the wagons had made in former days when they hauled the fallen timber to the pulp-mill. In places it was so

vague and faint as to be hardly a trail; in others,
where the wheel tracks remained visible, the trees had
sent out a new growth of lower branches in the place
of those lopped away, and almost forbade the advance
of foot-passengers. The ladies said they did not see
how Jeff was ever going to get through with the
wagon, and they expressed fears for the lunch he was
bringing, which seemed only too well grounded.

But Whitwell, who was leading them on, said:
" You let a Durgin alone to do a thing when he's made
up his mind to it. I guess you'll have your lunch all
right "; and by the time that they had got enough of
Browning, they heard the welcome sound of wheels
crashing upon dead boughs, and swishing through the
underbrush, and in the pauses of these pleasant noises,
the voice of Jeff Durgin encouraging his horses. The
children of the party broke away to meet him, and
then he came in sight ahead of his team, looking strong
and handsome in his keeping with the scene. Before
he got within hearing, the ladies murmured a hymn of
praise to his type of beauty; they said he looked like
a young Hercules, and Westover owned with an inward smile that Jeff had certainly made the best of
himself for the time being. He had taken a leaf from
the book of the summer folks; his stalwart calves revealed themselves in thick-ribbed stockings; he wore
knickerbockers and a Norfolk jacket of corduroy; he
had style as well as beauty, and he had the courage of
his clothes and looks. Westover was still in the first
surprise of the American facts, and he wondered just
what part in the picnic Jeff was to bear socially. He

was neither quite host or guest; but no doubt in the easy play of the life, which Westover was rather proud to find so charming, the question would solve itself rationally and gracefully.

"Where do you want the things?" the young fellow asked of the company at large, as he advanced upon them from the green portals of the roadway, pulling off his soft wool hat, and wiping his wet forehead with his blue-bordered white handkerchief.

"Oh, right here, Jeff." The nimblest of the nymphs sprang to her feet from the lounging and crouching circle about Westover. She was a young nymph no longer, but with a daughter not so much younger than herself as to make the contrast of her sixteen years painful. Westover recognized the officious, self-approving kind of the woman, but he admired the brisk efficiency with which she had taken possession of the affair from the beginning and inspired every one to help, in strict subordination to herself.

When the cloths were laid on the smooth, elastic moss, and the meal was spread, she heaped a plate without suffering any interval in her activities.

"I suppose you've got to go back to your horses, Jeff, and you shall be the first served," she said, and she offered him the plate with a bright smile and friendly grace, which were meant to keep him from the hurt of her intention.

Jeff did not offer to take the plate which she raised to him from where she was kneeling, but looked down at her with perfect intelligence. "I guess I don't

want anything," he said, and turned and walked away
into the woods.

The ill-advised woman remained kneeling for a
moment with her ingratiating smile hardening on her
face, while the sense of her blunder petrified the rest.
She was the first to recover herself, and she said with
a laugh that she tried to make reckless, " Well, friends,
I suppose the rest of you are hungry; I know *I* am,"
and she began to eat.

The others ate, too, though their appetites might
well have been affected by the diplomatic behavior of
Whitwell. He would not take anything, just at present, he said, and got his lank length up from the root
of a tree where he had folded it down. " I don't seem
to care much for anything in the middle of the day;
breakfast's my best meal," and he followed Jeff off
into the woods.

" Really," said the lady, " what did they expect ? "
But the question was so difficult that no one seemed
able to make the simple answer.

The incident darkened the day, and spoiled its
pleasure; it cast a lessening shadow into the evening
when the guests met round the fire in the large, ugly
new parlor at the hotel.

The next morning the ladies assembled again on the
piazza to decide what should be done with the beautiful day before them. Whitwell stood at the foot of
the flag-staff with one hand staying his person against
it, like a figure posed in a photograph to verify pro-
portions in the different features of a prospect.

The heroine of the unhappy affair of the picnic

could not forbear authorizing herself to invoke his
opinion at a certain point of the debate, and "Mr.
Whitwell!" she called to him, "won't you please come
here a moment?"

Whitwell slowly pulled himself across the grass to
the group, and at the same moment, as if she had been
waiting for him to be present, Mrs. Durgin came out
of the office door and advanced towards the ladies.

"Mrs. Marven," she said, with the stony passivity
which the ladies used to note in her when they came
over to Lion's Head farm in the tally-hoes, "the stage
leaves here at two o'clock to get the down train at
three. I want you should have your trunks ready to
go on the wagon a little before two."

"You want I should have my— What do you
mean, Mrs. Durgin?"

"I want your rooms."

"You want my *rooms*?"

Mrs. Durgin did not answer. She let her steadfast
look suffice; and Mrs. Marven went on in a rising flutter: "Why, you can't *have* my rooms! I don't understand you. I've taken my rooms for the whole of
August, and they are mine; and—"

"I have got to have your rooms," said Mrs. Durgin.

"Very well, then, I won't give them up," said the
lady. "A bargain's a bargain, and I have your agree-
ment—"

"If you're not out of your rooms by two o'clock,
your things will be put out; and after dinner to-day
you will not eat another bite under my roof."

Mrs. Durgin went in, and it remained for the com-

pany to make what they could of the affair. Mrs.
Marven did not wait for the result. She was not a
dignified person, but she rose with hauteur and
whipped away to her rooms, hers no longer, to make
her preparations. She knew at least how to give her
going the effect of quitting the place with disdain and
abhorrence.

The incident of her expulsion was brutal, but it was
clearly meant to be so. It made Westover a little
sick, and he would have liked to pity Mrs. Marven
more than he could. The ladies said that Mrs. Durgin's behavior was an outrage, and they ought all to
resent it by going straight to their own rooms and
packing their things and leaving on the same stage
with Mrs. Marven. None of them did so, and their
talk veered round to something extenuating if not jus-
tifying Mrs. Durgin's action.

"I suppose," one of them said, "that she felt more
indignant about it, because she *has* been so very good
to Mrs. Marven, and her daughter, too. They were
both sick on her hands here for a week, after they
came, first one and then the other, and she looked after
them and did for them like a mother."

"And yet," another lady suggested, "what could
Mrs. Marven have done? What *did* she do? He wasn't
asked to the picnic, and I don't see why he should
have been treated as a guest. He was there, purely
and simply, to bring the things and take them away.
And besides, if there *is* anything in distinctions, in
differences, if we are to choose who is to associate
with us—or our daughters—"

"That is true," the ladies said, in one form or another, with the tone of conviction; but they were not so deeply convinced but they wanted a man's opinion, and they all looked at Westover.

He would not respond to their look, and the lady who had argued for Mrs. Marven had to ask, "What do *you* think, Mr. Westover?"

"Ah, it's a difficult question," he said. "I suppose that as long as one person believes himself or herself socially better than another, it must always be a fresh problem what to do in every given case."

The ladies said they supposed so, and they were forced to make what they could of wisdom in which they might certainly have felt a want of finality.

Westover went away from them in a perplexed mind which was not simplified by the contempt he had at the bottom of all for something unmanly in Jeff, who had carried his grievance to his mother like a slighted boy, and provoked her to take up arms for him.

The sympathy for Mrs. Marven mounted again when it was seen that she did not come to dinner, or permit her daughter to do so, and when it became known later that she had refused for both the dishes sent to their rooms. Her farewells to the other ladies, when they gathered to see her off on the stage, were airy rather than cheery; there was almost a demonstration in her behalf, but Westover was oppressed by a kind of inherent squalor in the incident.

At night he responded to a knock which he supposed that of Frank Whitwell with ice-water, and Mrs. Durgin came into his room, and sat down in one of his two chairs. "Mr. Westover," she said, "if you knew all I had done for that woman and her daughter, and how much she had pretended to think of us all, I don't believe you'd be so ready to judge me."

"Judge you!" cried Westover. "Bless my soul, Mrs. Durgin! I haven't said a word that could be tormented into the slightest censure."

"But you think I done wrong?"

"I have not been at all able to satisfy myself on that point, Mrs. Durgin. I think it's always wrong to revenge one's self."

"Yes, I suppose it is," said Mrs. Durgin, humbly; and the tears came into her eyes. "I got the tray ready with my own hands, that was sent to her room; but she wouldn't touch it. I presume she didn't like having *a plate prepared for her!* But I did feel sorry for her. She a'n't over and above strong, and I'm afraid she'll be sick; there a'n't any rest'rant at our depot."

Westover fancied this a fit mood in Mrs. Durgin for her further instruction, and he said, "And if you'll excuse me, Mrs. Durgin, I don't think what you did was quite the way to keep a hotel."

More tears flashed into Mrs. Durgin's eyes, but they were tears of wrath now. "I would 'a' done it," she said, "if I thought every single one of 'em would 'a' left the house the next minute, for there a'n't one that has the first word to say against me, any other way. It wa'n't that I cared whether she thought my son was good enough to eat with her or not; I know what *I* think, and that's enough for *me*. He wa'n't invited to the picnic, and he a'n't one to put himself forward. If she didn't want him to stay, all she had to do was to do nothin'.   But to make him up a plate before everybody, and hand it to him to eat with the horses, like a tramp, or a dog—"   Mrs. Durgin filled to the throat with her wrath, and the sight of her made West- over keenly unhappy.

"Yes, yes," he said. "It was a miserable business." He could not help adding, "If Jeff could have kept it to himself,—but perhaps that wasn't possible."

"Mr. Westover!" said Mrs. Durgin, sternly. "Do you think Jeff would come to me, like a great cry- baby, and complain of my lady boarders and the way they used him?   It was Mr. Whit'ell that let it out, or I don't know as I should *ever* known about it."

"I'm glad Jeff didn't tell you," said Westover, with a revulsion of good feeling toward him.

"He'd 'a' died first," said his mother.   "But Mr. Whit'ell done just right all through, and I sha'n't soon forget it.   Jeff's give me a proper goin' over for what I done; both the boys have. But I couldn't help it, and I should do just so again. All is, I wanted you should know just what you was blamin' me for—"

"I don't know that I blame you.   I only wish you *could* have helped it—managed some other way."

"I did try to get over it, and all I done was to lose a night's rest.   Then, this morning, when I see her settin' there so cool and mighty with the boarders, and takin' the lead as usual, I just waited till she got Whit'ell across, and nearly everybody was there that saw what she done to Jeff, and then I flew out on her."

Westover could not suppress a laugh. "Well, Mrs. Durgin, your retaliation was complete; it was dramatic."

"I don't know what you mean by that," said Mrs. Durgin, rising and resuming her self-control; she did not refuse herself a grim smile. "But I guess she thought it was pretty perfect herself—or she will, when she's able to give her mind to it. I'm sorry for her daughter; I never had anything against her; or her mother either, for that matter, before. Franky look after you pretty well? I'll send him up with your ice-water. Got everything else you want?"

"I should have to invent a want, if I wished to complain," said Westover.

"Well, I should like to have you do it. We can't ever do too much for *you*. Well, good-night, Mr. Westover."

"Good-night, Mrs. Durgin."

XIII.

Jeff Durgin entered Harvard that fall, with fewer conditions than most students have to work off. This was set down to the credit of Lovewell Academy, where he had prepared for the University; and some observers in such matters were interested to note how thoroughly the old school in a remote town had done its work for him.

None who formed personal relations with him at that time conjectured that he had done much of the work for himself, and even to Westover, when Jeff came to him some weeks after his settlement in Cambridge, he seemed painfully out of his element, and unamiably aware of it. For the time, at least, he had lost the jovial humor, not too kindly always, which largely characterized him, and expressed itself in sallies of irony which were not so unkindly either. The painter perceived that he was on his guard against his own friendly interest; Jeff made haste to explain that he came because he had told his mother that he would do so. He scarcely invited a return of his visit, and he left Westover wondering at the sort of vague rebellion against his new life which he seemed to be in. The painter went out to see him in Cambridge, not long after, and was rather glad to find him rooming with some other rustic Freshman in a humble street running from the square towards the river; for he thought Jeff must have taken his lodging for its cheapness, out of regard to his mother's means. But Jeff was not glad to be found there, apparently; he said at once that he expected to get a room in the Yard the next year, and eat at Memorial Hall. He spoke scornfully of his boarding-house as a place where they were all a lot of jays together; and Westover thought him still more at odds with his environment than he had before. But Jeff consented to come in and dine with him at his restaurant, and afterwards go to the theatre with him.

When he came, Westover did not quite like his despatch of the half-bottle of California claret served each of them with the Italian table d'hôte. He did not like his having already seen the play he proposed; and he found some difficulty in choosing a play which Jeff had not seen. It appeared then that he had been at the theatre two or three times a week for the last month, and that it was almost as great a passion with him as with Westover himself. He had become already a critic of acting, with a rough good sense of it, and a decided opinion. He knew which actors he preferred, and which actresses, better still. It was some consolation for Westover to find that he mostly took an admission ticket when he went to the theatre; but though he could not blame Jeff for showing his own fondness for it, he wished that he had not his fondness.

So far Jeff seemed to have spent very few of his evenings in Cambridge, and Westover thought it would be well if he had some acquaintance there. He made favor for him with a friendly family, who asked him to dinner. They did it to oblige Westover, against their own judgment and knowledge, for they said it was always the same with Freshmen; a single act of hospitality finished the acquaintance. Jeff came, and he behaved with as great indifference to the kindness meant him as if he were dining out every night; he excused himself very early in the evening on the ground that he had to go into Boston, and he never paid his dinner-call. After that Westover tried to consider his whole duty to him fulfilled, and not to trouble himself further. Now and then, however, Jeff disappointed the expectation Westover had formed of him, by coming to see him, and being apparently glad of the privilege. But he did not make the painter think that he was growing in grace or wisdom, though he apparently felt an increasing confidence in his own knowledge of life.

Westover could only feel a painful interest tinged with amusement in his grotesque misconceptions of the world where he had not yet begun to right himself. Jeff believed lurid things of the society wholly unknown to him; to his gross credulity, Boston houses which at the worst were the homes of a stiff and cold exclusiveness, were the scenes of riot only less scandalous than the dissipation to which fashionable ladies

abandoned themselves at champagne suppers in the
Back Bay hotels, and on their secret visits to the Chinese opium-joints in Kingston Street.

Westover tried to make him see how impossible his
fallacies were; but he could perceive that Jeff thought
him either wilfully ignorant or helplessly innocent;
and of far less authority than a barber who had the
entrée of all these swell families as hair-dresser, and
who corroborated the witness of a hotel night-clerk
(Jeff would not give their names) to the depravity of
the upper classes. He had to content himself with
saying: "I hope you will be ashamed some day of
having believed such rot. But I suppose it's something you've got to go through. You may take my
word for it, though, that it isn't going to do you any
good. It's going to do you harm, and that's why I
hate to have you think it, for your own sake. It can't
hurt any one else."

What disgusted the painter most was that, with all
his belief in the wickedness of the fine world, it was
clear that Jeff would have willingly been of it; and he
divined that if he had any strong aspirations they were
for society and for social acceptance. He had fancied,
when the fellow seemed to care so little for the studies
of the University, that he might come forward in its
sports. Jeff gave more and more the effect of tremendous strength in his peculiar physique, though there
was always the disappointment of not finding him tall.
He was of the middle height, but he was hewn out and
squared upward massively. He felt like stone to any
accidental contact, and the painter brought away a

bruise from the mere brunt of his shoulders. He learned that Jeff was a frequenter of the gymnasium, where his strength must have been known, but he could not make out that he had any standing among the men who went in for athletics. If Jeff had even this, the sort of standing in college which he failed of would easily have been won too. But he had been falsely placed at the start, or some quality of his nature neutralized other qualities that would have made him a leader in college, and he remained one of the least forward men in it. Other jays won favor and liking, and ceased to be jays; Jeff continued a jay. He was not chosen into any of the nicer societies; those that he joined when he thought they were swell he could not care for when he found they were not.

Westover came into a knowledge of the facts through his casual and scarcely voluntary confidences, and he pitied him somewhat while he blamed him a great deal more, without being able to help him at all. It appeared to him that the fellow had gone wrong more through ignorance than perversity, and that it was a stubbornness of spirit rather than a badness of heart that kept him from going right. He sometimes wondered whether it was not more a baffled wish to be justified in his own esteem than anything else that made him overvalue the things he missed. He knew how such an experience as that with Mrs. Marven rankles in the heart of youth, and will not cease to smart till some triumph in kind brings it ease; but between the man of thirty and the boy of twenty there is a gulf fixed, and he could not ask. He did not know

that a college man often goes wrong in his first year,
out of no impulse that he can very clearly account for
himself, and then when he ceases to be merely of his
type and becomes more of his character, he pulls up
and goes right. He did not know how much Jeff had
been with a set that was fast without being fine. The
boy had now and then a book in his hand when he
came ; not always such a book as Westover could have
wished, but still a book ; and to his occasional questions about how he was getting on with his college
work, Jeff made brief answers, which gave the notion
that he was not neglecting it.

Towards the end of his first year he sent to Westover one night from a station-house, where he had
been locked up for breaking a street-lamp in Boston.
By his own showing he had not broken the lamp, or
assisted, except through his presence, at the misdeed
of the tipsy students who had done it. His breath
betrayed that he had been drinking too ; but otherwise
he seemed as sober as Westover himself, who did not
know whether to augur well or ill for him from the
proofs he had given before of his ability to carry off
a bottle of wine with a perfectly level head.   Jeff
seemed to believe Westover a person of such influence
that he could secure his release at once, and he was
abashed to find that he must pass the night in the
cell, where he conferred with Westover through the
bars.

In the police court, where his companions were
fined, the next morning, he was discharged for want of
evidence against him; but the University authorities

did not take the same view as the civil authorities.
He was suspended, and for the time he passed out of
Westover's sight and knowledge.

He expected to find him at Lion's Head, where he
went to pass the month of August—in painting those
pictures of the mountain which had in some sort, almost in spite of him, become his specialty.   But Mrs.
Durgin employed the first free moments after their
meeting in explaining that Jeff had got a chance to
work his way to London on a cattle-steamer, and had
been abroad the whole summer.   He had written home
that the voyage had been glorious, with plenty to eat
and little to do; and he had made favor with the captain for his return by the same vessel in September.
By other letters it seemed that he had spent the time
mostly in England; but he had crossed over into
France for a fortnight, and had spent a week in Paris.
His mother read some passages from his letters aloud
to show Westover how Jeff was keeping his eyes open.
His accounts of his travel were a mixture of crude
sensations in the presence of famous scenes and objects
of interest, hard-headed observation of the facts of
life, narrow-minded misconception of conditions, and
wholly intelligent and adequate study of the art of inn-
keeping in city and country.

Mrs. Durgin seemed to feel that there was some
excuse due for the relative quantity of the last.   " He
knows that's what I'd care for the most; and Jeff a'n't
one to forget his mother."   As if the word reminded
her, she added, after a moment, " We sha'n't any of
us soon forget what you done for Jeff—that time."

" ' JEFF TOLD ME EVERY WORD ABOUT IT ' "

"I didn't do anything for him, Mrs. Durgin; I couldn't," Westover protested.

"You done what you could, and I know that you saw the thing in the right light, or you wouldn't 'a' tried to do anything. Jeff told me every word about it. I know he was with a pretty harum-scarum crowd. But it was a lesson to him; and I wa'n't goin' to have him come back here, right away, and have folks, talkin' about what they couldn't understand, after the way the paper had it."

"Did it get into the papers?"

"Mm." Mrs. Durgin nodded. "And some dirty, sneakin' thing, here, wrote a letter to the paper and told a passel o' lies about Jeff, and all of us; and the paper printed Jeff's picture with it: I don't know *how* they got a hold of it. So when he got that chance to go, I just said, 'Go.' You'll see he'll keep all straight enough after this, Mr. Westover."

"Old woman read you any of Jeff's letters?" Whitwell asked, when his chance for private conference with Westover came. "What *was* the rights of that scrape he got into?"

Westover explained as favorably to Jeff as he could; the worst of the affair was the bad company he was in.

"Well, where there's smoke there's some fire. Cou't discharged him, and college suspended him. That's about where it is? I guess he'll keep out o' harm's way, next time. Read you what he said about them scenes of the Revolution in Paris?"

"Yes; he seems to have looked it all up pretty thoroughly."

" Done it for me, I guess, much as anything. I
was always talkin' it up with him. Jeff's kep' his
eyes open, that's a fact. He's got a head on him,
more'n I ever thought."

Westover decided that Mrs. Durgin's prepotent behavior towards Mrs. Marven the summer before had
not hurt her materially, with the witnesses even.
There were many new boarders, but most of those
whom he had already met were again at Lion's Head.
They said there was no air' like it; and no place so
comfortable. If they had sold their birthright for a
mess of pottage, Westover had to confess that the
pottage was very good. Instead of the Irish woman
at ten dollars a week who had hitherto been Mrs. Durgin's cook, under her personal surveillance and direction, she had now a man cook, whom she boldly called
a *chef*, and paid eighty dollars a month. He wore the
white apron and white cap of his calling, but Westover
heard him speak Yankee through his nose to one of
the stablemen as they exchanged hilarities across the
space between the basement and the barn door.
" Yes," Mrs. Durgin admitted, " he's an American;
and he learnt his trade at one of the best hotels in
Portland. He's pretty headstrong, but I guess he
does what he's told—in the end. The menyous? Oh,
Franky Whitwell prints *them*. He's got an amature
printing-office in the stable-loft."

XIV.

ONE morning towards the end of August, Whitwell, who was starting homeward, after leaving his
ladies, burdened with their wishes and charges for the
morrow, met Westover coming up the hill with his
painting-gear in his hand. " Say ! " he hailed him.
" Why don't you come down to the house to-night?
Jackson's goin' to come, and if you ha'n't seen him
work the plantchette for a spell, you'll be surprised.
There a'n't hardly anybody he can't have up. You'll
come? Good enough! "

What affected Westover first of all at the séance,
and perhaps most of all, was the quality of the air in
the little house; it was close and stuffy, mixed with
an odor of mould and an ancient smell of rats. The
kerosene-lamp set in the centre of the table, where
Jackson afterwards placed his planchette, devoured
the little life that was left in it. At the gasps which
Westover gave, with some despairing glances at the
closed windows, Whitwell said: " Hot ? Well, I guess
it is, a little. But you see Jackson has got to be careful about the night air; but I guess I can fix it for
you." He went out into the ell, and Westover heard

him raising a window. He came back and asked,
"That do? It'll get around in here, directly," and
Westover had to profess relief.

Jackson came in presently with the little Canuck,
whom Whitwell presented to Westover: "Know Jombateeste?"

The two were talking about a landslide which had
taken place on the other side of the mountain; the
news had just come that they had found among the
ruins the body of the farm-hand who had been missing
since the morning of the slide; his funeral was to be
the next day.

Jackson put his planchette on the table, and sat
down before it with a sigh; the Canuck remained
standing, and on foot he was scarcely a head higher
than the seated Yankees. "Well," Jackson said, "I
suppose he knows all about it now," meaning the dead
farm-hand.

"Yes," Westover suggested, "if he knows anything."

"Know anything!" Whitwell shouted. "Why,
man! Don't you believe he's as much alive as ever
he was?"

"I hope so," said Westover, submissively.

"Don't you *know* it?"

"Not as I know other things. In fact, I *don't* know
it," said Westover, and he was painfully aware of having shocked his hearers by the agnosticism so common
among men in towns that he had confessed it quite
simply and unconsciously. He perceived that faith
in the soul and life everlasting was as quick as ever

in the hills, whatever grotesque or unwonted form it wore. Jackson sat with closed eyes, and his head fallen back; Whitwell stared at the painter, with open mouth; the little Canuck began to walk up and down impatiently; Westover felt a reproach, almost an abhorrence, in all of them.

Whitwell asked, " Why, don't you think there's any proof of it?"

" Proof? Oh, yes! There's testimony enough to carry conviction to the stubbornest mind on any other point. But it's very strange about all that. It doesn't convince anybody but the witnesses. If a man tells me he's seen a disembodied spirit, I can't believe him. I must see the disembodied spirit myself."

" That's something so," said Whitwell, with a relenting laugh.

" If one came back from the dead, to tell us of a life beyond the grave, we should want the assurance that he'd really been dead, and not merely dreaming."

Whitwell laughed again, in the delight the philosophic mind finds even in the reasoning that baffles it.

The Canuck felt perhaps the simpler joy that the average man has in any strange notion that he is able to grasp. He stopped in his walk, and said, " Yes, and if you was dead, and went to heaven, and stayed so long you smelt, like Lazarus, and you come back and tol' 'em what you saw, nobody goin' believe you."

" Well, I guess you're right there, Jombateeste," said Whitwell, with pleasure in the Canuck's point. After a moment he suggested to Westover, " Then I s'pose if you feel the way you do, you don't care much about plantchette ? "

"Oh, yes, I do," said the painter. "We never know when we may be upon the point of revelation. I wouldn't miss any chance."

Whether Whitwell felt an ironic slant in the words or not, he paused a moment before he said, "Want to start her up, Jackson ? "

Jackson brought to the floor the fore feet of his chair, which he had tilted from it in leaning back, and without other answer put his hand on the planchette. It began to fly over the large sheet of paper spread upon the table, in curves and angles and eccentrics.

"Feels pootty lively to-night," said Whitwell, with a glance at Westover.

The little Canuck, as if he had now no further concern in the matter, sat down in a corner and smoked silently. Whitwell asked, after a moment's impatience, "Can't you git her down to business, Jackson ? "

Jackson gasped, "She'll come down when she wants to."

The little instrument seemed, in fact, trying to control itself. Its movements became less wild and large ; the zigzags began to shape themselves into something like characters. Jackson's wasted face gave no token of interest ; Whitwell laid half his gaunt length across the table in the endeavor to make out some meaning in them ; the Canuck, with his hands crossed on his stomach, smoked on, with the same gleam in his pipe and eye.

The planchette suddenly stood motionless.

"She done?" murmured Whitwell.

"I guess she is, for a spell, anyway," said Jackson, wearily.

"Let's try to make out what she says." Whitwell drew the sheet towards himself and Westover, who sat next him. "You've got to look for the letters everywhere. Sometimes she'll give you fair and square writin', and then again she'll slat the letters down every which way, and you've got to hunt 'em out for yourself. Here's a B I've got. That begins along pretty early in the alphabet. Let's see what we can find next."

Westover fancied he could make out an F and a T; Whitwell exulted in an unmistakable K and N; and he made sure of an R and an E. The painter was not so sure of an S. "Well, call it an S," said Whitwell. "And I guess I've got an O here, and an H. Hello! Here's an A, as large as life. Pootty much of a mixture."

"Yes; I don't see that we're much better off than we were before," said Westover.

"Well, I don't know about that," said Whitwell. "Write 'em down in a row, and see if we can't pick out some sense. I've had worse finds than this; no vowels at all sometimes; but here's three."

He wrote the letters down, while Jackson leaned back against the wall, in patient quiet.

"Well, sir," said Whitwell, pushing the paper, where he had written the letters in a line, to Westover, "make anything out of 'em?"

Westover struggled with them a moment. "I can make out one word, *shaft*."

"Anything else?" demanded Whitwell, with a glance of triumph at Jackson.

Westover studied the remaining letters. "Yes, I get one other word: *broken.*"

"Just what I done! But I wanted you to speak first. It's Broken Shaft. Jackson, she caught right on to what we was talkin' about. This life," he turned to Westover, in solemn exegesis, "is a broken shaft, when death comes. It rests upon the earth, but you got to look for the top of it in the skies. That's the way I look at it. What do you think, Jackson? Jombateeste?"

"Me, I think anybody can't see that, better go and get some heye-glass."

Westover remained in a shameful minority. He said, meekly, "It suggests a beautiful hope."

Jackson brought his chair legs down again, and put his hand on the planchette.

"Feel that tinglin'?" asked Whitwell, and Jackson made yes, with silent lips. "After he's been workin' the plantchette for a spell, and then leaves off, and she wants to say something more," Whitwell explained to Westover, "he seems to feel a kind of tinglin' in his arm, as if it was asleep, and then he's got to tackle her again. Writin' steady enough, now, Jackson!" he cried, joyously. "Let's see!" He leaned over and read, "*Thomas Jefferson*—" The planchette stopped. "My, I didn't go to do that," said Whitwell, apologetically. "You much acquainted with Jefferson's writin's?" he asked of Westover.

The painter had to own his ignorance of all except

the dictum that the government is best which governs least; but he was not in a position to deny that Jefferson had ever said anything about a broken shaft.

"It may have come to him on the other side," said Whitwell.

"Perhaps," Westover assented.

The planchette began to stir itself again. "She's goin' ahead!" cried Whitwell. He leaned over the table so as to get every letter as it was formed. "D— Yes! Death. Death is the Broken Shaft. Go on!" After a moment of faltering the planchette formed another letter. It was a U, and it was followed by an R, and so on, till Durgin had been spelled.—"Thunder!" cried Whitwell. "If anything's happened to Jeff!"

Jackson lifted his hand from the planchette.

"Oh, go on, Jackson!" Whitwell entreated. "Don't leave it so!"

"I can't seem to go on," Jackson whispered, and Westover could not resist the fear that suddenly rose among them. But he made the first struggle against it. "This is nonsense. Or if there's any sense in it, it means that Jeff's ship has broken her shaft, and put back."

Whitwell gave a loud laugh of relief. "That's so! You've hit it, Mr. Westover."

Jackson said, quietly: "He didn't mean to start home till to-morrow. And how could he send any message unless he was—"

"Easily!" cried Westover. "It's simply an instance of mental impression—of telepathy, as they call it."

"That's *so!*" shouted Whitwell, with eager and instant conviction.

Westover could see that Jackson still doubted. "If you believe that a disembodied spirit can communicate with you, why not an embodied spirit? If anything has happened to your brother's ship, his mind would be strongly on you at home, and why couldn't it convey its thought to you?"

"Because he ha'n't started yet," said Jackson.

Westover wanted to laugh; but they all heard voices without, which seemed to be coming nearer, and he listened with the rest. He made out Frank Whitwell's voice, and his sister's; and then another voice, louder and gayer, rose boisterously above them. Whitwell flung the door open and plunged out into the night. He came back, hauling Jeff Durgin in by the shoulder.

"Here, now," he shouted to Jackson, "you just let this feller and plantchette fight it out together!"

"What's the matter with plantchette?" said Jeff. before he said to his brother, "Hello, Jackson," and to the Canuck, "Hello, Jombateeste." He shook hands conventionally with them both, and then with the painter, whom he greeted with greater interest. "Glad to see *you*, here, Mr. Westover. Did I take you by surprise?" he asked of the company at large.

"No, sir," said Whitwell. "Didn't surprise *us* any if you *are* a fortnight ahead of time," he added, with a wink at the others.

"Well, I took a notion I wouldn't wait for the cattle-ship, and I started back on a French boat. Thought

I'd try it. They *live* well. But I hoped I should astonish you a little, too. I might as well waited."

Whitwell laughed. "We heard from you—plantchette kept right round after you."

"That so?" asked Jeff, carelessly.

"Fact. Have a good voyage?" Whitwell had the air of putting a casual question.

"First rate," said Jeff. "Plantchette say not?"

"No. Only about the broken shaft."

"Broken shaft? We didn't have any broken shaft! Plantchette's got mixed a little. Got the wrong ship."

After a moment of chopfallenness, Whitwell said: "Then somebody been makin' free with your name. Curious how them devils cut up oftentimes."

He explained, and Jeff laughed uproariously, when he understood the whole case. "Plantchette's been havin' fun with you."

Whitwell gave himself time for reflection. "No, sir, I don't look at it that way. I guess the wires got crossed, some way. If there's such a thing as the spirits o' the livin' influencin' plantchette, accordin' to Mr. Westover's say, here, I don't see why it wa'n't Jeff's being so near that got control of her, and made her sign his name to somebody else's words. It shows there's something in it."

"Well, I'm glad to come back alive, anyway," said Jeff, with a joviality new to Westover. "I tell you, there a'n't many places finer than old Lion's Head, after all. Don't you think so, Mr. Westover? I want to get the daylight on it, but it does well by moonlight, even." He looked round at the tall girl, who

had been lingering to hear the talk of planchette; at
the backward tilt he gave his head, to get her in range,
she frowned as if she felt his words a betrayal, and
slipped out of the room; the boy had already gone, and
was making himself heard in the low room overhead.
"There's a lot of folks here, this summer, mother
says," he appealed from the check he had got to Jackson. "Every room taken, for the whole month, she
says."

"We've been pretty full all July, too," said Jackson, blankly.

"Well, it's a great business; and I've picked up a
lot of hints, over there. We're not so smart as we
think we are. The Swiss can teach us a thing or two.
They know how to keep a hotel."

"Go to Switzerland?" asked Whitwell.

"I slipped over into the edge of it."

"I want to know! Well, now them Alps, now:
they so much bigger'n the White Hills, after all?"

"Well, I don't know about all of 'em," said Jeff.
"There may be some that would compare with our
hills, but I should say that you could take Mount
Washington up and set it in the lap of almost any one
of the Alps I saw, and it would look like a baby on
its mother's knee."

"I want to know!" said Whitwell again. His tone
expressed disappointment, but impartiality; he would
do justice to foreign superiority if he must. "And
about the ocean. What about waves runnin' mountains
high?"

"Well, we didn't have it very rough. But I don't

believe I saw any waves much higher than Lion's
Head." Jeff laughed to find Whitwell taking him
seriously. " Won't that satisfy you ? "

" Oh, it satisfies *me*. Truth always does. But, now,
about London. You didn't seem to say so much about
London in your letters, now. *Is* it so big as they let
on ? Big, that is, to the naked eye, as you may say ? "

" There a'n't any one place where you can get a complete bird's-eye view of it," said Jeff, " and two-thirds
of it would be hid in smoke, anyway. You've got to
think of a place that would take in the whole popula-
tion of New England, outside of Massachusetts, and
not feel as if it had more than a comfortable meal."
Whitwell laughed for joy in the bold figure. " I'll
tell you ! When you've landed and crossed up from
Liverpool, and struck London, you feel as if you'd gone
to sea again. It's an ocean : a whole Atlantic of houses."

" That's right ! " crowed Whitwell. " That's the
way I thought it was. Growin' any ? "

Jeff hesitated. " It grows in the night. You've
heard about Chicago growing ? "

" Yes ! "

" Well, London grows a whole Chicago every night."

" Good ! " said Whitwell. " That suits *me*. And
about Paris, now. Paris strike you the same way ? "

" It don't need to," said Jeff. " That's a place
where I'd like to *live*. Everybody's at home, there.
It's a man's house and his front yard, and I tell you
they keep it clean. Paris is washed down every morning ; scrubbed and mopped and rubbed dry. You
couldn't find any more dirt than you could in mother's

kitchen after she's hung out her wash.   That so, Mr.
Westover?"

Westover confirmed in general Jeff's report of the
cleanliness of Paris.

"And beautiful!   You don't know what a good-
looking town is till you strike Paris.   And they're
proud of it, too!   Every man acts as if he owned it.
They've had the statue of Alsace—in that Place de la
Concorde of yours, Mr. Whitwell, where they had the
guillotine—all draped in black, ever since the war
with Germany ; and they mean to have her back, some
day."

"Great country, Jombateeste!" Whitwell shouted to
the Canuck.

The little man roused himself from the muse in
which he was listening and smoking.   "Me, I'm
Frantsh," he said.

"Yes, that's what Jeff was sayin'," said Whitwell.
"I *meant* France."

"Oh," answered Jombateeste impatiently, "I
thought you mean the Hunited State."

"Well, not this time," said Whitwell amid the general laughter.

"Good for Jombateeste," said Jeff.   "Stand up for
Canada every time, John.   It's the livest country in
the world, three months of the year and the ice keeps
it perfectly sweet the other nine."

Whitwell could not brook a diversion from the high
and serious inquiry they had entered upon.   "It must
have made this country look pretty slim, when you got
back.   How'd New York look, after Paris?"

"Like a pig-pen," said Jeff.   He left his chair, and
walked round the table towards a door opening into
the adjoining room.   For the first time Westover noticed a figure in white seated there, and apparently
rapt in the talk which had been going on.   At the
approach of Jeff, and before he could have made
himself seen at the doorway, a tremor seemed to
pass over the figure; it fluttered to its feet, and then it
vanished into the farther dark of the room.   When
Jeff disappeared within, there was a sound of rustling
skirts and skurrying feet and the crash of a closing
door, and then the free rise of laughing voices without.   After a discreet interval Westover said: "Mr.
Whitwell, I must say good-night.   I've got another
day's work before me.   It's been a most interesting
evening."

"You must try it again," said Whitwell, hospitably.
"We ha'n't got to the bottom of that broken shaft
yet.   You'll see 't plantchette 'll have something more
to say about it.   Heigh, Jackson?"   He rose to receive Westover's good-night; the others nodded to
him.

As the painter climbed the hill to the hotel he saw
two figures on the road below; the one in white dra-
pery looked severed by a dark line slanting across it
at the waist.   In the country, he knew, such an appearance might mark the earliest stages of love-mak-
ing, or mere youthful tenderness, in which there was
nothing more implied or expected.   But whatever the
fact was, Westover felt a vague distaste for it, which,
as it related itself to a more serious possibility, deep-

ened to something like pain.   It was probable that it
should come to this between those two, but Westover
rebelled against the event with a sense of its unfitness
for which he could not give himself any valid reason;
and in the end he accused himself of being a fool.

XV.

Two ladies sat on the veranda of the hotel, and watched a cloud-wreath trying to lift itself from the summit of Lion's Head. In the effort it thinned away to transparency in places; in others it tore its frail texture asunder, and let parts of the mountain show through; then the fragments knitted themselves loosely together, and the vapor lay again in dreamy quiescence.

The ladies were older and younger, and apparently mother and daughter. The mother had kept her youth in face and figure so admirably that in another light she would have looked scarcely the elder. It was the candor of the morning which confessed the fine vertical lines running up and down to her lips, only a shade paler than the girl's, and that showed her hair a trifle thinner in its coppery brown, her blue eyes a little dimmer. They were both very graceful, and they had soft, caressing voices; they now began to talk very politely to each other, as if they were strangers, or as if strangers were by. They talked of the landscape, and of the strange cloud effect before them. They said that they supposed they should see the Lion's Head when the cloud lifted, and they were both sure they had never been quite so near a cloud before. They agreed that this was because in Switzerland the mountains were so much higher and farther off. Then the daughter said, without changing the direction of her eyes or the tone of her voice, "The gentleman who came over from the station with us last night," and the mother was aware of Jeff Durgin advancing towards the corner of the veranda where they sat.

"I hope you have got rested," he said, with the jovial bluntness which was characteristic of him with women.

"Oh, yes, indeed," said the elder lady. Jeff had spoken to her, but had looked chiefly at the younger. "I slept beautifully. So quiet here, and with this delicious air! Have you just tasted it?"

"No; I've been up ever since daylight, driving round," said Jeff. "I'm glad you like the air," he said, after a certain hesitation. "We always want to have people do that at Lion's Head. There's no air like it, though perhaps I shouldn't say so."

"Shouldn't?" the lady repeated.

"Yes; we own the air here, this part of it." Jeff smiled easily down at the lady's puzzled face.

"Oh! Then you are—are you a son of the house?"

"Son of the hotel, yes," said Jeff, with increasing ease. The lady continued her question in a look, and he went on: "I've been scouring the country for butter and eggs this morning. We shall get all our supplies from Boston next year, I hope, but we depend on the neighbors, a little, yet."

"How very interesting," said the lady. "You must

have a great many queer adventures," she suggested in a provisional tone.

"Well, nothing's queer to me in the hill country. But you see some characters here." He nodded over his shoulder to where Whitwell stood by the flag-staff, waiting the morning impulse of the ladies. "There's one of the greatest of them, now."

The lady put up a lorgnette and inspected Whitwell. "What are those strange things he has got in his hat-band?"

"The flowers and the fungi of the season," said Jeff. "He takes parties of the ladies walking, and that collection is what he calls his almanac."

"Really?" cried the girl. "That's charming!"

"Delightful!" said the mother, moved by the same impulse, apparently.

"Yes," said Jeff. "You ought to hear him talk. I'll introduce him to you after breakfast, if you like."

"Oh, we should only be too happy!" said the mother, and her daughter, from her inflection, knew that 'she would be willing to defer her happiness.

But Jeff did not. "Mr. Whitwell!" he called out, and Whitwell came across the grass to the edge of the veranda. "I want to introduce you to Mrs. Vostrand —and Miss Vostrand."

Whitwell took their slim hands successively into his broad, flat palm, and made Mrs. Vostrand repeat her name to him. "Strangers at Lion's Head, I presume?" Mrs. Vostrand owned as much; and he added: "Well, I guess you won't find a much sightlier place anywhere; though accordin' to Jeff's say, here,

they've got *bigger* mountains on the other side.   Ever
been in Europe ? "

"Why, yes," said Mrs. Vostrand, with a little
mouth of deprecation.   "In fact, we've just come
home!   We've been living there."

"That so ? " returned Whitwell, in humorous toleration.   "Glad to get back, I presume ? "

"Oh, yes—yes," said Mrs. Vostrand, in a sort of
willowy concession, as if the character before her were
not to be crossed or gainsaid.

"Well, it'll do you good here," said Whitwell.
"'N' the young lady, too.   A few tramps over these
hills'll make you look like another woman." He added,
as if he had perhaps made his remarks too personal
to the girl, "Both of you."

"Oh, yes," the mother assented fervently.   "We shall
count upon your showing us all their—mysteries."

Whitwell looked pleased.   "I'll do my best—whenever you're ready."   He went on : "Why, Jeff, here,
has just got back, too.   Jeff, what was the name of
that French boat you said you crossed on ?   I want to
see if I can't make out what plantchette meant by that
broken shaft.   She must have meant something, and
if I could find out the name of the ship—   Tell the
ladies about it ? "   Jeff laughed, with a shake of the
head, and Whitwell continued, "Why, it was like
this," and he possessed the ladies of a fact which they
professed to find extremely interesting.   At the end
of their polite expressions, he asked Jeff again, "What
did you say the name was ? "

"*Acquitaine*," said Jeff briefly.

"Why, *we* came on the *Acquitaine!*" said Mrs. Vostrand, with a smile for Jeff. "But how did we happen not to see each other?"

"Oh, I came second-cabin," said Jeff. "I worked my way over on a cattle-ship to London, and when I decided not to work my way back, I found I hadn't enough money for a first-cabin passage. I was in a hurry to get back in time to get settled at Harvard, and so I came second-cabin. It wasn't bad. I used to see you across the rail."

"Well!" said Whitwell.

"How very—amusing!" said Mrs. Vostrand. "What a small world it is." With these words she fell into a vagary; her daughter recalled her from it with a slight movement. "Breakfast? How impatient you are, Genevieve! Well!" She smiled the sweetest parting to Whitwell, and suffered herself to be led away by Jeff.

"And you're at Harvard! I'm so interested. My own boy will be going there soon."

"Well, there's no place like Harvard," said Jeff. "I'm in my Sophomore year, now."

"Oh, a Sophomore! Fancy!" cried Mrs. Vostrand, as if nothing could give her more pleasure. "My son is going to prepare at St. Mark's. Did you prepare there?"

"No, I prepared at Lovewell Academy, over here." Jeff nodded in a southerly direction.

"Oh, indeed!" said Mrs. Vostrand, as if she knew where Lovewell was, and instantly recognized the name of the ancient school.

They had reached the dining-room, and Jeff pushed
the screen-door open with one hand, and followed the
ladies in.   He had the effect of welcoming them like
invited guests; he placed the ladies himself at a window, where he said Mrs. Vostrand would be out of the
draughts, and they could have a good view of Lion's
Head.   He leaned over between them, when they were
seated, to get sight of the mountain, and "There!"
he said.   "That cloud's gone at last."   Then, as if it
would be modester in the proprietor of the view to
leave them to their flattering raptures in it, he moved
away, and stood talking a moment with Cynthia Whitwell near the door of the serving-room.   He talked
gayly, with many tosses of the head and turns about,
while she listened with a vague smile motionlessly.

"She's very pretty," said Miss Vostrand to her mother.

"Yes.   The New England type," murmured the
mother.

"They all have the same look, a good deal," said
the girl, glancing over the room where the waitresses
stood ranged against the wall with their hands folded
at their waists.   "They have better faces than figures,
but she is beautiful every way.   Do you suppose they
are all school-teachers?   They look intellectual.   Or
is it their glasses?"

"I don't know," said the mother.   "They used to
be; but things change here so rapidly, it may all be
different.   Do you like it?"

"I think it's charming here," said the younger lady,
evasively.   "Everything is so exquisitely clean.   And

the food is very good. Is this corn-bread—that you've told me about so much ?"

"Yes, this is corn-bread. You will have to get accustomed to it."

"Perhaps it won't take long. I could fancy that girl knowing about everything. Don't you like her looks ?"

"Oh, very much !" Mrs. Vostrand turned for another glance at Cynthia.

"What say ?" Their smiling waitress came forward from the wall where she was leaning, as if she thought they had spoken to her.

"Oh, we were speaking—the young lady to whom Mr. Durgin was talking—she is—"

"She's the housekeeper—Miss Whitwell."

"Oh, indeed ! She seems so young—"

"I guess she knows what to do-o-o," the waitress chanted. "*We* think she's about ri-i-ght !" She smiled tolerantly upon the misgiving of the stranger, if it was that, and then retreated when the mother and daughter began talking together again.

They had praised the mountain with the cloud off, to Jeff, very politely, and now the mother said, a little more intimately, but still with the deference of a society acquaintance, "He seems very gentlemanly, and I am sure he is very kind. I don't quite know what to do about it, do you ?"

"No, I don't. It's all strange to me, you know."

"Yes, I suppose it must be. But you will get used to it if we remain in the country. Do you think you will dislike it ?"

"Oh, no! It's very different."

"Yes, it's different. He is very handsome, in a certain way." The daughter said nothing, and the mother added, "I wonder if he was trying to conceal that he had come second-cabin, and was not going to let us know that he crossed with us?"

"Do you think he was bound to do so?"

"No. But it was very odd, his not mentioning it. And his going out on a cattle-steamer," the mother observed.

"Oh, but that's very *chic*, I've heard," the daughter replied. "I've heard that the young men like it, and think it a great chance. They have great fun. It isn't at all like second-cabin."

"You young people have your own world," the mother answered, caressingly.

XVI.

WESTOVER met the ladies coming out of the dining-room as he went in rather late to breakfast; he had been making a study of Lion's Head in the morning light after the cloud lifted from it. He was always doing Lion's Heads, it seemed to him; but he loved the mountain and he was always finding something new in it.

He was now seeing it inwardly with so exclusive a vision that he had no eyes for these extremely pretty women till they were out of sight. Then he remembered noticing them, and started with a sense of recognition, which he verified by the hotel register when he had finished his meal. It was in fact Mrs. James W. Vostrand, and it was Miss Vostrand, whom West-over had known ten years before in Italy. Mrs. Vostrand had then lately come abroad for the education of her children, and was pausing in doubt at Florence whether she should educate them in Germany or Switzerland. Her husband had apparently abandoned this question to her, and he did not contribute his presence to her moral support during her struggle with a problem which Westover remembered as having a tendency

to solution in the direction of a permanent stay in
Florence.

In those days he liked Mrs. Vostrand very much,
and at twenty he considered her at thirty distinctly
middle-aged. For one winter she had a friendly little
salon, which was the most attractive place in Florence
to him, then a cub painter sufficiently unlicked. He
was aware of her children being a good deal in the
salon: a girl of eight who was like her mother, and
quite a savage little boy of five, who may have been
like his father. If he was, and the absent Mr. Vostrand had the same habit of sulking and kicking at
people's shins, Westover could partly understand why
Mrs. Vostrand had come to Europe for the education
of her children. It all came vividly back to him, while
he went about looking for Mrs. Vostrand and her
daughter on the verandas and in the parlors. But he
did not find them, and he was going to send his name
to their rooms when he came upon Jeff Durgin figur-
ing about the office in a fresh London conception of
an outing costume.

"You're very swell," said Westover, halting him to
take full note of it.

"Like it? Well, I knew you'd understand what it
meant. Mother thinks it's a little too rowdy-looking.
Her idea is black broadcloth frock-coat and doeskin
trousers, for a gentleman, you know." He laughed
with a young joyousness; and then became serious.
"Couple of ladies here, somewhere, I'd like to introduce you to. Came over with me from the depot
last night. Very nice people, and I'd like to make it

pleasant for them—get up something—go somewhere, and when you see their style you can judge what it had better be.   Mrs. Vostrand and her daughter."

"Thank you," said Westover.   "I think I know them already—at least one of them.   I used to go to Mrs. Vostrand's house in Florence."

"That so?   Well, fact is, I crossed with them; but I came second-cabin, because I'd spent all my money, and I didn't get acquainted with them on the ship, but we met in the train coming up, last night.   Said they had heard of Lion's Head on the other side from friends.   But it was quite a coincidence, don't you think!   I'd like to have them see what this neighborhood really is; and I wish, Mr. Westover, you'd find out, if you can, what they'd like.   If they're for walking, we could get Whitwell to personally conduct a party, and if they're for driving, I'd like to show them a little mountain-coaching myself."

"I don't know whether I'd better not leave the whole thing to you, Jeff," Westover said, after a moment's reflection.   "I don't see exactly how I could bring the question into a first interview."

"Well, perhaps it would be rather rushing it.   But if I get up something, you'll come, Mr. Westover?"

"I will, with great pleasure," said Westover, and he went to make his call.

A half-hour later he was passing the door of the old parlor which Mrs. Durgin still kept for hers, on his way up to his room, when a sound of angry voices came out to him.   Then the voice of Mrs. Durgin defined itself in the words: "I'm not goin' to have to

ask any more folks for their rooms on your account,
Jeff Durgin— Mr. Westover!   Mr. Westover, is that
you?" her voice broke off to call after him as he hurried by.   "Won't you come in here, a minute?"

He hesitated, and then Jeff called, "Yes, come in,
Mr. Westover."

The painter found him sitting on the old hair-cloth
sofa, with his stick between his hands and knees, con-
fronting his mother, who was rocking excitedly to and
fro in the old hair-cloth easy-chair.

"You know these folks that Jeff's so crazy about?"
she demanded.

"Crazy!" cried Jeff, laughing and frowning at the
same time.   "What's crazy in wanting to go off on a
drive, and choose your own party?"

"Do you know them?" Mrs. Durgin repeated to
Westover.

"The Vostrands?   Why, yes.   I knew Mrs. Vostrand in Italy a good many years ago, and I've just
been calling on her and her daughter, who was a little
girl, then."

"What kind of folks are they?"

"What kind?   Really!   Why, they're very charming people—"

"So Jeff seems to think.   Any call to show them
any particular attention?"

"I don't know if I quite understand—"

"Why, it's just this.   Jeff, here, wants to make a
picnic for them, or something, and I can't see the
sense of it.   You remember what happened at that
other picnic, with that Mrs. Marven "—Jeff tapped the

floor with his stick, impatiently, and Westover felt sorry for him—" and I don't want it to happen again, and I've told Jeff so. I presume he thinks it'll set him right with them, if they're thinkin' demeaning of him because he came over second-cabin on their ship."

Jeff set his teeth and compressed his lips to bear as best he could the give-away which his mother could not appreciate in its importance to him.

"They're not the kind of people to take such a thing shabbily," said Westover. "They didn't happen to mention it, but Mrs. Vostrand must have got used to seeing young fellows in straits of all kinds during her life abroad. I know that I sometimes made the cup of tea and biscuit she used to give me in Florence do duty for a dinner, and I believe she knew it."

Jeff looked up at Westover with a grateful, side-long glance.

His mother said, " Well, then, that's all right, and Jeff needn't do anything for them on that account. And I've made up my mind about one thing: whatever the hotel does has got to be done for the whole hotel. It can't pick and choose amongst the guests." Westover liked so little the part of old family friend which he seemed, whether he liked it or not, to bear with the Durgins, that he would gladly have got away now, but Mrs. Durgin detained him with a direct appeal. " Don't you think so, Mr. Westover ? "

Jeff spared him the pain of a response. " Very well," he said to his mother, " I'm not the hotel, and you never want me to be. I can do this on my own account."

" Not with my coach and not with my hosses," said his mother.

Jeff rose. " I might as well go on down to Cambridge, and get to work on my conditions."

" Just as you please about that," said Mrs. Durgin, with the same impassioned quiet that showed in her son's handsome face and made it one angry red to his yellow hair. " We've got along without you so far, this summer, and I guess we can the rest of the time. And the sooner you work off your conditions the better, I presume."

The next morning Jeff came to take leave of him, where Westover had pitched his easel and camp-stool on the slope behind the hotel.

" Why, are you really going?" he asked. " I was in hopes it might have blown over."

" No, things don't blow over so easy with mother," said Jeff, with an embarrassed laugh, but no resentment. " She generally means what she says."

" Well, in this case, Jeff, I think she was right."

" Oh, I guess so," said Jeff, pulling up a long blade of grass, and taking it between his teeth. " Anyway, it comes to the same thing as far as I'm concerned. It's for her to say what shall be done and what sha'n't be done in her own house, even if it *is* a hotel. That's what I shall do in mine. We're used to these little differences; but we talk it out, and that's the end of it. I shouldn't really go, though, if I didn't think I ought to get in some work on those conditions before the thing begins regularly. I should have liked to help here a little, for I've had a good time and I ought

" ' WELL, GOOD-BY, MR. WESTOVER ' "

to be willing to pay for it.   But she's in good hands.
Jackson's well—for him—and she's got Cynthia."

The easy security of tone with which Jeff pronounced
the name vexed Westover.   "I suppose your mother
would hardly know how to do without her, even if you
were at home," he said, dryly.

"Well, that's a fact," Jeff assented, with a laugh
for the hit.   "And Jackson thinks the world of her.
I believe he trusts her judgment more than he does
mother's about the hotel.   Well, I must be going.
You don't know where Mrs. Vostrand is going to be
this winter, I suppose?"

"No, I don't," said Westover.   He could not help
a sort of blind resentment in the situation.   If he
could not feel that Jeff was the best that could be for
Cynthia, he had certainly no reason to regret that his
thoughts could be so lightly turned from her.   But
the fact anomalously incensed him as a slight to the
girl, who might have been still more sacrificed by
Jeff's constancy.   He forced himself to add, "I fancy
Mrs. Vostrand doesn't know herself."

"I wish I didn't know where *I* was going to be,"
said Jeff.   "Well, good-by, Mr. Westover.   I'll see
you in Boston."

"Oh, good-by."   The painter freed himself from
his brush and palette for a parting handshake, reluctantly.

Jeff plunged down the hill, waving a final adieu
from the corner of the hotel before he vanished round
it.

Mrs. Vostrand and her daughter were at breakfast

when Westover came in after the early light had been
gone some time.   They entreated him to join them at
their table, and the mother said : " I suppose you were
up soon enough to see young Mr. Durgin off.   Isn't
it too bad he has to go back to college when it's so
pleasant in the country ? "

" Not bad for him," said Westover.   " He's a young
man who can stand a great deal of hard work."   Partly
because he was a little tired of Jeff, and partly because
he was embarrassed in their presence by the reason of
his going, he turned the talk upon the days they had
known together.

Mrs. Vostrand was very willing to talk of her past,
even apart from his, and she told him of her sojourn
in Europe since her daughter had left school.   They
spent their winters in Italy and their summers in
Switzerland, where it seemed her son was still at his
studies in Lausanne.   She wished him to go to Harvard, she said, and she supposed he would have to
finish his preparation at one of the American schools;
but she had left the choice entirely to Mr. Vostrand.

This seemed a strange event after twelve years'
stay in Europe for the education of her children, but
Westover did not feel authorized to make any comment upon it.   He fell rather to thinking how very
pleasant both mother and daughter were, and to wondering how much wisdom they had between them.
He reflected that men had very little wisdom, as far
as he knew them, and he questioned whether, after
all, the main difference between men and women might
not be that women talked their follies and men acted

theirs.   Probably Mrs. Vostrand, with all her babble, had done fewer foolish things than her husband, but here Westover felt his judgment disabled by the fact that he had never met her husband; and his mind began to wander to a question of her daughter, whom he had there before him.   He found himself bent upon knowing more of the girl, and trying to eliminate her mother from the talk, or at least to make Genevieve lead in it.   But apparently she was not one of the natures that like to lead; at any rate she remained discreetly in abeyance, and Westover fancied she even respected her mother's opinions and ideas.   He thought this very well for both of them, whether it was the effect of Mrs. Vostrand's merit or Miss Vostrand's training.   They seemed both of one exquisite gentleness, and of one sweet manner, which was rather elaborate and formal in expression.   They deferred to each other as politely as they deferred to him, but, if anything, the daughter deferred most.

XVII.

The Vostrands did not stay long at Lion's Head. Before the week was out Mrs. Vostrand had a letter summoning them to meet her husband at Montreal, where that mysterious man, who never came into the range of Westover's vision, somehow, was kept by business from joining them in the mountains.

Early in October the painter received Mrs. Vostrand's card at his studio in Boston, and learned from the scribble which covered it that she was with her daughter at the Hotel Vendôme. He went at once to see them there, and was met, almost before the greetings were past, with a prayer for his opinion.

"Favorable opinion?" he asked.

"Favorable? Oh, yes; of course. It's simply this. When I sent you my card, we were merely birds of passage, and now I don't know but we are— What is the opposite of birds of passage?"

Westover could not think, and said so.

"Well, it doesn't matter. We were walking down the street, here, this morning, and we saw the sign of an apartment to let, in a window, and we thought, just for amusement we would go in and look at it."

"And you took it?"

"No, not quite so rapid as that.   But it was *lovely;* in such a pretty *hôtel garni*, and so exquisitely furnished! We didn't really think of staying in Boston; we'd quite made up our minds on New York; but this apartment is a temptation."

"Why not yield, then?" said Westover.   "That's the easiest way with a temptation. Confess, now, that you've taken the apartment already!"

"No, no, I haven't yet," said Mrs. Vostrand.

"And if I advised not, you wouldn't?"

"Ah, that's another thing!"

"When are you going to take possession, Mrs. Vostrand?"

"Oh, at once, I suppose—if we do!"

"And may I come in when I'm hungry, just as I used to do in Florence, and will you stay me with flagons in the old way?"

"There never was anything but tea, you know well enough."

"The tea had rum in it."

"Well, perhaps it will have rum in it here, if you're very good."

"I will try my best, on condition that you'll make any and every possible use of me. Mrs. Vostrand, I can't tell you how very glad I am you're going to stay," said the painter, with a fervor that made her impulsively put out her hand to him.   He kept it while he could add, "I don't forget—I can never forget—how good you were to me in those days," and at that she gave his hand a quick pressure. "If I can do any-

thing at all for you, you *will* let me, won't you.   I'm
afraid you'll be so well provided for that there won't
be anything.   Ask them to slight you, to misuse you
in something, so that I can come to your rescue."

"Yes, I will," Mrs. Vostrand promised. "And may
we come to your studio to implore your protection?"

"The sooner the better."   Westover got himself
away with a very sweet friendship in his heart for this
rather anomalous lady, who, more than half her daughter's life, had lived away from her daughter's father,
upon apparently perfectly good terms with him, and
so discreetly and self-respectfully that no breath of
reproach had touched her.   Until now, however, her
position had not really concerned Westover, and it
would not have concerned him now, if it had not been
for a design that formed itself in his mind as soon as
he knew that Mrs. Vostrand meant to pass the winter
in Boston. He felt at once that he could not do things
by halves for a woman who had once done them for
him by wholes and something over, and he had instantly decided that he must not only be very pleasant
to her himself, but he must get his friends to be pleasant, too.   His friends were some of the nicest people
in Boston; nice in both the personal and the social
sense; he knew they would not hesitate to sacrifice
themselves for him in a good cause, and that made
him all the more anxious that the cause should be
good beyond question.

Since his last return from Paris he had been rather
a fad as a teacher, and his class had been kept quite
strictly to the ladies who got it up and to such as they

chose to let enter it. These were not all chosen for
wealth or family; there were some whose gifts gave
the class distinction, and the ladies were glad to have
them. It would be easy to explain Mrs. Vostrand to
these, but the others might be more difficult; they
might have their anxieties, and Westover meant to ask
the leader of the class to help him receive at the studio
tea he had at once imagined for the Vostrands, and
that would make her doubly responsible.

He found himself drawing a very deep and long
breath before he began to mount the many stairs to
his studio, and wishing either that Mrs. Vostrand had
not decided to spend the winter in Boston, or else
that he were of a slacker conscience and could wear
his gratitude more lightly. But there was some relief
in thinking that he could do nothing for a month yet.
He gained a degree of courage by telling the ladies,
when he went to find them in their new apartment, that
he should want them to meet a few of his friends at
tea as soon as people began to get back to town; and
he made the most of their instant joy in accepting his
invitation.

His pleasure was somehow dashed a little, before
he left them, by the announcement of Jeff Durgin's
name.

"I felt bound to send him my card," said Mrs.
Vostrand, while Jeff was following his up in the eleva-
tor. "He was so very kind to us the day we arrived
at Lion's Head; and I—didn't know but he might be
feeling a little sensitive about coming over second-
cabin in our ship; and—"

"How like you, Mrs. Vostrand!" cried Westover, and he was now distinctly glad he had not tried to sneak out of doing something for her. "Your kindness won't be worse wasted on Durgin than it was on me, in the old days, when I supposed I had taken a second-cabin passage for the voyage of life. There's a great deal of good in him; I don't mean to say he got through his Freshman year without trouble with the college authorities, but the Sophomore year generally brings wisdom."

"Oh," said Mrs. Vostrand, "they're always a little wild at first, I suppose."

Later, the ladies brought Jeff with them when they came to Westover's studio, and the painter perceived that they were very good friends, as if they must have met several times since he had seen them together. He interested himself in the growing correctness of Jeff's personal effect. During his Freshman year, while the rigor of the unwritten Harvard law yet forbade him a silk hat or a cane, he had kept something of the boy, if not the country boy. Westover had noted that he had always rather a taste for clothes, but in this first year he did not get beyond a derby-hat and a sack-coat, varied towards the end by a cutaway. In the outing dress he wore at home he was always effective, but there was something in Jeff's figure which did not lend itself to more formal fashion; something of herculean proportion which would have marked him of a classic beauty perhaps if he had not been in clothes at all, or of a yeomanly vigor and force if he had been clad for work, but which seemed

to threaten the more worldly conceptions of the tailor
with danger.   It was as if he were about to burst out
of his clothes, not because he wore them tight, but
because there was somehow more of the man than
the citizen in him; something native, primitive, something that Westover could not find quite a word for,
characterized him physically and spiritually.   When
he came into the studio after these delicate ladies, the
robust Jeff Durgin wore a long frock-coat, with a flower in his button-hole, and in his left hand he carried
a silk hat turned over his forearm as he must have
noticed people whom he thought stylish carrying their
hats.   He had on dark-gray trousers and sharp-pointed
enamelled-leather shoes; and Westover grotesquely
reflected that he was dressed, as he stood, to lead
Genevieve Vostrand to the altar.

Westover saw at once that when he made his studio
tea for the Vostrands he must ask Jeff; it would be
cruel, and for several reasons impossible, not to do so;
and he really did not see why he should not.   Mrs.
Vostrand was taking him on the right ground, as a
Harvard student, and nobody need take him on any
other.   Possibly people would ask him to teas at their
own houses, from Westover's studio, but he could not
feel that he was concerned in that.   Society is interested in a man's future, not his past, as it is interested
in a woman's past, not her future.

But when he gave his tea it went off wonderfully
well in every way, perhaps because it was one of the
first teas of the fall.   It brought people together in
their autumnal freshness before the winter had begun

to wither their resolutions to be amiable to one another, to dull their wits, to stale their stories, or to give so wide a currency to their sayings that they could not freely risk them with every one.

Westover had thought it best to be frank with the leading lady of his class, when she said she should be delighted to receive for him, and would provide suitable young ladies to pour: a brunette for the tea, and a blonde for the chocolate. She took his scrupulosity very lightly when he spoke of Mrs. Vostrand's educational sojourn in Europe; she laughed and said she knew the type, and the situation was one of the most obvious phases of the American marriage.

He protested in vain that Mrs. Vostrand was not the type; she laughed again, and said, Oh, types were never typical. But she was hospitably gracious both to her and to Miss Genevieve; she would not allow that the mother was not the type when Westover challenged her experience, but she said they were charming, and made haste to get rid of the question with the vivid demand, " But who was your young friend who ought to have worn a lion-skin and carried a club?"

Westover by this time disdained palliation. He said that Jeff was the son of the landlady at Lion's Head Mountain, which he had painted so much, and he was now in his second year at Harvard, where he was going to make a lawyer of himself; and this interested the lady. She asked if he had talent, and a number of other things about him and about his mother; and Westover permitted himself to be rather graphic in telling of his acquaintance with Mrs. Durgin.

XVIII.

AFTER all, it was rather a simple-hearted thing of Westover to have either hoped or feared very much for the Vostrands. Society, in the sense of good society, can always take care of itself, and does so perfectly. In the case of Mrs. Vostrand some ladies who liked Westover and wished to be civil to him asked her and her daughter to other afternoon teas, shook hands with them at their coming, and said, when they went, they were sorry they must be going so soon. In the crowds people recognized them now and then, both of those who had met them at Westover's studio, and of those who had met them at Florence and Lausanne. But if these were merely people of fashion they were readily rid of the Vostrands, whom the dullest among them quickly perceived not to be of their own sort, somehow. Many of the ladies of Westover's class made Genevieve promise to let them paint her; and her beauty and her grace availed for several large dances at the houses of more daring spirits, where the daughters made a duty of getting partners for her, and discharged it conscientiously. But there never was an approach to more intimate hospitalities, and towards

the end of February, when good society in Boston
goes southward to indulge a Lenten grief at Old Point
Comfort, Genevieve had so many vacant afternoons
and evenings at her disposal that she could not have
truthfully pleaded a previous engagement to the invitations Jeff Durgin made her.   They were chiefly for
the theatre, and Westover saw him with her and her
mother at different plays; he wondered how Jeff had
caught on to the notion of asking Mrs. Vostrand to
come with them.

Jeff's introductions at Westover's tea had not been
many, and they had not availed him at all.   He had
been asked to no Boston houses, and when other students, whom he knew, were going in to dances, the
whole winter he was socially as quiet, but for the Vostrands, as at the Mid-year Examinations.   Westover
could not resent the neglect of society in his case, and
he could not find that he quite regretted it; but he
thought it characteristically nice of Mrs. Vostrand to
make as much of the friendless fellow as she fitly
could.   He had no doubt but her tact would be equal
to his management in every way, and that she could
easily see to it that he did not become embarrassing
to her daughter or herself.

One day, after the east wind had ceased to blow the
breath of the ice-fields of Labrador against the New
England coast, and the buds on the trees along the
mall between the lawns of the avenue were venturing
forth in a hardy experiment of the Boston May, Mrs.
Vostrand asked Westover if she had told him that Mr.
Vostrand was actually coming on to Boston.   He

"THEY WERE SORRY THEY MUST BE GOING SO SOON"

rejoiced with her in this prospect, and he reciprocated the wish which she said Mr. Vostrand had always had for a meeting with himself.

A fortnight later, when the leaves had so far inured themselves to the weather as to have fully expanded, she announced another letter from Mr. Vostrand, saying that after all he should not be able to come to Boston, but hoped to be in New York before she sailed.

"Sailed!" cried Westover.

"Why, yes! Didn't you know we were going to sail in June? I thought I had told you!"

"No—"

"Why, yes. We must go out to poor Checco, now; Mr. Vostrand insists upon that. If ever we are a united family again, Mr. Westover—if Mr. Vostrand can arrange his business, when Checco is ready to enter Harvard—I mean to take a house in Boston. I'm sure I should be contented to live nowhere else in America. The place has quite bewitched me—dear old, sober, charming Boston! I'm sure I should like to live here all the rest of my life. But why in the world do people go out of town so early? Those houses over there have been shut for a whole month past!"

They were sitting at Mrs. Vostrand's window looking out on the avenue, where the pale globular electrics were swimming like jelly-fish in the clear evening air, and above the ranks of low trees the houses on the other side were close-shuttered from basement to attic.

Westover answered, "Some go because they have

such pleasant houses at the shore, and some because they want to dodge their taxes."

"To dodge their taxes?" she repeated, and he had to explain how if people were in their country-houses before the first of May they would not have to pay the high personal tax of the city; and she said that she would write that to Mr. Vostrand; it would be another point in favor of Boston. Women, she declared, would never have thought of such a thing; she denounced them as culpably ignorant of so many matters that concerned them, especially legal matters. "And you think," she asked, "that Mr. Durgin will be a good lawyer? That he will—distinguish himself?"

Westover thought it rather a short-cut to Jeff from the things they had been talking of, but if she wished to speak of him he had no reason to oppose her wish. "I've heard it's all changed a good deal. There are still distinguished lawyers, and lawyers who get on, but they don't distinguish themselves in the old way so much, and they get on best by becoming counsel for some powerful corporation."

"And you think he has talent?" she pursued. "For that, I mean."

"Oh, I don't know," said Westover. "I think he has a good head. He can do what he likes within certain limits, and the limits are not all on the side I used to fancy. He baffles me. But of late, I fancy you've seen rather more of him than I have."

"I have urged him to go more to you. But," said Mrs. Vostrand, with a burst of frankness, "he thinks you don't like him."

"He's wrong," said Westover. "But I might dislike him very much."

"I see what you mean," said Mrs. Vostrand, "and I'm glad you've been so frank with me. I've been so interested in Mr. Durgin, *so* interested! Isn't he very young?"

The question seemed a bit of indirection to Westover. But he answered directly enough. "He's rather old for a Sophomore, I believe. He's twenty-two."

"And Genevieve is twenty. Mr. Westover, may I trust you with something?"

"With everything, I hope, Mrs. Vostrand."

"It's about Genevieve. Her father is so opposed to her making a foreign marriage. It seems to be his one great dread. And of course she's very much exposed to it, living abroad so much with me, and I feel doubly bound on that account to respect her father's opinions, or even prejudices. Before we left Florence —in fact, last winter—there was a most delightful young officer wished to marry her. I don't know that she cared anything for him, though he was everything that *I* could have wished: handsome, brilliant, accomplished, good family; everything *but* rich, and that was what Mr. Vostrand objected to; or, rather, he objected to putting up, as he called it, the sum that Captain Grassi would have had to deposit with the government before he was allowed to marry. You know how it is with the poor fellows in the army, there; I don't understand the process exactly, but the sum is something like sixty thousand francs, I believe; and poor Gigi hadn't it: I always called him Gigi, but his name is Count Luigi de' Popolani Grassi ; and he is descended from one of the old republican families of Florence.   He is *so* nice !   Mr. Vostrand was opposed to him from the beginning, and as soon as he heard of the sixty thousand francs, he utterly refused. He called it buying a son-in-law, but I don't see why he need have looked at it in that light.   However, it was broken off, and we left Florence—more for poor Gigi's sake than for Genevieve's, I must *say*.   He was quite heart-broken ; I pitied him."

Her voice had a tender fall in the closing words, and Westover could fancy how sweet she would make her compassion to the young man.   She began several sentences aimlessly, and he suggested, to supply the broken thread of her discourse rather than to offer consolation, while her eyes seemed to wander with her mind, and ranged the avenue up and down, " Those foreign marriages are not always successful."

" No, they are not," she assented.   " But don't you think they're better with Italians than with Germans, for instance."

" I don't suppose the Italians expect their wives to black their boots, but I've heard that they beat them, sometimes."

" In exaggerated cases, perhaps they do," Mrs. Vostrand admitted.   " And, of course," she added, thoughtfully, " there is nothing like a purely American marriage, for happiness."

Westover wondered how she really regarded her own marriage, but she never betrayed any consciousness of its variance from the type.

XIX.

A YOUNG couple came strolling down the avenue
who to Westover's artistic eye first typified grace and
strength, and then to his more personal perception
identified themselves as Genevieve Vostrand and Jeff
Durgin.

They faltered before one of the benches beside the
mall, and he seemed to be begging her to sit down.
She cast her eyes round till they must have caught the
window of her mother's apartment; then, as if she felt
safe under it, she sank into the seat and Jeff put himself beside her. It was quite too early yet for the
simple lovers who publicly notify their happiness by
the embraces and hand-clasps everywhere evident in
our parks and gardens; and a Boston pair of social
tradition would not have dreamed of sitting on a bench
in Commonwealth Avenue at any hour. But two such
aliens as Jeff and Miss Vostrand might very well do
so; and Westover sympathized with their bohemian
impulse.

Mrs. Vostrand and he watched them awhile, in talk
that straggled away from them, and became more and

more distraught in view of them. Jeff leaned forward, and drew on the ground with the point of his stick; Genevieve held her head motionless at a pensive droop. It was only their backs that Westover could see, and he could not of course make out a syllable of what was effectively their silence; but all the same he began to feel as if he were peeping and eavesdropping.

Mrs. Vostrand seemed not to share his feeling, and there was no reason why he should have it if she had not. He offered to go, but she said, No, no; he must not think of it till Genevieve came in; and she added some banalities about her always scolding when she had missed one of his calls; they would be so few, now, at the most.

"Why, do you intend to go so soon?" he asked.

She did not seem to hear him, and he could see that she was watching the young people intently. Jeff had turned his face up towards Genevieve, without lifting his person, and was saying something she suddenly shrank back from. She made a start as if to rise, but he put out his hand in front of her, beseechingly or compellingly, and she sank down again. But she slowly shook her head at what he was saying, and turned her face towards him so that it gave her profile to the spectators. In that light and at that distance it was impossible to do more than fancy anything fateful in the words which she seemed to be uttering; but Westover chose to fancy this. Jeff waited a moment in apparent silence, after she had spoken. He sat erect, and faced her, and this gave his profile, too.

He must have spoken, for she shook her head again ; and then, at other words from him, nodded assentingly. Then she listened motionlessly while he poured a rapid stream of visible but inaudible words. He put out his hand, as if to take hers, but she put it behind her ; Westover could see it white there against the belt of her dark dress.

Jeff went on more vehemently, but she remained steadfast, slowly shaking her head. When he ended she spoke, and with something of his own energy ; he made a gesture of submission, and when she rose, he rose too. She stood a moment, and with a gentle and almost entreating movement she put out her hand to him. He stood looking down with both his hands resting on the top of his stick, as if ignoring her proffer. Then he suddenly caught her hand, held it a moment, dropped it and walked quickly away without looking back. Genevieve ran across the lawn and roadway towards the house.

" Oh, *must* you go ? " Mrs. Vostrand said to Westover. He found that he had probably risen in sympathy with Jeff's action. He was not aware of an intention of going, but he thought he had better not correct Mrs. Vostrand's error.

" Yes, I really must, now," he said.

" Well, then," she returned distractedly, " do come often."

He hurried out to avoid meeting Genevieve. He passed her on the public stairs of the house, but he saw that she did not recognize him in the dim light.

Late that night he was startled by steps that seemed

to be seeking their way up the stairs to his landing,
and then by a heavy knock on his door.

He opened it, and confronted Jeff Durgin.

"May I come in, Mr. Westover?" he asked with
unwonted deference.

"Yes, come in," said Westover, with no great relish, setting his door open, and then holding on to it a
moment, as if he hoped that, having come in, Jeff
might instantly go out again.

His reluctance was lost upon Jeff, who said, unconscious of keeping his hat on, "I want to talk with
you—I want to tell you something—"

"All right. Won't you sit down?"

At this invitation Jeff seemed reminded to take his
hat off, and he put it on the floor beside his chair.
"I'm not in a scrape, this time; or, rather, I'm in the
worst kind of a scrape, though it isn't the kind that
you want bail for."

"Yes," Westover prompted.

"I don't know whether you've noticed—and if you
haven't it don't make any difference—that I've seemed
to—care a good deal for Miss Vostrand?"

Westover saw no reason why he should not be
frank, and said, "Too much, I've fancied sometimes,
for a student in his Sophomore year."

"Yes, I know that. Well, it's over, whether it was
too much or too little." He laughed in a joyless,
helpless way, and looked deprecatingly at Westover.
"I guess I've been making a fool of myself; that's
all."

"It's better to make a fool of one's self than to

make a fool of some one else," said Westover, oracu-
larly.

"Yes," said Jeff, apparently finding nothing more
definite in the oracle than people commonly find in
oracles. "But I think," he went on with a touch of
bitterness, " that her mother might have told me that
she was engaged—or the same as engaged."

"I don't know that she was bound to take you seriously, or to suppose you took yourself so, at your
age, and with your prospects in life.　If you want to
know "—Westover faltered, and then went on—" she
began to be kind to you because she was afraid that
you might think she didn't take your coming home
second-cabin in the right way; and one thing led to
another.　You mustn't blame her for what's happened."

Westover defended Mrs. Vostrand, but he did not
feel strong in her defence; he was not sure that Durgin was quite wrong, absurd as he had been.　He sat
down and looked up at his visitor under his brows.
"What are you here for, Jeff?　Not to complain of
Mrs. Vostrand?"

Jeff gave a short, shamefaced laugh.　"No, it's this.
You're such an old friend of Mrs. Vostrand's that I
thought she'd be pretty sure to tell you about it; and
I wanted to ask—to ask—that you wouldn't say anything to mother."

"You *are* a boy!　I shouldn't think of meddling
with your affairs," said Westover; he got up again,
and Jeff rose too.

Before noon the next day, a district messenger

brought Westover a letter which he easily knew, from
the now belated tall, angular hand, to be from Mrs.
Vostrand. It announced on a much criss-crossed little
sheet that she and Genevieve were inconsolably taking
a very sudden departure, and were going on the twelve-
o'clock train to New York, where Mr. Vostrand was
to meet them. " In regard to that affair which I men-
tioned last night, he withdraws his objections (we
have had an overnight telegram), and so I suppose all
will *go well*. I cannot tell you how sorry we both are
not to see you again ; you have been such a dear, good
friend to us ; and if you don't hear from us again at
New York, you will from the other side. Genevieve
had some very strange news when she came in, and we
both feel very sorry for the poor young fellow. You
must console him from us all you can. I did not know
before how much she was attached to Gigi : but it
turned out very fortunately that she could say she considered herself bound to him, and did everything to
save Mr. D.'s feelings."

XX.

WESTOVER was not at Lion's Head again till the summer before Jeff's graduation. In the meantime the hotel had grown like a living thing. He could not have imagined wings in connection with the main edifice, but it had put forth wings, one that sheltered a new and enlarged dining-room, with two stories of chambers above, and another that hovered a parlor and ball-room under a like provision of chambers. An ell had been pushed back on the level behind the house; the barn had been moved farther to the southward, and on its old site a laundry built, with quarters for the help over it. All had been carefully, frugally, yet sufficiently done, and Westover was not surprised to learn that it was all the effect of Jackson Durgin's ingenuity and energy. Mrs. Durgin confessed to having no part in it; but she had kept pace, with Cynthia Whitwell's help, in the housekeeping. As Jackson had cautiously felt his way to the needs of their public in the enlargement and rearrangement of the hotel, the two housewives had watchfully studied, not merely the demands, but the half-conscious instincts of their guests, and had responded to them simply and adequately, in the spirit of Jackson's exterior and structural improvements. The walls of the new rooms were left unpapered and their floors uncarpeted ; there were thin rugs put down ; the wood-work was merely stained. Westover found that he need not to ask especially for some hot dish at night; there was almost the abundance of a dinner, though dinner was still at one o'clock.

Mrs. Durgin asked him the first day if he would not like to go into the serving-room and see it while they were serving dinner. She tried to conceal her pride in the busy scene—the waitresses pushing in through one valve of the double-hinged doors with their empty trays, and out through the other with the trays full laden; delivering their dishes with the broken victual at the wicket, where the untouched portions were put aside and the rest poured into the waste ; following in procession along the reeking steam-table, with its great tanks of soup and vegetables, where the carvers stood with the joints and the trussed fowls smoking before them, which they sliced with quick sweeps of their blades, or waiting their turn at the board where the little plates with portions of fruit and dessert stood ready. All went regularly on amid a clatter of knives and voices and dishes ; and the clashing rise and fall of the wire baskets plunging the soiled crockery into misty depths, whence it came up clean and dry without the touch of finger or towel. Westover could not deny that there were elements of the picturesque in it, so that he did not respond quite in kind to Jeff's suggestion, " Scene for a painter, Mr. Westover."

The young fellow followed satirically at his mother's
elbow, and made a mock of her pride in it, trying to
catch Westover's eye when she led him through the
kitchen with its immense range, and introduced him to
a new *chef*, who wiped his hand on his white apron to
offer it to Westover.

"Don't let him get away without seeing the laundry, mother," her son jeered at a final air of absent-
mindedness in her, and she defiantly accepted his
challenge.

"Jeff's mad because he wasn't consulted," she explained, "and because we don't run the house like his
one-horse European hotels."

"Oh, I'm not in it at all, Mr. Westover," said the
young fellow. "I'm as much a passenger as you are.
The only difference is that I'm allowed to work my
passage."

"Well, one thing," said his mother, "is that we've
got a higher class of boarders than we ever had before.
You'll see, Mr. Westover, if you stay on here till
August. There's a class that boards all the year
round, and that knows what a hotel is—about as well
as Jeff, I guess. You'll find 'em at the big city houses,
the first of the winter, and then they go down to Flor-
idy or Georgy for February and March; and they get
up to Fortress Monroe in April, and work along north
about the middle of May to them family hotels in the
suburbs around Boston; and they stay there till it's
time to go to the shore. They stay at the shore
through July, and then they come here in August, and
stay till the leaves turn. They're folks that live on

their money, and they're the very highest class, I
guess. It's a round of gayety with 'em the whole
year through."

Jeff, from the vantage of his greater worldly experience, was trying to exchange looks of intelligence
with Westover concerning those hotel-dwellers whom
his mother revered as aristocrats ; but he did not openly
question her conceptions. "They've told me how they
do, some of the ladies have," she went on. "They've
got the money for it, and they know how to get the
most for their money. Why, Mr. Westover, we've
got rooms in this house, now, that we let for thirty-
five to fifty dollars a week, for two persons, and folks
like that take 'em right along through August and
September, and want a room apiece. It's different
now, I can tell you, from what it was when folks
thought we was killin' 'em if we wanted ten or twelve
dollars."

Westover had finished his dinner before this tour
of the house began, and when it was over the two men
strolled away together.

"You see, it's on the regular American lines," Jeff
pursued, after parting with his mother. "Jackson's
done it, and he can't imagine anything else. I don't
say it isn't well done in its way, but the way's wrong ;
it's stupid and clumsy." When they were got so far
from the hotel as to command a prospect of its un-
gainly mass sprawled upon the plateau, his smoulder-
ing disgust burst out. "Look at it ! Did you ever
see anything like it ? I wish the damned thing would
burn up—or down ! "

Westover was aware in more ways than one of Jeff's exclusion from authority in the place, where he was constantly set aside from the management as if his future were so definitely dedicated to another calling that not even his advice was desired or permitted; and he could not help sympathizing a little with him when he chafed at his rejection. He saw a great deal of him, and he thought him quite up to the average of Harvard Seniors in some essentials. He had been sobered apparently by experience; his unfortunate love-affair seemed to have improved him, as the phrase is.

They had some long walks and long talks together, and in one of them Jeff opened his mind, if not his heart, to the painter. He wanted to be the Landlord of the Lion's Head, which he believed he could make the best hotel in the mountains. He knew, of course, that he could not hope to make any changes that did not suit his mother and his brother, as long as they had the control, but he thought they would let him have the control sooner if his mother could only be got to give up the notion of his being a lawyer. As nearly as he could guess, she wanted him to be a lawyer because she did not want him to be a hotel-keeper, and her prejudice against that was because she believed that selling liquor made her father a drunkard.

" Well, now you know enough about me, Mr. Westover, to know that drink isn't my danger."

" Yes, I think I do," said Westover.

" I went a little wild in my Freshman year, and I got into that scrape; but I've never been the worse for liquor since. Fact is, I never touch it now. There isn't any more reason why I should take to drink because I keep a hotel than Jackson; but just that one time has set mother against it, and I can't seem to make her understand that once is enough for me. Why, I should keep a temperance house, here, of course; you can't do anything else in these days. If I was left to choose between hotel-keeping and any other life that I know of, I'd choose it every time," Jeff went on after a moment of silence. "I *like* a hotel. You can be your own man from the start; the start's made here, and I've helped to make it. All you've got to do is to have common-sense in the hotel business, and you're sure to succeed. I believe I've got common-sense, and I believe I've got some ideas that I can work up into a great success. The reason that most people fail in the hotel business is that they waste so much, and the landlord that wastes on his guests can't treat them well. It's got so now that in the big city houses they can't make anything on feeding people, and so they try to make it up on the rooms. I should feed them well—I believe I know how—and I should make money on my table, as they do in Europe. I've thought a good many things out; my mind runs on it all the time; but I'm not going to bore you with it now."

"Oh, not at all," said Westover. "I'd like to know what your ideas are."

"Well, some time I'll tell you. But look here, Mr. Westover, I wish if mother gets to talking about me with you, that you'd let her know how I feel. We can't talk together, she and I, without quarrelling about

it; but I guess you could put in a word that would
show her I wasn't quite a fool.   She thinks I've gone
crazy from seeing the way they do things in Europe;
that I'm conceited and unpatriotic, and I don't know
what all."

Jeff laughed as if with an inner fondness for his
mother's wrongheadedness.

"And would you be willing to settle down here in
the country for the rest of your life, and throw away
your Harvard training on hotel-keeping?"

"What do the other fellows do with their Harvard
training when they go into business, as nine-tenths of
them do?   Business is business, whether you keep a
hotel or import dry-goods, or manufacture cotton, or
run a railroad, or help a big trust to cheat legally.
Harvard has got to take a back seat when you get out
of Harvard.   But you don't suppose that keeping a
summer hotel would mean living in the country the
whole time, do you?   That's the way mother does,
but I shouldn't.   It isn't good for the hotel, even.   If
I had such a place as Lion's Head, I should put a man
and his family into it for the winter to look after it,
and I should go to town myself—to Boston or New
York, or I might go to London or Paris.   They're not
so far off, and it's so easy to get to them that you can
hardly keep away."   Jeff laughed, and looked up at
Westover from the log where he sat, whittling a pine
stick; Westover sat on the stump from which the log
had been felled eight or ten years before.

"You *are* modern," he said.

"That's what I should do at first.   But I don't be-

lieve I should have Lion's Head very long before I had
another hotel—in Florida, or the Georgia uplands, or
North Carolina, somewhere. I should take my help
back and forth; it would be as easy to run two hotels
as one; easier! It would keep my hand in. But if
you want to know, I'd rather stick here in the country,
year in and year out, and run Lion's Head, than to be
a lawyer and hang round trying to get a case for nine
or ten years. Who's going to support me? Do you
suppose I want to live on mother till I'm forty? She
don't think of that. She thinks I can go right into
court, and begin distinguishing myself, if I can fight
the people off from sending me to Congress. I'd
rather live in the country, anyway. I think town's
the place for winter, or two-three months of it, and
after that I haven't got any use for it. But mother,
she's got this old-fashioned ambition to have me go to
a city, and set up there. She thinks that if I was a
lawyer in Boston I should be at the top of the heap.
But I know better than that, and so do you; and I
want you to give her some little hint of how it really
is: how it takes family, and money, and a lot of influence to get to the top in any city."

It occurred to Westover, and not for the first time,
that the frankest thing in Jeff Durgin was his disposition to use his friends. It seemed to him that Jeff
was always asking something of him, and it did not
change the fact that in this case he thought him altogether in the right. He said that if Mrs. Durgin spoke
to him of the matter he would not keep the light from
her. He looked about him, now, for the first time,

in recognition of the place where they had stopped.
" Why, this is Whitwell's Clearing."

" Didn't you know it ? " Jeff asked.   " It changes
a good deal every year, and you haven't been here for
a while, have you ? "

" Not since Mrs. Marven's picnic," said Westover,
and he added quickly, to efface the painful association
which he must have called up by his heedless words,
" The woods have crowded back upon it so.   It can't
be more than half its old size."

" No," Jeff assented.   He struck his heel against a
fragment of the pine bough he had been whittling,
and drove it into the soft ground beside the log, and
said, without looking up from it, " I met that woman
at a dance last winter.   It wasn't her dance, but she
was running it as if it were, just the way she did with
the picnic.   She seemed to want to let bygones be bygones, and I danced with her daughter.   She's a nice
girl.   I thought mother did wrong about that."   Now
he looked at Westover.   " She couldn't help it, but
it wasn't the thing to do.   A hotel is a public house,
and you can't act as if it wasn't.   If mother hadn't
known how to keep a hotel so well in other ways, she
might have ruined the house by not knowing in a
thing like that.   But we've got some of the people
with us this year that used to come here when we first
took farm-boarders; mother don't know that they're
ever so much nicer, socially, than the people that take
the fifty-dollar rooms."   He laughed, and then he
said, seriously, " If I ever had a son, I don't believe I
should let my pride in him risk doing him mischief.

And if you've a mind to let her understand that you believe I'm set against the law for good and all—"

"I guess I shall not be your ambassador, so far as that. Why don't you tell her yourself?"

"She won't believe me," said Jeff, with a laugh. "She thinks I don't know my mind. And I don't like the way we differ when we differ. We differ more than we mean to. I don't pretend to say I'm always right. She was right about that other picnic—the one I wanted to make for Mrs. Vostrand. I suppose," he ended unexpectedly, "that you hear from them, now and then?"

"No, I don't. I haven't heard from them for a year; not since— You knew Genevieve was married?"

"Yes, I knew that," said Jeff, steadily.

"I don't quite make it all out. Mr. Vostrand was very much opposed to it, Mrs. Vostrand told me; but he must have given way at last; and he must have put up the money." Jeff looked puzzled, and Westover explained. "You know the officers in the Italian army —and all the other armies in Europe, for that matter —have to deposit a certain sum with the government before they can marry—and in the case of Count Grassi, Mr. Vostrand had to furnish the money."

Jeff said after a moment, "Well, *she* couldn't help that."

"No, the girl wasn't to blame. I don't know that any one was to blame. But I'm afraid our girls wouldn't marry many titles if their fathers didn't put up the money."

"Well, I don't see why they shouldn't spend their

money that way as well as any other," said Jeff, and
this proof of his impartiality suggested to Westover
that he was not only indifferent to the mercenary international marriages, which are a scandal to so many
of our casuists, but had quite outlived his passion for
the girl concerned in this.

"At any rate," Jeff added, "I haven't got anything
to say against it.   Mr. Westover, I've always wanted
to say one thing to you.   When I came to your room
that night, I wanted to complain of Mrs. Vostrand for
not letting me know about the engagement; and I
wasn't man enough to acknowledge that what you said
would account for their letting me make a fool of myself.   But I believe I am now, and I want to say it."

"I'm glad you can see it in that way," said Westover, "and since you do, I don't mind saying that I
think Mrs. Vostrand might have been a little franker
with you without being less kind.   She was kind, but
she wasn't quite frank."

"Well, it's all over now," said Jeff, and he rose up
and brushed the whittlings from his knees.   "And I
guess it's just as well."

XXI.

THAT afternoon Westover saw Jeff helping Cynthia Whitwell into his buckboard, and then, after his lively horse had made some paces of a start, spring to the seat beside her and bring it to a stand. "Can I do anything for you over at Lovewell, Mr. Westover?" he called, and he smiled towards the painter. Then he lightened the reins on the mare's back; she squared herself for a start in earnest, and flashed down the sloping hotel road to the highway below, and was lost to sight in the clump of woods to the southward.

"That's a good friend of yours, Cynthy," he said, leaning towards the girl with a simple comfort in her proximity. She was dressed in a pale pink color, with a hat of yet paler pink; without having a great deal of fashion, she had a good deal of style. She looked bright and fresh; there was a dash of pink in her cheeks, which suggested the color of the sweetbrier, its purity and sweetness, and if there was something in Cynthia's character and temperament that suggested its thorns too, one still could not deny that she was like that flower. She liked to shop, and she liked to ride after a good horse, as the neighbors would have said; she was going over to Lovewell to buy a number of things, and Jeff Durgin was driving her there with the swift mare that was his peculiar property. She smiled upon him without the usual reservations she contrived to express in her smiles.

"Well, I don't know anybody I'd rather have for my friend than Mr. Westover." She added, "He acted like a friend the very first time I saw him."

Jeff laughed with shameless pleasure in the reminiscence her words suggested. "Well, I did get my come-uppings that time. And I don't know but he's been a pretty good friend to me, too. I'm not sure he likes me; but Mr. Westover is a man that could be your friend if he didn't like you."

"What have you done to make him like you?" asked the girl.

"Nothing!" said Jeff, with a shout of laughter in his conviction. "I've done a lot of things to make him despise me from the start. But if you like a person yourself, you want him to like you whether you deserve it or not."

"I don't know as I do."

"You say that because you always deserve it. You can't tell how it is with a fellow like me. I should want you to like me, Cynthy, whatever you thought of me." He looked round into her face, but she turned it away.

They had struck the level, long for the hill country, at the foot of the hotel road, and the mare, that found herself neither mounting nor descending a steep, dropped from the trot proper for an acclivity into a rapid walk.

" This mare can walk like a Kentucky horse," said Jeff. " I believe I could teach her single-foot." He added, with a laugh, " If I knew how," and now Cynthia laughed with him.

" I was just going to say that."

" Yes, you don't lose many chances to give me a dig, do you ? "

" Oh, I don't know as I look for them. Perhaps I don't need to." The pine woods were deep on either side. They whispered in the thin, sweet wind, and gave out their odor in the high, westering sun. They covered with their shadows the road that ran velvety between them.

" This is nice," said Jeff, letting himself rest against the back of the seat. He stretched his left arm along the top, and presently it dropped and folded itself about the waist of the girl.

" You may take your arm away, Jeff," she said, quietly.

" Why ? "

" Because it has no right there, for one thing ! " She drew herself a little aside, and looked round at him. " You wouldn't put it round a town girl if you were riding with her."

" I shouldn't be riding with her. Girls don't go buggy-riding in town any more," said Jeff, brutally.

" Then I shall know what to do the next time you ask me."

" Oh, they'd go quick enough if I asked them up

here in the country. Etiquette don't count with them
when they're on a vacation."

"I'm not on a vacation; so it counts with me.
Please take your arm away," said Cynthia.

"Oh, all right. But I shouldn't object to your
putting your arm around me."

"You will never have the chance."

"Why are you so hard on me, Cynthy?" asked Jeff.
"You didn't used to be so."

"People change."

"Do I?"

"Not for the better."

Jeff was dumb. She was pleased with her hit, and
laughed. But her laugh did not encourage him to put
his arm round her again. He let the mare walk on,
and left her to resume the conversation at whatever
point she would.

She made no haste to resume it. At last she said,
with sufficient apparent remoteness from the subject
they had dropped, "Jeff, I don't know whether you
want me to talk about it. But I guess I ought to, even
if it isn't my place exactly. I don't think Jackson's
very well, this summer."

Jeff faced round towards her. "What makes you
think he isn't well?"

"He's weaker. Haven't you noticed it?"

"Yes, I have noticed that. He's worked down;
that's all."

"No, that isn't all. But if you don't think so—"

"I want to know what *you* think, Cynthy," said
Jeff, with the amorous resentment all gone from his

voice. " Sometimes folks outside notice the signs
more— I don't mean that you're an outsider, as far
as we're concerned—"

She put by that point. " Father's noticed it, too ;
and he's with Jackson a good deal."

" I'll look after it. If he isn't so well, he's got to
have a doctor. That medium's stuff can't do him any
good. Don't you think he ought to have a doctor ? "

" Oh, yes."

" You don't think a doctor can do him much good ? "

" He ought to have one," said the girl, non-commit-
tally.

" Cynthia, I've noticed that Jackson was weak, too ;
and it's no use pretending that he's simply worked
down. I believe he's worn out. Do you think mother's ever noticed it ? "

" I don't believe she has."

" It's the one thing I can't very well make up my
mind to speak to her about. I don't know what she
would do." He did not say, " If she lost Jackson,"
but Cynthia knew he meant that, and they were both
silent. " Of course," he went on, " I know that she
places a great deal of dependence upon you, but Jackson's her main stay. He's a good man, and he's a
good son. I wish I'd always been half as good."

Cynthia did not protest against his self-reproach as
he possibly hoped she would. She said, " I think
Jackson's got a very good mind. He reads a great
deal, and he's thought a great deal, and when it comes
to talking, I never heard any one express themselves
better. The other night, we were out looking at the

stars—I came part of the way home with him; I didn't
like to let him go alone, he seemed so feeble—and he
got to showing me Mars.   He thinks it's inhabited,
and he's read all that the astronomers say about it, and
the seas and the canals that they've found on it.   He
spoke very beautifully about the other life, and then
he spoke about death."   Cynthia's voice broke, and
she pulled her handkerchief out of her belt, and put it
to her eyes.   Jeff's heart melted in him at the sight;
he felt a tender affection for her, very unlike the gross
content he had enjoyed in her presence before, and he
put his arm round her again, but this time almost unconsciously, and drew her towards him.   She did not
repel him; she even allowed her head to rest a moment on his shoulder; though she quickly lifted it, and
drew herself away, not resentfully, it seemed, but for
her greater freedom in talking.

"I don't believe he's going to die," Jeff said, con-
solingly, more as if it were her brother than his that
he meant.   "But he's a very sick man, and he's got
to knock off, and go somewhere.   It won't do for him
to pass another winter here.   He must go to California, or Colorado; they'd be glad to have him there,
either of them; or he can go to Florida, or over to
Italy.   It won't matter how long he stays—"

"What are you talking about, Jeff Durgin?" Cynthia demanded, severely.   "What would your mother
do?   What would she do this winter?"

"That brings me to something, Cynthia," said Jeff,
"and I don't want you to say anything till I've got
through.   I guess I could help mother run the place

as well as Jackson, and I could stay here next winter."

"You?"

"Now, you let me talk! My mind's made up about one thing: I'm not going to be a lawyer. I don't want to go back to Harvard. I'm going to keep a hotel, and if I don't keep one here at Lion's Head, I'm going to keep it somewhere else."

"Have you told your mother?"

"Not yet. I wanted to hear what you would say first."

"I? Oh, I haven't got anything to do with it," said Cynthia.

"Yes, you have! You've got everything to do with it, if you'll say one thing first. Cynthia, you know how I feel about you. It's been so ever since we were boy and girl here. I want you to promise to marry me. Will you?"

The girl seemed neither surprised nor very greatly pleased; perhaps her pleasure had spent itself in that moment of triumphant expectation when she foresaw what was coming, or perhaps she was preoccupied in clearing the way in her own mind to a definite result.

"What do you say, Cynthia?" Jeff pursued, with more injury than misgiving in his voice at her delay in answering. "Don't you—care for me?"

"Oh, yes, I presume I've always done that—ever since we were boy and girl, as you say. But—"

"Well?" said Jeff, patiently, but not insecurely.

"Have *you?*"

"Have I what?"

" Always cared for *me*."

He could not find his voice quite as promptly as
before. He cleared his throat before he asked, " Has
Mr. Westover been saying anything about me ? "

" I don't know what you mean, exactly ; but I presume *you* do."

" Well, then—I always expected to tell you—I did
have a fancy for that girl, for Miss Vostrand, and I—
told her so. It's like something that never happened.
She wouldn't have me. That's all."

" And you expect me to take what she wouldn't
have ? "

" If you like to call it that. But I should call it
taking a man that had been out of his head for a while,
and had come to his senses again."

" I don't know as I should ever feel safe with a man
that had been out of his head once."

" You wouldn't find many men that hadn't," said
Jeff, with a laugh that was rather scornful of her ignorance.

" No, I presume not," she sighed. " She was beautiful, and I believe she was good, too. She was very
nice. Perhaps I feel strangely about it. But if she
hadn't been so nice, I shouldn't have been so willing
that you should have cared for her."

" I suppose I don't understand," said Jeff, " but I
know I was hard hit. What's the use ? It's over. She's
married. I can't go back and unlive it all. But if
you want time to think—of course you do—*I* 've taken
time enough—"

He was about to lift the reins on the mare's back as

a sign to her that the talk was over for the present, and to quicken her pace, when Cynthia put out her hand and laid it on his, and said with a certain effect of authority: " I shouldn't want you should give up your last year in Harvard."

" Just as you say, Cynthy ; " and in token of intelligence he wound his arm round her neck and kissed her. It was not the first kiss by any means ; in the country kisses are not counted very serious, or at all binding, and Cynthia was a country girl ; but they both felt that this kiss sealed a solemn troth between them, and that a common life began for them with it

XXII.

CYNTHIA came back in time to go into the dining-room and see that all was in order there for supper before the door opened. The waitresses knew that she had been out riding, as they called it, with Jeff Durgin; the fact had spread electrically to them where they sat in a shady angle of the hotel listening to one who read a novel aloud, and skipped all but the most exciting love parts. They conjectured that the pair had gone to Lovewell, but they knew nothing more, and the subtlest of them would not have found reason for further conjecture in Cynthia's behavior, when she came in and scanned the tables and the girls' dresses and hair, where they stood ranged against the wall. She was neither whiter nor redder than usual, and her nerves and her tones were under as good control as a girl's ever are after she has been out riding with a fellow. It was not such a great thing, anyway, to ride with Jeff Durgin. First and last, nearly all the young lady boarders had been out with him, upon one errand or another to Lovewell.

After supper, when the girls had gone over to their

rooms in the helps' quarters, and the guests had gathered in the wide, low office, in the light of the fire kindled on the hearth to break the evening chill, Jeff joined Cynthia in her inspection of the dining-room. She always gave it a last look, to see that it was in perfect order for breakfast, before she went home for the night. Jeff went home with her; he was impatient of her duties, but he was in no hurry when they stole out of the side door together under the stars, and began to stray sidelong down the hill over the dewless grass.

He lingered more and more as they drew near her father's house, in the abandon of a man's love. He wished to give himself solely up to it, to think and to talk of nothing else, after a man's fashion. But a woman's love is no such mere delight. It is serious, practical. For her it is all future, and she cannot give herself wholly up to any present moment of it, as a man does.

"Now, Jeff," she said, after a certain number of partings, in which she had apparently kept his duty clearly in mind, "you had better go home and tell your mother."

"Oh, there's time enough for that," he began.

"I want you to tell her right away, or there won't *be* anything to tell."

"Is that so?" he joked back. "Well, if I must, I must, I suppose. But I didn't think you'd take the whip-hand so soon, Cynthia."

"Oh, I don't ever want to take the whip-hand with you, Jeff. Don't make me!"

"'NOW, JEFF, YOU HAD BETTER GO HOME AND TELL YOUR
MOTHER'"

"Well, I won't, then. But what are you in such a hurry to have mother know for? She's not going to object. And if she does—"

"It isn't that," said the girl. "If I had to go round a single day with your mother hiding this from her, I should begin to hate you. I couldn't bear the concealment. I shall tell father as soon as I go in."

"Oh, your father 'll be all right, of course."

"Yes, he'll be all right, but if he wouldn't, and I knew it, I should have to tell him, all the same. Now, *good*-night. Well, there, then; and there! Now, *let* me go!"

She paused for a moment in her own room, to smooth her tumbled hair, and try to identify herself in her glass. Then she went into the sitting-room, where she found her father pulled up to the table, with his hat on, and poring over a sheet of hieroglyphics, which represented the usual evening with planchette.

"Have you been to help Jackson up?" she asked.

"Well, I wanted to, but he wouldn't hear of it. He's feelin' ever so much better to-night, and he wanted to go alone. I just come in."

"Yes, you've got your hat on yet."

Whitwell put his hand up and found that his daughter was right. He laughed, and said, "I guess I must 'a' forgot it. We've had the most *interestin'* season with plantchette that I guess we've about ever had. She's said something here—"

"Well, never mind; I've got something more important to say than plantchette has," said Cynthia, and she pulled the sheet away from under her father's eyes.

This made him look up at her. "Why, what's happened?"

"Nothing.   Jeff Durgin has asked me to marry him."

"He *has!*" The New England training is not such as to fit people for the expression of strong emotion, and the best that Whitwell found himself able to do in view of the fact was to pucker his mouth for a whistle which did not come.

"Yes—this afternoon," said Cynthia, lifelessly. The tension of her nerves relaxed in a languor which was evident even to her father, though his eyes still wandered to the sheet she had taken from him.

"Well, you don't seem over and above excited about it.   Did—did you—   What did you *say?*"

"How should I know what I said?   What do you think of it, father?"

"I don't know as I ever give the subject much attention," said the philosopher.   "I always meant to take it out of him, somehow, if he got to playin' the fool."

"Then you wanted I should accept him?"

"What difference 'd it make what I wanted?   That what you done?"

"Yes, I've accepted him," said the girl, with a sigh. "I guess I've always expected to."

"Well, I thought likely it would come to that, myself.   All I can say, Cynthy, is 't he's a lucky feller."

Whitwell leaned back, bracing his knees against the table, which was one of his philosophic poses.   "I *have* sometimes believed that Jeff Durgin was goin' to turn out a blackguard. He's got it *in* him. He's as like his gran'father as two peas, and he *was* an old devil. But you got to account in all these here heredity cases for counteractin' influences. The Durgins are as good as wheat, right along, all of 'em; and I guess Mis' Durgin's mother must have been a pretty good woman too. Mis' Durgin's all right, too, if she *has* got a will of her own." Whitwell returned from his scientific inquiry to ask, "How'll she take it?"

"I don't know," said Cynthia, dreamily, but without apparent misgiving. "That's Jeff's lookout."

"So 'tis. I guess she won't make much fuss. A woman never likes to see her son get married; but you've been a kind of daughter to her so long. Well, I guess *that* part of it'll be all right. Jackson," said Whitwell, in a tone of relief, as if turning from an irrelevant matter to something of real importance, "was down here to-night tryin' to ring up some them spirits from the planet Mars. Martians, he calls 'em. His mind's got to runnin' a good deal on Mars lately. I guess it's this apposition that they talk about that does it. Mars comin' so much nearer the earth by a million of miles or so, it stands to reason that he should be more influenced by the minds on it. I guess it's a case o' that telepathy that Mr. Westover tells about. I judge that if he kept at it before Mars gits off too far again he might make something out of it. I couldn't seem to find much sense in what plantchette done to-night; we couldn't either of us; but she has her spells when you can't make head or tail of her. But mebbe she's just leadin' up to something, the way she did about that broken shaft when Jeff come home. We ha'n't ever made out exactly what she meant by that yet."

Whitwell paused, and Cynthia seized the advantage of his getting round to Jeff again. "He wanted to give up going to Harvard this last year, but I wouldn't let him."

"*Jeff* did?" asked her father. "Well, you done a good thing that time, anyway, Cynthy. His mother 'd never get over it."

"There's something else she's got to get over, and I don't know how she ever *will*. He's going to give up the law."

"Give up the *law!*"

"Yes. Don't tease, father! He says he's never cared about it, and he wants to keep a hotel. I thought that I'd ought to tell him how we felt about Jackson's having a rest, and going off somewhere; and he wanted to begin at once. But I said if he left off the last year at Harvard I wouldn't have anything to do with him."

Whitwell put his hand in his pocket for his knife, and mechanically looked down for a stick to whittle. In default of any, he scratched his head. "I guess she'll make it warm for him. She's had her mind set on his studyin' law so long, 't she won't give up in a hurry. She can't see that Jackson ain't fit to help her run the hotel, any more—till he's had a rest, anyway —and I believe she thinks her and Frank could run it —and you. She'll make an awful kick," said Whitwell, solemnly. "I hope you didn't encourage him Cynthy?"

"I *should* encourage him," said the girl. "He's got the right to shape his own life, and nobody else has got the right to do it; and I should tell his mother so, if she ever said anything to me about it."

"All right," said Whitwell. "I suppose you know what you're about."

"I do, father. Jeff would make a good landlord; he's got ideas about a hotel, and I can see that they're the right ones. He's been out in the world, and he's kept his eyes open. He will make Lion's Head the best hotel in the mountains."

"It's that already."

"He doesn't think it's half as good as he can make it."

"It wouldn't be half what it is now, if it wa'n't for you and Frank."

"I guess he understands that," said Cynthia. "Frank would be the clerk."

"Got it all mapped out!" said Whitwell proudly, in his turn. "Look out you don't slip up in your calculations. That's all."

"I guess we sha'n't slip up."

XXIII.

JEFF came into the ugly old family parlor, where his mother sat mending by the kerosene-lamp which she had kept through all the household changes, and pushed enough of her work aside from the corner of the table to rest his arm upon it.

"Mother, I want you to listen to me, and to wait till I get done. Will you?"

She looked up at him over her spectacles from the stocking she was darning; the china egg gleamed through the frayed place. "What notion have you got in your head, now?"

"It's about Jackson. He isn't well. He's got to leave off work, and go away."

The mother's hand dropped at the end of the yarn she had drawn through the stocking heel, and she stared at Jeff. Then she resumed her work with the decision expressed in her tone. "Your father lived to be sixty years old, and Jackson a'n't forty! The doctor said there wa'n't any reason why he shouldn't live as long as his father did."

"I'm not saying he won't live to a hundred. I'm saying he oughtn't to stay another winter here."

Mrs. Durgin was silent for a time, and then she said, "Jeff, is that *your* notion about Jackson, or *whose* is it?"

"It's mine, now."

Mrs. Durgin waited a moment. Then she began, with a feeling quite at variance with her words: "Well, I'll thank Cynthy Whit'ell to mind her own business! Of course," she added, and in what followed her feeling worked to the surface in her words, "I know 't she thinks the world of Jackson, and he does of her; and I presume she means well. I guess she'd be more apt to notice, if there was any change, than what I should. What did she say?"

Jeff told, as nearly as he could remember, and he told what Cynthia and he had afterwards jointly worked out as to the best thing for Jackson to do. Mrs. Durgin listened frowningly, but not disapprovingly, as it seemed; though at the end she asked, "And what am I going to do, with Jackson gone?"

Jeff laughed, with his head down. "Well, I guess you and Cynthy could run it, with Frank and Mr. Whitwell."

"Mr. Whit'ell!" said Mrs. Durgin, concentrating in her accent of his name the contempt she could not justly pour out on the others.

"Or," Jeff went on, "I *did* think that *I* could take hold with you, if you could bring yourself to let me off this last year at Harvard."

"Jeff!" said his mother, reproachfully. "You know you don't mean that you'd give up your last year in college?"

"I do mean it, but I don't expect you to do it; and
I don't ask it. I suggested it to Cynthy, when we
got to talking it over, and she saw it wouldn't do."

"Well, she showed some sense *that* time," Mrs.
Durgin said.

"I don't know when Cynthy hasn't shown sense,
except once, and then I guess it was my fault."

"What do you mean?"

"Why, this afternoon I asked her to marry me
sometime, and she said she would." He looked at
his mother and laughed, and then he did not laugh.
He had expected her to be pleased; he had thought
to pave the way with this confession for the declaration
of his intention not to study law, and to make his
engagement to Cynthia serve him in reconciling his
mother to the other fact. But a menacing suspense
followed his words.

His mother broke out at last: "You asked Cynthy
Whit'ell to marry you! And she said she would!
Well, I can tell her she won't, then!"

"And I can tell you she *will!*" Jeff stormed back.
He rose to his feet and stood over his mother.

She began steadily, as if he had not spoken. "If
that designin'—"

"Look out, mother! Don't you say anything
against Cynthia! She's been the best girl to you in
the world, and you know it. She's been as true to
you as Jackson has himself. She hasn't got a selfish
bone in her body, and she's so honest she couldn't
design anything against you or any one, unless she
told you first. Now you take that back! Take it

back!   She's no more designing than—than *you* are!"

Mrs. Durgin was not moved by his storming, but she was inwardly convinced of error.   "I do take it back. Cynthy is all right. She's all you say and more. It's *your* fault, then, and you've got yourself to thank, for whosever fault it is, she'll pack—"

"If Cynthy packs, *I* pack!" said Jeff. "Understand that. The moment she leaves this house I leave it too, and I'll marry her anyway. Frank 'd leave and—and— Pshaw! What do you care for that? But I don't know what you mean!   I always thought you liked Cynthy and respected her.   I didn't believe I could tell you a thing that would please you better than that she had said she would have me.   But if it don't, all right."

Mrs. Durgin held her peace in bewilderment; she stared at her son with dazed eyes, under the spectacles lifted above her forehead.   She felt a change of mood in his unchanged tone of defiance, and she met him half-way.   "I tell you I take back what I called Cynthy, and I told you so.   But—but I didn't ever expect you to marry her."

"Why didn't you?   There isn't one of the summer folks to compare with her.   She's got more sense than all of 'em.   I've known her ever since I can remember. Why didn't you expect it?"

"I didn't expect it."

"Oh, I know!   You thought I'd see somebody in Boston—some swell girl.   Well, they wouldn't any of them look at me, and if they would, they wouldn't look at *you*."

" I shouldn't care whether they looked at me or not."

" I tell you they wouldn't look at *me*. You don't understand about these things, and I do. They marry their own kind, and I'm not their kind, and I shouldn't be if I was Daniel Webster himself. Daniel Webster! Who remembers him, or cares for him, or ever did? You don't believe it? You think that because I've been at Harvard— Oh, *can't* I make you see it? I'm what they call a *jay* in Harvard, and Harvard don't count if you're a jay."

His mother looked at him without speaking. She would not confess the ambition he taxed her with, and perhaps she had nothing so definite in her mind. Perhaps it was only her pride in him, and her faith in a splendid future for him, that made her averse to his marriage in the lot she had always known, and on a little lower level in it than her own. She said at last: " I don't know what you mean by being a jay. But I guess we better not say anything more about this to-night."

" All right," Jeff returned. There never were any formal good-nights between the Durgins, and he went away now without further words.

His mother remained sitting where he left her. Two or three times she drew her empty darning-needle through the heel of the stocking she was mending.

She was still sitting there when Jackson passed on his way to bed, after leaving the office in charge of the night porter. He faltered, as he went by, and as he stood on the threshold she told him what Jeff had told her.

"That's good," he said, lifelessly. "Good for Jeff," he added, thoughtfully, conscientiously.

"Why a'n't it good for her, too?" demanded Jeff's mother, in quick resentment of the slight put upon him.

"I didn't say it wa'n't," said Jackson. "But it's better for Jeff."

"She may be very glad to get him!"

"I presume she is. She's always cared for him, I guess. She'll know how to manage him."

"I don't know," said Mrs. Durgin, "as I like to have you talk so, about Jeff. He was here, just now, wantin' to give up his last year in Harvard, so 's to let you go off on a vacation. He thinks you've worked yourself down."

Jackson made no recognition of Jeff's professed self-sacrifice. "I don't want any vacation. I'm feeling first rate now. I guess that stuff I had from the writin' medium has begun to take hold of me. I don't know when I've felt so well. I believe I'm going to get stronger than ever I was. Jeff say I needed a rest?"

Something like a smile of compassion for the delusion of his brother dawned upon the sick man's wasted face, which was blotched with large freckles, and stared with dim, large eyes from out a framework of grayish hair, and grayish beard cut to the edges of the cheeks and chin.

XXIV.

Mrs. Durgin and Cynthia did not seek any formal meeting the next morning. The course of their work brought them together, but it was not till after they had transacted several household affairs of pressing importance that Mrs. Durgin asked, "What's this about you and Jeff?"

"Has he been telling you?" asked Cynthia, in her turn, though she knew he had.

"Yes," said Mrs. Durgin, with a certain dryness, which was half humorous. "I presume, if you two are satisfied, it's all right."

"I guess we're satisfied," said the girl, with a tremor of relief which she tried to hide.

Nothing more was said, and there was no physical demonstration of affection or rejoicing between the women. They knew that the time would come when they would talk over the affair down to the bone together, but now they were content to recognize the fact, and let the time for talking arrive when it would. "I guess," said Mrs. Durgin, "you'd better go over

to the helps' house and see how that youngest Miller
girl's gittin' along.   She'd ought to give up and go
home if she a'n't fit for her work."

"I'll go and see her," said Cynthia.   "I don't believe she's strong enough for a waitress, and I have
got to tell her so."

"Well," returned Mrs. Durgin, glumly, after a moment's reflection, "I shouldn't want you should hurry
her.   Wait till she's out of bed, and give her another
chance."

"All right."

Jeff had been lurking about for the event of the interview, and he waylaid Cynthia on the path to the
helps' house.

"I'm going over to see that youngest Miller girl,"
she explained.

"Yes, I know all about that," said Jeff.   "Well,
mother took it just right, didn't she?   You can't always count on her; but I hadn't much anxiety in this
case.   She likes you, Cynthia."

"I guess so," said the girl, demurely; and she
looked away from him to smile her pleasure in the fact.

"But I believe if she hadn't known you were with
her about my last year in Harvard—it would have
been different.   I could see, when I brought it in that
you wanted me to go back, her mind was made up for
you."

"Why need you say anything about that?"

"Oh, I knew it would clinch her.   I understand
mother.   If you want something from her you mustn't
ask it straight out.   You must propose something very

disagreeable. Then when she refuses that, you can
come in for what you were really after and get it."

"I don't know," said Cynthia, "as I should like to
think that your mother had been tricked into feeling
right about me."

"Tricked!" The color flashed up in Jeff's face.

"Not that, Jeff," said the girl, tenderly. "But you
know what I mean. I hope you talked it all out fully
with her."

"Fully? I *don't* know what you mean."

"About your not studying law, and—everything."

"I don't believe in crossing a river till I come to
it," said Jeff. "I didn't say anything to her about
that."

"You didn't!"

"No. What had it got to do with our being engaged?"

"What had your going back to Harvard to do with
it? If your mother thinks I'm with her in that, she'll
think I'm with her in the other. And I'm not. I'm
with *you*." She let her hand find his, as they walked
side by side, and gave it a little pressure.

"It's the greatest thing, Cynthy," he said, breath-
lessly, "to *have* you with me in that. But if you said
I ought to study law, I should do it."

"I shouldn't say that, for I believe you're right;
but even if I believed you were wrong, I shouldn't say
it. You have a right to make your life what you want
it; and your mother hasn't. Only she must know it,
and you must tell her at once."

"At once?"

"Yes—now. What good will it do to put it off? You're not *afraid* to tell her!"

"I don't like you to use that word."

"And I don't like to use it. But I know how it is. You're afraid that the brunt of it will come on *me*. She'll think you're all right, but I'm all wrong because I agree with you."

"Something like that."

"Well, now, I'm not afraid of anything she can say; and what could she do? She can't part us, unless you let her, and then *I* should let her, too."

"But what's the hurry? What's the need of doing it right off?"

"Because it's a deceit not to do it. It's a lie!"

"I don't see it in that light. I might change my mind, and still go on and study law."

"You know you never will. Now, Jeff! Why do you act so?"

Jeff did not answer at once. He walked beside her with a face of trouble that finally became one of resolve in the set jaws. "I guess you're right, Cynthy. She's got to know the worst, and the sooner she knows it the better."

"Yes!"

He had another moment of faltering. "You don't want I should talk it over with Mr. Westover?"

"What has he got to do with it?"

"That's true!"

"If you want to see it in the right light, you can think you've let it run on till after you're out of college, and then you've got to tell her. Suppose she

asked you how long you had made up your mind
against the law, how should you feel? And if she
asked me whether I'd known it all along, and I had to
say I had, and that I'd supported and encouraged you
in it, how should *I* feel?"

"She mightn't ask any such question," said Jeff,
gloomily. Cynthia gave a little impatient "Oh!" and
he hastened to add: "But you're right; I've got to
tell her. I'll tell her to-night—"

"Don't wait till to-night; do it now."

"Now?"

"Yes; and I'll go with you as soon as I've seen the
youngest Miller girl." They had reached the helps'
house now, and Cynthia said: "You wait outside here,
and I'll go right back with you. Oh, I hope it isn't
doing wrong to put it off till I've seen that girl!"
She disappeared through the door, and Jeff waited by
the steps outside, plucking up one long grass stem
after another, and biting it in two. When Cynthia
came out she said: "I guess she'll be all right. Now
come, and don't lose another second."

"You're afraid I sha'n't do it if I wait any longer!"

"I'm afraid *I* sha'n't." There was a silence after
this.

"Do you know what I think of you, Cynthy?"
asked Jeff, hurrying to keep up with her quick steps.
"You've got more courage—"

"Oh, don't praise me or I shall break down!"

"I'll see that you don't break down," said Jeff, tenderly. "It's the greatest thing to have you go with
me!"

"'I'M SORRY A SON OF MINE HAD TO BE TOLD HOW TO ACT WITH HIS MOTHER'"

" Why don't you *see?* " she lamented. " If you went alone, and told your mother that I approved of it, you would look as if you were afraid, and wanted to get behind me ; and I'm not going to have that."

They found Mrs. Durgin in the dark entry of the old farm-house, and Cynthia said, with involuntary imperiousness, " Come in here, Mrs. Durgin ; I want to tell you something."

She led the way to the old parlor, and she checked Mrs. Durgin's question, " Has that Miller girl—"

" It isn't about her," said Cynthy, pushing the door to. " It's about me—and Jeff."

Mrs. Durgin became aware of Jeff's presence with an effect of surprise. " There a'n't anything *more,* is there ? "

" Yes, there is ! " Cynthia shrilled. " Now, Jeff ! "

" It's just this, mother. Cynthy thinks I ought to tell you—and she thinks I ought to have told you last night—she expected me to—that I'm not going to study law."

" And I approve of his not doing it," Cynthia promptly followed, and she put herself beside Jeff where he stood in front of his mother's rocking-chair.

She looked from one to the other of the faces before her. " I'm sorry a son of mine," she said, with dignity, " had to be told how to act with his mother. But if he had, I don't know as anybody had a better right to do it than the girl that's going to marry him. And I'll say this, Cynthia Whitwell, before I say anything else : you've begun *right.* I wish I could say Jeff had."

There was an uncomfortable moment before Cynthia
said, " He *expected* to tell you."

" Oh, yes, I know," said his mother, sadly. She
added, sharply, " And did he expect to tell me what
he intended to do for a livin' ? "

Jeff took the word. " Yes, I did. I intend to keep
a hotel."

" What hotel ? " asked Mrs. Durgin, with a touch
of taunting in her tone.

" This one."

The mother of the bold, rebellious boy that Jeff had
been stirred in Mrs. Durgin's heart, and she looked at
him with the eyes that used to condone his mischief.
But she said, " I guess you'll find out that there's
more than one has to agree to that."

" Yes, there are two; you and Jackson; and I don't
know but what three, if you count Cynthy, here."

His mother turned to the girl. " You think this
fellow's got sense enough to keep a hotel ? "

" Yes, Mrs. Durgin, I do. I think he's got good
ideas about a hotel."

" And what's he goin' to do with his college education ? "

Jeff interposed. " You think that all the college
graduates turn out lawyers and doctors and professors ? Some of 'em are mighty glad to sweep out banks
in hopes of a clerkship; and some take any sort of a
place in a mill or a business house, to work up; and
some bum round out West on cattle ranches; and
some, if they're lucky, get newspaper reporters' places
at ten dollars a week."

Cynthia followed with the generalization : " I don't believe anybody can know too much to keep a hotel. It won't hurt Jeff if he's been to Harvard, or to Europe, either."

" I guess there's a pair of you," said Mrs. Durgin, with superficial contempt. She was silent for a time, and they waited. " Well, there ! " she broke out again. " I've got something to chew upon for a spell, I guess. Go along, now, both of you ! And the next time you've got to face your mother, Jeff, don't you come in lookin' round anybody's petticoats ! I'll see you later about all this."

They went away with the joyful shame of children who have escaped punishment.

" That's the last of it, Cynthy," said Jeff.

" I guess so," the girl assented, with a certain grief in her voice. " I wish you *had* told her first ! "

" Oh, never mind that now ! " cried Jeff, and in the dim passageway he took her in his arms and kissed her.

He would have released her, but she lingered in his embrace. " Will you promise that if there's ever anything like it again, you *won't* wait for me to make you ? "

" I like your having made me, but I promise," he said.

Then she tightened her arms round his neck and kissed him.

XXV.

THE will of Jeff's mother relaxed its grip upon the purpose so long held, as if the mere strain of the tenacity had wearied and weakened it. When it finally appeared that her ambition for her son was not his ambition for himself and would never be, she abandoned it. Perhaps it was the easier for her to forego her hopes of his distinction in the world, because she had learned before that she must forego her hopes of him in other ways. She had vaguely fancied that with the acquaintance his career at Harvard would open to him Jeff would make a splendid marriage. She had followed darkling and stumbling his course in society as far as he would report it to her, and when he would not suffer her to glory in it, she believed that he was forbidding her from a pride that would not recognize anything out of the common in it. She exulted in his pride, and she took all his snubbing reserves tenderly, as so many proofs of his success.

At the bottom of her heart she had both fear and contempt of all towns-people, whom she generalized from her experience of them as summer-folks of a greater or lesser silliness. She often found herself

unable to cope with them, even when she felt that she
had twice their sense; she perceived that they had
something from their training that with all her un-
disciplined force she could never hope to win from her
own environment.   But she believed that her son
would have the advantages which baffled her in them,
for he would have their environment; and she had
wished him to rivet his hold upon those advantages
by taking a wife from among them, and by living the
life of their world.   Her wishes, of course, had no
such distinct formulation, and the feeling she had
towards Cynthia as a possible barrier to her ambition
had no more definition.   There had been times when
the fitness of her marriage with Jeff had moved the
mother's heart to a jealousy that she always kept
silent, while she hoped for the accident or the providence which should annul the danger.   But Genevieve
Vostrand had not been the kind of accident or providence that she would have invoked, and when she
saw Jeff's fancy turning towards her, Mrs. Durgin had
veered round to Cynthia.   All the same she kept a
keen eye upon the young ladies among the summer-
folks who came to Lion's Head, and tacitly canvassed
their merits and inclinations with respect to Jeff in
the often-imagined event of his caring for any one of
them.   She found that her artfully casual references
to her son's being in Harvard scarcely affected their
mothers in the right way.   The fact made them think
of the head waiters whom they had met at other hotels, and who were working their way through Dartmouth or Williams or Yale, and it required all the

force of Jeff's robust personality to dissipate their
erroneous impressions of him.   He took their daughters out of their arms and from under their noses on
long drives upon his buckboard, and it became a convention with them to treat his attentions somewhat
like those of a powerful but faithful vassal.

Whether he was indifferent, or whether the young
ladies were coy, none of these official flirtations came
to anything.   He seemed not to care for one more
than another; he laughed and joked with them all, and
had an official manner with each which served somewhat like a disparity of years in putting them at their
ease with him.   They agreed that he was very handsome, and some thought him very talented; but they
questioned whether he was quite what you would call
a gentleman.   It is true that this misgiving attacked
them mostly in the mass; singly, they were little or
not at all troubled by it, and they severally behaved
in an unprincipled indifference to it.

Mrs. Durgin had the courage of her own purposes,
but she had the fear of Jeff's.   After the first pang of
the disappointment which took final shape from his
declaration that he was going to marry Cynthia, she
did not really care much.   She had the habit of the girl;
she respected her, she even loved her.   The children,
as she thought of them, had known each other from
their earliest days; Jeff had persecuted Cynthia
throughout his graceless boyhood, but he had never
intimidated her; and his mother, with all her weakness for him, felt that it was well for him that his wife
should be brave enough to stand up against him.

She formulated this feeling no more than the others, but she said to Westover, whom Jeff bade her tell of the engagement: " It a'n't exactly as I could 'a' wished it to be. But I don't know as mothers are ever quite suited with their children's marriages. I presume it's from always kind of havin' had her round under my feet ever since she was born, as you may say, and seein' her family always so shiftless. Well, I can't say that of Frank, either. He's turned out a fine boy; but the father! Cynthy *is* one of the most capable girls, smart as a trap, and bright as a biscuit. She's masterful, too; she *need* to have a will of her own with Jeff."

Something of the insensate pride that mothers have in their children's faults, as their quick tempers, or their wastefulness, or their revengefulness, expressed itself in her tone; and it was perhaps this that irritated Westover.

" I hope he'll never let her know it. I don't think a strong will is a thing to be prized, and I shouldn't consider it one of Cynthia's good points. The happiest life for her would be one that never forced her to use it."

" I don't know as I understand you exactly," said Mrs. Durgin, with some dryness. " I know Jeff's got rather of a domineering disposition, but I don't believe but she can manage him without meetin' him on his own ground, as you may say."

" She's a girl in a thousand," Westover returned, evasively.

" Then you think he's shown sense in choosin' of

her?" pursued Jeff's mother, resolute to find some praise of him in Westover's words.

"He's a very fortunate man," said the painter.

"Well, I guess you're right," Mrs. Durgin acquiesced, as much to Jeff's advantage as she could. "You know I was always afraid he would make a fool of himself, but I guess he's kept his eyes pretty well open all the while. Well!" She closed the subject with this exclamation. "Him and Cynthy's been at me about Jackson," she added, abruptly. "They've cooked it up between 'em that he's out of health, or run down, or something."

Her manner referred the matter to Westover, and he said: "He isn't looking so well this summer. He ought to go away somewhere."

"That's what *they* thought," said Mrs. Durgin, smiling in her pleasure at having their opinion confirmed by the old and valued friend of the family. "Whereabouts do you think he'd best go?"

"Oh, I don't know. Italy—or Egypt—"

"I guess if you could get Jackson to go away at all, it would be to some of them old Bible countries," said Mrs. Durgin. "We've got to have a fight to get him off, make the best of it, and I've thought it over since the children spoke about it, and I couldn't seem to see Jackson willin' to go out to Californy or Colorady, to either of his brothers. But I guess he would go to Egypt. That a good climate for the—his complaint?"

She entered eagerly into the question, and Westover promised to write to a Boston doctor, whom he

knew very well, and report Jackson's case to him, and
get his views of Egypt.

"Tell him how it is," said Mrs. Durgin, "and the
tussle we shall have to have anyway to make Jackson
believe he'd ought to have a rest.   He'll go to Egypt
if he'll go anywheres, because his mind keeps runnin'
on Bible questions, and it 'll interest him to go out
there; and we can make him believe it's just to bange
around for the winter.   He's terrible hopeful."   Now
that she began to speak, all her long-repressed anxiety
poured itself out, and she hitched her chair nearer to
Westover and wistfully clutched his sleeve.   "That's
the worst of Jackson.   You can't make him believe anything's the matter.   Sometimes I can't bear to hear him
go on about himself as if he was a well young man.
He expects that medium's stuff is goin' to cure him!"

"People sick in that way are always hopeful," said
Westover.

"Oh, don't I know it!   Ha'n't I seen my children
and my husband—   Oh, do ask that doctor to answer
as quick as he can!"

XXVI.

WESTOVER had a difficulty in congratulating Jeff which he could scarcely define to himself, but which was like that obscure resentment we feel towards people whom we think unequal to their good fortune. He was ashamed of his grudge, whatever it was, and this may have made him overdo his expressions of pleasure. He was sensible of a false cordiality in them, and he checked himself in a flow of forced sentiment to say, more honestly: "I wish you'd speak to Cynthia for me. You know how much I think of her, and how much I want to see her happy. You ought to be a very good fellow, Jeff!"

"I'll tell her that; she'll like that," said Jeff. "She thinks the world of you."

"Does she? Well!"

"And I guess she'll be glad you *sent* word. She's been wondering what you would say; she's always so afraid of you."

"Is she? *You're* not afraid of me, are you? But perhaps you don't think so much of me."

"I guess Cynthia and I think alike on that point," said Jeff, without abating Westover's discomfort.

There was a stress of sharp cold that year about the

Realistic Look ob Nature

20th of August. Then the weather turned warm again, and held fine till the beginning of October, within a week of the time when Jackson was to sail. It had not been so hard to make him consent when he knew where the doctor wished him to go, and he had willingly profited by Westover's suggestions about getting to Egypt. His interest in the matter, which he tried to hide at first under a mask of decorous indifference, mounted with the fire of Whitwell's enthusiasm, and they held nightly councils together, studying his course on the map, and consulting planchette upon the points at variance that rose between them, while Jombateeste sat with his chair tilted against the wall, and pulled steadily at his pipe, which mixed its strong fumes with the smell of the kerosene lamp and the perennial odor of potatoes in the cellar under the low room where the companions forgathered.

Towards the end of September Westover spent the night before he went back to town with them. After a season with planchette, their host pushed himself back with his knees from the table till his chair reared upon its hind-legs, and shoved his hat up from his forehead in token of a philosophical mood.

"I tell you, Jackson," he said, "you'd ought to get hold o' some them occult devils out there, and squeeze their science out of 'em. Any Buddhists in Egypt, Mr. Westover?"

"I don't think there are," said Westover. "Unless Jackson should come across some wandering Hindoo. Or he might push on, and come home by the way of India."

"Do it, Jackson!" his friend conjured him. "May cost you something more, but it 'll be worth the money. If it's true, what some them Blavetsky fellers claim, you can visit us here in your astral body—git in with 'em the right way. I should like to have you try it. What's the reason India wouldn't be as good for him as Egypt, anyway?" Whitwell demanded of Westover.

"I suppose the climate's rather too moist; the heat would be rather trying to him there."

"That so?"

"And he's taken his ticket for Alexandria," Westover pursued.

"Well, I guess that's so." Whitwell tilted his backward sloping hat to one side, so as to scratch the northeast corner of his head, thoughtfully.

"But as far as that is concerned," said Westover, "and the doctrine of immortality generally is concerned, Jackson will have his hands full if he studies the Egyptian monuments."

"What they got to do with it?"

"Everything. Egypt is the home of the belief in a future life; it was carried from Egypt to Greece. He might come home by way of Athens."

"Why, man!" cried Whitwell. "Do you mean to say that them old Hebrew saints, Joseph's brethren, that went down into Egypt after corn, didn't know about immortality, and them Egyptian devils *did?*"

"There's very little proof in the Old Testament that the Israelites knew of it."

Whitwell looked at Jackson. "That the idee *you* got?"

"I guess he's right," said Jackson. "There's something a little about it in Job, and something in the Psalms: but not a great deal."

"And we got it from them Egyptian d—"

"I don't say that," Westover interposed. "But they had it before we had. As we imagine it, we got it through Christianity."

Jombateeste, who had taken his pipe out of his mouth in a controversial manner, put it back again.

Westover added, "But there's no question but the Egyptians believed in the life hereafter, and in future rewards and punishments for the deeds done in the body, thousands of years before our era."

"Well, I'm dumned," said Whitwell.

Jombateeste took his pipe out again. "Hit show they got good sense. They know—they feel it in their bone—what goin' 'appen—when you dead. Me, I guess they got some prophet find it hout for them; then they goin' take the credit."

"I guess that's something so, Jombateeste," said Whitwell. "It don't stand to reason that folks without any alphabet, as you may say, and only a lot of pictures for words, like Injuns, could figure out the immortality of the soul. They got the idee by inspiration somehow. Why, here! It's like this. Them Pharaohs must have always been clawin' out for the Hebrews before they got a hold of Joseph, and when they found out the true doctrine, they hushed up where they got it, and their priests went on teachin' it as if it was their own."

"That's w'at I say. Got it from the 'Ebrew."

"Well, it don't matter a great deal where they got it, so they got it," said Jackson, as he rose.

"I believe I'll go with you," said Westover.

"All there is about it," said the sick man, solemnly, with a frail effort to straighten himself, to which his sunken chest would not respond, "is this. No man ever did figure that out for himself. A man sees folks die, and as far as his senses go, they don't live again. But somehow he knows they *do ;* and his knowledge comes from somewhere else ; it's inspired—"

"That's w'at I say," Jombateeste hastened to interpose. "Got it from the 'Ebrew. Feel it in 'is bone."

Out under the stars Jackson and Westover silently mounted the hill-side together. At one of the thank-you-marms in the road, the sick man stopped, like a weary horse, to breathe. He took off his hat, and wiped the sweat of weakness that had gathered upon his forehead, and looked round the sky, powdered with the constellations and the planets. "It's sightly," he whispered.

"Yes, it *is* fine," Westover assented. "But the stars of our Northern nights are nothing to what you'll see in Egypt."

Jackson repeated vaguely : "Egypt ! Where I *should* like to go is Mars." He fixed his eyes on the flaming planet, in a long stare. "But I suppose they have their own troubles, same as we do. They must get sick and die, like the rest of us. But I should like to know more about 'em. You believe it's inhabited, don't you ? "

Westover's agnosticism did not, somehow, extend to Mars. "Yes, I've no doubt of it."

Jackson seemed pleased. "I've read everything I can lay my hands on about it. I've got a notion that if there's any choosin', after we get through here, I should like to go to Mars for a while, or as long as I was a little homesick still, and wanted to keep as near the earth as I could," he added, quaintly.

Westover laughed. "You could study up the subject of irrigation, there; they say that's what keeps the parallel markings green on Mars; and telegraph a few hints to your brother in Colorado, after the Martians perfect their signal code."

Perhaps the invalid's fancy flagged. He drew a long, ragged breath. "I don't know as I care to leave home, much. If it wa'n't a kind of duty, I shouldn't." He seemed impelled by a sudden need to say, "How do you think Jefferson and mother will make it out together?"

"I've no doubt they'll manage," said Westover.

"They're a good deal alike," Jackson suggested.

Westover preferred not to meet his overture. "You'll be back, you know, almost as soon as the season commences, next summer."

"Yes," Jackson assented, more cheerfully. "And now, Cynthy's sure to be here."

"Yes, she will be here," said Westover, not so cheerfully.

Jackson seemed to find the opening he was seeking, in Westover's tone. "What do you think of gettin' married, anyway, Mr. Westover?" he asked.

"We haven't either of us thought so well of it as to try it, Jackson," said the painter, jocosely.

"Think it's a kind of chance?"

"It's a chance."

Jackson was silent. Then, "I a'n't one of them," he said, abruptly, "that think a man's goin' to be made over by marryin' this woman or that. If he a'n't goin' to be the right kind of a man himself, he a'n't because his wife's a good woman. Sometimes I think that a man's wife is the last person in the world that can change his disposition. She can influence him about this and about that, but she can't change him. It seems as if he couldn't let her, if he tried, and after the first start-off he don't try."

"That's true," Westover assented. "We're terribly inflexible. Nothing but something like a change of heart, as they used to call it, can make us different, and even then we're apt to go back to our old shape. When you look at it in that light, marriage seems impossible. Yet it takes place every day!"

"It's a great risk for a woman," said Jackson, putting on his hat and stirring for an onward movement. "But I presume that if the man is honest with her it's the best thing she can have. The great trouble is for the man to be honest with her."

"Honesty is difficult," said Westover.

He made Jackson promise to spend a day with him in Boston, on his way to take the Mediterranean steamer at New York. When they met he yielded to an impulse which the invalid's forlornness inspired, and went on to see him off. He was glad that he did that, for though Jackson was not sad at parting, he was visibly touched by Westover's kindness.

Of course he talked away from it. "I guess I've left 'em in pretty good shape for the winter at Lion's Head," he said. "I've got Whitwell to agree to come up and live in the house with mother, and she'll have Cynthy with her, anyway; and Frank and Jombateeste can look after the hosses easy enough."

He had said something like this before, but Westover could see that it comforted him to repeat it, and he encouraged him to do so in full. He made him talk about getting home in the spring, after the frost was out of the ground, but he questioned involuntarily, while the sick man spoke, whether he might not then be lying under the sands that had never known a frost since the glacial epoch. When the last warning for visitors to go ashore came, Jackson said, with a wan smile, while he held Westover's hand, "I sha'n't forget this very soon."

"Write to me," said Westover.

XXVII.

JACKSON kept his promise to write to Westover, but he was better than his word to his mother, and wrote to her every week that winter.

"I seem just to live from letter to letter. It's ridic-'lous," she said to Cynthia once when the girl brought the mail in from the barn, where the men-folks kept it till they had put away their horses after driving over from Lovewell with it. The trains on the branch road were taken off in the winter, and the post-office at the hotel was discontinued. The men had to go to the town by cutter, over a highway that the winds sifted half full of snow after it had been broken out by the ox-teams in the morning. But Mrs. Durgin had studied the steamer days and calculated the time it would take letters to come from New York to Love-well; and, unless a blizzard was raging, some one had to go for the mail when the day came. It was usually Jombateeste, who reverted in winter to the type of *habitant* from which he had sprung. He wore a blue woollen cap, like a large sock, pulled over his ears and close to his eyes, and below it his clean-shaven brown face showed. He had blue woollen mittens, and boots of russet leather, without heels, came to his knees; he got a pair every time he went home on St. John's day. His lean little body was swathed in several short jackets, and he brought the letters buttoned into one of the innermost pockets. He produced the letter from Jackson promptly enough when Cynthia came out to the barn for it, and then he made a show of getting his horse out of the cutter shafts, and shouting international reproaches at it, till she was forced to ask, "Haven't you got something for me, Jombateeste?"

"You expec' some letter?" he said, unbuckling a strap and shouting louder.

"You know whether I do. Give it to me."

"I don' know. I think I drop something on the road. I saw something white; maybe snow; good deal of snow."

"Don't plague! Give it here!"

"Wait I finish unhitch. I can't find any letter till I get some time to look."

"Oh, now, Jombateeste! *Give* me my letter!"

"W'at you want letter for? Always same thing. Well! 'Old the 'oss; I goin' to feel."

Jombateeste felt in one pocket after another, while Cynthia clung to the colt's bridle, and he was uncertain till the last whether he had any letter for her. When it appeared she made a flying snatch at it, and ran; and the comedy was over, to be repeated in some form the next week.

The girl somehow always possessed herself of what was in her letters before she reached the room where Mrs. Durgin was waiting for hers. She had to read that aloud to Jackson's mother, and in the evening she

had to read it again to Mrs. Durgin, and Whitwell and
Jombateeste and Frank, after they had done their
chores, and they had gathered in the old farm-house
parlor, around the air-tight sheet-iron stove, in a heat
of eighty degrees. Whitwell listened, with planchette
ready on the table before him, and he consulted it for
telepathic impressions of Jackson's actual mental state
when the reading was over.

He got very little out of the perverse instrument.
" I can't seem to work her. If Jackson was here—"

" We shouldn't need to ask plantchette about him,"
Cynthia once suggested, with the spare sense of humor
that sometimes revealed itself in her.

" Well, I guess that's something so," her father
candidly admitted. But the next time he consulted
the helpless planchette as hopefully as before. " You
can't tell, you can't tell," he urged.

" The trouble seems to be that plantchette can't
tell," said Mrs. Durgin, and they all laughed. They
were not people who laughed a great deal, and they
were each intent upon some point in the future that
kept them from pleasure in the present. The little
Canuck was the only one who suffered himself a con-
temporaneous consolation. His early faith had so far
lapsed from him that he could hospitably entertain the
wild psychical conjectures of Whitwell without an accusing sense of heresy, and he found the winter of
northern New England so mild after that of Lower
Canada that he experienced a high degree of animal
comfort in it, and looked forward to nothing better.
To be well fed, well housed, and well heated ; to smoke

" ' GIVE ME MY LETTERS ' "

successive pipes while the others talked, and to catch
through his smoke wreaths vague glimpses of their
meanings, was enough.   He felt that in being promoted to the care of the stables in Jackson's absence
he occupied a dignified and responsible position, with
a confidential relation to the exile which justified him
in sending special messages to him, and attaching peculiar value to Jackson's remembrances.

The exile's letters said very little about his health,
which in the sense of no news his mother held to be
good news, but they were full concerning the monuments and the ethnological interest of life in Egypt.
They were largely rescripts of each day's observations
and experiences, close and full, as his mother liked
them in regard to fact, and generously philosophized
on the side of politics and religion for Whitwell.   The
Eastern question became in the snow-choked hills of
New England the engrossing concern of this speculative mind, and he was apt to spring it upon Mrs. Durgin and Cynthia at meal-times and other defenceless
moments.   He tried to debate it with Jombateeste,
who conceived of it as a form of spiritualistic inquiry,
and answered from the hay-loft, where he was throwing down fodder for the cattle to Whitwell, volubly
receiving it on the barn floor below, that he believed,
him, everybody got a hastral body, English same as
Mormons.

"Guess you mean Moslems," said Whitwell, and
Jombateeste asked the difference, defiantly.

The letters which came to Cynthia could not be
made as much a general interest, and, in fact, no one

else cared so much for them as for Jackson's letters,
not even Jeff's mother.   After Cynthia got one of
them, she would ask, perfunctorily, what Jeff said, but
when she was told there was no news she did not
press her question.

"If Jackson don't get back in time next summer,"
Mrs. Durgin said, in one of the talks she had with the
girl, " I guess I shall have to let Jeff and you run the
house alone."

" I guess we shall want a little help from you,"
said Cynthia, demurely.   She did not refuse the implication of Mrs. Durgin's words, but she would not
assume that there was more in them than they expressed.

When Jeff came home for the three days' vacation
at Thanksgiving, he wished again to relinquish his
last year at Harvard, and Cynthia had to summon all
her forces to keep him to his promise of staying. He
brought home the books with which he was working
off his conditions, with a half-hearted intention of
study, and she took hold with him, and together they
fought forward over the ground he had to gain.   His
mother was almost willing at last that he should give
up his last year in college.

"What is the use?" she asked.   "He's give up
the law, and he might as well commence here first as
last, if he's goin' to."

The girl had no reason to urge against this; she
could only urge her feeling that he ought to go back,
and take his degree with the rest of his class.

" If you're going to keep Lion's Head the way you

pretend you are," she said to him, as she could not say to his mother, "you want to keep all your Harvard friends, don't you, and have them remember you? Go back, Jeff, and don't you come here again till after you've got your degree. Never mind the Christmas vacation, nor the Easter. Stay in Cambridge, and work off your conditions. You can do it, if you try. Oh, don't you suppose *I* should like to have you here?" she reproached him.

He went back, with a kind of grudge in his heart, which he confessed in his first letter home to her, when he told her that she was right and he was wrong. He was sure now, with the impulse which their work on them in common had given him, that he should get his conditions off, and he wanted her and his mother to begin preparing their minds to come to his Class Day. He planned how they could both be away from the hotel for that day. The house was to be opened on the 20th of June, but it was not likely that there would be so many people at once that they could not give the 21st to Class Day; Frank and his father could run Lion's Head somehow, or, if they could not, then the opening could be postponed till the 24th. At all events, they must not fail to come. Cynthia showed the whole letter to his mother, who refused to think of such a thing, and then asked, as if the fact had not been fully set before her, "*When* is it to be?"

"The 21st of June."

"Well, he's early enough with his invitation," she grumbled.

"Yes, he is," said Cynthia; and she laughed for shame and pleasure as she confessed, "I was thinking he was rather late."

She hung her head, and turned her face away. But Mrs. Durgin understood. "You be'n expectin' it all along, then."

"I guess so."

"I presume," said the elder woman, "that he's talked to you about it. He never tells me much. I don't see why you should want to go. What's it like?"

"Oh, I don't know. But it's the day the graduating class have to themselves, and all their friends come."

"Well, I don't know why anybody should want to go," said Mrs. Durgin. "I sha'n't. Tell him he won't want to own me when he sees me. What *am* I goin' to wear, I should like to know? What *you* goin' to wear, Cynthy?"

XXVIII.

JEFF's place at Harvard had been too long fixed among the jays to allow the hope of wholly retrieving his condition now. It was too late for him to be chosen in any of the nicer clubs or societies, but he was not beyond the mounting sentiment of comradery, which begins to tell in the last year among college men, and which had its due effect with his class. One of the men, who had always had a foible for humanity, took advantage of the prevailing mood in another man, and wrought upon him to ask, among the fellows he was asking to a tea at his rooms, several fellows who were distinctly and almost typically jay. The tea was for the aunt of the man who gave it, a very pretty woman from New York, and it was so richly qualified by young people of fashion from Boston that the infusion of the jay flavor could not spoil it, if it would not rather add an agreeable piquancy. This college mood coincided that year with a benevolent emotion in the larger world, from which fashion was not exempt. Society had just been stirred by the reading of a certain book, which had then a very great vogue, and several people had been down among

the wretched at the North End doing good in a con-
science-stricken effort to avert the millenium which
the book in question seemed to threaten. The lady
who matronized the tea was said to have done more
good than you could imagine at the North End, and
she caught at the chance to meet the college jays in
a spirit of Christian charity. When the man who
was going to give the tea rather sheepishly confessed
what the altruistic man had got him in for, she praised
him so much that he went away feeling like the hero
of a holy cause. She promised the assistance and
sympathy of several brave girls, who would not be
afraid of all the jays in college.

After all, only one of the jays came. Not many,
in fact, had been asked, and when Jeff Durgin actually appeared, it was not known that he was both the
first and the last of his kind. The lady who was
matronizing the tea recognized him, with a throe of
her quickened conscience, as the young fellow whom
she had met two winters before at the studio tea which
Mr. Westover had given to those queer Florentine
friends of his, and whom she had never thought of
since, though she had then promised herself to do
something for him. She had then even given him
some vague hints of a prospective hospitality, and
she confessed her sin of omission in a swift but
graphic retrospect to one of her brave girls, while Jeff
stood blocking out a space for his stalwart bulk amid
the alien elegance just within the doorway, and the
host was making his way towards him, with an out-
stretched hand of hardy welcome.

At an earlier period of his neglect and exclusion,
Jeff would not have responded to the belated overture
which had now been made him, for no reason that he
could divine. But he had nothing to lose by accepting the invitation, and he had promised the altruistic
man, whom he rather liked; he did not dislike the
giver of the tea so much as some other men, and so
he came.

The brave girl whom the matron was preparing to
devote to him stood shrinking with a trepidation which
she could not conceal at sight of his strange massive-
ness, with his rust-gold hair coming down towards his
thick yellow brows and mocking blue eyes in a dense
bang, and his jaw squaring itself under the rather in-
solent smile of his full mouth. The matron felt that
her victim was perhaps going to fail her, when a voice
at her ear said, as if the question were extorted,
" Who in the world is *that?* "

She instantly turned, and flashed out in a few inspired syllables the fact she had just imparted to her
treacherous heroine. " *Do* let me introduce him, Miss
Lynde. I must do something for him, when he gets
up to me, if he ever does."

" By all means," said the girl, who had an impulse
to laugh at the rude force of Jeff's face and figure, so
disproportioned to the occasion, and she vented it at
the matron's tribulation. The matron was shaking
hands with people right and left, and exchanging inaudible banalities with them. She did not know what
the girl said in answer, but she was aware that she
remained near her. She had professed her joy at

seeing Jeff again, when he reached her, and she turned
with him and said, "Let me present you to Miss
Lynde, Mr. Durgin," and so abandoned them to each
other.

As Jeff had none of the anxiety for social success
which he would have felt at an earlier period, he now
left it to Miss Lynde to begin the talk, or not, as she
chose. He bore himself with so much indifference
that she was piqued to an effort to hold his eyes, that
wandered from her to this face and that in the crowd.

"Do you find many people you know, Mr. Durgin?"

"I don't find any."

"I supposed you didn't from the way you looked
at them."

"How did I look at them?"

"As if you wanted to eat them, and one never
wants to eat one's friends."

"Why?"

"Oh, I don't know.   They wouldn't agree with
one."

Jeff laughed, and he now took fuller note of the
slender girl who stood before him, and swayed a little
backward, in a graceful curve.   He saw that she had
a dull, thick complexion, with liquid eyes, set wide
apart and slanted upwards slightly, and a nose that was
deflected inward from the straight line ; but her mouth
was beautiful and vividly red like a crimson blossom.

"Couldn't you find me some place to sit down, Mr.
Durgin?" she asked.

He had it on his tongue to say, "Well, not unless
you want to sit down on some enemy," but he did not

venture this: when it comes to daring of that sort,
the boldest man is commonly a little behind a timid
woman.

Several of the fellows had clubbed their rooms, and
lent them to the man who was giving the tea; he used
one of the apartments for a cloak-room, and he meant
the other for the social overflow from his own. But
people always prefer to remain dammed-up together
in the room where they are received, and Miss Lynde
looked between the neighboring heads, and over the
neighboring shoulders, and saw the borrowed apartment quite empty. At the moment of this discovery
the host came fighting his way up to make sure that
Jeff had been provided for in the way of introductions. He promptly introduced him to Miss Lynde.
She said: "Oh, that's been done! Can't you think
of something new?" Jeff liked the style of this.
"*I* don't mind it, but I'm afraid Mr. Durgin must find
it monotonous."

"Oh, well, do something original yourself, then,
Miss Lynde!" said the host. "Start a movement for
that room across the passage; that's mine, too, for the
occasion; and save some of these people's lives. It's
suffocating in here."

"I don't mind saving Mr. Durgin's," said the girl,
"if he wants it saved."

"Oh, I know he's just dying to have you save it,"
said the host, and he left them, to inspire other
people to follow their example. But such as glanced
across the passage into the overflow room seemed to
think it now the possession solely of the pioneers of

the movement. At any rate, they made no show of joining them; and after Miss Lynde and Jeff had looked at the pictures on the walls and the photographs on the mantel of the room where they found themselves, they sat down on chairs fronting the open door and the door of the room they had left. The window-seat would have been more to Jeff's mind, and he had proposed it, but the girl seemed not to have heard him; she took the deep easy-chair in full view of the company opposite, and left him to pull up a chair beside her.

"I always like to see the pictures in a man's room," she said, with a little sigh of relief from their inspection and a partial yielding of her figure to the luxury of the chair. "Then I know what the man is. This man—I don't know whose room it is—seems to have spent a good deal of *his* time at the theatre."

"Isn't that where most of them spend their time?" asked Jeff.

"I'm sure I don't know. Is that where you spend yours?"

"It used to be. I'm not spending my time anywhere just now." She looked questioningly, and he added, "I haven't got any to spend."

"Oh, indeed! Is that a reason? Why don't you spend somebody else's?"

"Nobody has any, that I know."

"You're all working off conditions, you mean?"

"That's what I'm doing, or trying to."

"Then it's never certain whether you can do it, after all?"

" Not so certain as to be free from excitement,"
said Jeff, smiling.

" And are you consumed with the melancholy that
seems to be balling up all the men at the prospect of
having to leave Harvard and go out into the hard, cold
world ? "

" I don't look it, do I ? " Jeff asked.

" No, you don't. And you don't feel it ? You're
not trying concealment, and so forth ? "

" No ; if I'd had my own way, I'd have left Harvard
before this." He could see that his bold assumption
of difference, or indifference, told upon her. " I
couldn't get out into the hard, cold world too soon."

" How fearless ! Most of them don't know what
they're going to do in it."

" I do."

" And what *are* you going to do ? Or perhaps you
think that's asking ! "

" Oh, no. I'm going to keep a hotel."

He had hoped to startle her, but she asked, rather
quietly, " What do you mean ? " and she added, as if
to punish him for trying to mystify her : " I've heard
that it requires gifts for that. Isn't there some prov-
erb ? "

" Yes. But I'm going to try to do it on experience."
He laughed, and he did not mind her trying to hit
him, for he saw that he had made her curious.

" Do you mean that you *have* kept a hotel ? "

" For three generations," he returned, with a gravity that mocked her from his bold eyes.

" I'm sure *I* don't know what you mean," she said,

indifferently. "Where is your hotel? In Boston—
New York—Chicago?"

"It's in the country—it's a summer hotel," he said,
as before.

She looked away from him towards the other room.
"There's my brother. I didn't know he was coming."

"Shall I go and tell him where you are?" Jeff
asked, following the direction of her eyes.

"No, no; he can find me," said the girl, sinking
back in her chair again. He left her to resume the
talk where she chose, and she said, " If it's something
ancestral, of course—"

"I don't know as it's that, exactly. My grandfather
used to keep a country tavern, and so it's in the blood,
but the hotel I mean is something that we've worked
up into from a farm boarding-house."

"You don't talk like a country person," the girl
broke in, abruptly.

"Not in Cambridge. I do in the country."

"And so," she prompted, "you're going to turn it
into a hotel, when you've got out of Harvard."

"It's a hotel already, and a pretty big one; but I'm
going to make the right kind of hotel of it when I
take hold of it."

"And what is the right kind of a hotel?"

"That's a long story. It would make you tired."

"It might, but we've got to spend the time somehow. You could begin, and then if I couldn't stand
it you could stop."

"It's easier to stop first, and begin some other time.
I guess I'll let you imagine my hotel, Miss Lynde."

" Oh, I understand now," said the girl. " The table will be the great thing. You will stuff people."

" Do you mean that I'm trying to stuff you ? "

" How do I know? You never can tell what men really mean."

Jeff laughed with mounting pleasure in her audacity, that imparted a sense of tolerance for him such as he had experienced very seldom from the Boston girls he had met; after all, he had met but few. It flattered him to have her doubt what he had told her in his reckless indifference; it implied that he was fit for better things than hotel-keeping.

" You never can tell how much a woman believes," he retorted.

" And you keep trying to find out ? "

" No, but I think that they might believe the truth."

" You'd better try them with it ! "

" Well, I will. Do you really want to know what I'm going to do when I get through ? "

" Let me see ! " Miss Lynde leaned forward, with her elbow on her knee and her chin in her hand, and softly kicked the edge of her skirt with the toe of her shoe, as if in deep thought. Jeff waited for her to play her comedy through. " Yes," she said, " I think I *did* wish to know—at one time."

" But you don't now ? "

" Now? How can I tell? It was a great while ago ! "

" I see you don't."

Miss Lynde did not make any reply. She asked, " Do you know my aunt, Mr. Durgin ? "

" I didn't know you had one."

"Yes, everybody has an aunt—even when they haven't a mother, if you can believe the Gilbert operas. I ask because I happen to live with my aunt, and if you knew her she might—ask you to call." Miss Lynde scanned Jeff's face for the effect of this.

He said, gravely, " If you'll introduce me to her, I'll ask her to let me."

"Would you, really?" said the girl. " I've half a mind to try. I wonder if you'd really have the courage."

" I don't think I'm easily rattled."

"You mean that I'm trying to rattle you."

"No—"

" I'm not. My aunt is just what I've said."

"You haven't said what she was. Is she here ? "

" No ; that's the worst of it. If she were, I should introduce you, just to see if you'd dare. Well, some other time I *will*."

"You think there'll be some other time?" Jeff asked.

"I don't know. There are all kinds of times. By-the-way, what time *is* it?"

Jeff looked at his watch. " Quarter after six."

"Then I must go." She jumped to her feet, and faced about for a glimpse of herself in the little glass on the mantel, and put her hand on the large pink roses massed at her waist. One heavy bud dropped from its stem to the floor, where, while she stood, the edge of her skirt pulled and pushed it. She moved a little aside, to peer over at a photograph. Jeff stooped and picked up the flower, which he offered her.

"You dropped it," he said, bowing over it.

"Did I?" She looked at it with an effect of surprise and doubt.

"I thought so, but if you don't, I shall keep it."

The girl removed her careless eyes from it. "When they break off so short, they won't go back."

"If I were a rose, I should want to go back," said Jeff.

She stopped in one of her many aversions and reversions, and looked at him steadily across her shoulder. "You won't have to keep a poet, Mr. Durgin."

"Thank you. I always expected to write the circulars myself. I'll send you one."

"Do."

"With this rose pressed between the leaves, so you'll know."

"That would be very pretty. But you must take me to Mrs. Bevidge, now, if you can."

"I guess I can," said Jeff; and in a minute or two they stood before the matronizing hostess, after a passage through the babbling and laughing groups that looked as impossible after they had made it as it looked before.

Mrs. Bevidge gave the girl's hand a pressure distinct from the official touch of parting, and contrived to say, for her hearing alone: "Thank you *so* much, Bessie. You've done missionary work."

"I shouldn't call it that."

"It will do for *you* to say so! He wasn't really so bad, then? Thank you again, dear!"

Jeff had waited his turn. But now, after the girl

had turned away, as if she had forgotten him, his eyes followed her, and he did not know that Mrs. Bevidge was speaking to him.   Miss Lynde had slimly lost herself in the mass, till she was only a graceful tilt of hat, before she turned with a distraught air.   When her eyes met Jeff's they lighted up with a look that comes into the face when one remembers what one has been trying to think of.   She gave him a brilliant smile that seemed to illumine him from head to foot, and before it was quenched he felt as if she had kissed her hand to him from her rich mouth.

Then he heard Mrs. Bevidge asking something about a hall, and he was aware of her bending upon him a look of the daring humanity that had carried her triumphantly through her good works at the North End.

"Oh, I'm not in the Yard," said Jeff, with belated intelligence.

"Then will just Cambridge reach you?"

He gave his number and street, and she thanked him with the benevolence that availed so much with the lower classes.   He went away thrilling and tingling, with that girl's tones in his ear, her motions in his nerves, and the colors of her face filling his sight, which he printed on the air whenever he turned, as one does with a vivid light after looking at it.

XXIX.

When Jeff reached his room he felt the need of writing to Cynthia, with whatever obscure intention of atonement. He told her of the college tea he had just come from, and made fun of it, and the kind of people he had met, especially the affected girl who had tried to rattle him; he said he guessed she did not think she had rattled him a great deal.

While he wrote he kept thinking how this Miss Lynde was nearer his early ideal of fashion, of high life, which Westover had pretty well snubbed out of him, than any woman he had seen yet; she seemed a girl who would do what she pleased, and would not be afraid if it did not please other people. He liked her having tried to rattle him, and he smiled to himself in recalling her failure. It was as if she had laid hold of him with her little hands to shake him, and had shaken herself. He laughed out in the dark when this image came into his mind; its intimacy flattered him; and he believed that it was upon some hint from her that Mrs. Bevidge had asked his address. She must be going to ask him to her house, and very soon, for it was part of Jeff's meagre social experience that this was the way swells did; they might never ask you twice, but they would ask you promptly.

The thing that Mrs. Bevidge asked Jeff to, when her note reached him the second day after the tea, was a meeting to interest young people in the work at the North End, and Jeff swore under his breath at the disappointment and indignity put upon him. He had reckoned upon an afternoon tea, at least, or even, in the flights of fancy which he now disowned to himself, a dance after the Mid-Years, or possibly an earlier reception of some sort. He burned with shame to think of a theatre party, which he had fondly specialized, with a seat next Miss Lynde.

He tore Mrs. Bevidge's note to pieces, and decided not to answer it at all, as the best way of showing how he had taken her invitation. But Mrs. Bevidge's benevolence was not wanting in courage; she believed that Jeff should pay his footing in society, such as it was, and should allow himself to be made use of, the first thing; when she had no reply from him, she wrote him again, asking him to an adjourned meeting of the first convocation, which had been so successful in everything but numbers. This time she baited her hook, in hoping that the young men would feel something of the interest the young ladies had already shown in the matter. She expressed the fear that Mr. Durgin had not got her earlier letter, and she sent this second to the care of the man who had given the tea.

Jeff's resentment was now so far past that he would have civilly declined to go to the woman's house; but all his hopes of seeing that girl, as he always called

Miss Lynde in his thought, were revived by the mention of the young ladies interested in the cause. He accepted, though all the way into Boston he laid wagers with himself that she would not be there; and up to the moment of taking her hand he refused himself any hope of winning.

There was not much business before the meeting; that had really been all transacted before; it was mainly to make sure of the young men, who were present in the proportion of one to five young ladies at least. Mrs. Bevidge explained that she had seen the wastefulness of amateur effort among the poor, and announced that hereafter she was going to work with the established charities. These were very much in want of visitors, especially young men, to go about among the applicants for relief, and inquire into their real necessities, and get work for them. She was herself going to act as secretary for the meetings during the coming month, and apparently she wished to signalize her accession to the regular forces of charity by bringing into camp as large a body of recruits as she could.

But Jeff had not come to be made use of, or as a jay who was willing to work for his footing in society. He had come in the hope of meeting Miss Lynde, and now that he had met her he had no gratitude to Mrs. Bevidge as a means, and no regret for the defeat of her good purposes so far as she intended their fulfilment in him. He was so cool and self-possessed in excusing himself, for reasons that he took no pains to make seem unselfish, that the altruistic man who had

got him asked to the college tea as a friendless jay
felt it laid upon him to apologize for Mrs. Bevidge's
want of tact.

"She means well, and she's very much in earnest,
in this work; but I must say she can make herself
very offensive—when she doesn't try! She has a right
to ask our help, but not to parade us as the captives
of her bow and spear."

"Oh, that's all right," said Jeff. He perceived that
the amiable fellow was claiming for all an effect that
Jeff knew really implicated himself alone. "I couldn't
load up with anything of that sort, if I'm to work off
my conditions, you know."

"Are *you* in that boat?" said the altruist, as if he
were, too; and he put his hand compassionately on
Jeff's iron shoulder, and left him to Miss Lynde, whose
side he had not stirred from since he had found her.

"It seems to me," she said, "that where there are
so many of you in the same boat, you might manage
to get ashore somehow."

"Yes, or all go down together." Jeff laughed, and
ate Mrs. Bevidge's bread-and-butter, and drank her
tea, with a relish unaffected by his refusal to do what
she asked him. He was right, perhaps, and perhaps
she deserved nothing better at his hands, but the altruist, when he glanced at him from the other side of
the room, thought that he had possibly wasted his
excuses upon Jeff's self-complacence.

He went away in a halo of young ladies; several of
the other girls grouped themselves in their departure;
and it happened that Miss Lynde and Jeff took leave

together. Mrs. Bevidge said to her, with the caressing tenderness of one in the same set, "Good-by, dear!" To Jeff she said, with the cold conscience of those whom their nobility obliges, "I am always at home on Thursdays, Mr. Durgin."

"Oh, thank you," said Jeff. He understood what the words and the manner meant together, but both were instantly indifferent to him when he got outside and found that Miss Lynde was not driving. Something, which was neither look, nor smile, nor word, of course, but nothing more at most than a certain pull and tilt of the shoulder, as she turned to walk away from Mrs. Bevidge's door, told him from her that he might walk home with her if he would not seem to do so.

It was one of the pink evenings, dry and clear, that come in the Boston December, and they walked down the side-hill street, under the delicate tracery of the elm boughs in the face of the metallic sunset. In the section of the Charles that the perspective of the street blocked out, the wrinkled current showed as if glazed with the hard color. Jeff's strong frame rejoiced in the cold with a hale pleasure when he looked round into the face of the girl beside him, with the gray film of her veil pressed softly against her red mouth by her swift advance. Their faces were nearly on a level, as they looked into each other's eyes, and he kept seeing the play of the veil's edge against her lips as they talked.

"Why sha'n't you go to Mrs. Bevidge's Thursdays?" she asked. "They're very nice."

"How do you know I'm not going?" he retorted.

"By the way you thanked her."

"Do you advise me to go?"

"I haven't got anything to do with it. What do you mean by that?"

"I don't know. Curiosity, I suppose."

"Well, I do advise you to go," said the girl.

"Shall you be there next Thursday?"

"I? *I* never go to Mrs. Bevidge's Thursdays!"

"*Touché*," said Jeff, and they both laughed. "Can you always get in at an enemy that way?"

"Enemy?"

"Well, friend. It's the same thing."

"I see," said the girl. "You belong to the pessimistic school of Seniors."

"Why don't you try to make an optimist of me?"

"Would it be worth while?"

"That isn't for me to say."

"Don't be diffident! That's staler yet."

"I'll be anything you like."

"I'm not sure you could." For an instant Jeff did not feel the point, and he had not the magnanimity, when he did, to own himself touched again. Apparently, if this girl could not rattle him, she could beat him at fence, and the will to dominate her began to stir in him. If he could have thought of any sarcasm, no matter how crushing, he would have come back at her with it. He could not think of anything, and he walked at her side, inwardly chafing for the chance which would not come.

When they reached her door there was a young

man at the lock with a latch-key, which he was not
making work, for, after a bated blasphemy of his failure, he turned and twitched the bell impatiently.

Miss Lynde laughed provokingly, and he looked
over his shoulder at her and at Jeff, who felt his injury
increased by the disadvantage this young man put him
at. Jeff was as correctly dressed; he wore a silk hat
of the last shape, and a long frock-coat; he was prop-
erly gloved and shod; his clothes fitted him, and were
from the best tailor; but at sight of this young man
in clothes of the same design he felt ill-dressed. He
was in like sort aware of being rudely blocked out
physically, and coarsely colored as to his blond tints
of hair and eye and cheek. Even the sinister something in the young man's look had distinction, and
there was style in the signs of dissipation in his handsome face which Jeff saw with a hunger to outdo him.

Miss Lynde said to Jeff, "My brother, Mr. Durgin,"
and then she added to the other, "You ought to ring
first, Arthur, and try your key afterwards."

"The key's all right," said the young man, without
paying any attention to Jeff beyond a glance of recognition; he turned his back, and waited for the door to
be opened.

His sister suggested, with an amiability which Jeff
felt was meant in reparation to him, "Perhaps a night-
latch never works before dark—or very well before
midnight." The door was opened, and she said to
Jeff, with winning entreaty, "Won't you come in, Mr.
Durgin?"

Jeff excused himself, for he perceived that her

politeness was not so much an invitation to him as a
defiance to her brother; he gave her credit for no
more than it was worth, and he did not wish any the
less to get even with her because of it.

XXX.

At dinner, in the absence of the butler, Alan Lynde attacked his sister across the table for letting herself be seen with a jay, who was not only a jay, but a cad, and personally so offensive to most of the college men that he had never got into a decent club or society; he had been suspended the first year, and if he had not had the densest kind of cheek he would never have come back. Lynde said he would like to know where she had picked the fellow up.

She answered that she had picked him up, if that was the phrase he liked, at Mrs. Bevidge's; and then Alan swore a little, so as not to be heard by their aunt, who sat at the head of the table, and looked down its length between them, serenely ignorant, in her slight deafness, of what was going on between them. To her perception Alan was no more vehement than usual, and Bessie no more smilingly self-contained. He said he supposed that it was some more of Lancaster's damned missionary work, then, and he wondered that a gentleman like Morland had ever let Lancaster work such a jay in on him; he had seen her *afficher* herself with the fellow at Morland's tea; he

commanded her to stop it; and he professed to speak
for her good.

Bessie returned that she knew how strongly he felt
from the way he had misbehaved when she introduced
him to Mr. Durgin, but that she supposed he had been
at the club and his nerves were unstrung. Was that
the reason, perhaps, why he could not make his latch-
key work? Mr. Durgin might be a cad, and she would
not say he was not a jay, but so far he had not sworn
at her; and if he had been suspended and come back,
there were some people who had not been suspended
or come back either, though that might have been for
want of cheek.

She ended by declaring she was used to going into
society without her brother's protection, or even his
company, and she would do her best to get on without his advice. Or was it his conduct he wished her
to profit by?

It had come to the fish going out by this time, and
Alan, who had eaten with no appetite, and drunken
feverishly of apollinaris, flung down his napkin and
went out too.

"What is the matter?" asked his aunt, looking after him.

Bessie shrugged, but she said, presently, with her
lips more than her voice, "I don't think he feels very
well."

"Do you think he—"

The girl frowned assent, and the meal went on to
its end. Then she and her aunt went into the large,
dull library, where they passed the evenings which

Bessie did not spend in some social function.   These
evenings were growing rather more frequent, with her
advancing years, for she was now nearly twenty-five,
and there were few Seniors so old.   She was not the
kind of girl to renew her youth with the Sophomores
and Freshmen in the classes succeeding the class with
which she had danced through college; so far as she
had kept up the old relation with students, she continued it with the men who had gone into the law-
school.   But she saw less and less of these without
seeing more of other men, and perhaps in the last
analysis she was not a favorite.   She was allowed to be
fascinating, but she was not felt to be flattering, and
people would rather be flattered than fascinated.   In
fact, the men were mostly afraid of her; and it has
been observed of girls of this kind that the men who
are not afraid of them are such as they would do well
to be afraid of.   Whether that was quite the case with
Bessie Lynde or not, it was certain that she who was
always the cleverest girl in the room, and if not the
prettiest, then the most effective, had not the best men
about her.   Her men were apt to be those whom the
other girls called stupid or horrid, and whom it would
not be easy, though it might be more just, to classify
otherwise.   The other girls wondered what she could
see in them; but perhaps it was not necessary that
she should see anything in them, if they could see all
she wished them to see, and no more, in her.

The room where tea was now brought and put before her was volumed round by the collections of her
grandfather, except for the spaces filled by his portrait

and that of earlier ancestors, going back to the time
when Copley made masterpieces of his fellow-Bostoni-
ans.   Her aunt herself looked a family portrait of the
middle period, a little anterior to her father's, but sub-
sequent to her great-grandfather's.   She had a comely
face, with large, smooth cheeks and prominent eyes;
the edges of her decorous brown wig were combed
rather near their corners, and a fitting cap palliated
but did not deny the wig.   She had the quiet but
rather dull look of people slightly deaf, and she had
perhaps been stupefied by a life of unalloyed prosperity and propriety.   She had grown an old maid naturally, but not involuntarily, and she was without the
sadness or the harshness of disappointment.   She had
never known much of the world, though she had always lived in it.   She knew that it was made up of
two kinds of people—people who were like her and
people who were not like her; and she had lived solely
in the society of people who were like her, and in the
shelter of their opinions and ideals.   She did not contemn or exclude the people who were unlike her, but
she had never had any more contact with them than
she now had with the weather of the streets, as she
sat, filling her large arm-chair full of her ladylike correctness, in the library of the handsome house her
father had left her.   The irruption of her brother's
son and daughter into its cloistered quiet had scarcely
broken its invulnerable order.   It was right and fit
they should be there after his death, and it was not
strange that in the course of time they should both
show certain unregulated tendencies which, since they

were not known to be Lynde tendencies, must have
been derived from the Southwestern woman her brother had married during his social and financial periclita-
tions in a region wholly inconceivable to her.   Their
mother was dead, too, and their aunt's life closed
about them with full acceptance, if not complacence,
as part of her world.   They had grown to manhood
and womanhood without materially discomposing her
faith in the old-fashioned Unitarian deity, whose service she had always attended.

When Alan left college in his Freshman year, and
did not go back, but went rather to Europe and Egypt
and Japan, it appeared to her myopic optimism that
his escapades had been pretty well hushed up by time
and distance.   After he came home and devoted himself to his club, she could have wished that he had
taken up some profession or business; but since there
was money enough, she waited in no great disquiet
until he showed as decided a taste for something else
as he seemed for the present to have only for horses.
In the meanwhile, from time to time, it came to her
doctor's advising his going to a certain retreat.   But
he came out the first time so much better and remained
well so long that his aunt felt a kind of security in
his going again and again, whenever he became at all
worse.   He always came back better.   As she took
the cup of tea that Bessie poured out for her, she
recurred to the question that she had partly asked
already:

"Do you think Alan is getting worse again?"

"Not so very much," said the girl, candidly.   "He's

been at the club, I suppose, but he left the table partly
because I vexed him."

"Because you what?"

"Because I *vexed* him. He was scolding me, and
I wouldn't stand it."

Her aunt tasted her tea, and found it so quite what
she liked that she said, from a natural satisfaction with
Bessie, "I don't see what he had to scold you about."

"Well," returned Bessie, and she got her pretty
voice to the level of her aunt's hearing, with some
straining, and kept it there, "when he is in that state,
he has to scold *some* one; and I had been rather an-
noying, I suppose."

"What had you been doing?" asked her aunt,
making out her words more from the sight than from
the sound, after all.

"I had been walking home with a jay, and we found
Alan trying to get in at the front door with his key,
and I introduced him to the jay."

Miss Louisa Lynde had heard the word so often
from her niece and nephew, that she imagined herself
in full possession of its meaning. She asked, "Where
had you met him?"

"I met him first," said the girl, "at Willie Morland's tea, last week, and to-day I found him at Mrs.
Bevidge's altruistic toot."

"I didn't know," said her aunt, after a momentary
attention to her tea, "that jays were interested in that
sort of thing."

The girl laughed. "I believe they're not. It hasn't
quite reached them, yet; and I don't think it will ever

reach *my* jay.   Mrs. Bevidge tried to work him into
the cause, but he refused so promptly, and so—intelligently, don't you know—and so almost brutally, that
poor Freddy Lancaster had to come and apologize to
him for her want of tact."   Bessie enjoyed the fact,
which she had colored a little, in another laugh, but
she had apparently not possessed her aunt of the humor
of it.   She remained seriously attentive, and the girl
went on.   " He was not the least abashed at having
refused; he stayed till the last, and as we came out together and he was going my way, I let him walk home
with me.   He's a jay, but he isn't a *common* jay."
Bessie leaned forward and tried to implant some notion of Jeff's character and personality in her aunt's
mind.

Miss Lynde listened attentively enough, but she
merely asked, when all was said, " And why was Alan
vexed with you about him ? "

" Well," said the girl, falling back into her chair,
" generally because this man's a jay, and particularly
because he's been rather a baddish jay, I believe.   He
was suspended in his first year for something or other,
and you know poor Alan's *very* particular !   But Molly
Enderby says Freddy Lancaster gives him the best of
characters now."   Bessie pulled down her mouth, with
an effect befitting the notion of repentance and atonement.   Then she flashed out: " Perhaps he had been
drinking when he got into trouble.   Alan could never
forgive him for *that*."

" I think," said her aunt, " it is to your brother's
credit that he is anxious about your associations."

"Oh, very much!" shouted Bessie, with a burst of laughter. "And as he isn't practically so, I ought to have been more patient with his theory. But when he began to scold me, I lost *my* temper, and I gave him a few wholesome truths in the guise of taunts. That was what made him go away, I suppose."

"But I don't really see," her aunt pursued, "what occasion he had to be angry with you in this instance."

"Oh, *I* do!" said Bessie. "Mr. Durgin isn't one to inspire the casual beholder with the notion of his spiritual distinction. His face is so rude and strong, and he has such a primitive effect in his clothes, that you feel as if you were coming down the street with a prehistoric man that the barbers and tailors had put a *fin de siècle* surface on." At the mystification which appeared in her aunt's face, the girl laughed again. "I should have been quite as anxious, if I had been in Alan's place, and I shall tell him so, some time. If I had not been so interested in the situation I don't believe I could have kept my courage. Whenever I looked round, and found that prehistoric man at my elbow, it gave me the creeps, a little, as if he were really carrying me off to his cave. I shall try to express that to Alan."

XXXI.

THE ladies finished their tea, and the butler came and took the cups away. Miss Lynde remained silent in her chair at her end of the library table, and by-and-by Bessie got a book and began to read. When her aunt woke up it was half-past nine. " Was that Alan coming in ? " she asked.

" I don't think he's been out," said the girl. " It isn't late enough for him to come in—or early enough."

" I believe I'll go to bed," Miss Lynde returned. " I feel rather drowsy."

Bessie did not smile at a comedy which was apt to be repeated every evening that she and her aunt spent at home together ; they parted for the night with the decencies of family affection, and Bessie delivered the elder lady over to her maid. Then the girl sank down again, and lay musing in her deep chair before the fire with her book shut on her thumb. She looked rather old and worn in her reverie ; her face lost the air of gay banter which, after the beauty of her queer eyes and her vivid mouth, was its charm. The eyes were rather dull now, and the mouth was a little withered.

She was waiting for her brother to come down, as
he was apt to do if he was in the house, after their
aunt went to bed, to smoke a cigar in the library. He
was in his house-shoes when he shuffled into the room,
but her ear had detected his presence before a hiccough announced it. She did not look up, but let him
make several failures to light his cigar, and damn the
matches under his breath, before she pushed the drop-
light to him in silent suggestion. As he leaned over
her chair-back to reach its chimney with his cigar in
his mouth, she said, " *You're* all right, Alan."

He waited till he got round to his aunt's easy-chair
and dropped into it before he answered, "So are you,
Bess."

" I'm not so sure of that," said the girl, " as I
should be if you were still scolding me. I knew that
he was a jay, well enough, and I'd just seen him behaving very like a cad to Mrs. Bevidge."

" Then I don't understand how you came to be with
him."

" Oh, yes, you do, Alan. You mustn't be logical!
You might as well say you can't understand how you
came to be more serious than sober." The brother
laughed helplessly. " It was the excitement."

" But you can't give way to that sort of thing,
Bess," said her brother, with the gravity of a man
feeling the consequences of his own errors.

" I know I can't, but I do," she returned. " I know
it's bad for me, if it isn't for other people. Come!
I'll swear off if you will! "

" I'm always ready to swear off," said the young

man, gloomily. He added, "But you've got brains, Bess, and I hate to see you playing the fool."

"Do you really, Alan?" asked the girl, pleased perhaps as much by his reproach as by his praise. "Do you think I've got brains?"

"You're the only girl that has."

"Oh, I didn't mean to ask so much as that! But what's the reason I can't do anything with them? Other girls draw, and play, and write. I don't do anything but go in for the excitement that's bad for me. I wish you'd explain it."

Alan Lynde did not try. The question seemed to turn his thoughts back upon himself to dispiriting effect. "I've got brains, too, I believe," he began.

"Lots of them!" cried his sister, generously. "There isn't any of the men to compare with you. If I had you to talk with all the time, I shouldn't want jays. I don't mean to flatter. You're a constant feast of reason; I don't care for flows of soul. You always take right views of things when you're yourself, and even when you're somebody else you're not stupid. You could be anything you chose."

"The devil of it is I can't choose," he replied.

"Yes, I suppose that's the devil of it," said the girl.

"You oughtn't to use such language as that, Bess," said her brother, severely.

"Oh, I don't with everybody," she returned. "*Never* with ladies!"

He looked at her out of the corner of his eye with a smile at once rueful and comic.

"You've got me, I guess, that time," he owned.

"'*Touché*,' Mr. Durgin says. He fences, it seems, and he speaks French. It was like an animal speaking French; you always expect them to speak English. But *I* don't mind your swearing before me; I know that it helps to carry off the electricity." She laughed, and made him laugh with her.

"Is there anything to him?" he growled, when they stopped laughing.

"Yes, a good deal," said Bessie, with an air of thoughtfulness; and then she went on to tell all that Jeff had told her of himself, and she described his aplomb in dealing with the benevolent Bevidge, as she called her, and sketched his character, as it seemed to her. The sketch was full of shrewd guesses, and she made it amusing to her brother, who from the vantage of his own baddishness no doubt judged the original more intelligently.

"Well, you'd better let him alone, after this," he said, at the end.

"Yes," she pensively assented. "I suppose it's as if you took to some very common kind of whiskey, isn't it? I see what you mean. If one must, it ought to be champagne."

She turned upon him a look of that keen but limited knowledge which renders women's conjectures of evil always so amusing, or so pathetic, to men.

"Better let the champagne alone, too," said her brother, darkly.

"Yes, I know that," she admitted, and she lay back in her chair, looking dreamily into the fire. After a

" ' NO MORE JAYS FOR ME, NO MORE JAGS FOR YOU ' "

while she asked, abruptly, "Will you give it up if I will?"

"I am afraid I couldn't."

"You could try."

"Oh, I'm used to that."

"Then it's a bargain," she said. She jumped from her chair and went over to him, and smoothed his hair over his forehead and kissed the place she had smoothed, though it was unpleasantly damp to her lips. "Poor boy, poor boy! Now, remember! No more jays for me, and no more jags for you. Good-night."

Her brother broke into a wild laugh at her slanging, which had such a bizarre effect in relation to her physical delicacy.

XXXII.

JEFF did not know whether Miss Bessie Lynde meant to go to Mrs. Bevidge's Thursdays or not. He thought she might have been bantering him by what she said, and he decided that he would risk going to the first of them on the chance of meeting her. She was not there, and there was no one there whom he knew. Mrs. Bevidge made no effort to enlarge his acquaintance, and after he had drunk a cup of her tea he went away with rage against society in his heart, which he promised himself to vent at the first chance of refusing its favors. But the chance seemed not to come. The world which had opened its gates to him was fast shut again, and he had to make what he could of renouncing it. He worked pretty hard, and he renewed himself in his fealty to Cynthia, while his mind strayed curiously to that other girl. But he had almost abandoned the hope of meeting her again, when a large party was given on the eve of the Harvard Mid-Year Examinations, which end the younger gayeties of Boston, for a fortnight at least, in January. The party was so large that the invitations overflowed the strict bounds of society at some points. In

the case of Jeff Durgin the excess was intentional beyond the vague benevolence which prompted the giver
of the party to ask certain other outsiders.   She was
a lady of a soul several sizes larger than the souls of
some other society leaders; she was not afraid to do
as she liked; for instance, she had not only met the
Vostrands at Westover's tea, several years before, but
she had afterwards offered some hospitalities to those
ladies which had discharged her whole duty towards
them without involving her in any disadvantages.   Jeff
had been presented to her at Westover's, but she dis-
liked him so promptly and decidedly that she had
left him out of even the things that she asked some
other jays to, like lectures and parlor readings for good
objects.   It was not until one of her daughters met
him, first at Willie Morland's tea and then at Mrs.
Bevidge's meeting, that her social conscience concerned itself with him.   At the first her daughter had
not spoken to him, as might very well have happened,
since Bessie Lynde had kept him away with her nearly
all the time; but at the last she had bowed pleasantly
to him across the room, and Jeff had responded with
a stiff obeisance, whose coldness she felt the more for
having been somewhat softened herself in Mrs. Bevidge's altruistic atmosphere.

"I think he was hurt, mamma," the girl explained
to her mother, "that you've never had him to anything.   I suppose they must feel it."

"Oh, well, send him a card, then," said her mother;
and when Jeff got the card, rather near the eleventh
hour, he made haste to accept, not because he cared

to go to Mrs. Enderby's house, but because he hoped
he should meet Miss Lynde there.

Bessie was the first person he met after he turned
from paying his duty to the hostess. She was with
her aunt, and she presented him, and promised him a
dance, which she let him write on her card. She sat
out another dance with him, and he took her to supper.

To Westover, who had gone with the increasing
forlornness a man feels in such pleasures after thirty-
five, it seemed as if the two were in each other's
company the whole evening. The impression was so
strong with him that when Jeff restored Bessie to her
aunt for the dance that was to be for some one else,
and came back to the supper-room, the painter tried
to satisfy a certain uneasiness by making talk with
him. But Jeff would not talk; he got away with a
bottle of champagne, which he had captured, and a
plate heaped with croquettes and pease, and galantine
and salad. There were no ladies left in the room by
that time, and few young men; but the oldsters
crowded the place, with their bald heads devoutly
bowed over their victual, or their frosty mustaches
bathed in their drink, singly or in groups; the noise
of their talk and laughter mixed with the sound of
their eating and drinking, and the clash of the knives
and dishes. Over their stooped shoulders and past
their rounded stomachs Westover saw Alan Lynde
vaguely making his way with a glass in his hand, and
looking vaguely about for wine; he saw Jeff catch his
wandering eye, and make offer of his bottle, and then
saw Lynde, after a moment of haughty pause, unbend

and accept it.   His thin face was flushed, and his hair tossed over his forehead, but Jeff seemed not to take note of that.   He laughed boisterously at something Lynde said, and kept filling his glass for him.   His own color remained clear and cool.   It was as if his powerful physique absorbed the wine before it could reach his brain.

Westover wanted to interfere, and so far as Jeff was concerned he would not have hesitated; but Lynde was concerned, too, and you cannot save such a man from himself without offense.   He made his way to the young man, hoping he might somehow have the courage he wanted.

Jeff held up the bottle, and called to him, " Get yourself a glass, Mr. Westover."   He put on the air of a host, and would hardly be denied.   " Know Mr. Westover, Mr. Lynde?   Just talking about you," he explained to Westover.

Alan had to look twice at the painter.   " Oh, yes, Mr. Durgin, here—telling me about his place in the mountains.   Says you've been there.   Going—going myself in the summer.   See his—horses."   He made pauses between his words as some people do when they try to keep from stammering.

Westover believed Lynde understood Jeff to be a country gentleman of sporting tastes, and he would not let that pass.   " Yes, it's the pleasantest little hotel in the mountains."

" Strictly—temperance, I suppose ? " said Alan, trying to smile with lips that obeyed him stiffly.   He appeared not to care who or what Jeff was; the cham-

pagne had washed away all differences between them.
He went on to say that he had heard of Jeff's intention
of running the hotel himself when he got out of Harvard. He held it to be damned good stuff.

Jeff laughed. "Your sister wouldn't believe me
when I told her."

"I think I didn't mention Miss Lynde," said Alan,
haughtily.

Jeff filled his glass; Alan looked at it, faltered, and
then drank it off. The talk began again between the
young men, but it left Westover out, and he had to go
away. Whether Jeff was getting Lynde beyond himself from the love of mischief, such as had prompted
him to tease little children in his boyhood, or was
trying to ingratiate himself with the young fellow
through his weakness, or doing him harm out of mere
thoughtlessness, Westover came away very unhappy at
what he had seen. His unhappiness connected itself
so distinctly with Lynde's family that he went and
sat down beside Miss Lynde from an obscure impulse
of compassion, and tried to talk with her. It would
not have been so hard if she were merely deaf, for
she had the skill of deaf people in arranging the conversation so that a nodded yes or no would be all that
was needed to carry it forward. But to Westover she
was terribly dull, and he was gasping, as in an ex-
hausted receiver, when Bessie came up with a smile of
radiant recognition for his extremity. She got rid of
her partner, and devoted herself at once to Westover.
"How *good* of you!" she said, without giving him
the pain of an awkward disclaimer.

He could counter in equal sincerity and ambiguity, "How beautiful of *you*."

"Yes," she said, "I *am* looking rather well, to-night; but don't you think *effective* would have been a better word?" She smiled across her aunt at him out of a cloud of pink, from which her thin shoulders and slender neck emerged, and her arms, gloved to the top, fell into her lap; one of them seemed to terminate naturally in the fan, which sensitively shared the inquiescence of her person.

"I will say effective too, if you insist," said Westover. "But at the same time you're the most beautiful person here."

"How lovely of you, even if you don't mean it," she sighed. "If girls could have more of those things said to them, they would be better, don't you think? Or at least *feel* better."

Westover laughed. "We might organize a society —they have them for nearly everything now—for saying pleasant things to young ladies with a view to the moral effect."

"Oh, do!"

"But it ought to be done conscientiously, and you couldn't go round telling every one that she was the most beautiful girl in the room."

"Why not? She'd believe it!"

"Yes; but the effect on the members of the society?"

"Oh, yes; that! But you could vary it so as to save your conscience. You could say, 'How divinely you're looking!' or 'How angelic!' or 'You're the

very poetry of motion,' or 'You are grace itself,' or
'Your gown is a perfect dream,' or any little commonplace, and every one would take it for praise of her
personal appearance, and feel herself a great beauty,
just as I do now, though I know very well that I'm
all out of drawing, and just *chicqued* together."

"I couldn't allow any one but you to say that, Miss
Bessie; and I only let it pass because you say it so
well."

"Yes; you're always so good! You wouldn't con-
tradict me even when you turned me out of your
class."

"Did I turn you out of my class?"

"Not just in so many words, but when I said I
couldn't do anything in art, you didn't insist that it
was because I *wouldn't*, and of course then I had to
go. I've never forgiven you, Mr. Westover, never!
*Do keep on talking very excitedly; there's a man com-
ing up to us that I don't want to think I see him, or
he'll stop.* There! He's veered off! Where were
you, Mr. Westover?"

"Ah, Miss Bessie," said the painter, delighted at
her drama. "There isn't anything you couldn't do if
you would."

"You mean parlor entertainments; impersonations;
impressions; that sort of thing? I *have* thought of it.
But it would be too easy. I want to try something
difficult."

"For instance."

"Well, being very, very good. I want something
that would really tax my powers. I should like to be

an example. I tried it the other night just before I
went to sleep, and it was fine. I became an example
to others. But when I woke up—I went on in the
old way. I want something *hard*, don't you know;
but I want it to be *easy!*"

She laughed, and Westover said: "I am glad you're
not serious. No one ought to be an example to others.
To be exemplary is as dangerous as to be compliment-
ary."

"It certainly isn't so agreeable to the object," said
the girl. "But it's fine for the subject as long as it
lasts. How metaphysical we're getting! The object-
ive and the subjective. It's quite what I should expect
of talk at a Boston dance if I were a New-Yorker.
Have you seen anything of my brother, within the last
hour or so, Mr. Westover?"

"Yes; I just left him in the supper-room. Shall I
go get him for you?" When he had said this, with
the notion of rescuing him from Jeff, Westover was
sorry, for he doubted if Alan Lynde were any longer
in the state to be brought away from the supper-room,
and he was glad to have Bessie say:

"No, no. He'll look us up in the course of the
evening—or the morning."

A young fellow came to claim her for a dance, and
Westover had not the face to leave Miss Lynde, all
the less because she told him he must not think of
staying. He stayed till the dance was over, and
Bessie came back to him.

"What time is it, Mr. Westover? I see my aunt
beginning to nod on her perch."

Westover looked at his watch. " It's ten minutes past two."

"How early!" sighed the girl. "I'm tired of it, aren't you?"

"Very," said Westover. "I was tired an hour ago."

Bessie sank back in her chair with an air of nervous collapse, and did not say anything. Westover saw her watching the young couples who passed in and out of the room where the dancing was, or found corners on sofas, or window-seats, or sheltered spaces beside the doors and the chimney-piece, the girls panting and the men leaning forward to fan them. She looked very tired of it; and when a young fellow came up and asked her to dance, she told him that she was provisionally engaged. "Come back and get me, if you can't do better," she said, and he answered there was no use trying to do better, and said he would wait till the other man turned up, or didn't, if she would let him. He sat down beside her, and some young talk began between them.

In the midst of it Jeff appeared. He looked at Westover first, and then approached with an embarrassed face.

Bessie got vividly to her feet. "No apologies, Mr. Durgin, please! But in just another moment you'd have lost your dance."

Westover saw what he believed a change pass in Jeff's look from embarrassment to surprise and then to flattered intelligence. He beamed all over; and he went away with Bessie towards the ballroom, and left

Westover to a wholly unsupported belief that she had not been engaged to dance with Jeff. He wondered what her reckless meaning could be, but he had always thought her a young lady singularly fitted by nature and art to take care of herself, and when he reasoned upon what was in his mind he had to own that there was no harm in Jeff's dancing with her.

He took leave of Miss Lynde, and was going to get his coat and hat for his walk home when he was mysteriously stopped in a corner of the stairs by one of the caterer's men whom he knew. It is so unnatural to be addressed by a servant at all unless he asks you if you will have something to eat or drink, that Westover was in a manner prepared to have him say something startling. " It's about young Mr. Lynde, sor. We've got um in one of the rooms up-stairs, but he ain't fit to go home alone, and I've been lookin' for somebody that knows the family to help get um into a car'ge. He won't go for anny of us, sor."

" Where is he ? " asked Westover, in anguish at being unable to refuse the appeal, but loathing the office put upon him.

" I'll show you, sor," said the caterer's man, and he sprang up the stairs before Westover, with glad alacrity.

XXXIII.

In a little room at the side of that where the men's hats and coats were checked, Alan Lynde sat drooping forward in an arm-chair, with his head fallen on his breast. He roused himself at the flash of the burner which the man turned up. " What's all this ? " he demanded, haughtily. " Where's the carriage ? What's the matter ? "

" Your carriage is waiting, Lynde," said Westover. " I'll see you down to it," and he murmured hopelessly to the caterer's man, " Is there any back way ? "

" There's the wan we got um up by."

" It will do," said Westover, as simply.

But Lynde called out defiantly : " Back way ; I sha'n't go down back way. Inshult to guest. I wish —say—good-night to—Mrs. Enderby. Who you, anyway ? Damn caterer's man ? "

" I'm Westover, Lynde," the painter began, but the young fellow broke in upon him, shaking his hand and then taking his arm.

" Oh, Westover ! All right ! I'll go down back way with *you*. Thought—thought it was damn caterer's man. No—offense."

"No. It's all right." Westover got his arm under
Lynde's elbow, and, with the man going before for
them to fall upon jointly in case they should stumble,
he got him down the dark and twisting stairs and
through the basement hall, which was vaguely haunted
by the dispossessed women servants of the family, and
so out upon the pavement of the moonlighted streets.

"Call Miss Lynde's car'ge," shouted the caterer's
man to the barker, and escaped back into the basement, leaving Westover to stay his helpless charge on
the sidewalk.

It seemed a publication of the wretch's shame when
the barker began to fill the night with hoarse cries of,
"Miss Lynde's carriage; carriage for Miss Lynde!"
The cries were taken up by a coachman here and there
in the rank of vehicles whose varnished roofs shone
in the moon up and down the street.   After a time
that Westover of course felt to be longer than it was,
Miss Lynde's old coachman was roused from his sleep
on the box and started out of the rank.   He took in
the situation with the eye of custom, when he saw
Alan supported on the sidewalk by a stranger at the
end of the canopy covering the pavement.

He said, "Oh, ahl right, sor!" and when the two
white-gloved policemen from either side of it helped
Westover into the carriage with Lynde, he set off at a
quick trot.   The policemen clapped their hands together, and smiled across the strip of carpet that separated them, and winks and nods of intelligence passed
among the barkers to the footmen about the curb and
steps.   There were none of them sorry to see a gen-

tleman in that state; some of them had perhaps seen Alan in that state before.

Half-way home he roused himself and put his hand on the carriage-door latch. "Tell the coachman drive us to—the—club. Make night of it."

"No, no," said Westover, trying to restrain him. "We'd better go right on to your house."

"Who—who—who are you?" demanded Alan.

"Westover."

"Oh, yes—Westover. Thought we left Westover at Mrs.—Enderby's. Thought it was that jay— What's his name? Durgin. He's awful jay, but civil to me, and I want be civil to him. You're not—jay? No? That's right. Fellow made me sick; but I took his—champagne; and I must—show him some—attention." He released the door-handle, and fell back against the cushioned carriage wall. " He's a blackguard!" he said, sourly. "Not—simple jay—blackguard, too. No—no—business bring in my sister's name, hey? You—you say it's—Westover? Oh, yes, Westover. Old friend of family. Tell you good joke, Westover—my sister's. No more jays for me, no more jags for you. That's what she say—just between her and me, you know; she's a lady, Bess is; knows when to use—slang. Mark—mark of a lady know when to use—slang. Pretty good—jays and jags. Guess we didn't count this time—either of us."

When the carriage pulled up before Miss Lynde's house, Westover opened the door. "You're at home, now, Lynde. Come, let's get out."

Lynde did not stir. He asked Westover again who

he was, and when he had made sure of him, he said, with dignity, Very well; now they must get the other fellow. Westover entreated; he even reasoned; Lynde lay back in the corner of the carriage, and seemed asleep.

Westover thought of pulling him up and getting him in-doors by main force. He appealed to the coachman to know if they could not do it together.

"Why, you see, I couldn't leave me harsses, sor," said the coachman. "What's he wants, sor?" He bent urbanely down from his box and listened to the explanation that Westover made him, standing in the cold on the curb-stone, with one hand on the carriage door. "Then it's no use, sor," the man decided. "Whin he's that way, ahl hell couldn't stir um. Best go back, sor, and try to find the gentleman."

This was in the end what Westover had to do, feeling all the time that a thing so frantically absurd could not be a waking act, but helpless to escape from its performance. He thought of abandoning his charge and leaving him to his fate when he opened the carriage door before Mrs. Enderby's house; but with the next thought he perceived that this was on all accounts impossible. He went in, and began his quest for Jeff, sending various serving-men about with vague descriptions of him, and asking for him of departing guests, mostly young men he did not know, but who, he thought, might know Jeff.

He had to take off his overcoat at last, and reappear at the ball. The crowd was still great, but visibly less dense than it had been. By a sudden inspiration he made his way to the supper-room, and he found Jeff there, filling a plate, as if he were about to carry it off somewhere. He commanded Jeff's instant presence in the carriage outside; he told him of Alan's desire for him.

Jeff leaned back against the wall with the plate in his hand and laughed till it half slipped from his hold. When he could get his breath, he said: "I'll be back in a few minutes; I've got to take this to Miss Bessie Lynde. But I'll be right back."

Westover hardly believed him. But when he got on his own things again, Jeff joined him in his hat and overcoat, and they went out together.

It was another carriage that stopped the way now, and once more the barker made the night ring with what Westover felt his heartless and shameless cries for Miss Lynde's carriage. After a maddening delay, it lagged up to the curb and Jeff pulled the door open.

"Hello!" he said. "There's nobody here!"

"Nobody there?" cried Westover, and they fell upon the coachman with wild question and reproach; the policeman had to tell him at last that the carriage must move on, to make way for others.

The coachman had no explanation to offer: he did not know how or when Mr. Alan had got away.

"But you can give a guess where he's gone?" Jeff suggested, with a presence of mind which Westover mutely admired.

"Well, sor, I know where he do be gahn, some-times," the man admitted.

"Well, that will do; take me there," said Jeff. "You go in and account for me to Miss Lynde," he instructed Westover, across his shoulder. "I'll get him home before morning, somehow; and I'll send the carriage right back for the ladies, now."

Westover had the forethought to decide that Miss Bessie should ask for Jeff if she wanted him, and this simplified matters very much. She asked nothing about him. At sight of Westover coming up to her where she sat with her aunt, she merely said, "Why, Mr. Westover! I thought you took leave of this scene of gayety long ago."

"Did you?" Westover returned provisionally, and she saved him from the sin of framing some deceit in final answer by her next question.

"Have you seen anything of Alan lately?" she asked, in a voice involuntarily lowered.

Westover replied in the same octave, "Yes, I saw him going a good while ago."

"Oh!" said the girl. "Then I think my aunt and I had better go, too."

Still she did not go, and there was an interval in which she had the air of vaguely waiting. To Westover's vision, the young people still passing to and from the ballroom were like the painted figures of a picture quickened with sudden animation. There were scarcely any elders to be seen now, except the chaperons, who sat in their places with iron fortitude; Westover realized that he was the only man of his age left. He felt that the lights ought to have grown dim, but the place was as brilliant as ever. A window had been

opened somewhere, and the cold breath of the night
was drawing through the heated rooms.

He was content to have Bessie stay on, though he
was almost dropping with sleep, for he was afraid that
if she went at once, the carriage might not have got
back, and the whole affair must somehow be given
away; at last, if she were waiting, she decided to wait
no longer, and then Westover did not know how to
keep her.   He saw her rise and stoop over her aunt,
putting her mouth to the elder lady's ear, and he heard
her saying, "I am going home, Aunt Louisa."   She
turned sweetly to him.   "Won't you let us set you
down, Mr. Westover?"

"Why, thank you, I believe I prefer walking.   But
do let me have your carriage called," and again he
hurried himself into his overcoat and hat, and ran
down-stairs, and the barker a third time sent forth his
lamentable cries in summons of Miss Lynde's carriage.

While he stood on the curb-stone eagerly peering
up and down the street, he heard, without being able
either to enjoy or resent it, one of the policemen say
across him to the other, " Miss Lynde seems to be doin' a livery-stable business to-night."

Almost at the moment a carriage drove up, and he
recognized Miss Lynde's coachman, who recognized
him.   " Just got back, sor," he whispered, and a minute later Bessie came daintily out over the carpeted
way with her aunt.

"How good of you!" she said, and "Good-night,
Mr. Westover," said Miss Lynde, with an implication
in her voice that virtue was peculiarly its own reward

for those who performed any good office for her or hers.

Westover shut them in, the carriage rolled off, and he started on his homeward walk with a long sigh of relief.

XXXIV.

Bessie asked the sleepy man who opened her aunt's door whether her brother had come in yet, and found that he had not. She helped her aunt off up-stairs with her maid, and when she came down again she sent the man to bed; she told him she was going to sit up and she would let her brother in. The caprices of Alan's latch-key were known to all the servants, and the man understood what she meant. He said he had left a light in the reception-room and there was a fire there; and Bessie tripped on down from the library floor, where she had met him. She had put off her ball dress and had slipped into the simplest and easiest of breakfast frocks, which was by no means plain. Bessie had no plain frocks for any hour of the day; her frocks all expressed in stuff and style and color, and the bravery of their flying laces and ribbons, the audacity of spirit with which she was herself *chicqued* together, as she said. This one she had on now was something that brightened her dull complexion, and brought out the best effect of her eyes and mouth, and seemed the effluence of her personal dash and grace.

It made the most of her, and she liked it beyond all
her other négligées for its complaisance.

She got a book, and sat down in a long, low chair
before the fire and crossed her pretty slippers on the
warm hearth. It was a quarter after three by the clock
on the mantel; but she had never felt more eagerly
awake. The party had not been altogether to her
mind, up to midnight, but after that it had been a
series of rapid and vivid emotions, which continued
themselves still in the tumult of her nerves, and seemed
to demand an indefinite sequence of experience. She
did not know what state her brother might be in when
he came home; she had not seen anything of him after
she first went out to supper; till then, though, he had
kept himself straight, as he needs must; but she could
not tell what happened to him afterwards. She hoped
that he would come home able to talk, for she wished
to talk. She wished to talk about herself; and as she
had already had flattery enough, she wanted some
truth about herself; she wanted Alan to say what he
thought of her behavior the whole evening with that
jay. He must have seen something of it in the beginning, and she should tell him all the rest. She
should tell him just how often she had danced with
the man, and how many dances she had sat out with
him; how she had pretended once that she was engaged when another man asked her, and then danced
with the jay, to whom she pretended that he had engaged her for the dance. She had wished to see how
he would take it; for the same reason she had given
to some one else a dance that was really his. She

would tell Alan how the jay had asked her for that
last dance, and then never come near her again.   That
would give him the whole situation, and she would
know just what he thought of it.

What she thought of herself she hardly knew, or
made believe she hardly knew.   She prided herself
upon not being a flirt; she might not be very good, as
goodness went, but she was not despicable, and a flirt
was despicable.   She did not call the audacity of her
behavior with the jay flirting; he seemed to understand
it as well as she, and to meet her in her own spirit;
she wondered now whether this jay was really more interesting than the other men one met, or only different;
whether he was original, like Alan himself, or merely
novel, and would soon wear down to the tiresomeness
that seemed to underlie them all, and made one
wish to do something dreadful.   In the jay's presence
she had no wish to do anything dreadful.   Was it
because he was dreadful enough for both, all the time,
without doing anything?   She would like to ask Alan
that, and see how he would take it.   Nothing seemed
to put the jay out, so far as she had tried, and she
had tried some bold impertinences with him.   He was
very jolly through them all, and at the worst of them
he laughed and asked her for that dance, which he
never came to claim, though in the meantime he
brought her some belated supper, and was devoted to
her and her aunt, inventing services to do for them.
Then suddenly he went off and did not return, and
Mr. Westover mysteriously reappeared, and got their
carriage.

She heard a scratching at the key-hole of the outside door; she knew it was Alan's latch. She had
left the inner door ajar that there might be no uncertainty of hearing him, and she ran out into the space
between that and the outer door where the fumbling
and scraping kept on.

"Is that you, Alan?" she called, softly, and if she
had any doubt before, she had none when she heard
her brother outside, cursing his luck with his key as
usual.

She flung the door open, and confronted him with
another man, who had his arms around him as if he
had caught him from falling with the inward pull of
the door. Alan got to his feet and grappled with the
man, and insisted that he should come in and make a
night of it.

Bessie saw that it was Jeff, and they stood a moment, looking at each other. Jeff tried to free himself
with an appeal to Bessie: "I beg your pardon, Miss
Lynde. I walked home with your brother, and I was
just helping him to get in—I didn't think that
you—"

Alan said, with his measured distinctness: "Nobody cares what you think. Come in, and get something to carry you over the bridge. Cambridge cars
stopped running long ago. I say you *shall!*" He
began to raise his voice. A light flashed in a window
across the way, and a sash was lifted; some one must
be looking out.

"Oh, come in with him!" Bessie implored, and at
a little yielding in Jeff, her brother added:

" Come in, you damn jay ! " He pulled at Jeff.

Jeff made haste to shut the door behind them. He was laughing ; and if it was from mere brute insensibility to what would have shocked another in the situation, his frank recognition of its grotesqueness was of better effect than any hopeless effort to ignore it would have been. People adjust themselves to their trials ; it is the pretence of the witness that there is no trial which hurts, and Bessie was not wounded by Jeff's laugh.

" There's a fire here in the reception-room," she said. " Can you get him in ? "

" I guess so."

Jeff lifted Alan into the room and stayed him on foot there, while he took off his hat and overcoat, and then he let him sink into the low easy-chair Bessie had just risen from. All the time, Alan was bidding her ring and have some champagne and cold meat set out on the side-board, and she was lightly promising and coaxing. But he drowsed quickly in the warmth, and the last demand for supper died half uttered on his lips.

Jeff asked across him : " Can't I get him up-stairs for you ? I can carry him."

She shook her head, and whispered back, " I can leave him here," and she looked at Jeff with a moment's hesitation. " Did you—do you think that— any one noticed him, at Mrs. Enderby's ? "

" No ; they had got him in a room by himself—the caterer's men had."

" And you found him there ? "

" 'COME IN, YOU DAMN JAY' "

"Mr. Westover found him there," Jeff answered.

"I don't understand."

"Didn't he come to you after I left?"

"Yes."

"I told him to excuse me—"

"He didn't."

"Well, I guess he was pretty badly rattled." Jeff stopped himself in the vague laugh of one who remembers something ludicrous, and turned his face away.

"Tell me what it was!" she demanded, nervously.

"Mr. Westover had been home with him once, and he wouldn't stay.   He made Mr. Westover come back for me."

"What did he want with you?"

Jeff shrugged.

"And then what?"

"We went out to the carriage, as soon as I could get away from you; but he wasn't in it.   I sent Mr. Westover back to you and set out to look for him."

"That was very good of you.   And I—thank you for your kindness to my brother.   I shall not forget it.   And I wish to beg your pardon."

"What for?" asked Jeff, bluntly.

"For blaming you when you didn't come back for the dance."

If Bessie had meant nothing but what was fitting to the moment some inherent lightness of nature played her false.   But even the histrionic touch which she could not keep out of her voice, her manner, another sort of man might have found merely pathetic.

Jeff laughed with subtle intelligence. "Were you very hard on me?"

"Very," she answered in kind, forgetting her brother, and the whole terrible situation.

"Tell me what you thought of me," he said, and he came a little nearer to her, looking very handsome and very strong. "I should like to know."

"I said I should never speak to you again."

"And you kept your word," said Jeff. "Well, that's all right. Good-night—or good-morning, whichever it is." He took her hand, which she could not withdraw, or feigned to herself that she could not withdraw, and looked at her with a silent laugh, and a hardy, sceptical glance that she felt take in every detail of her prettiness, her plainness. Then he turned and went out, and she ran quickly and locked the door upon him.

XXXV.

Bessie crept up to her room, where she spent the rest of the night in her chair, amidst a tumult of emotion which she would have called thinking. She asked herself the most searching questions, but she got no very candid answers to them, and she decided that she must see the whole fact with some other's eyes before she could know what she had meant or what she had done.

When she let the daylight into her room, it showed her a face in her mirror that bore no trace of conflicting anxieties. Her complexion favored this effect of inward calm; it was always thick; and her eyes seemed to her all the brighter for their vigils.

A smile, even, hovered on her mouth as she sat down at the breakfast-table, in the pretty négligée she had worn all night, and poured out Miss Lynde's coffee for her.

"That's always very becoming to you, Bessie," said her aunt. "It's the nicest breakfast gown you have."

"Do you think so?" Bessie looked down at it, first on one side and then on the other, as a woman always does when her dress is spoken of.

"Mr. Alan said he would have his breakfast in his

room, miss," murmured the butler, in husky respect-
fulness, as he returned to Bessie from carrying Miss
Lynde's cup to her.   " He don't want anything but a
little toast and coffee."

She perceived that the words were meant to make
it easy for her to ask, " Isn't he very well, Andrew ? "

"About as usual, miss," said Andrew, a thought
more sepulchral than before.   " He's going on—about
as usual."

She knew this to mean that he was going on from
bad to worse, and that his last night's excess was the
beginning of a debauch which could end only in one
way.   She must send for the doctor; he would decide
what was best, when he saw how Alan came through
the day.

Late in the afternoon she heard Mary Enderby's
voice in the reception-room, bidding the man say that
if Miss Bessie were lying down she would come up to
her, or would go away, just as she wished.   She flew
down-stairs with a glad cry of " Molly!   What an inspiration!   I was just thinking of you, and wishing
for you.   But I didn't suppose you were up yet! "

" It's pretty early," said Miss Enderby.   " But I
should have been here before if I could, for I knew I
shouldn't wake you, Bessie, with your habit of turning
night into day, and getting up any time in the forenoon."

" How dissipated you sound ! "

" Yes, don't I ?   But I've been thinking about you
ever since I woke, and I had to come and find out if
you were alive, anyhow."

"Come up-stairs and see!" said Bessie, holding her friend's hand on the sofa where they had dropped down together, and going all over the scene of last night in that place, for the thousandth time.

"No, no; I really mustn't. I hope you had a good time?"

"At *your* house!"

"How dear of you! But, Bessie, I got to thinking you'd been rather sacrificed. It came into my mind the instant I woke, and gave me this severe case of conscience. I suppose it's a kind of conscience."

"Yes, yes. Go on! I like having been a martyr, if I don't know what about."

"Why, you know, Bessie, or if you don't you will presently, that it was I who got mamma to send him a card; I felt rather sorry for him, that day at Mrs. Bevidge's, because she'd so obviously got him there to use him, and I got mamma to ask him. Everything takes care of itself, at a large affair, and I thought I might trust in Providence to deal with him after he came; and then I saw you made a *means* the whole evening! I didn't reflect that there always has to be a *means!*"

"It's a question of Mr. Durgin?" said Bessie, coldly thrilling at the sound of a name that she pronounced so gayly in a tone of sympathetic amusement.

Miss Enderby bobbed her head. "It shows that we ought never to do a good action, doesn't it? But, poor thing! How *you* must have been swearing off!"

"I don't know. Was it so very bad? I'm trying to think," said Bessie, thinking that after this begin-

ning it would be impossible to confide in Mary Enderby.

"Oh, now, Bessie! Don't *you* be patient, or I shall
begin to lose my faith in human nature. Just say at
once that it was an outrage, and I'll forgive you!
You see," Miss Enderby went on, "it isn't merely that
he's a jay; but he isn't a very *nice* jay. None of the
men like him—except Freddy Lancaster, of course;
he likes everybody, on principle; he doesn't count. I
thought that perhaps, although he's so crude and
blunt, he might be sensitive and high-minded; you're
always reading about such things; but they say he
isn't, in the least; oh, not the *least!* They say he
goes with a set of fast jays, and that he's *dreadful;*
though he has a very good mind, and could do very
well if he chose. That's what cousin Jim said to-day;
he's just been at our house; and it was so extremely
telepathic that I thought I must run round and prevent your having the man on your conscience if you
felt you had had too much of him. You *won't* lay
him up against us, *will* you?" She jumped to her
feet.

"You dear!" said Bessie, keeping Mary Enderby's
hand, and pressing it between both of hers against her
breast as they now stood face to face. "Do come up
and have some tea!"

"No, no! Really, I can't."

They were both involuntarily silent. The door had
been opened to some one, and there was a brief parley,
which ended in a voice they knew to be the doctor's,
saying, "Then I'll go right up to his room." Both

the girls broke into laughing adieux, to hide their
consciousness that the doctor was going up to see
Alan Lynde, who was never sick except in the one
way.

Miss Enderby even said, " I was so glad to see Alan
looking so well, last night."

" Yes, he had such a good time," said Bessie, and
she followed her friend to the door, where she kissed
her reassuringly, and thanked her for taking all the
trouble she had, bidding her not be the least anxious
on her account.

It seemed to her that she should sink upon the stairs
in mounting them to the library.   Mary Enderby had
told her only what she had known before ; it was what
her brother had told her; but then it had not been
possible for the man to say that he had brought Alan
home tipsy, and been alone in the house with her at
three o'clock in the morning.   He would not only
boast of it to all that vulgar comradehood of his, but
it might get into those terrible papers, which published
the society scandals.   There would be no way but to
appeal to his pity, his generosity.   She fancied herself
writing to him, but he could show her note, and she
must send for him to come and see her, and try to
put him on his honor.   Or, that would not do, either.
She must make it happen that they should be thrown
together, and then speak to him.   Even that might
make him think she was afraid of him ; or he might
take it wrong, and believe that she cared for him.   He
had really been very good to Alan, and she tried to
feel safe in the thought of that.   She did feel safe for

a moment; but if she had meant nothing but to make him believe her grateful, what must he infer from her talking to him in the light way she did about forgiving him for not coming back to dance with her.   Her manner, her looks, her tone, had given him the right to say that she had been willing to flirt with him there, at that hour, and in those dreadful circumstances.

She found herself lying in a deep arm-chair in the library, when she was aware of Dr. Lacy pausing at the door and looking tentatively in upon her.

"Come in, doctor," she said, and she knew that her face was wet with tears, and that she spoke with the voice of weeping.

He came forward and looked narrowly at her, without sitting down.   "There's nothing to be alarmed about, Miss Bessie," he said.   "But I think your brother had better leave home again, for a while."

"Yes," she said, blankly.   Her mind was not on his words.

"I will make the arrangements."

"Thank you," said Bessie, listlessly.

The doctor had made a step backward, as if he were going away, and now he stopped.   "Aren't you feeling quite well, Miss Bessie?"

"Oh, yes," she said, and she began to cry.

The doctor came forward, and said, cheerily, "Let me see."   He pulled a chair up to hers, and took her wrist between his fingers.   "If you were at Mrs. Enderby's last night, you'll need another night to put you just right. But you're pretty well, as it is."   He let her wrist softly go, and said: "You mustn't dis-

tress yourself about your brother's case. Of course,
it's hard to have it happen now after he's held up so
long; longer than it has been before, I think, isn't it?
But it's something that it has been so long.   The next
time, let us hope, it will be longer still."

The doctor made as if to rise. Bessie put her hand
out to stay him. "What is it makes him do it?"

"Ah, that's a great mystery," said the doctor. "I
suppose you might say, the excitement."

"Yes!"

"But it seems to me very often, in such cases, as
if it were to *escape* the excitement. I think you're
both keyed up pretty sharply by nature, Miss Bessie,"
said the doctor, with the personal kindness he felt for
the girl, and the pity softening his scientific spirit.

"I know!" she answered. "We're alike. Why
don't I take to drinking, too?"

The doctor laughed at such a question from a young
lady, but with an inner seriousness in his laugh, as if,
coming from a patient, it was to be weighed. "Well,
I suppose it isn't the habit of your sex, Miss Bessie."

"Sometimes it is. Sometimes women get drunk,
and then I think they do less harm than if they did
other things to get away from the excitement."   She
longed to confide in him; the words were on her
tongue; she believed he could help her, tell her what
to do; out of his stores of knowledge and experience
he must have some suggestion, some remedy; he could
advise her; he could stand her friend, so far.   People
told their doctors all kinds of things, silly things.
Why should she not tell her doctor this?

It would have been easier if it had been an older man, who might have had a daughter of her age. But he was in that period of the early forties when a doctor sometimes has a matter-of-fact, disagreeable wife whose idea stands between him and the spiritual intimacy of his patients, so that it seems as if they were delivering their confidences rather to her than to him. He was able, he was good, he was extremely acute, he was even with the latest facts and theories; but as he sat straight up in his chair his stomach defined itself as a half-moon before him, and he said to the quivering heap of emotions beside him, "You mean like breaking hearts, and such little matters?"

It was fatally stupid, and it beat her back into herself.

"Yes," she said, with a contempt that she easily hid from him, "that's worse than getting drunk, isn't it?"

"Well, it isn't so regarded," said the doctor, who supposed himself to have made a sprightly answer, and laughed at it. "I wish, Miss Bessie, you'd take a little remedy I'm going to send you. You've merely been up too late, but it's a very good thing for people who've been up too late."

"Thank you. And about my brother?"

"Oh! I'll send a man to look after him to-night, and to-morrow I really think he'd better go."

XXXVI.

Miss Lynde had gone earlier than usual to bed, when Bessie heard Alan's door open, and then heard him feeling his way fumblingly down-stairs. She surmised that he had drunk up all that he had in his room, and was making for the sideboard in the dining-room.

She ran and got the two decanters, one of whiskey and one of brandy, which he was in the habit of carrying back to his room from such an incursion.

"Alan!" she called to him, in a low voice.

"Where are you?" he answered back.

"In the library," she said. "Come in here, please."

He came, and stood looking gloomily in from the doorway. He caught sight of the decanters and the glasses on the library table. "Oh!" he said, and gave a laugh cut in two by a hiccough.

"Come in, and shut the door, Alan," she said. "Let's make a night of it. I've got the materials here." She waved her hand towards the decanters.

Alan shrugged. "*I* don't know what you mean." But he came forward, and slouched into one of the deep chairs.

" Well, I'll tell you what," said Bessie, with a laugh.
" We're both excited, and we want to get away from
ourselves.   Isn't that what's the matter with you when
it begins ?   Doctor Lacy thinks it is."

"Does he ? " Alan asked.   " I didn't suppose he
had so much sense.   What of it ? "

" Nothing.   Merely that I'm going to drink a glass
of whiskey and a glass of brandy for every glass that
you drink to-night."

" You mustn't play the fool, Bess," said her brother, with dignified severity.

" But I'm really serious, Alan.   Shall I give you
something ?   Which shall we begin on ?   And we'd
better begin soon, for there's a man coming from the
doctor to look after you, and then you won't get anything."

" Don't be ridiculous !   Give me those decanters ! "
Alan struggled out of his chair, and trembled over to
where she had them on the table beside her.

She caught them up, one in either hand, and held
them as high as she could lift them.   " If you don't
sit down and promise to keep still, I'll smash them
both on the hearth.   You know I will."

Her strange eyes gleamed, and he hesitated; then
he went back to his chair.

" I don't see what's got into you to-night.   *I* don't
want anything," he said.   He tried to brave it out,
but presently he cast a piteous glance at the decanters
where she had put them down beside her again.   " Does
the doctor think I'd better go again ? " he asked.

" Yes."

"'I'LL SMASH THEM BOTH ON THE HEARTH'"

" When ? "

" To-morrow."

He looked at the decanters. " And when is that fellow coming ? "

" He may be here any moment."

" It's pretty rough," he sighed. " Two glasses of that stuff would drive you so wild you wouldn't know where you were, Bess," he expostulated.

" Well, I *wish* I didn't know where I was. I wish I wasn't anywhere." He looked at her, and then dropped his eyes, with the effect of giving up a hopeless conundrum.

But he asked, " What's the matter ? "

She scanned him keenly before she answered: " Something that I should like to tell you—that you ought to know. Alan, do you think you are fit to judge of a very serious matter ? "

He laughed pathetically. " I don't believe I'm in a very judicial frame of mind to-night, Bess. To-morrow—"

" Oh, to-morrow ! Where will you be to-morrow ? "

" That's true ! Well, what is it ? I'll try to listen. But if you knew how my nerves were going." His eyes wandered from hers back to the decanters. " If I had just one glass—"

" I'll have one, too," she said, with a motion towards the decanter next her.

He threw up his arms. " Oh, well, go on. I'll listen as well as I can." He sank down in his chair and stretched his little feet out toward the fire. " Go on ! "

She hesitated before she began. "Do you know who brought you home last night, Alan?"

"Yes," he answered, quickly. "Westover."

"Yes, Mr. Westover brought you, and you wouldn't stay. You don't remember anything else?"

"No. What else?"

"Nothing for you, if you don't remember." She sat in silent hopelessness for a while, and her brother's eyes dwelt on the decanters, which she seemed to have forgotten. "Alan!" she broke out abruptly. "I'm worried, and if I can't tell you about it, there's no one I can."

The appeal in her voice must have reached him, though he seemed scarcely to have heeded her words. "What is it?" he asked, kindly.

"You went back to the Enderbys' after Mr. Westover brought you home, and then some one else had to bring you again."

"How do you know?"

"I was up, and let you in—"

"Did you, Bessie? That was *like* you," he said, tenderly.

"And I had to let *him* in, too. You pulled him into the house, and you made such a disturbance at the door that he had to come in for fear you would bring the police."

"What a beast!" said Alan, of himself, as if it were some one else.

"He came in with you. And you wanted him to have some supper. And you fell asleep before the fire in the reception-room."

"That—that was the dream!" said Alan, severely. 'What are you talking that stuff for, Bessie?"

"Oh, no!" she retorted with a laugh, as if the pleasure of its coming in so fitly were compensation for the shame of the fact. "The dream was what happened afterwards. The dream was that you fell asleep there, and left me there with him—"

"Well, poor old Westover; he's a gentleman! You needn't be worried about *him*—"

"You're *not* fit!" cried the girl. "I give it up." She got upon her feet, and stood a moment listless.

"No, I'm not, Bessie. I can't pull my mind together to-night. But look here!" He seemed to lose what he wanted to say. He asked: "Is it something I've got you in for? Do I understand that?"

"Partly," she said.

"Well, then, I'll help you out. You can trust me, Bessie; you can, indeed. You don't believe it?"

"Oh, I believe you think I can trust you."

"But this time you *can*. If you need my help I will stand by you, right or wrong. If you want to tell me now, I'll listen, and I'll advise you the best I can—"

"It's just something I've got nervous about," she said, while her eyes shone with sudden tears. "But I won't trouble you with it to-night. There's no such great hurry. We can talk about it in the morning if you're better then. Or, I forgot! You're going away!"

"No," said the young man, with pathetic dignity, "I'm not going if you need my help. But you're right about me to-night, Bessie. I'm not fit. I'm

afraid I can't grasp anything to-night. Tell me in
the morning. Oh, don't be afraid!" he cried out at
the glance she gave the decanters. "That's over, now;
you could put them in my hands and be safe enough.
I'm going back to bed, and in the morning—"

He rose and went towards the door. "If that doctor's man comes to-night you can send him away
again. He needn't bother."

"All right, Alan," she said, fondly. "Good-night.
Don't worry about me. Try to get some sleep."

"And you must sleep, too. You can trust me,
Bessie."

He came back after he got out of the room and
looked in. "Bess, if you're anxious about it, if you
don't feel perfectly sure of me, you can take those
things to your room with you." He indicated the
decanters with a glance.

"Oh, no! I shall leave them here. It wouldn't be
any use your just keeping well overnight. You'll have
to keep well a long time, Alan, if you're going to help
me. And that's the reason I'd rather talk to you
when you can give your whole mind to what I say."

"Is it something so serious?"

"I don't know. That's for you to judge. Not very
—not at all, perhaps."

"Then I won't fail you, Bessie. I shall ' keep well,'
as you call it, as long as you want me. Good-night."

"Good-night. I shall leave these bottles here, remember."

"You needn't be afraid. You might put them
beside my bed."

Bessie slept soundly, from exhaustion, and in that provisional fashion in which people who have postponed a care to a given moment are able to sleep. But she woke early, and crept down-stairs before any one else was astir, and went to the library. The decanters stood there on the table, empty. Her brother lay a shapeless heap in one of the deep arm-chairs.

XXXVII.

WESTOVER got home from the Enderby dance at last with the forecast of a violent cold in his system, which verified itself the next morning. He had been housed a week, when Jeff Durgin came to see him. "Why didn't you let me know you were sick?" he demanded. " I'd have come and looked after you."

"Thank you," said Westover, with as much stiffness as he could command in his physical limpness. " I shouldn't have allowed you to look after me; and I want you to understand, now, that there can't be any sort of friendliness between us till you've accounted for your behavior with Lynde, the other night."

"You mean at the party?" Jeff asked, tranquilly.

"Yes!" cried Westover. " If I had not been shut up ever since, I should have gone to see you and had it out with you. I've only let you in, now, to give you the chance to explain; and I refuse to hear a word from you till you do." Westover did not think that this was very forcible, and he was not much surprised that it made Jeff smile.

"Why, I don't know what there is to explain. I suppose you think I got him drunk; I know what you

thought that night.   But he was pretty well loaded
when he struck my champagne.   It wasn't a question
of what he was going to do any longer, but how he
was going to do it.   I kept an eye on him, and at the
right time I helped the caterer's man to get him up
into that room where he wouldn't make any trouble.
I expected to go back and look after him, but I forgot
him."

"I don't suppose, really, that you're aware what a
devil's argument that is," said Westover.   "You got
Lynde drunk, and then you went back to his sister,
and allowed her to treat you as if you were a gentleman, and didn't deserve to be thrown out of the
house."   This at last was something like what Westover had imagined he would say to Jeff, and he looked
to see it have the imagined effect upon him.

"Do you suppose," asked Jeff, with cheerful cyni-
cism, "that it was the first time she was civil to a man
her brother got drunk with?"

"No!   But all the more you ought to have considered her helplessness.   It ought to have made her the
more sacred "—Jeff gave an exasperating shrug—" to
you, and you ought to have kept away from her for
decency's sake."

"I was engaged to dance with her."

"I can't allow you to be trivial with me, Durgin,"
said Westover.   "You've acted like a blackguard, and
worse, if there is anything worse."

Jeff stood at a corner of the fire, leaning one elbow
on the mantel, and he now looked thoughtfully down
on Westover, who had sunk weakly into a chair before

the hearth. " I don't deny it from your point of view, Mr. Westover," he said, without the least resentment in his tone. " You believe that everything is done from a purpose, or that a thing is intended because it's done. But I see that most things in this world are not thought about, and not intended. They happen, just as much as the other things that we call accidents."

" Yes," said Westover, " but the wrong things don't happen from people who are in the habit of meaning the right ones."

" I believe they do, fully half the time," Jeff returned; " and as far as the grand result is concerned you might as well think them and intend them as not. I don't mean that you ought to do it; that's another thing, and if I had tried to get Lynde drunk, and then gone to dance with his sister, I should have been what you say I am. But I saw him getting worse without meaning to make him so; and I went back to her because—I wanted to."

" And you think, I suppose," said Westover, " that she wouldn't have cared any more than you cared if she had known what you did."

" I can't say anything about that."

The painter continued, bitterly : " You used to come in here, the first year, with notions of society women that would have disgraced a Goth, or a gorilla. Did you form your estimate of Miss Lynde from those premises ? "

" I'm not a boy now," Jeff answered, " and I haven't stayed *all* the kinds of a fool I was."

"Then you don't think Miss Lynde would speak to you, or look at you, after she knew what you had done?"

"I should like to tell her and see," said Jeff, with a hardy laugh. "But I guess I sha'n't have the chance. I've never been a favorite in society, and I don't expect to meet her again."

"Perhaps you'd like to have *me* tell her?"

"Why, yes, I believe I should, if you could tell me what she *thought*—not what she *said* about it."

"You *are* a brute," answered Westover, with a puzzled air. What puzzled him most and pleased him least was the fellow's patience under his severity, which he seemed either not to feel or not to mind. It was of a piece with the behavior of the rascally boy whom he had cuffed for fr'ghtening Cynthia and her little brother long ago, and he wondered what final malvolence it portended.

Jeff said, as if their controversy were at an end and they might now turn to more personal things: "You look pretty slim, Mr. Westover. A'n't there something I can do for you—get you? I've come in with a message from mother. She says if you ever want to get that winter view of Lion's Head, now's your time. She wants you to come up there; she and Cynthia both do. They can make you as comfortable as you please, and they'd like to have a visit from you. Can't you go?"

Westover shook his head ruefully. "It's good of them, and I want you to thank them for me. But I don't know when I'm going to get out again."

"Oh, you'll soon get out," said Jeff. "I'm going to look after you a little," and this time Westover was too weak to protest. He did not forbid Jeff's taking off his overcoat; he suffered him to light his spirit-lamp and make a punch of the whiskey which he owned the doctor was giving him; and when Jeff handed him the steaming glass, and asked him, "How's that?" he answered with a pleasure in it which he knew to be deplorable, "It's fine."

Jeff stayed the whole evening with him, and made him more comfortable than he had been since his cold began. Westover now talked seriously and frankly with him, but no longer so harshly, and in his relenting he felt a return of his old illogical liking for him. He fancied in Durgin's kindness to himself an indirect regret, and a desire to atone for what he had done, and he said: "The effect is in you—the worst effect. I don't think either of the young Lyndes very exemplary people. But you'd be doing yourself a greater wrong than you've done them if you didn't recognize that you had been guilty towards them."

Jeff seemed struck by this notion. "What do you want me to do? What can I do? Chase myself out of society? Something like that? I'm willing. It's too easy, though. As I said, I've never been wanted much, there, and I shouldn't be missed."

"Well, then, how would you like to leave it to the people at Lion's Head to say what you should do?" Westover suggested.

"I shouldn't like it," said Jeff, promptly. "They'd judge it as you do—as if they'd done it themselves.

That's the reason women are not fit to judge." His
gay face darkened. "But tell 'em if you want to."

"Bah!" cried the painter. "Why should I want
to? I'm not a woman in everything."

"I beg your pardon, Mr. Westover. I didn't mean
that. I only meant that you're an idealist. I look at
this thing as if some one else had done it; I believe
that's the practical way; and I shouldn't go in for
punishing any one else for such a thing very severely."
He made another punch—for himself this time, he
said; but Westover joined him in a glass of it.

"It won't do to take that view of your faults, Jeff,"
he said, gravely.

"What's the reason?" Jeff demanded; and now
either the punch had begun to work in Westover's
brain, or some other influence of like force and quality.
He perceived that in this earth-bound temperament
was the potentiality of all the success it aimed at.
The acceptance of the moral fact as it was, without
the unconscious effort to better it, or to hold himself
strictly to account for it, was the secret of the power
in the man which would bring about the material re-
sults he desired; and this simplicity of the motive
involved had its charm. Westover was aware of liking
Durgin at that moment much more than he ought, and
of liking him helplessly. In the light of his good-
natured selfishness, the injury to the Lyndes showed
much less a sacrilege than it had seemed; Westover
began to see it with Jeff's eyes, and to see it with
reference to what might be low and mean in them,
instead of what might be fine and high.

He was sensible of the growth Jeff had made intellectually. He had not been at Harvard nearly four years for nothing. He had phrases and could handle them. In whatever obscure or perverse fashion, he had profited by his opportunities. The fellow who could accuse him of being an idealist, and could in some sort prove it, was no longer a naughty boy to be tutored and punished. The revolt latent in him would be violent in proportion to the pressure put upon him, and Westover began to be without the wish to press his fault home to him so strongly. In the optimism generated by the punch, he felt that he might leave the case to Jeff himself; or else in the comfort we all experience in sinking to a lower level, he was unwilling to make the effort to keep his own moral elevation. But he did make an effort to save himself by saying: "You can't get what you've done before yourself as you can the action of some one else. It's part of you, and you have to judge the motive as well as the effect."

"Well, that's what I'm doing," said Jeff; "but it seems to me that you're trying to have me judge of the effect from a motive I didn't have. As far as I can make out, I hadn't any motive at all.

He laughed, and all that Westover could say was, "Then you're still responsible for the result." But this no longer appeared so true to him.

XXXVIII.

It was not a condition of Westover's welcome at
Lion's Head that he should seem peculiarly the friend
of Jeff Durgin, but he could not help making it so,
and he began to overact the part as soon as he met
Jeff's mother. He had to speak of him in thanking
her for remembering his wish to paint Lion's Head in
the winter, and he had to tell her of Jeff's thoughtfulness during the past fortnight; he had to say that he
did not believe he should ever have got away if it had
not been for him. This was true; Durgin had even
come in from Cambridge to see him off on the train;
he behaved as if the incident with Lynde and all their
talk about it had cemented the friendship between
Westover and himself, and he could not be too devoted. It now came out that he had written home all
about Westover, and made his mother put up a stove
in the painter's old room, so that he should have the
instant use of it when he arrived.

It was an air-tight wood-stove, and it filled the
chamber with a heat in which Westover drowsed as
soon as he entered it. He threw himself on the bed,
and slept away the fatigue of his railroad journey and

the cold of his drive with Jombateeste from the station.   His nap was long, and he woke from it in a
pleasant languor, with the dream-clouds still hanging
in his brain.   He opened the damper of his stove, and
set it roaring again ; then he pulled down the upper
sash of his window and looked out on a world whose
elements of wood and snow and stone he tried to co-
ordinate.   There was nothing else in that world but
these things, so repellent of one another.   He suffered
from the incongruity of the wooden bulk of the hotel,
with the white drifts deep about it, and with the granite cliffs of Lion's Head before it, where the gray crags
darkened under the pink afternoon light which was
beginning to play upon its crest from the early sunset.
The wind that had seemed to bore through his thick
cap and his skull itself, and that had tossed the dry
snow like dust against his eyes on his way from the
railroad, had now fallen, and an incomparable quiet
wrapped the solitude of the hills.   A teasing sense of
the impossibility of the scene, as far as his art was
concerned, filled him full of a fond despair of rendering its feeling.   He could give its light and color and
form in a sufficiently vivid suggestion of the fact, but
he could not make that pink flush seem to exhale, like
a long breath, upon those rugged shapes ; he could
not impart that sentiment of delicacy, almost of elegance which he found in the wilderness, while every
detail of civilization physically distressed him.   In
one place the snow had been dug down to the pine
planking of the pathway round the house ; and the
contact of this woodenness with the frozen ground

pierced his nerves and set his teeth on edge like a
harsh noise.   When once he saw it he had to make
an effort to take his eyes from it, and in a sort unknown to him in summer he perceived the offence of
the hotel itself amidst the pure and lonely beauty of
the winter landscape.   It was a note of intolerable
banality, of philistine pretence and vulgar convention,
such as Whitwell's low, unpainted cottage at the foot
of the hill did not give, nor the little red school-house,
on the other hand, showing through the naked trees.
There should have been really no human habitation
visible except a wigwam in the shelter of the pines,
here and there; and when he saw Whitwell making
his way up the hill-side road, Westover felt that if
there must be any human presence it should be some
savage clad in skins, instead of the philosopher in his
rubber boots and his clothing-store ulster.   He preferred the small, wiry shape of Jombateeste, in his
blue woollen cap, and his Canadian foot-gear, as he
ran round the corner of the house towards the barn,
and left the breath of his pipe in the fine air behind
him.

The light began to deepen from the pale pink to a
crimson which stained the tops and steeps of snow,
and deepened the dark of the woods massed on the
mountain slopes between the irregular fields of white.
The burnished brown of the hard-wood trees, the dull
carbon shadows of the evergreens, seemed to wither
to one black as the red strengthened in the sky.
Westover realized that he had lost the best of any
possible picture in letting that first delicate color

escape him. This crimson was harsh and vulgar in comparison; it would have almost a chromo quality; he censured his pleasure in it as something gross and material, like that of eating; and on a sudden he felt hungry. He wondered what time they would give him supper, and he took slight account of the fact that a caprice of the wind had torn its hood of snows from the mountain summit, and that the profile of the Lion's Head showed almost as distinctly as in summer. He stood before the picture which for that day at least was lost to him, and questioned whether there would be a hearty meal, something like a dinner, or whether there would be something like a farm-house supper, mainly of doughnuts and tea.

He pulled up his window and was going to lie down again, when some one knocked, and Frank Whitwell stood at the door. " Do you want we should bring your supper to you here, Mr. Westover, or will you—"

" Oh, let me join you all! " cried the painter eagerly. " Is it ready—shall I come now ? "

" Well, in about five minutes, or so." Frank went away, after setting down in the room the lamp he had brought. It was a lamp which Westover thought he remembered from the farm-house period, and on his way down he realized as he had somehow not done in his summer sojourns, the entirety of the old house in the hotel which had encompassed it. The primitive cold of its stairways and passages struck upon him as soon as he left his own room, and he found the parlor door closed against the chill. There was a hot stove-fire within, and a kerosene-lamp turned low, but there

was no one there, and he had the photograph of his
first picture of Lion's Head to himself in the dim
light.   The voices of Mrs. Durgin and Cynthia came
to him from the dining-room, and from the kitchen
beyond, with the occasional clash of crockery, and
the clang of iron upon iron about the stove, and the
quick tread of women's feet upon the bare floor.
With these pleasant noises came the smell of cooking,
and later there was an opening and shutting of doors,
with a thrill of the freezing air from without, and the
dull thumping of Whitwell's rubber boots, and the
quicker flapping of Jombateeste's soft leathern soles.
Then there was the sweep of skirted feet at the parlor
door, and Cynthia Whitwell came in without perceiv-
ing him.   She went to the table by the darkening
window, and quickly turned up the light of the lamp.
In her ignorance of his presence, he saw her as if she
had been alone, almost as if she were out of the body;
he received from her unconsciousness the impression
of something rarely pure and fine, and he had a sudden compassion for her, as for something precious that
is fated to be wasted or misprized.   At a little movement which he made to relieve himself from a sense
of eavesdropping, she gave a start, and shut her lips
upon the little cry that would have escaped from another sort of woman.

"I didn't know you were here," she said; and she
flushed with the shyness of him which she always
showed at first.   She had met him already with the
rest, but they had scarcely spoken together; and he
knew of the struggle she must now be making with

herself when she went on : " I didn't know you had been called. I thought you were still sleeping."

" Yes. I seemed to sleep for centuries," said West-over, " and I woke up feeling coeval with Lion's Head. But I hope to grow younger again."

She faltered, and then she asked, " Did you see the light on it when the sun went down ? "

" I wish I hadn't. I could never get that light— even if it ever came again."

" It's there every afternoon, when it's clear."

" I'm sorry for that; I shall have to try for it, then."

" Wasn't that what you came for ? " she asked, by one of the efforts she was making with everything she said. He could have believed he saw the pulse throb-bing in her neck. But she held herself stone-still, and he divined her resolution to conquer herself, if she should die for it.

" Yes, I came for that," said Westover. " That's what makes it so dismaying. If I had only happened on it, I shouldn't have been responsible for the failure I shall make of it."

She smiled, as if she liked his lightness, but doubted if she ought. " We don't often get Lion's Head clear of snow."

" Yes ; that's another hardship," said the painter. " Everything is against me ! If we don't have a snow overnight, and a cloudy day to-morrow, I shall be in despair."

She played with the little wheel of the wick; she looked down, and then, with a glance flashed at him,

she gasped, "I shall have to take your lamp for the
table—tea is ready."

"Oh, well, if you will only take me with it. I'm
frightfully hungry."

Apparently she could not say anything to that. He
tried to get the lamp to carry it out for her, but she
would not let him. "It isn't heavy," she said, and
hurried out before him.

It was all nothing, but it was all very charming, and
Westover was richly content with it; and yet not content, for he felt that the pleasure of it was not truly
his, but was a moment of merely borrowed happiness.

The table was laid in the old farm-house sitting-
room where he had been served alone when he first
came to Lion's Head. But now he sat down with the
whole family, even to Jombateeste, who brought in a
faint odor of the barn with him.

They had each been in contact with the finer world
which revisits nature in the summer-time, and they
must all have known something of its usages, but they
had reverted in form and substance to the rustic living
of their neighbors. They had steak for Westover,
and baked potatoes; but for themselves they had such
farm fare as Mrs. Durgin had given him the first time
he supped there. They made their meal chiefly of
doughnuts and tea, and hot biscuit, with some sweet
dishes of a festive sort added in recognition of his
presence; and there was mince-pie for all. Mrs. Durgin and Whitwell ate with their knives, and Jombateeste filled himself so soon with every implement at
hand that he was able to ask excuse of the others if he

left them for the horses before they had half finished.
Frank Whitwell fed with a kind of official or func-
tional conformity to the ways of summer folks; but
Cynthia, at whom Westover glanced with anxiety, only
drank some tea and ate a little bread-and-butter.   He
was ashamed of his anxiety, for he had owned that it
ought not to have mattered if she had used her knife
like her father; and it seemed to him as if he had
prompted Mrs. Durgin by his curious glance to say:
"We don't know half the time how the child lives.
Cynthy!   Take something to eat!"

Cynthia pleaded that she was not hungry; Mrs.
Durgin declared that she would die if she kept on
as she was going; and then the girl escaped to the
kitchen on one of the errands which she made from
time to time between the stove and the table.

"I presume it's your coming, Mr. Westover,"
Mrs. Durgin went on, with the comfortable superiority of elderly people to all the trials of the young.
"I don't know why she should make a stranger of
you, every time.   You've known her pretty much all
her life."

"Ever since you give Jeff what he deserved for
scaring her and Frank here with his dog," said Whitwell.

"Poor Fox!" Mrs. Durgin sighed.   "He did have
the least sense for a dog I ever saw.   And Jeff used
to be so fond of him!   Well, I guess *he* got tired of
him, *too*, towards the last."

"He's gone to the happy hunting-grounds now.
Colorady didn't agree with him—or old age," said

Whitwell. "I don't see why the Injuns wa'n't right," he pursued, thoughtfully. "If they've got souls, why ha'n't their dogs? I suppose Mr. Westover here would say there wa'n't any certainty about the Injuns themselves!"

"You know my weak point, Mr. Whitwell," the painter confessed. "But I can't *prove* they haven't."

"Nor dogs, neither, I guess," said Whitwell, tolerantly. "It's curious, though, if animals have got souls, that we ha'n't ever had any communications from 'em. You might say that ag'in the idea."

"No, I'll let *you* say it," returned Westover. "But a good many of the communications seem to come from the lower intelligences, if not the lower animals."

Whitwell laughed out his delight in the thrust. "Well, I guess that's something so. And them old Egyptian devils, over there, that you say discovered the doctrine of immortality, seemed to think a cat was about as good as a man. What's that," he appealed to Mrs. Durgin, "Jackson said in his last letter about their cat mummies?"

"Well, I guess I'll finish my supper first," said Mrs. Durgin, whose nerves Westover would not otherwise have suspected of faintness. "But Jackson's letters," she continued, loyally, "are about the *best* letters!"

"Know they'd got some of 'em in the papers?" Whitwell asked; and at the surprise that Westover showed he told him how a fellow who was trying to make a paper go over at the Huddle, had heard of

Jackson's letters and teased for some of them, and had printed them as neighborhood news in that side of his paper which he did not buy ready printed in Boston.

Mrs. Durgin studied with modest deprecation the effect of the fact upon Westover, and seemed satisfied with it. "Well, of course, it's interestin' to Jackson's old friends in the country, here. They know he'd look at things, over there, pretty much as they would. Well, I had to lend the letters round, so much, anyway, it was a kind of a relief to have 'em in the paper, where everybody could see 'em, and be done with it. Mr. Whit'ell here, he fixes 'em up so's to leave out the family part, and I guess they're pretty well thought of."

Westover said he had no doubt they were, and he should want to see all the letters they could show him, in print and out of print.

"If Jackson only had Jeff's health and opportunities—" the mother began, with a suppressed passion in her regret.

Frank Whitwell pushed back his chair. "I guess I'll ask to be excused," he said to the head of table.

"There! I a'n't goin' to say any more about that, if that's what you're afraid of, Frank," said Mrs. Durgin. "Well, I presume I do talk a good deal about Jackson when I get goin', and I presume it's natural Cynthy shouldn't want I should talk about Jeff before folks. Frank, a'n't you goin' to wait for that plate of hot biscuit?—if she ever *gits* it here!"

"I guess I don't care for anything more," said

Frank, and he got himself out of the room more in-
articulately than he need, Westover thought.

His father followed his retreat with an eye of humorous intelligence. " I guess Frank don't want to
keep the young ladies waitin' a great while.   There's
a church sociable over 't the Huddle," he explained
to Westover.

" Oh, that's it, is it ? " Mrs. Durgin put in.   " Why
didn't he say so ? "

" Well, the young folks don't any of 'em seem to
want to talk about such things nowadays, and I don't
know as they ever did."   Whitwell took Westover
into his confidence with a wink.

The biscuit that Cynthia brought in were burned a
little on top, and Mrs. Durgin recognized the fact with
the question, " Did you get to studyin', out there ?
Take one, do, Mr. Westover !   You ha'n't made half
a meal !   If I didn't keep round after her, I don't
know what would become of us all.   The young ladies
down at Boston, any of 'em, try to keep up with the
fellows in college ? "

" I suppose they do in the Harvard Annex," said
Westover, simply, in spite of the glance with which
Mrs. Durgin tried to convey a covert meaning.   He
understood it afterwards, but for the present his sin-
gle-mindedness spared the girl.

She remained to clear away the table, when the
rest left it, and Westover followed Mrs. Durgin into
the parlor, where she indemnified herself for refrain-
ing from any explicit allusion to Jeff before Cynthia.
" The boy," she explained, when she had made him

ransack his memory for every scrap of fact concerning her son, "don't hardly ever write to me, and I guess he don't give Cynthy very *much* news. I presume he's workin' harder than ever this year. And I'm glad he's goin' about a little, from what you say. I guess he's got to feelin' a little better. It did worry me for him to feel so what you may call meechin' about folks. You see anything that made you think he wa'n't appreciated?"

After Westover got back into his own room, some one knocked at his door, and he found Whitwell outside. He scarcely asked him to come in, but Whitwell scarcely needed the invitation. "Got everything you want? I told Cynthy I'd come up and see after you; Frank won't be back in time." He sat down and put his feet on top of the stove, and struck the heels of his boots on its edge, from the habit of knocking the caked snow off them in that way on stove-tops. He did not wait to find out that there was no responsive sizzling before he asked, with a long nasal sigh, "Well, how is Jeff gettin' along?"

He looked across at Westover, who had provisionally seated himself on his bed.

"Why, in the old way." Whitwell kept his eye on him, and he added, "I suppose we don't any of us change; we develop."

Whitwell smiled with pleasure in the loosely philosophic suggestion. "You mean that he's the same kind of a man that he was a boy? Well, I guess that's so. The question is, what kind of a boy was he? I've been mullin' over that consid'able since

"'GOT EVERYTHING YOU WANT?'"

Cynthy and him fixed it up together. Of course, I
know it's their business, and all that; but I presume
I've got a right to spec'late about it?"

He referred the point to Westover, who knew an
inner earnestness in it, in spite of Whitwell's habit of
outside jocosity. "Every right in the world, I should
say, Mr. Whitwell," he answered, seriously.

"Well, I'm glad you feel that way," said Whitwell,
with a little apparent surprise. "I don't want to
meddle, any; but I know what Cynthy is—I no need
to brag her up—and I don't feel so over and above
certain 't I know what *he* is. He's a good deal of a
mixture, if you want to know how he strikes me. I
don't mean I don't like him; I do; the fellow's got a
way with him that makes me kind of like him when
I *see* him. He's good-natured and clever; and he's
willin' to take any amount of trouble for you; but you
can't tell where to have him." Westover denied the
appeal for explicit assent in Whitwell's eye, and he
went on: "If I'd done that fellow a good turn, in
spite of him, or if I'd held him up to something that
he allowed was right, and consented to, I should want
to keep a sharp lookout that he didn't play me some
ugly trick for it. He's a comical devil," Whitwell
ended, rather inadequately. "How d's it look to
you? Seen anything lately that seemed to tally with
my idee?"

"No, no; I can't say that I have," said Westover,
reluctantly. He wished to be franker than he now
meant to be, but he consulted a scruple that he did
not wholly respect; a mere convention it seemed to

him, presently. He said: "I've always felt that charm in him, too, and I've seen the other traits, though not so clearly as you seem to have done. He has a powerful will, yes—"

He stopped, and Whitwell asked, "Been up to any deviltry lately?"

"I can't say he has. Nothing that I can call intentional."

"No," said Whitwell. "What's he done, though?"

"Really, Mr. Whitwell, I don't know that you have any right to expect me to talk him over, when I'm here as his mother's guest—his own guest—"

"No. *I* ha'n't," said Whitwell. "What about the father of the girl he's goin' to marry?"

Westover could not deny the force of this. "You'd be anxious if I didn't tell you what I had in mind, I dare say, more than if I did." He told him of Jeff's behavior with Alan Lynde, and of his talk with him about it. "And I think he was honest. It was something that happened, that wasn't meant."

Whitwell did not assent directly, somewhat to Westover's surprise. He asked, "Fellow ever done anything to Jeff?"

"Not that I know of. I don't know that they ever met before."

Whitwell kicked his heels on the edge of the stove again. "Then it might been an accident," he said, dryly.

Westover had to break the silence that followed, and he found himself defending Jeff, though somehow not for Jeff's sake. He urged that if he had the

strong will they both recognized in him, he would
never commit the errors of a weak man, which were
usually the basest.

"How do you know that a strong-willed man a'n't a
weak one?" Whitwell astonished him by asking.
" A'n't what we call a strong will just a kind of a bull-
dog clinch that the dog himself can't unloose? I take
it a man that has a *good* will is a strong man. If Jeff
done a right thing against his will, he wouldn't rest
easy till he'd showed that he wa'n't obliged to, by
some mischief worse 'n what he was kept out of. I
tell you, Mr. Westover, if I'd made that fellow toe
the mark anyway, I'd be afraid of him." Whitwell
looked at Westover with eyes of significance, if not
of confidence. Then he rose with a prolonged
" M-wel-l-l! We're all born, but we a'n't all buried.
This world is a queer place. But I guess Jeff 'll come
out right in the end."

Westover said, " I'm sure he will!" and he shook
hands warmly with the father of the girl Jeff was going to marry.

Whitwell came back, after he had got some paces
away, and said, "Of course, this is between you and
me, Mr. Westover."

" Of course!"

" I don't mean Mis' Durgin. I shouldn't care what
she thought of my talkin' him over with you. I don't
know," he continued, putting up his hand against the
door-frame, to give himself the comfort of its support
while he talked, " as you understood what she meant
by the young ladies at Boston keepin' up with the

fellows in college.   Well, that's what Cynthy's doin'
with Jeff, right along; and if he ever works off them
conditions of his, and gits his degree, it'll be because
she helped him to.   I tell you, there's more than one
kind of telepathy in this world, Mr. Westover. That's
all."

XXXIX.

WESTOVER understood from Whitwell's after-
thought that it was Cynthia he was anxious to keep
ignorant of his misgiving, if they were so much as
misgivings. But the importance of this fact could
not stay him against the tide of sleep which was bear-
ing him down. When his head touched the pillow it
swept over him, and he rose from it in the morning
with a gayety of heart which he knew to be returning
health. He jumped out of bed, and stuffed some
shavings into his stove from the wood-box beside it,
and laid some logs on them; he slid the damper open,
and then lay down again, listening to the fire that
showed its red teeth through the slats and roared and
laughed to the day which sparkled on the white world
without. When he got out of bed a second time, he
found the room so hot that he had to pull down his
window-sash, and he dressed in a temperature of
twenty degrees below zero without knowing that the
dry air was more than fresh. Mrs. Durgin called to
him through the open door of her parlor, as he entered
the dining-room : " Cynthy will give you your breakfast, Mr. Westover. We're all done long ago, and I'm

busy in here," and the girl appeared with the coffee-
pot and the dishes she had been keeping hot for him
at the kitchen stove. She seemed to be going to leave
him when she had put them down before him, but
she faltered, and then she asked, " Do you want I
should pour your coffee for you ? "

" Oh, yes ! Do ! " he begged, and she sat down
across the table from him. " I'm ashamed to make
this trouble for you," he added. " I didn't know it
was so late."

" Oh, we have the whole day fur our work," she
answered, tolerantly.

He laughed, and said : " How strange that seems !
I suppose I shall get used to it. But in town we seem
never to have a whole day for a day's work ; we always
have to do part of it at night, or the next morning.
Do you ever have a day here that's too large a size
for its work ? "

" You can nearly always find something to do about
a house," she returned, evasively. " But the time
doesn't go the way it does in the summer."

" Oh, I know how the country is in the winter," he
said. " I was brought up in the country."

" I didn't know that," she said, and she gave him
a stare of surprise before her eyes fell.

" Yes. Out in Wisconsin. My people were emi-
grants, and I lived in the woods, there, till I began to
paint my way out. I began pretty early, but I was
in the woods till I was sixteen."

" I didn't know that," she repeated. " I always
thought that you were—"

"Summer folks, like the rest? No, I'm all-the-
year-round folks originally. But I haven't been in
the country in the winter since I was a boy, and it's
all been coming back to me, here, like some one else's
experience."

She did not say anything, but the interest in her
eyes, which she could not keep from his face now,
prompted him to go on.

"You can make a beginning in the West easier
than you can in the East, and some people who came
to our lumber camp discovered me, and gave me a
chance to begin. I went to Milwaukee first, and they
made me think I was somebody. Then I came on to
New York, and they made me think I was nobody. I
had to go to Europe to find out which I was; but after
I had been there long enough I didn't care to know.
What I was trying to do was the important thing to
me; not the fellow who was trying to do it."

"Yes," she said, with intelligence.

"I met some Boston people in Italy, and I thought
I should like to live where that kind of people lived.
That's the way I came to be in Boston. It all seems
very simple now, but I used to think it might look
romantic from the outside. I've had a happy life;
and I'm glad it began in the country. I shouldn't
care if it ended there. I don't know why I've both-
ered you with my autobiography, though. Perhaps
because I thought you knew it already."

She looked as if she would have said something fitting if she could have ruled herself to it; but she said
nothing at all. Her failure seemed to abash her, and

she could only ask him if he would not have some more coffee, and then excuse herself, and leave him to finish his breakfast alone.

That day he tried for his picture from several points out-of-doors before he found that his own window gave him the best. With the window open, and the stove warm at his back, he worked there in great comfort nearly every afternoon. The snows kept off, and the clear sunsets burned behind the summit day after day. He painted frankly and faithfully, and made a picture which, he said to himself, no one would believe in, with that warm color tender upon the frozen hills. The soft suffusion of the winter scene was improbable to him when he had it in nature before his eyes; when he looked at it as he got it on his canvas it was simply impossible.

In the forenoons he had nothing to do, for he worked at his picture only when the conditions renewed themselves with the sinking sun. He tried to be in the open air, and get the good of it; but his strength for walking had failed him, and he kept mostly to the paths broken around the house. He went a good deal to the barn with Whitwell and Jombateeste to look after the cattle and the horses, whose subdued stamping and champing gave him a sort of animal pleasure. The blended odors of the hay-mows and of the creatures' breaths came to him with the faint warmth which their bodies diffused through the cold obscurity.

When the wide doors were rolled back, and the full day was let in, he liked the appeal of their startled eyes, and the calls they made to one another from their stalls, while the men spoke back to them in terms which they seemed to have in common with them, and with the poultry that flew down from the barn lofts to the barn floor and out into the brilliant day, with loud clamor and affected alarm.

In these simple experiences he could not imagine the summer life of the place. It was nowhere more extinct than in the hollow verandas, where the rocking-chairs swung in July and August, and where Westover's steps in his long tramps up and down woke no echo of the absent feet. In-doors he kept to the few stove-heated rooms where he dwelt with the family, and sent only now and then a vague conjecture into the hotel built round the old farm-house. He meant, before he left, to ask Mrs. Durgin to let him go through the hotel, but he put it off from day to day, with a physical shrinking from its cold and solitude.

The days went by in the swiftness of monotony. His excursions to the barn, his walks on the verandas, his work on his picture, filled up the few hours of the light, and when the dark came he contentedly joined the little group in Mrs. Durgin's parlor. He had brought two or three books with him, and sometimes he read from one of them; or he talked with Whitwell on some of the questions of life and death that engaged his speculative mind. Jombateeste preferred the kitchen for the naps he took after supper before his early bedtime. Frank Whitwell sat with his books there, where Westover sometimes saw his sister helping him at his studies. He was loyally faithful and obedient to her in all things. He helped her with the dishes, and was not ashamed to be seen at this work; she had charge of his goings and comings in society; he submitted to her taste in his dress, and accepted her counsel on many points which he referred to her, and discussed with her in low-spoken conferences. He seemed a formal, serious boy, shy like his sister; his father let fall some hints of a religious cast of mind in him. He had an ambition beyond the hotel; he wished to study for the ministry; and it was not alone the chance of going home with the girls that made him constant at the evening meetings. "*I* don't know where he gits it," said his father with a shake of the head that suggested doubt of the wisdom of the son's preference of theology to planchette.

Cynthia had the same care of her father as of her brother; she kept him neat, and held him up from lapsing into the slovenliness to which he would have tended if she had not, as Westover suspected, made constant appeals to him for the respect due their guest. Mrs. Durgin, for her part, left everything to Cynthia, with a contented acceptance of her future rule and an abiding trust in her sense and strength, which included the details of the light work that employed her rather luxurious leisure. Jombateeste himself came to Cynthia with his mending, and her needle kept him tight and firm against the winter which it amused Westover to realize was the Canuck's native element, insomuch that there was now something incongruous in the notion of Jombateeste and any other season.

The girl's motherly care of all the household did not

leave Westover out. Buttons appeared on garments
long used to shifty contrivances for getting on without them; button-holes were restored to their proper
limits; his overcoat pockets were searched for gloves,
and the gloves put back with their finger-tips drawn
close as the petals of a flower which had decided to
shut and be a bud again.

He wondered how he could thank her for his share
of the blessing that her passion for motherly care was
to all the house. It was pathetic, and he used sometime to forecast her self-devotion with a tender indignation, which included a due sense of his own present
demerit. He was not reconciled to the sacrifice because it seemed the happiness, or at least the will, of
the nature which made it. All the same it seemed a
waste, in its relation to the man she was to marry.

Mrs. Durgin and Cynthia sat by the lamp and sewed
at night, or listened to the talk of the men. If Westover read aloud, they whispered together from time
to time about some matter remote from it, as women
always do where there is reading. It was quiet, but
it was not dull for Westover, who found himself in no
hurry to get back to town.

Sometimes he thought of the town with repulsion;
its unrest, its vacuous, troubled life haunted him like
a memory of sickness; but he supposed that when he
should be quite well again all that would change, and
be as it was before. He interested himself, with the
sort of shrewd ignorance of it that Cynthia showed in
the questions she asked about it now and then when
they chanced to be left alone together. He fancied

that she was trying to form some intelligible image of Jeff's environment there, and was piecing together from his talk of it the impressions she had got from summer folks. He did his best to help her, and to construct for her a veritable likeness of the world as far as he knew it.

A time came when he spoke frankly of Jeff in something they were saying, and she showed no such shrinking as he had expected she would; he reflected that she might have made stricter conditions with Mrs. Durgin than she expected to keep herself in mentioning him. This might well have been necessary with the mother's pride in her son which knew no stop when it once began to indulge itself. What struck Westover more than the girl's self-possession when they talked of Jeff was a certain austerity in her with regard to him. She seemed to hold herself tense against any praise of him, as if she should fail him somehow if she relaxed at all in his favor.

This, at least, was the rather mystifying impression which Westover got from her evident wish to criticise and understand exactly all that he reported, rather than to flatter herself from it. Whatever her motive was, he was aware that through it all she permitted herself a closer and fuller trust of himself. At times it was almost too implicit; he would have liked to deserve it better by laying open all that had been in his heart against Jeff. But he forbore, of course, and he took refuge, as well as he could, in the respect by which she held herself at a reverent distance from him when he could not wholly respect himself.

XL.

ONE morning Westover got leave from Mrs. Durgin to help Cynthia open the dim rooms and cold corridors at the hotel to the sun and air. She promised him he should take his death, but he said he would wrap up warm, and when he came to join the girl in his overcoat and fur cap, he found Cynthia equipped with a woollen cloud tied around her head, and a little shawl pinned across her breast.

" Is that all? " he reproached her. " I ought to have put on a single wreath of artificial flowers and some sort of a blazer for this expedition. Don't you think so, Mrs. Durgin? "

" I believe women can stand about twice as much cold as you can, the best of you," she answered, grimly.

" Then I must try to keep myself as warm as I can with work," he said. " You must let me do all the rough work of airing out, won't you, Cynthia? "

" There isn't any rough work about it," she answered, in a sort of motherly toleration of his mood, without losing anything of her filial reverence.

She took care of him, he perceived, as she took care of her brother and her father, but with a delicate respect for his superiority, which was no longer shyness.

They began with the office and the parlor, where they flung up the windows, and opened the doors, and then they opened the dining-room, where the tables stood in long rows, with the chairs piled on them legs upwards. Cynthia went about with many sighs for the dust on everything, though to Westover's eyes it all seemed frigidly clean. "If it goes on as it has for the past two years," she said, "we shall have to add on a new dining-room. I don't know as I like to have it get so large!"

"I never wanted it to go beyond the original farmhouse," said Westover. "I've been jealous of every boarder but the first. I should have liked to keep it for myself, and let the world know Lion's Head from my pictures."

"I guess Mrs. Durgin thinks it was your picture that began to send people here."

"And do you blame me, too? What if the thing I'm doing now should make it a winter resort? Nothing could save you, then, but a fire. I believe that's Jeff's ambition. Only he would want to put another hotel in place of this; something that would be more popular. Then the ruin I began would be complete, and I shouldn't come any more; I couldn't bear the sight."

"I guess Mrs. Durgin wouldn't think it was Lion's Head if you stopped coming," said Cynthia.

"But you would know better than that," said

Westover; and then he was sorry he had said it, for it seemed to ask something of different quality from her honest wish to make him know their regard for him.

She did not answer, but went down a long corridor to which they had mounted, to raise the window at the end, while he raised another at the opposite extremity. When they met at the stairway again to climb to the story above, he said, " I am always ashamed when I try to make a person of sense say anything silly," and she flushed, still without answering, as if she understood him, and his meaning pleased her. " But fortunately a person of sense is usually equal to the temptation. One ought to be serious when he tries it with a person of the other sort; but I don't know that one is ! "

" Do you feel any draught between these windows ? " asked Cynthia, abruptly. " I don't want you should take cold."

" Oh, I'm all right," said Westover.

She went into the rooms on one side of the corridor, and put up their windows, and flung the blinds back. He did the same on the other side. He got a peculiar effect of desolation from the mattresses pulled down over the foot of the bedsteads, and the dismantled interiors reflected in the mirrors of the dressing-cases; and he was going to speak of it when he rejoined Cynthia at the stairway leading to the third story, when she said, " Those were Mrs. Vostrand's rooms I came out of the last." She nodded her head over her shoulder towards the floor they were leaving.

" Were they indeed!   And do you remember people's rooms so long? "

" Yes; I always think of rooms by the name of
people that have them, if they're any way peculiar."

He thought this bit of uncandor charming, and
accepted it as if it were the whole truth.   " And Mrs.
Vostrand was certainly peculiar.   Tell me, Cynthia,
what did you think of her? "

" She was only here a little while."

" But you wouldn't have come to think of her
rooms by her name if she hadn't made a strong impression on you! "   She did not answer, and he said,
" I see you didn't like her! "

The girl would not speak, and Mr. Westover went
on : " She used to be very good to me, and I think she
used to be better to herself than she is now."   He
knew that Jeff must have told Cynthia of his affair
with Genevieve Vostrand, and he kept himself from
speaking of her by a resolution he thought creditable,
as he mounted the stairs to the upper story in the
silence to which Cynthia left his last remark.   At the
top she made a little pause in the obscurer light of the
close-shuttered corridor, while she said, " I liked her
daughter the best."

" Yes? " he returned.   " I never felt very well acquainted with her, I believe.   One couldn't get far
with her.   Though, for the matter of that, one didn't
get far with Mrs. Vostrand herself.   Did you think
Genevieve was much influenced by her mother? "

" She didn't seem a strong character."

" No, that was it.   She was what her mother wished

her to be. I've often wondered how much she was interested in the marriage she made."

Cynthia let a rustic silence ensue, and Westover shrank again from the inquisition he longed to make.

It was not Genevieve Vostrand's marriage which really concerned him, but Cynthia's engagement, and it was her mind that he would have liked to look into. It might well be supposed that she regarded it in a perfect matter-of-fact way, and with no ambition beyond it. She was a country girl, acquainted from childhood with facts of life which town-bred girls would not have known without a blunting of the sensibilities, and why should she be different from other country girls? She might be as good and as fine.as he saw her, and yet be insensible to the spiritual toughness of Jeff, because of her love for him. Her very goodness might make his badness unimaginable to her, and if her refinement were from the conscience merely, and not from the tastes and experiences, too, there was not so much to dread for her in her marriage with such a man. Still, he would have liked, if he could, to tell her what he had told her father of Durgin's behavior with Lynde, and let her bring the test of her self-devotion to the case with a clear understanding. He had sometimes been afraid that Whitwell might not be able to keep it to himself ; but now he wished that the philosopher had not been so discreet. He had all this so absorbingly in mind that he started presently with the fear that she had said something and he had not answered, but when he asked her he found that she had not spoken. They

were standing at an open window looking out upon
Lion's Head, when he said: "I don't know how I
shall show my gratitude to Mrs. Durgin and you for
thinking of having me up here. I've done a picture
of Lion's Head that might be ever so much worse;
but I shouldn't have dreamed of getting at it if it
hadn't been for you, though I've so often dreamed of
doing it. Now I shall go home richer in every sort
of way—thanks to you."

She answered, simply, "You needn't thank anybody; but it was Jeff who thought of it; we were
ready enough to ask you."

"That was very good of him," said Westover, whom
her words confirmed in a suspicion he had had all
along. But what did it matter that Jeff had suggested their asking him, and then attributed the notion
to them? It was not so malign for him to use that
means of ingratiating himself with Westover, and of
making him forget his behavior with Lynde, and it
was not unnatural. It was very characteristic; at the
worst it merely proved that Jeff was more ashamed of
what he had done than he would allow, and that was
to his credit.

He heard Cynthia asking, "Mr. Westover, have
you ever been at Class Day? He wants us to come."

"Class Day? Oh, Class Day!" He took a little
time to gather himself together. "Yes, I've been at
a good many. If you care to see something pretty,
it's the prettiest thing in the world. The students'
sisters and mothers come from everywhere; and
there's fashion and feasting and flirting, from ten in

the morning till ten at night. I'm not sure there's so much happiness; but I can't tell. The young people know about that. I fancy there's a good deal of defeat and disappointment in it all. But if you like beautiful dresses, and music and dancing, and a great flutter of gayety, you can get more of it at Class Day than you can in any other way. The good time depends a great deal upon the acquaintance a student has, and whether he is popular in college." Westover found this road a little impassable, and he faltered.

Cynthia did not apparently notice his hesitation. "Do you think Mrs. Durgin would like it?"

"Mrs. Durgin?" Westover found that he had been leaving her out of the account, and had been thinking only of Cynthia's pleasure or pain. "Well, I don't suppose—it would be rather fatiguing— Did Jeff want her to come too?"

"He said so."

"That's very nice of him. If he could devote himself to her; but— And would she like to go?"

"To please him, she would." Westover was silent, and the girl surprised him by the appeal she suddenly made to him. "Mr. Westover, do you believe it would be very well for either of us to go? I think it would be better for us to leave all that part of his life alone. It's no use in pretending that we're like the kind of people he knows, or that we know their ways, and I don't believe—"

Westover felt his heart rise in indignant sympathy. "There isn't any one he knows to compare with you!" he said, and in this he was thinking mainly of Bessie

Lynde. "You're worth a thousand— If I were—if he's half a man he would be proud— I beg your pardon! I don't mean—but you understand—"

Cynthia put her head far out of the window, and looked along the steep roof before them. "There is a blind off one of the windows. I heard it clapping in the wind the other night. I must go and see the number of the room." She drew her head in quickly and ran away without letting him see her face.

He followed hèr. "Let me help you put it on again!"

"No, no!" she called back. "Frank will do that, or Jombateeste, when they come to shut up the house."

XLI.

Westover did not meet Durgin for several days after his return from Lion's Head. He brought messages for him from his mother and from Whitwell, and he waited for him to come and get them so long that he had to blame himself for not sending them to him. When Jeff appeared, at the end of a week, Westover had a certain embarrassment in meeting him, and the effort to overcome this carried him beyond his sincerity. He was aware of feigning the cordiality he showed, and of having less real liking for him than ever before. He suggested that he must be busier every day, now, with his college work, and he resented the air of social prosperity which Jeff put on in saying, Yes, there was that, and then he had some engagements which kept him from coming in sooner.

He did not say what the engagements were, and they did not recur to the things they had last spoken of. Westover could not do so without Jeff's leading, and he was rather glad that he gave none. He stayed only a little time, which was spent mostly in a show of interest on both sides, and the hollow hilarities which people use to mask their indifference to one another's being and doing. Jeff declared that he had

never seen Westover looking so well, and said he
must go up to Lion's Head again; it had done him
good. As for his picture, it was a corker; it made
him feel as if he were there! He asked about all the
folks, and received Westover's replies with vague
laughter, and an absence in his bold eye, which made
the painter wonder what his mind was on, without the
wish to find out. He was glad to have him go, though
he pressed him to drop in soon again, and said they
would take in a play together.

Jeff said he would like to do that, and he asked at
the door whether Westover was going to the tea at
Mrs. Bellingham's. He said he had to look in there,
before he went out to Cambridge; and left Westover
in mute amaze at the length he had apparently gone in
a road that had once seemed no thoroughfare for him.
Jeff's social acceptance, even after the Enderby ball,
which was now some six or seven weeks past, had been
slow; but of late, for no reason that he or any one else
could have given, it had gained a sudden precipitance;
and people who wondered why they met him at other
houses began to ask him to their own.

He did not care to go to their houses, and he went
at first in the hope of seeing Bessie Lynde again. But
this did not happen for some time, and it was a mid-
Lenten tea that brought them together. As soon as he
caught sight of her he went up to her and began to
talk as if they had been in the habit of meeting constantly. She could not control a little start at his approach, and he frankly recognized it.

" What's the matter ? "

" HE CONTINUED TO GO WITH HER "

" Oh—the window—"

" It isn't open," he said, trying it. "Do you want to try it yourself ? "

" I think I can trust you," she answered, but she sank a little into the shelter of the curtains, not to be seen talking with him, perhaps, or not to be interrupted—she did not analyze her motive closely.

He remained talking to her until she went away, and then he contrived to go with her. She did not try to escape him after that; each time they met she had the pleasure of realizing that there had never been any danger of what never happened. But beyond this she could perhaps have given no better reason for her willingness to meet him again and again than the bewildered witnesses of the fact. In her set people not only never married outside of it, but they never flirted outside of it. For one of themselves, even for a girl like Bessie, whom they had not quite known from childhood, to be apparently amusing herself with a man like that, so wholly alien in origin, in tradition, was something unheard of; and it began to look as if Bessie Lynde was more than amused. It seemed to Mary Enderby that wherever she went she saw that man talking to Bessie. She could have believed that it was by some evil art that he always contrived to reach Bessie's side, if anything could have been less like any kind of art than the bold push he made for her as soon as he saw her in a room. But sometimes Miss Enderby feared that it was Bessie who used such *finesse* as there was, and always put herself where he could see her. She waited

with trembling for her to give the affair sanction by
making her aunt ask him to something at her house.
On the other hand, she could not help feeling that
Bessie's flirtation was all the more deplorable for the
want of some such legitimation.

She did not even know certainly whether Jeff ever
called upon Bessie at her aunt's house, till one day
the man let him out at the same time he let her in.

"Oh, come up, Molly!" Bessie sang out from the
floor above, and met her half-way down the stairs,
where she kissed her and led her embraced into the
library.

"You don't like my jay, do you, dear?" she asked
promptly.

Mary Enderby turned her face, the mirror of conscience upon her, and asked, "*Is* he your jay?"

"Well, no; not just in that sense, Molly. But suppose he was?"

"Then I should have nothing to say."

"And suppose he wasn't?"

Still Mary Enderby found herself with nothing of
all she had a thousand times thought she should say
to Bessie if she had ever the slightest chance. It always seemed so easy, till now, to take Bessie in her
arms, and appeal to her good sense, her self-respect,
her regard for her family and friends; and now it
seemed so impossible.

She heard herself answering very stiffly: "Perhaps
I'd better apologize for what I've said already. You
must think I was very unjust the last time we men-
tioned him."

"Not at all!" cried Bessie, with a laugh that sounded very mocking and very unworthy to her friend. "He's all that you said, and worse. But he's more than you said, and better."

"I don't understand," said Mary, coldly.

"He's very interesting ; he's original ; he's different !"

"Oh, every one says that."

"And he doesn't flatter me, or pretend to think much of me. If he did, I couldn't bear him. You know how I am, Molly. He keeps me interested, don't you understand, and prowling about in the great unknown where he has his weird being."

Bessie put her hand to her mouth, and laughed at Mary Enderby with her slanted eyes ; a sort of Parisian version of a Chinese motive in eyes.

"I suppose," her friend said, sadly, "You won't tell me more than you wish."

"I won't tell you more than I know—though I'd like to," said Bessie. She gave Mary a sudden hug. "You dear ! There isn't anything of it, if that's what you mean."

"But isn't there danger that there will be, Bessie?" her friend entreated.

"Danger? I shouldn't call it *danger*, exactly !"

"But if you don't *respect* him, Bessie—"

"Why, how *can* I? He doesn't respect *me!*"

"I know you're teasing, now, said Mary Enderby, getting up, "and you're quite right. I have no business to—"

Bessie pulled her down upon the seat again. "Yes,

you have! Don't I tell you, over and over? He
doesn't respect me, because I don't know how to make
him, and he wouldn't like it, if I did. But now, I'll
try to make you understand. I don't believe I care
for him the least; but mind, I'm not certain, for I've
never cared for any one, and I don't know what it's
like. You know I'm not sentimental; I think sentiment's funny; and I'm not dignified—"

"You're divine," murmured Mary Enderby, with
reproachful adoration.

"Yes, but you see how my divinity could be improved," said Bessie with a wild laugh. "I'm not
sentimental, but I'm emotional, and he gives me emotions. He's a riddle, and I'm all the time guessing at
him. You get the answer to the kind of men we know
easily; and it's very nice, but it doesn't amuse you so
much as trying. Now, Mr. Durgin—what a name! I
can see it makes you creep—is no more like one of us
than a—bear is; and his attitude towards us is that
of a bear who's gone so much with human beings that
he thinks he's a human being. He's delightful, that
way. And, do you know, he's intellectual! He actually brings me books, and wants to read passages to
me out of them! He has brought me the plans of
the new hotel he's going to build. It's to be very æs-
thetic, and it's going to be called The Lion's Head
Inn. There's to be a little theatre, for amateur dra-
matics, which I could conduct, and for all sorts of
professional amusements. If you should ever come,
Molly, I'm sure we shall do our best to make you
comfortable."

Mary Enderby would not let Bessie laugh upon her shoulder after she said this. "Bessie Lynde," she said, severely, "if you have no regard for yourself, you ought to have some regard for him. You may say you are not encouraging him, and you may believe it—"

"Oh, I shouldn't say it if I didn't *believe* it," Bessie broke in with a mock air of seriousness.

"I must be going," said Mary, stiffly, and this time she succeeded in getting to her feet.

Bessie laid hold of her again. "You think you've been trifled with, don't you, dear?"

"No—"

"Yes, you do! Don't *you* try to be slippery, Molly. The plain pikestaff is *your* style, morally speaking—if any one knows what a pikestaff *is*. Well, now, listen! You're anxious about me."

"You know how I feel, Bessie," said Mary Enderby, looking her in the eyes.

"Yes, I do," said Bessie. "The trouble is, I don't know how *I* feel. But if I ever do, Molly, I'll tell you! Is that fair?"

"Yes—"

"I'll give you ample warning. At the least little consciousness in the region of the pericardium, off will go a note by a district messenger, and when you come I'll do whatever you say. There!"

"Oh, Bessie!" cried her friend, and she threw her arms round her, "you always *were* the most fascinating creature in the world!"

"Yes," said Bessie, "that's what I try to have *him* think."

XLII.

Towards the end of April most people who had places at the Shore were mostly in them, but they came up to town on frequent errands, and had one effect of evanescence with people who still remained in their Boston houses provisionally, and seemed more than half absent. The Enderbys had been at the Shore for a fortnight, and the Lyndes were going to be a fortnight longer in Boston, yet, as Bessie made her friend observe, when Mary ran in for lunch, or stopped for a moment on her way to the train, every few days, they were both of the same transitory quality.

" It might as well be I as you," Bessie said one day, " if we only think so. It's all very weird, dear, and I'm not sure but it *is* you who sit day after day at my lonely casement and watch the sparrows examining the fuzzy buds of the Jap ivy to see just how soon they can hope to build in the vines. Do you object to the ivy buds looking so very much like snipped woollen rags? If you do, I'm sure it's you, here in my place, for when I come up to town in your personality, it sets my teeth on edge. In fact, that's

the worst thing about Boston now—the fuzzy ivy
buds; there's so much ivy! When you can forget
the buds, there are a great many things to make you
happy. I feel quite as if we were spending the summer in town; and I feel very adventurous and very
virtuous, like some sort of self-righteous bohemian.
You don't know how I look down on people who have
gone out of town. I consider them very selfish and
heartless; I don't know why, exactly. But when we
have a good marrow-freezing northeasterly storm, and
the newspapers come out with their ironical congrat-
ulations to the tax-dodgers at the Shore, I feel that
Providence is on my side, and I'm getting my reward,
even in *this* world." Bessie suddenly laughed. "I
see by your expression of fixed inattention, Molly,
that you're thinking of Mr. Durgin!"

Mary gave a start of protest, but she was too honest to deny the fact outright, and Bessie ran on:

"No, we *don't* sit on a bench in the Common, or
even in the Garden, or on the walk in Commonwealth
Avenue. If we come to it later, as the season advances, I shall make him stay quite at the other end
of the bench, and not put his hand along the top.
You needn't be afraid, Molly; all the proprieties shall
be religiously observed. Perhaps I shall ask Aunt
Louisa to let us sit out on her front steps, when the
evenings get warmer; but I assure you it's much more
comfortable in-doors yet, even in town, though you'll
hardly believe it at the Shore. Shall you come up to
Class Day?"

"Oh, I don't know," Mary began, with a sigh of

the baffled hope and the inextinguishable expectation which the mention of Class Day stirs in the heart of every Boston girl past twenty.

"Yes!" said Bessie, with a sigh burlesqued from Mary's. "That is what we all say, and it is certainly the most maddening of human festivals. I suppose, if we were quite left to ourselves, we shouldn't go; but we seem never to be, quite. After every Class Day I say to myself that nothing on earth could induce me to go to another; but when it comes round again, I find myself grasping at any straw of a pretext. I'm pretending now that I've a tender obligation to go because it's *his* Class Day."

"Bessie!" cried Mary Enderby. "You don't mean it!"

"Not if I *say* it, Mary dear. What did I promise you about the pericardiac symptoms? But I feel—I feel that if *he* asks me I must go. Shouldn't you like to go and see a *jay* Class Day—be part of it? Think of going once to the Pi Ute spread—or whatever it is! And dancing in their tent! And being left out of the Gym, and Beck! Yes, I ought to go, so that it can be brought home to me, and I can have a realizing sense of what I am doing, and be stayed in my mad career."

"Perhaps," Mary Enderby suggested colorlessly, "he will be devoted to his own people." She had a cold fascination in the picture Bessie's words had conjured up, and she was saying this less to Bessie than to herself.

"And I should meet them—his mothers and sisters!" Bessie dramatized an excess of anguish. "Oh, Mary, that is the very thorn I have been trying *not* to press my heart against; and does *your* hand commend it to my embrace? His folks! Yes, they would be *folks ;* and *what* folks! I think I am getting a realizing sense. Wait! Don't speak—don't move, Molly!" Bessie dropped her chin into her hand, and stared straight forward, gripping Mary Enderby's hand.

Mary withdrew it. "I shall have to go, Bessie," she said. "How is your aunt?"

"Must you? Then I shall always say that it was your fault that I couldn't get a realizing sense—that you prevented me, just when I was about to see myself as others see me—as you see me. She's very well!" Bessie sighed in earnest, and her friend gave her hand a little pressure of true sympathy. "But of course it's rather dull here, now."

"I hate to have you staying on. Couldn't you come down to us for a week?"

"No. We both think it's best to be here when Alan gets back. We want him to go down with us." Bessie had seldom spoken openly with Mary Enderby about her brother; but that was rather from Mary's shrinking than her own; she knew that everybody understood his case. She went so far now as to say: "He's ever so much better than he has been. We have such hopes of him, if he can keep well, when he gets back this time."

"Oh, I know he *will*," said Mary. fervently. "I'm *sure* of it. Couldn't *we* do something for you, Bessie?"

"No, there isn't anything. But—thank you. I know you always think of me, and that's worlds. When are you coming up again?"

"I don't know.   Next week, some time."

"Come in and see me—and Alan, if he should be at home.   He likes you, and he will be so glad."

Mary kissed Bessie for consent.   "You know how much I admire Alan.   He could be anything."

"Yes, he could.   *If* he could!"

Bessie seldom put so much earnest in anything, and Mary loved (as she would have said) the sad sincerity, the honest hopelessness of her tone.   "We must help him.   I know we can."

"We must try.   But people who could—*if* they could—"   Bessie stopped.

Her friend divined that she was no longer speaking wholly of her brother, but she said: "There isn't any if about it; and there are no ifs about anything if we only think so.   It's a sin not to think so."

The mixture of severity and of optimism in the nature of her friend had often amused Bessie, and it did not escape her tacit notice in even so serious a moment as this.   Her theory was that she was shocked to recognize it now, because of its relation to her brother, but her theories did not always agree with the facts.

That evening, however, she was truly surprised when, after a rather belated ring at the door, the card of Mr. Thomas Jefferson Durgin came up to her from the reception-room.   Her aunt had gone to bed, and she had a luxurious moment in which she reaped all

the reward of self-denial by supposing herself to have
foregone the pleasure of seeing him, and sending
down word that she was not at home.   She did not
wish, indeed, to see him, but she wished to know how
he felt warranted in calling in the evening, and it was
this unworthy curiosity which she stifled for that luxurious moment.   The next, with undiminished dignity,
she said, "Ask him to come up, Andrew," and she
waited in the library for him to offer a justification
of the liberty he had taken.

He offered none whatever, but behaved at once as
if he had always had the habit of calling in the evening, or as if it was a general custom which he need
not account for in his own case.   He brought her a
book which they had talked of at their last meeting,
but he made no excuse or pretext of it.

He said it was a beautiful night, and that he had
found it rather warm walking in from Cambridge.
The exercise had moistened his whole rich, red color,
and fine drops of perspiration stood on his clean-shav-
en upper-lip and in the hollow between his under-lip
and his bold chin ; he pushed back the coarse, dark-
yellow hair from his forehead with his handkerchief,
and let his eyes mock her from under his thick, straw-
colored eyebrows.   She knew that he was enjoying
his own impudence, and he was so handsome that she
could not refuse to enjoy it with him.   She asked him
if he would not have a fan, and he allowed her to get
it for him from the mantel.   "Will you have some
tea ? "

"No ; but a glass of water, if you please," he said,

and Bessie rang and sent for some Apollinaris, which Jeff drank a great goblet of when it came. Then he lay back in the deep chair he had taken, with the air of being ready for any little amusing thing she had to say.

"Are you still a pessimist, Mr. Durgin?" she asked, tentatively, with the effect of innocence that he knew meant mischief.

"No," he said. "I'm a reformed optimist."

"What is that?"

"It's a man who can't believe all the good he would like, but likes to believe all the good he can."

Bessie said it over, with burlesque thoughtfulness "There was a girl here to-day," she said, solemnly, "who must have been a reformed pessimist, then, for she said the same thing."

"Oh! Miss Enderby," said Jeff.

Bessie started. "You're preternatural! But what a pity you should be mistaken. How came you to think of her?"

"She doesn't like me, and you always put me on trial after she's been here."

"Am I putting you on trial now? It's your guilty conscience! Why shouldn't Mary Enderby like you?"

"Because I'm not good enough."

"Oh! And what has that to do with people's liking you? If that was a reason, how many friends do you think you would have?"

"I'm not sure that I should have any."

"And doesn't that make you feel badly?"

"Very."   Jeff's confession was a smiling one.

"You don't show it!"

"I don't want to grieve you."

"Oh, I'm not sure *that* would grieve me."

"Well, I thought I wouldn't risk it."

"How considerate of you!"

They had come to a little barrier, up that way, and could go no further.   Jeff said, "I've just been interviewing another reformed pessimist."

"Mr. Westover?"

"You're preternatural, too.   And you're not mistaken, either.   Do you ever go to his studio?"

"No; I haven't been there since he told me it would be of no use to come as a student.   He can be terribly frank."

"Nobody knows that better than I do," said Jeff, with a smile for the notion of Westover's frankness as he had repeatedly experienced it.   "But he means well."

"Oh, that's what they always say.   But *all* the frankness can't be well meant.   Why should uncandor be the only form of malevolence?"

"That's a good idea.   I believe I'll put that up on Westover the next time he's frank."

"And will you tell me what he says?"

"Oh, I don't know about that."   Jeff lay back in his chair at large ease and chuckled.   "I should like to tell you what he's just been saying to me, but I don't believe I can."

"Do!"

"You know he was up at Lion's Head in February,

and got a winter impression of the mountain. Did
you see it?"

"No. Was that what you were talking about?"

"We talked about something a great deal more interesting—the impression he got of me."

"Winter impression?"

"Cold enough. He had come to the conclusion
that I was very selfish and unworthy; that I used
other people for my own advantage, or let them use
themselves; that I was treacherous and vindictive, and
if I didn't betray a man I couldn't be happy till I had
beaten him. He said that if I ever behaved well, it
came after I had been successful one way or the
other."

"How perfectly fascinating!" Bessie rested her
elbow on the corner of the table, and her chin in the
palm of the hand whose thin fingers tapped her red
lips; the light sleeve fell down and showed her pretty,
lean little forearm. "Did it strike you as true, at all?"

"I could see how it might strike him as true."

"Now *you* are candid. But go on! What did he
expect you to do about it?"

"Nothing. He said he didn't suppose I could help
it."

"This is immense," said Bessie. "I hope I'm
taking it all in. How came he to give you this flattering little impression? So hopeful, too! Or, perhaps your frankness doesn't go any farther?"

"Oh, I don't mind saying. He seemed to think it
was a sort of abstract duty he owed to my people."

"Your—folks?" asked Bessie.

" Yes," said Jeff, with a certain dryness. But as her face looked blankly innocent, he must have decided that she meant nothing offensive. He relaxed into a broad smile. It's a queer household up there, in the winter. I wonder what you would think of it."

" You might describe it to me, and perhaps we shall see."

" You couldn't realize it," said Jeff, with a finality that piqued her. He reached out for the bottle of Apollinaris, with somehow the effect of being in another student's room, and poured himself a glass. This would have amused her, nine times out of ten, but the tenth time had come when she chose to resent it.

" I suppose," she said, " you are all very much excited about Class Day at Cambridge."

" That sounds like a remark made to open the way to conversation." Jeff went on to burlesque a reply in the same spirit. " Oh, very much so indeed, Miss Lynde! We are all looking forward to it *so* eagerly. Are you coming?"

She rejected his lead with a slight sigh so skilfully drawn that it deceived him when she said, gravely : " I don't know. It's apt to be a very baffling time at the best. All the men that you like are taken up with their own people, and even the men that you don't like over-value themselves, and think they're doing you a favor if they give you a turn at the Gym or bring you a plate of something."

" Well, they are, aren't they?"

" I suppose, yes, that's what makes me hate it. One doesn't like to have such men do one a favor.

And then, Juniors get younger every year! Even a nice Junior is only a Junior," she concluded, with a sad fall of her mocking voice."

" I don't believe there's a Senior in Harvard that wouldn't forsake his family and come to the rescue if your feelings could be known," said Jeff. He lifted the bottle at his elbow and found it empty, and this seemed to remind him to rise.

"Don't *make* them known, please," said Bessie. " I shouldn't want an ovation." She sat, after he had risen, as if she wished to detain him, but when he came up to take leave she had to put her hand in his. She looked at it there, and so did he; it seemed very little and slim, about one-third the size of his palm, and it seemed to go to nothing in his grasp. "*I* should think," she added, "that the jays wonld have the best time on Class Day. I should like to dance at one of their spreads, and do everything they did. It would be twice the fun, and there would be some nature in it. I should like to see a jay Class Day."

" If you'll come out, I'll show you one," said Jeff, without wincing.

" Oh, will you?" she said, taking away her hand. " That would be delightful. But what would become of your—folks?" She caught a corner of her mouth with her teeth, as if the word had slipped out.

" Do you call them folks?" asked Jeff, quietly.

" I—supposed— Don't you?"

" Not in Boston. I do at Lion's Head."

"Oh! Well—people."

" I don't know as they're coming."

"How delightful! I don't mean that; but if they're not, and if you really *knew* some jays, and could get me a little glimpse of their Class Day—"

"I think I could manage it for you." He spoke as before, but he looked at her with a mockery in his lips and eyes as intelligent as her own, and the latent change in his mood gave her the sense of being in the presence of a vivid emotion. She rose in her excitement; she could see that he admired her, and was enjoying her insolence too, in a way, though in a way that she did not think she quite understood; and she had the wish to make him admire her a little more.

She let a light of laughter come into her eyes, of harmless mischief played to an end. "I don't deserve your kindness, and I won't come. I've been very wicked, don't you think?"

"Not very—for *you*," said Jeff.

"Oh, how *good!*" she broke out. "But be frank now! I've offended you."

"How? I know I'm a jay, and in the country I've got folks."

"Ah, I see you're hurt at my joking, and I'm awfully sorry. I wish there was some way of making you forgive me. But it couldn't be that alone," she went on rather aimlessly as to her words, trusting to his answer for some leading, and willing meanwhile to prolong the situation for the effect in her nerves. It had been a very dull and tedious day, and she was finding much more than she could have expected in the mingled fear and slight which he inspired her with in such singular measure. These feminine subtleties of motive are beyond any but the finest natures in the other sex, and perhaps all that Jeff perceived was the note of insincerity in her words.

"Couldn't be what alone?" he asked.

"What I've said," she ventured, letting her eyes fall; but they were not eyes that fell effectively, and she instantly lifted them again to his.

"You haven't said anything, and if you've thought anything, what have I got to do with that? I think all sorts of things about people—or folks, as you call them—"

"Oh, thank you! Now you *are* forgiving me!"

"I think them about you—"

"Oh, *do* sit down and tell me the kind of things you think about me!" Bessie implored, sinking back into her chair.

"You mightn't like them."

"But if they would do me good?"

"What should I want to do you good for?"

"That's true," sighed Bessie, thoughtfully.

"People—folks—"

"Thank you *so* much!"

"Don't try to do each other good, unless they're cranks like Lancaster, or bores like Mrs. Bevidge—"

"You belong to the analytical school of Seniors! Go on!"

"That's all," said Jeff.

"And you don't think I've tried to do *you* good?"

He laughed. Her comedy was delicious to him. He had never found anybody so amusing; he almost respected her for it.

"If that is your opinion of me, Mr. Durgin," she said, very gravely, "I am sorry. May I remark that I don't see why you come, then?"

"I can tell you," said Jeff, and he advanced upon her where she sat so abruptly that she started and shrank back in her chair. "I come because you've got brains, and you're the only girl that has—here." They were Alan's words, almost his words, and for an instant she thought of her brother, and wondered what he would think of this jay's praising her in his terms. "Because," Jeff went on, "you've got more sense—and nonsense—than all the women here put together. Because it's better than a play to hear you talk—and act; and because you're graceful—and fascinating, and *chic*, and— Good-night, Miss Lynde." He put out his hand, but she did not take it as she rose haughtily. "We've said good-night once. I prefer to say good-by this time. I'm sure you will understand why after this I cannot see you again." She seemed to examine him for the effect of these words upon him before she went on.

"No, I don't understand," he answered, coolly; "but it isn't necessary I should; and I'm quite willing to say good-by, if you prefer. You haven't been so frank with me as I have with you; but that doesn't make any difference; perhaps you never meant to be, or couldn't be, if you meant. Good-by." He bowed and turned towards the door.

She fluttered between him and it. "I wish to know what you accuse me of!"

"I? Nothing."

"You imply that I have been unjust towards you.'

"*Oh*, no!"

"And I can't let you go till you prove it."

"Prove to a woman that— Will you let me pass?"

"No!" She spread her slender arms across the doorway.

"Oh, very well!" Jeff took her hands and put them both in the hold of one of his large, strong hands. Then, with the contact, it came to him, from a varied experience of girls in his rustic past, that this young lady, who was nothing but a girl after all, was playing her comedy with a certain purpose, however little she might know it or own it. He put his other large, strong hand upon her waist, and pulled her to him and kissed her. Another sort of man, no matter what he had believed of her, would have felt his act a sacrilege then and there. Jeff only knew that she had not made the faintest struggle against him; she had even trembled towards him, and he brutally exulted in the belief that he had done what she wished, whether it was what she meant or not.

She, for her part, realized that she had been kissed as once she had happened to see one of the maids kissed by the grocer's boy at the basement door. In an instant this man had abolished all her defences of family, of society, of personality, and put himself on a level with her in the most sacred things of life. Her mind grasped the fact and she realized it intellectually, while as yet all her emotions seemed paralyzed. She did not know whether she resented it as an abominable outrage or not; whether she hated the man for

"'WILL YOU LET ME PASS?'"

whi gived a shit?

it or not. But perhaps he was in love with her, and his love overpowered him ; in that case she could forgive him, if she were in love with him. She asked herself whether she was, and whether she had betrayed herself to him so that he was somehow warranted in what he did. She wondered if another sort of man would have done it, a gentleman, who believed she was in love with him. She wondered if she were as much shocked as she was astonished. She knew that there was everything in the situation to make the fact shocking, but she got no distinct reply from her jarred consciousness.

It ought to be known, and known at once ; she ought to tell her brother, as soon as she saw him ; she thought of telling her aunt, and she fancied having to shout the affair into her ear, and having to repeat, " He kissed me !   Don't you understand ?   *Kissed* me ! "   Then she reflected with a start that she could never tell any one, that in the midst of her world she was alone in relation to this ; she was as helpless and friendless as the poorest and lowliest girl could be. She was more so, for if she were like the maid whom the grocer's boy kissed she would be of an order of things in which she could advise with some one else who had been kissed ; and she would know what to feel.

She asked herself whether she was at all moved at heart ; till now it seemed to her that it had not been different with her towards him from what it had been towards all the other men whose meaning she would have liked to find out. She had not in the least respected them, and she did not respect him; but if it happened because he was overcome by his love for her, and could not help it, then perhaps she must forgive him whether she cared for him or not.

These ideas presented themselves with the simultaneity of things in a dream in that instant when she lingered helplessly in his hold, and she even wondered if by any chance Andrew had seen them; but she heard his step on the floor below; and at the same time it appeared to her that she must be in love with this man if she did not resent what he had done.

XLIII.

WESTOVER was sitting at an open window of his studio smoking out into the evening air, and looking down into the thinly foliaged tops of the public garden, where the electrics fainted and flushed and hissed. Cars trooped by in the troubled street, scraping the wires overhead that screamed as if with pain at the touch of their trolleys, and kindling now and again a soft planet, as the trolleys struck the batlike plates that connected the crossing lines. The painter was getting almost as much pleasure out of the planets as pain out of the screams, and he was in an after-dinner languor in which he was very reluctant to recognize a step, which he thought he knew, on his stairs and his stairs-landing. A knock at his door followed the sound of the approaching steps. He lifted himself, and called out inhospitably, "Come in!" and, as he expected, Jeff Durgin came in. Westover's meetings with him had been an increasing discomfort since his return from Lion's Head. The uneasiness which he commonly felt at the first moment of encounter with him yielded less and less to the influence of Jeff's cynical *bonhomie*, and it returned in force as soon as they parted.

It was rather dim in the place, except for the light thrown up into it from the turmoil of lights outside, but he could see that there was nothing of the smiling mockery on Jeff's face which habitually expressed his inner hardihood. It was a frowning mockery.

"Hello!" said Westover.

"Hello!" answered Jeff. "Any commands for Lion's Head?"

"What do you mean?"

"I'm going up there to-morrow. I've got to see Cynthia, and tell her what I've been doing."

Westover waited a moment before he asked, "Do you want me to ask what you've been doing?"

"I shouldn't mind it."

The painter paused again. "I don't know that I care to ask. Is it any good?"

"No!" shouted Jeff. "It's the worst thing yet, I guess you'll think. I couldn't have believed it myself, if I hadn't been through it. I shouldn't have supposed I was such a fool. I don't care for the girl; I never did."

"Cynthia?"

"Cynthia? No! Miss Lynde. Oh, try to take it in!" Jeff cried, with a laugh at the daze in Westover's face. "You must have known about the flirtation; if you haven't, you're the only one." His vanity in the fact betrayed itself in his voice. "It came to a crisis last week, and we tried to make each other believe that we were in earnest. But there won't be any real love lost."

Westover did not speak. He could not make out

whether he was surprised or whether he was shocked, and it seemed to him that he was neither surprised nor shocked. He wondered whether he had really expected something of the kind, sooner or later, or whether he was not always so apprehensive of some deviltry in Durgin that nothing he did could quite take him unawares. At last he said : " I suppose it's true—even though you say it. It's probably the only truth in you."

" That's something like," said Jeff, as if the contempt gave him a sort of pleasure; and his heavy face lighted up and then darkened again.

" Well," said Westover, " what are we going to do ? You've come to tell me."

" I'm going to break with her. I don't care for her —that!" He snapped his fingers. " I told her I cared because she provoked me to. It happened because she wanted it to and led up to it."

" Ah !" said Westover. " You put it on her !" But he waited for Durgin's justification with a dread that he should find something in it.

" Pshaw ! What's the use ? It's been a game from the beginning, and a question which should win. *I* won. She meant to throw me over, if the time came for her, but it came for me first, and it's only a question now which shall break first; we've both been near it once or twice already. I don't mean she shall get the start of me."

Westover had a glimpse of the innate enmity of the sexes in this game; of its presence in passion that was lived and of its prevalence in passion that was played.

But the fate of neither gambler concerned him; he was impatient of his interest in what Jeff now went on to tell him, without scruple concerning her, or palliation of himself. He scarcely realized that he was listening, but afterwards he remembered it all, with a little pity for Bessie and none for Jeff, but with more shame for her, too. Love seems more sacredly confided to women than to men; it is and must be a higher and finer as well as a holier thing with them; their blame for its betrayal must always be the heavier. He had sometimes suspected Bessie's willingness to amuse herself with Jeff, as with any other man who would let her play with him; and he would not have relied upon anything in him to defeat her purpose, if it had been anything so serious as a purpose.

At the end of Durgin's story he merely asked: "And what are you going to do about Cynthia?"

"I am going to tell her," said Jeff. "That's what I am going up there for."

Westover rose, but Jeff remained sitting where he had put himself astride of a chair, with his face over the back. The painter walked slowly up and down before him in the capricious play of the street light. He turned a little sick, and he stopped a moment at the window for a breath of air.

"Well?" asked Jeff.

"Oh! You want my advice?" Westover still felt physically incapable of the indignation which he strongly imagined. "I don't know what to say to you, Durgin? You transcend my powers. Are you able to see this whole thing yourself?"

"I guess so," Jeff answered. "I don't idealize it, though. I look at the facts; they're bad enough. You don't suppose that Miss Lynde is going to break her heart over—"

"I don't believe I care for Miss Lynde any more than I care for you. But I believe I wish you were not going to break with her."

"Why?"

"Because you and she are fit for each other. If you want my advice, I advise you to be true to her— if you can."

"And Cynthia?"

"Break with *her*."

"Oh!" Jeff gave a snort of derision.

"You're not fit for her. You couldn't do a crueler thing for her than to keep faith with her."

"Do you mean it?"

"Yes, I mean it. Stick to Miss Lynde—if she'll let you."

Jeff seemed puzzled by Westover's attitude, which was either too sincere or too ironical for him. He pushed his hat, which he had kept on, back from his forehead. "Damned if I don't believe she would," he mused aloud. The notion seemed to flatter him and repay him for what he must have been suffering. He smiled, but he said: "She wouldn't do, even if she were any good. Cynthia is worth a million of her. If she wants to give me up after she knows all about me, well and good. I sha'n't blame her. But I shall give her a fair chance, and I sha'n't whitewash myself; you needn't be afraid of that, Mr. Westover."

" Why should I care what you do ? " asked the painter, scornfully.

" Well, you can't, on my account," Durgin allowed. " But you do care on her account."

" Yes, I do," said Westover, sitting down again, and he did not say anything more.

Durgin waited a long while for him to speak before he asked, " Then that's really your advice, is it ? "

" Yes, break with her."

" And stick to Miss Lynde."

" If she'll let you."

Jeff was silent in his turn. He started from his silence with a laugh. " She'd make a daisy landlady for Lion's Head. I believe she would like to try it awhile just for the fun. But after the ball was over —well, it would be a good joke, if it was a joke. Cynthia is a woman—she a'n't any corpse-light. She understands me, and she don't overrate me either. She knew just how much I was worth, and she took me at her own valuation. I've got my way in life marked out, and she believes in it as much as I do. If anybody can keep me level and make the best of me, she can, and she's going to have the chance, if she wants to. I'm going to act square with her about the whole thing. I guess she's the best judge in a case like this, and I shall lay the whole case before her, don't you be afraid of that. And she's got to have a free field. Why, even if there wa'n't any question of *her*," he went on, falling more and more into his vernacular, " I don't believe I should care in the long-run for this other one. We couldn't make it go

for any time at all. She wants excitement, and after
the summer folks began to leave, and we'd been to
Florida for a winter, and then came back to Lion's
Head—well! This planet hasn't got excitement
enough in it for that girl, and I doubt if the solar
system has. At any rate, I'm not going to act as ad-
vance-agent for her."

"I see," said Westover, "that you've been reasoning it all out, and I'm not surprised that you've kept
your own advantage steadily in mind. I don't suppose you know what a savage you are, and I don't
suppose I could teach you. I sha'n't try, at any rate.
I'll take you on your own ground, and I tell you again
you had better break with Cynthia. I won't say that
it's what you owe her, for that won't have any effect
with you, but it's what you owe yourself. You can't
do a wrong thing and prosper on it—"

"Oh, yes you can," Jeff interrupted with a sneer-
ing laugh. "How do you suppose all the big fortunes
were made? By keeping the commandments?"

"No. But you're an unlucky man if life hasn't
taught you that you must pay in suffering of some
kind, sooner or later, for every wrong thing you do—"

"Now that's one of your old-fashioned supersti-
tions, Mr. Westover," said Jeff, with a growing kind-
liness in his tone, as if the pathetic delusion of such
a man really touched him. "You pay, or you don't
pay, just as it happens. If you get hit soon after
you've done wrong, you think it's retribution, and if
it holds off till you've forgotten all about it, you think
it's a strange Providence, and you puzzle over it, but

you don't reform. You keep right along in the old way. Prosperity and adversity, they've got nothing to do with conduct. If you're a strong man, you get there, and if you're a weak man, all the righteousness in the universe won't help you. But I propose to do what's right about Cynthia, and not what's wrong; and according to your own theory of life—which won't hold water a minute—I ought to be blessed to the third and fourth generation. I don't look for that, though. I shall be blessed if I look out for myself; and if I don't, I shall suffer for my want of foresight. But I sha'n't suffer for anything else. Well, I'm going to cut some of my recitations, and I'm going up to Lion's Head, to-morrow, to settle my business with Cynthia. I've got a little business to look after here with some one else first, and I guess I shall have to be about it. I don't know which I shall like the best." He rose, and went over to where Westover was sitting, and held out his hand to him.

"What is it?" asked Westover.

"Any commands for Lion's Head?" Jeff said, as at first.

"No," said Westover, turning his face away.

"Oh, all right." Durgin put his hand into his pocket unshaken.

XLIV.

"What is it, Jeff?" asked Cynthia, the next night, as they started out together after supper, and began to stroll down the hill towards her father's house. It lay looking very little and low in the nook at the foot of the lane, on the verge of the woods that darkened away to the northward from it, under the glassy night sky, lit with the spare young moon. The peeping of the frogs in the marshy places filled the air; the hoarse voice of the brook made itself heard at intervals through them.

"It's not so warm here, quite, as it is in Boston," he returned. "Are you wrapped up enough? This air has an edge to it."

"I'm all right," said the girl. "What is it?"

"You think there's something? You don't believe I've come up for rest over Sunday? I guess mother herself didn't, and I could see your father following up my little lies as if he wa'n't going to let one escape him. Well, you're right. There *is* something. Think of the worst thing you can, Cynthy!"

She pulled her hand out of his arm, which she had

taken, and halted him by her abrupt pause. " You're not going to get through ! "

" I'm all right on my conditions," said Jeff, with forlorn derision. " You'll have to guess again." He stood looking back over his shoulder at her face, which showed white in the moonlight, swathed airily round in the old-fashioned soft woollen cloud she wore.

" Is it some trouble you've got into ? I shall stand by you ! "

" Oh, you splendid girl ! The trouble's over, but it's something you can't stand by me in, I guess. You know that girl I wrote to you about—the one I met at the college tea, and—"

" Yes ! Miss Lynde ! "

" Come on ! We can't stay here talking. Let's go down and sit on your porch." She mechanically obeyed him, and they started on together down the hill again ; but she did not offer to take his arm, and he kept the width of the roadway from her.

" What about her ? " she quietly asked.

" Last night I ended up the flirtation I've been carrying on with her ever since."

" I want to know just what you mean, Jeff."

" I mean that last week I got engaged to her, and last night I broke with her." Cynthia seemed to stumble on something ; he sprang over and caught her, and now she put her hand in his arm, and stayed herself by him as they walked.

" Go on," she said.

" That's all there is of it."

"No!" She stopped, and then she asked with a kind of gentle bewilderment, "What did you want to tell me for?"

"To let you break with me—if you wanted to."

"Don't you care for me any more?"

"Yes, more than ever I did. But I'm not fit for you, Cynthia. Mr. Westover said I wasn't. I told him about it—"

"What did he say?"

"That I ought to break with you."

"But if you broke with her?"

"He told me to stick to her. He was right about *you*, Cynthy. I'm not fit for you, and that's a fact."

"What was it about that girl? Tell me everything." She spoke in a tone of plaintive entreaty, very unlike the command she once used with Jeff when she was urging him to be frank with her and true to himself. They had come to her father's house and she freed her hand from his arm again, and sat down on the step before the side door with a little sigh as of fatigue.

"You'll take cold," said Jeff, who remained on foot in front of her.

"No," she said, briefly. "Go on."

"Why," Jeff began, harshly, and with a note of scorn for himself and his theme in his voice, "there isn't any more of it, but there's no end to her. I promised Mr. Westover I shouldn't whitewash myself, and I sha'n't. I've been behaving badly, and it's no excuse for me because she wanted me to. I began to go for her as soon as I saw that she wanted me to, and that she liked the excitement. The excitement is all that she cared for; she didn't care for me except for the excitement of it. She thought she could have fun with me, and then throw me over; but I guess she found her match. You couldn't understand such a girl, and I don't brag of it. All she cared for was to flirt with me, and she liked it all the more because I was a jay and she could get something new out of it. I can't explain it; but I could see it right along. She fooled herself more than she fooled me."

"Was she—very good-looking?" Cynthia asked, listlessly.

"No!" shouted Jeff. "She wasn't good-looking at all. She was dark and thin, and she had little slanting eyes; but she was graceful, and she knew how to make herself go further than any girl I ever saw. If she came into a room, she made you look at her, or you had to somehow. She was bright too; and she had more sense than all the other girls there put together. But she was a fool, all the same." Jeff paused. "Is that enough?"

"It isn't all."

"No, it isn't all. We didn't meet much at first, but I got to walking home with her from some teas; and then we met at a big ball. I danced with her the whole while nearly, and—and I took her brother home— Pshaw! He was drunk; and I—well, he had got drunk drinking with me at the ball. The wine didn't touch me, but it turned his head; and I took him home; he's a drunkard, anyway. She let us in when we got to their house, and that kind of made a tie between us. She pretended to think she was under obligations to me, and so I got to going to her house."

"Did she know how her brother got drunk?"

"She does now. I told her last night."

"How came you to tell her?"

"I wanted to break with her. I wanted to stop it, once for all, and I thought that would do it, if anything would."

"Did that make her willing to give you up?"

Jeff checked himself in a sort of retrospective laugh. "I'm not so sure. I guess she liked the excitement of that, too. You couldn't understand the kind of girl she— She wanted to flirt with me that night I brought him home tipsy."

"I don't care to hear any more about her. Why did you give her up?"

"Because I didn't care for her, and I did care for you, Cynthy."

"I don't believe it." Cynthia rose from the step, where she had been sitting, as if with renewed strength. "Go up and tell father to come down here. I want to see him." She turned and put her hand on the latch of the door.

"You're not going in there, Cynthia," said Jeff. "It must be like death in there."

"It's more like death out here. But if it's the cold you mean, you needn't be troubled. We've had a fire to-day, airing out the house. Will you go?"

"But what do you—what are you going to say to me?"

"I don't know, yet. If I said anything now, I should tell you what Mr. Westover did: go back to that girl, if she'll let you. You're fit for each other, as he said. Did you tell her that you were engaged to some one else?"

"I did, last night."

"But before that she didn't know *how* false you were. Well, you're *not* fit for her, then; you're not good enough."

She opened the door and went in, closing it after her. Jeff turned and walked slowly away; then he came quickly back, as if he were going to follow her within. But through the window he saw her as she stood by the table with a lamp in her hand. She had turned up the light, which shone full in her face and revealed its severe beauty broken and writhen with the effort to repress her weeping. He might not have minded the severity or the beauty, but the pathos was more than he could stand. "Oh, *Lord!*" he said, with a shrug, and he turned again and walked slowly up the hill.

When Whitwell faced his daughter in the little sitting-room, whose low ceiling his hat almost touched as he stood before her, the storm had passed with her, and her tear-drenched visage wore its wonted look of still patience.

"Did Jeff tell you why I sent for you, father?"

"No. But I knew it was trouble," said Whitwell, with a dignity which his sympathy for her gave a countenance better adapted to the expression of the lighter emotions.

"'WHAT ARE YOU GOIN' TO DO?'"

"I guess you were right about him," she resumed. She went on to tell in brief the story that Jeff had told her. Her father did not interrupt her, but at the end he said, inadequately: "He's a comical devil. I knew about his gittin' that feller drunk. Mr. Westover told me when he was up here."

"Mr. Westover did!" said Cynthia, in a note of indignation.

"He didn't offer to," Whitwell explained. "I got it out of him in spite of him, I guess." He had sat down with his hat on, as his absent-minded habit was, and he now braced his knees against the edge of the table. Cynthia sat across it from him with her head drooped over it, drawing vague figures on the board with her finger. "What are you goin' to do?"

"I don't know," she answered.

"I guess you don't quite realize it yet," her father suggested, tenderly. "Well, I don't want to hurry you any. Take your time."

"I guess I realize it," said the girl.

"Well, it's a pootty plain case, that's a fact," Whitwell conceded. She was silent, and he asked, "How did he come to tell you?"

"It's what he came up for. He began to tell me at once. I was certain there was some trouble."

"Was it his notion to come, I wonder, or Mr. Westover's?"

"It was his. But Mr. Westover told him to break off with me, and keep on with her, if she would let him."

"I guess that was pootty good advice," said Whit-

well, letting his face betray his humorous relish of it.
" I guess there's a pair of 'em."

" She was not playing any one else false," said Cynthia, bitterly.

" Well, I guess that's so, too," her father assented.
" 'Ta'n't so much of a muchness as you might think,
in that light." He took refuge from the subject in
an undirected whistle.

After a moment the girl asked, forlornly, " What
should you do, father, if you were in my place?"

" Well, there I guess you got me, Cynthy," said
her father. " I don't believe 't any man, I don't care
how old he is, or how much experience he's had, knows
exactly how a girl feels about a thing like this, or has
got any call to advise her. Of course, the way I feel
is like takin' the top of his head off. But I d' know,"
he added, " as *that* would do a great deal of good,
either. *I* presume a woman's got rather of a chore to
get along with a man, anyway. We a'n't any of us
much to brag on. It's out o' sight, out o' mind, with
the best of us, *I* guess."

" It wouldn't be with Jackson—it wouldn't be with
Mr. Westover."

" There a'n't many men like Mr. Westover—well,
not a *great* many; or Jackson, either. Time! I wish
Jackson was home! He'd know how to straighten
this thing out, and he wouldn't weaken over Jeff much
—well, not *much*. But he a'n't here, and you've got
to act for yourself. The way I look at it is this: you
took Jeff when you knowed what a comical devil he
was, and I presume you ha'n't got quite the same right

to be disappointed in what he done as if you hadn't
knowed.   Now mind, I a'n't excusin' him.   But if
you knowed he was the feller to play the devil if he
got a chance, the question is whether—whether—"

"I know what you mean, father," said the girl,
"and I don't want to shirk my responsibility.   It was
everything to have him come right up and tell me."

"Well," said Whitwell, impartially, "as far forth
as that goes, I don't think he's strained himself.   He'd
know you would hear of it sooner or later anyway, and
he ha'n't just found out that he was goin' wrong.
Been keepin' it up for the last three months, and
writin' you all the while them letters you was so crazy
to get."

"Yes," sighed the girl.   "But we've got to be just
to his disposition as well as his actions.   I can see it
in one light that can excuse it some.   He can't bear
to be put down, and I know he's been left out a good
deal among the students, and it's made him bitter.
He told me about it; that's one reason why he wanted
to leave Harvard this last year.   He saw other young
men made much of, when he didn't get any notice;
and when he had the chance to pay them back with a
girl of their own set that was trying to make a fool of
him—"

"That was the time for him to remember *you*," said
Whitwell.

Cynthia broke under the defence she was trying to
make.   "Yes," she said, with an indrawn sigh, and
she began to sob piteously.

The sight of her grief seemed to kindle her father's

wrath to a flame. "Anyway you look at him, he's been a dumn blackguard; that's what he's been. You're a million times too good for him; and I—"

She sobbed herself quiet, and then she said; "Father, I don't like to go up there to-night. I want to stay here."

"All right, Cynthia. I'll come down and stay with you. You got everything we want here?"

"Yes. And I'll go up and get the breakfast for them in the morning. There won't be much to do."

"Dumn 'em! Let 'em get their own breakfast!" said Whitwell, recklessly.

"And, father," the girl went on as if he had not spoken, "don't you talk to Mrs. Durgin about it, will you?"

"No, no. I sha'n't speak to her. I'll just tell Frank you and me are goin' to stay down here to-night. She'll suspicion something, but she can figure it out for herself. Or she can make Jeff tell her. It can't be kept from her."

"Well, let him be the one to tell her. Whatever happens, I shall never speak of it to a soul besides you."

"All right, Cynthy. You'll have the night to think it over—I guess you won't sleep much—and I'll trust you to do what's the best thing about it."

XLV.

CYNTHIA found Mrs. Durgin in the old farm-house kitchen at work getting breakfast when she came up to the hotel in the morning. She was early, but the elder woman had been earlier still, and her heavy face showed more of their common night-long trouble than the girl's.

She demanded, at sight of her, "What's the matter with you and Jeff, Cynthy?"

Cynthia was unrolling the cloud from her hair. She said, as she tied on her apron, "You must get him to tell you, Mrs. Durgin."

"Then there *is* something?"

"Yes."

"Has Jeff been using you wrong?"

Cynthia stooped to open the oven door, and to turn the pan of biscuit she found inside. She shut the door sharply to, and said, as she rose: "I don't want to tell anything about it, and I sha'n't, Mrs. Durgin. He can do it, if he wants to. Shall I make the coffee?"

"Yes; you seem to make it better than I do. Do you think I shouldn't believe you was fair to him?"

" I wasn't thinking of that.   But it's his secret.   If
he wants to keep it, he can keep it, for all me."

" You ha'n't give each other up ? "

" I don't know."   Cynthia turned away with a
trembling chin, and began to beat the coffee up with
an egg she had dropped into the pot.   She put the
breakfast on the table when it was ready, but she
would not sit down with the rest.   She said she did
not want any breakfast, and she drank a cup of coffee
in the kitchen.

It fell to Jeff mainly to keep the talk going. He had
been out at the barn with Jombateeste since daybreak,
looking after the cattle, and the joy of the weather
had got into his nerves and spirits.   At first he had
lain awake after he went to bed, but he had fallen
asleep about midnight, and got a good night's rest.
He looked fresh and strong and very handsome.   He
talked resolutely to every one at the table, but Jombateeste was always preoccupied with eating at his
meals, and Frank Whitwell had on a Sunday silence,
which was perhaps deepened by a feeling that there
was something wrong between his sister and Jeff, and
it would be rash to commit himself to an open friendliness until he understood the case.   His father met
Jeff's advances with philosophical blandness and eva-
sion, and Mrs. Durgin was provisionally dry and severe both with the Whitwells and her son.   After
breakfast she went to the parlor, and Jeff set about a
tour of the hotel, inside and out.   He looked carefully
to the details of its winter keeping.   Then he came
back and boldly joined his mother where she sat be-

fore her stove, whose subdued heat she found pleasant in the lingering cold of the early spring.

He tossed his hat on the table beside her, and sat
down on the other side of the stove.   "Well, I must
say, the place has been well looked after.   I don't believe Jackson himself could have kept it in better
shape.   When was the last you heard from him?"

"I hope," said his mother, gravely, "you've been
lookin' after your end at Boston, too."

"Well, not as well as you have here, mother," said
Jeff, candidly.   "Has Cynthy told you?"

"I guess she expected you to tell me, if there *was*
anything."

"There's a lot; but I guess I needn't go over it all.
I've been playing the devil."

"Jeff!"

"Yes, I have.   I've been going with another girl
down there, one of the kind you wanted me to make
up to, and I went so far I—well, I made love to her;
and then I thought it over, and I found out I didn't
really care for her, and I had to tell her so, and then
I came up to tell Cynthy.   That's about the size of it.
What do you think of it?"

"D' you tell Cynthy?"

"Yes, I told her."

"What' d she say?"

"She said I'd better go back to the other girl."
Jeff laughed hardily, but his mother remained impas-
sive.

"I guess she's right; I guess you had."

"That seems to be the general opinion.   That's

what Mr. Westover advised. I seem to be the only
one against it. I suppose you mean that I'm not fit
for Cynthy. I don't deny it. All I say is I want her,
and I don't want the other one. What are you going
to do in a case like that ? "

"The way I should look at it," said his mother,
" is this : whatever you are, Cynthy made you. You
was a lazy, disobedient, worthless boy, and it was her
carin' for you from the first that put any spirit and
any principle into you. It was her that helped you
at school when you was little things together ; and
she helped you at the academy, and she's helped you
at college. I'll bet she could take a degree, or whatever it is, at Harvard better than you could now ;
and if you ever do take a degree, you've got her to
thank for it."

"That's so," said Jeff. "And what's the reason
you didn't want me to marry her when I came in here
last summer and told you I'd asked her to ? "

" You know well enough what the reason was. It
was part of the same thing as my wantin' you to be a
lawyer; but I might knowed that if you didn't have
Cynthy to go into court with you, and put the words
into your mouth, you wouldn't make a speech that
would "—Mrs. Durgin paused for a fitting figure—
" save a flea from the gallows."

Jeff burst into a laugh. "Well, I guess that's so,
mother. And now you want me to throw away the
only chance I've got of learning how to run Lion's
Head in the right way by breaking with Cynthy."

"Nobody wants you to run Lion's Head for a

while yet," his mother returned, scornfully. " Jackson is going to run Lion's Head. He'll be home the end of June, and *I'll* run Lion's Head till he gets here. You talk," she went on, " as if it was in your hands to break with Cynthy, or throw away the chance with her. The way I look at it, she's broke with you, and you ha'n't got any chance with her. Oh, Jeff," she suddenly appealed to him, " tell me all about it ! What *have* you been up to ? If I understood it once, I know I can make her see it in the right light."

" The better you understand it, mother, the less you'll like it; and I guess Cynthy sees it in the right light already. What did she say ? "

" Nothing. She said she'd leave it to you."

" Well, that's like Cynthy. I'll tell you, then," said Jeff; and he told his mother his whole affair with Bessie Lynde. He had to be very elemental, and he was aware, as he had never been before, of the difference between Bessie's world and his mother's world, in trying to make Bessie's world conceivable to her. He was patient in going over every obscure point, and illustrating from the characters and condition of different summer-folks the facts of Bessie's *entourage*. It is doubtful, however, if he succeeded in conveying to his mother a clear and just notion of the purely *chic* nature of the girl. In the end she seemed to conceive of her simply as a hussy, and so pronounced her, without limit or qualification, in spite of Jeff's laughing attempt to palliate her behavior, and to inculpate himself. She said she did not see what he

had done that was so much out of the way. That
thing had led him on from the beginning; she had
merely got her come-uppings, when all was said. Mrs.
Durgin believed Cynthia would look at it as she did, if
she could have it put before her rightly. Jeff shook
his head with persistent misgiving. His notion was
that Cynthia saw the affair only too clearly, and that
there was no new light to be thrown on it from her
point of view. Mrs. Durgin would not allow this;
she was sure that she could bring Cynthia round; and
she asked Jeff whether it was his getting that fellow
drunk that she seemed to blame him for the most. He
answered that he thought that was pretty bad, but he
did not believe that was the worst thing in Cynthia's
eyes. He did not forbid his mother's trying to do
what she could with her, and he went away for a walk,
and left the house to the two women. Jombateeste
was in the barn, which he preferred to the house, and
Frank Whitwell had gone to church over at the Huddle. As Jeff passed Whitwell's cottage in setting out
on his stroll he saw the philosopher through the window, seated with his legs on the table, his hat pushed
back, and his spectacles fallen to the point of his nose,
reading, and moving his lips as he read.

The forenoon sun was soft, but the air was cool.
There was still plenty of snow on the upper slopes of
the hills, and there was a drift here and there in a
corner of pasture wall in the valley; but the spring-
time green was beginning to hover over the wet places
in the fields; the catkins silvered the golden tracery
of the willow branches by the brook; there was a buzz

"SHE BLUSHED AND BRIDLED AT HIS BOW"

of bees about them, and about the maples, blackened
by the earlier flow of sap through the holes in the
bark made by the woodpeckers' bills.   Now and then
the tremolo of a bluebird shook in the tender light
and the keen air.   At one point in the road where the
sun fell upon some young pines in a sheltered spot a
balsamic odor exhaled from them.

These gentle sights and sounds and odors blended
in the influence which Jeff's spirit felt more and more.
He realized that he was a blot on the loveliness of the
morning.   He had a longing to make atonement and
to win forgiveness.   His heart was humbled towards
Cynthia, and he went wondering how his mother would
make it out with her, and how, if she won him any
advantage, he should avail himself of it and regain the
girl's trust; he had no doubt of her love.   He perceived that there was nothing for him hereafter but
the most perfect constancy of thought and deed, and
he desired nothing better.

At a turn of his road where it branched towards
the Huddle a group of young girls stood joking and
laughing; before Jeff came up with them they separated, and all but one continued on the way beyond
the turning.   She came towards Jeff, who gayly recognized her as she drew near.

She blushed and bridled at his bow and at his
beauty and splendor, and in her embarrassment pertly
said that she did not suppose he would have remembered her.   She was very young, but at fifteen a country girl is not so young as her town sister at eighteen
in the ways of the other sex.

Jeff answered that he should have known her anywhere, in spite of her looking so much older than she did in the summer when she had come with berries to the hotel.   He said she must be feeling herself quite a young lady now, in her long dresses, and he praised the dress which she had on.   He said it became her style; and he found such relief from his heavy thoughts in these harmless pleasantries that he kept on with them.   He had involuntarily turned with her to walk back to her house on the way he had come, and he asked her if he might not carry her catkins for her.   She had a sheaf of them in the hollow of her slender arm, which seemed to him very pretty, and after a little struggle she yielded them to him. The struggle gave him still greater relief from his self-reproach, and at her gate he begged her to let him keep one switch of the pussy-willows, and he stood a moment wondering whether he might not ask her for something else.   She chose one from the bundle, and drew it lightly across his face before she put it in his hand.   "You may have this for Cynthy," she said, and she ran laughingly up the pathway to her door.

XLVI.

CYNTHIA did not appear at dinner, and Jeff asked
his mother when he saw her alone if she had spoken
to the girl. "Yes, but she said she did not want to
talk yet."

"All right," he returned. "I'm going to take a
nap; I believe I feel as if I hadn't slept for a month."

He slept the greater part of the afternoon, and
came down rather dull to the early tea. Cynthia was
absent again, and his mother was silent and wore a
troubled look. Whitwell was full of a novel conception of the agency of hypnotism in interpreting the
life of the soul as it is intimated in dreams. He had
been reading a book that affirmed the consubstantial-
ity of the sleep-dream and the hypnotic illusion. He
wanted to know if Jeff, down at Boston, had seen
anything of the hypnotic doings that would throw
light on this theory.

It was still full light when they rose from the table,
and it was scarcely twilight when Jeff heard Cynthia
letting herself out at the back door. He fancied her
going down to her father's house, and he went out to
the corner of the hotel to meet her. She faltered a

moment at sight of him, and then kept on with
averted face.

He joined her, and walked beside her. "Well,
Cynthy, what are you going to say to me? I'm off
for Cambridge again to-morrow morning, and I suppose we've got to understand each other. I came up
here to put myself in your hands, to keep or to throw
away, just as you please. Well? Have you thought
about it?"

"Every minute," said the girl, quietly.

"Well?"

"If you had cared for me, it couldn't have happened."

"Oh, yes, it could. Now that's just where you're
mistaken. That's where a woman never can understand a man. I might carry on with half a dozen
girls, and yet never forget you, or think less of you,
although I could see all the time how pretty and
bright every one of 'em was. That's the way a man's
mind is built. It's curious, but it's true."

"I don't believe I care for any share in your mind,
then," said the girl.

"Oh, come, now! You don't mean that. You
know I was just joking; you know I don't justify
what I've done, and I don't excuse it. But I think
I've acted pretty square with you about it—about
telling you, I mean. I don't want to lay any claim,
but you remember when you made me promise that
if there was anything shady I wanted to hide from
you— Well, I acted on *that*. You do remember?"

"Yes," said Cynthia, and she pulled the cloud over

the side of her face next to him, and walked a little
faster.

He hastened his steps to keep up with her. "Cynthy, if you put your arms round me, as you did,
then—"

"I can't, Jeff!"

"You don't want to."

"Yes, I do! But you don't want me to, as you
did then. Do you?" She stopped abruptly and
faced him full. "Tell me honestly!"

Jeff dropped his bold eyes, and the smile left his
handsome mouth.

"You don't," said the girl, "for you know that if
you did, I would do it." She began to walk on again.
"It wouldn't be hard for me to forgive you anything
you've done against me—or against yourself; I should
care for you the same—if you were the same person;
but you're not the same, and you know it. I told
you then—that time—that I didn't want to make you
do what you knew was right, and I never shall try to
do it again. I'm sorry I did it then. I was wrong.
And I should be afraid of you if I did now. Some
time you would make me suffer for it, just as you've
made me suffer for making you do then what was
right."

It struck Jeff as a very curious fact that Cynthia
must always have known him better than he knew
himself in some ways, for he now perceived the truth
and accuracy of her words. He gave her mind credit
for the penetration due her heart; he did not understand that it is through their love women divine the

souls of men. What other witnesses of his character had slowly and carefully reasoned out from their experience of him she had known from the beginning, because he was dear to her.

He was silent, and then, with rare gravity, he said, "Cynthia, I believe you're right," and he never knew how her heart leaped towards him at his words. "I'm a pretty bad chap, I guess. But I want you to give me another chance—and I'll try not to make you pay for it, either," he added, with a flicker of his saucy humor.

"I'll give you a chance, then," she said, and she shrank from the hand he put out towards her. "Go back and tell that girl you're free now, and if she wants you she can have you."

"Is that what you call a chance?" demanded Jeff, between anger and injury. For an instant he imagined her deriding him and revenging herself.

"It's the only one I can give you. She's never tried to make you do what was right, and you'll never be tempted to hurt her."

"You're pretty rough on me, Cynthy," Jeff protested, almost plaintively. He asked, more in character, "Ain't *you* afraid of making me do right, now?"

"I'm not making you. I don't promise you anything, even if she won't have you."

"Oh!"

"Did you suppose I didn't *mean* that you were free? That I would put a lie in your mouth for you to be true with?"

"I guess you're too deep for me," said Jeff, after a

sulky silence. " Then it's all off between us ?   What do you say ? "

" What do you say ? "

" I say it's just as it was before, if you care for me."

" I care for you, but it can never be the same as it was before. What you've done, you've done. I wish I could help it, but I can't. I can't make myself over into what I was twenty-four hours ago. I seem another person, in another world; it's as if I died, and came to life somewhere else. I'm sorry enough, if that could help, but it can't. Go and tell that girl the truth : that you came up here to me, and I sent you back to her."

A gleam of amusement visited Jeff in the gloom where he seemed to be darkling. He fancied doing that very thing with Bessie Lynde, and the wild joy she would snatch from an experience so unique, so impossible. Then the gleam faded. " And what if I didn't want *her ?* " he demanded.

" Tell her that too," said Cynthia.

" I suppose," said Jeff, sulkily, " you'll let me go away and do as I please, if I'm free."

" Oh yes. I don't want you to do anything because I told you. I won't make that mistake again. Go and do what you are able to do of your own free will. You know what you ought to do as well as I do; and you know a great deal better what you *can* do."

They had reached Cynthia's house, and they were talking at the side door, as they had the night before, when there had been hope for her in the newness of her calamity, before she had yet fully imagined it.

Jeff made no answer to her last words. He asked,
" Am I going to see you again ? "

" I guess not. I don't believe I shall be up before
you start."

" All right. Good-by, then." He held out his
hand, and she put hers in it for the moment he chose
to hold it. Then he turned and slowly climbed the
hill.

Cynthia was still lying with her face in her pillow
when her father came into the dark little house, and
peered into her room with the newly lighted lamp in
his hand. She turned her face quickly over and
looked at him with dry and shining eyes.

" Well, it's all over with Jeff and me, father."

" Well, I'm satisfied," said Whitwell. " If you
could ha' made it up, so you could ha' felt right about
it, I shouldn't ha' had anything to say against it, but
I'm glad it's turned out the way it has. He's a comical devil, and he always was, and I'm glad you a'n't
takin' on about him any more. You used to have so
much spirit when you was little."

" Oh, spirit ! You don't know how much spirit I've
had, now."

" Well, I presume not," Whitwell assented.

" I've been thinking," said the girl, after a little
pause, " that we shall have to go away from here."

" Well, I guess *not*," her father began. " Not for
no Jeff Dur—"

" Yes, yes. We *must !* Don't make me talk about
it. We'll stay here till Jackson gets back in June,
and then—we must go somewhere else. We'll go

down to Boston, and I'll try to get a place to teach,
or something, and Frank can get a place."

" I presume," Whitwell mused, " that Mr. Westover
could—"

" *Father!* " cried the girl with an energy that startled him, as she lifted herself on her elbow. " Don't
ever *think* of troubling Mr. Westover! Oh," she
lamented, " I was thinking of troubling him myself!
But we mustn't. we mustn't! I should be so
ashamed! "

" Well," said Whitwell, " time enough to think
about all that. We got two good months yet to plan
it out before Jackson gets back, and I guess we can
think of something before that. I presume," he added, thoughtfully, " that when Mrs. Durgin hears that
you've give Jeff the sack, she'll make consid'able of a
kick. She done it when you got engaged."

XLVII.

AFTER he went back to Cambridge, Jeff continued mechanically in the direction given him by motives which had ceased for him. In the midst of his divergence with Bessie Lynde he had still kept an inner fealty to Cynthia, and tried to fulfil the purposes and ambition she had for him. The operation of this habitual allegiance now kept him up to his work, but the time must come when it could no longer operate, when his whole consciousness should accept the fact known to his intelligence, and he should recognize the close of that incident of his life as the bereaved finally accept and recognize the fact of death.

The event brought him relief, and it brought him freedom. He was sensible in his relaxation of having strained up to another's ideal, of having been hampered by another's will. His pleasure in the relief was tempered by a regret, not wholly unpleasant, for the girl whose aims, since they were no longer his, must be disappointed. He was sorry for Cynthia, and in his remorse he was fonder of her than he had ever been. He felt her magnanimity and clemency; he began to question, in that wordless deep of being where

volition begins, whether it would not be paying a kind
of duty to her if he took her at her word and tried to
go back to Bessie Lynde.   But for the present he did
nothing but renounce all notion of working at his
conditions, or attempting to take a degree.   That was
part of a thing that was past, and was no part of anything to come, so far as Jeff now forecast his future.

He did not choose to report himself to Westover,
and risk a scolding, or a snubbing.   He easily forgave
Westover for the tone he had taken at their last meeting, but he did not care to see him.   He would have
met him half-way, however, in a friendly advance, and
he was aware of much good-will towards him, which he
could not have been reluctant to show if chance had
brought them together.

Jeff missed Cynthia's letters which used to come so
regularly every Tuesday, and he had a half-hour every
Sunday which was at first rather painfully vacant since
he no longer wrote to her.   But in this vacancy he
had at least no longer the pang of self-reproach which
her letters always brought him, and he was not obliged
to put himself to the shame of concealment in writing
to her.   He had never minded that tacit lying on his
own account, but he hated it in relation to her; it
always hurt him as something incongruous and unfit.
He wrote to his mother now on Sunday, and in his
first letter, while the impression of Cynthia's dignity
and generosity was still vivid, he urged her to make
it clear to the girl that he wished her and her family
to remain at Lion's Head as if nothing had happened.
He put a great deal of real feeling into his request,

and he offered to go and spend a year in Europe, if
his mother thought that Cynthia would be more reconciled to his coming back at the end of that time.

His mother answered with a dryness to which his
ear supplied the tones of her voice, that she would try
to get along in the management of Lion's Head till
his brother got back, but that she had no objection to
his going to Europe for a year if he had the money
to spare. Jeff could not refuse her joke, as he felt it,
a certain applause, but he thought it pretty rough that
his mother should take part so decidedly against him
as she seemed to be doing. He had expected her to
be angry with him, but before they parted she had
seemed to find some excuse for him, and yet here she
was siding against her own son in what he might very
well consider an unnatural way. If Jackson had been
at home he would have laid it to his charge; but he
knew that Cynthia would have scorned even to speak
of him with his mother, and he knew too well his
mother's slight for Whitwell to suppose that he could
have influenced her. His mind turned in momentary
suspicion to Westover. Had Westover, he wondered,
with a purpose to pay him up for it forming itself
simultaneously with his question, been setting his
mother against him? She might have written to
Westover to get at the true inwardness of his behavior, and Westover might have written her something
that had made her harden her heart against him. But
upon reflection this seemed out of character for both
of them; and Jeff was thrown back upon his mother's
sober second thought of his misconduct for an expla-

nation of her coldness. He could not deny that he had grievously disappointed her in several ways.

But he did not see why he should not take a certain hint from her letter, or construct a hint from it, at one with a vague intent prompted by his own restless and curious vanity. Since he had parted with Bessie Lynde, on terms of humiliation for her which must have been anguish for him if he had ever loved her, or loved anything but his power over her, he had remained in absolute ignorance of her. He had not heard where she was or how she was; but now, as the few weeks before Class Day and Commencement crumbled away, he began to wonder why she made no sign. He believed that since she had been willing to go so far to get him, she would not be willing to give him up so easily. The thought of Cynthia had always intruded more or less effectively between them, but now that this thought began to fade into the past, the thought of Bessie began to grow out of it with no interposing shadow.

However, Jeff was in no hurry. It was not passion that moved him, and the mood in which he could play with the notion of getting back to his flirtation with Bessie Lynde was pleasanter after the violence of recent events than any renewal of strong sensations could be. He preferred to loiter in this mood, and he was meantime much more comfortable than he had been for a great while. He was rid of the disagreeable sense of disloyalty to Cynthia, and he was rid of the stress of living up to her conscience in various ways. He was rid of Bessie Lynde, too, and of the

trouble of forecasting and discounting her caprices.
His thought turned at times with a soft regret to
hopes, disappointments, experiences connected with
neither, and now tinged with a tender melancholy,
unalloyed by shame or remorse.   As he drew nearer
to Class Day he had a somewhat keener compunction
for Cynthia and the hopes he had encouraged her to
build and had then dashed.   But he was coming
more and more to regard it all as a fatality; and if
the chance that he counted upon to bring him and
Bessie together again had occurred he could have
more easily forgiven himself.

One of the jays, who was spreading on rather a large
scale, wanted Jeff to spread with him, but he refused,
because, as he said, he meant to keep out of it altogether; and for the same reason he declined to take
part in the spread of a rather jay society he belonged
to.   In his secret heart he trusted that some friendly
fortuity might throw an invitation to Beck Hall in his
way, or at least a card for the Gym, which, if no longer
the place it had been, was still by no means jay.   He
got neither; but as he felt all the joy of the June day
in his young blood he consoled himself very well with
the dancing at one of the halls, where the company
happened that year to be openly, almost recklessly
jay.   Jeff had some distinction among the fellows
who enviously knew of his social successes during the
winter, and especially of his affair with Bessie Lynde;
and there were some girls very pretty and very well
dressed among the crowd of girls who were neither.
They were from remote parts of the country, and in

the charge of chaperons ignorant of the differences so
poignant to local society.   Jeff went about among
them, and danced with the sisters and cousins of several men who seemed superior to the lost condition of
their kinswomen ; these were nice fellows enough, but
doomed by their grinding, or digging, or their want
of worldly wisdom, to a place among the jays, when
they really had some qualifications for a nobler standing.   He had a very good time, and he was enjoying
himself in his devotion to a lively young brunette
whom he was making laugh with his jokes about some
of the others, when his eye was caught by a group of
ladies who advanced among the jays with something
of that collective intrepidity and individual apprehension characteristic of people in slumming.   They had
the air of not knowing what might happen to them,
but the adventurous young Boston matron in charge
of the girls kept on a bold front behind her lorgnette,
and swept the strange company she found herself in
with an unshrinking eye as she led her band among
the promenaders, and past the couples seated along
the walls.   She hesitated a moment as her glance fell
upon Jeff, and then she yielded, at whatever risk, to
the comfort of finding a known face among so many
aliens.   " Why, Mr. Durgin ! " she called out.   " Bessie, here's Mr. Durgin," and she turned to the girl,
who was in her train, as Jeff had perceived by something finer than the senses from the first.

He rose from the side of his brunette, whose brother was standing near, and shook hands with the adventurous young matron, who seemed suddenly much

better acquainted with him than he had ever thought
her, and with Bessie Lynde; the others were New
York girls, and the matron presented him. "Are you
going on?" she asked, and the vague challenge with
the smile that accompanied it was sufficient invitation
for him.

"Why, I believe so," he said, and he turned to take
leave of his pretty brunette; but she had promptly
vanished with her brother, and he was spared the
trouble of getting rid of her. He would have been
equal to much more for the sake of finding himself
with Bessie Lynde again, whose excitement he could
see burning in her eyes, though her thick complexion
grew neither brighter nor paler. He did not know
what quality of excitement it might be, but he said,
audaciously, "It's a good while since we met!" and
he was sensible that his audacity availed.

"Is it?" she asked. He put himself at her side,
and he did not leave her again till he went to dress
for the struggle around the Tree. He found himself
easily included in the adventurous young matron's
party. He had not the elegance of some of the taller
and slenderer men in the scholar's gown, but the cap
became his handsome face. His affair with Bessie
Lynde had given him a certain note, and an adventurous young matron, who was naturally a little indis-
criminate, might very well have been willing to let him
go about with her party. She could not know how
impudent his mere presence was with reference to
Bessie, and the girl herself made no sign that could
have enlightened her. She accepted something more

than her share of his general usefulness to the party;
she danced with him whenever he asked her, and she
seemed not to scruple to publish her affair with him
in the openest manner. If he could have stilled a
certain shame for her which he felt, he would have
thought he was having the best kind of time. They
made no account of bygones in their talk, but she had
never been so brilliant, or prompted him to so many
of the effronteries which were the spirit of his humor.
He thought her awfully nice, with lots of sense; he
liked her letting him come back without any fooling
or fuss, and he began to admire instead of despising
her for it. Decidedly it was, as she would have said,
the chicquest sort of thing. What was the use, any
way? He made up his mind.

When he said he must go and dress for the Tree,
he took leave of her first, and he was aware of a vivid
emotion, which was like regret in her at parting with
him. She said, *Must* he? She seemed to want to
say something more to him; while he was dismissing
himself from the others, he noticed that once or twice
she opened her lips as if she were going to speak. In
the end she did nothing more important than to ask
if he had seen her brother; but after he had left the
party he turned and saw her following him with eyes
that he fancied anxious and even frightened in their
gaze.

The riot round the Tree roared itself through its
wonted events. Class after class of the undergradu-
ates filed in and sank upon the grass below the ter-
races and parterres of brilliantly dressed ladies within

the quadrangle of seats; the alumni pushed them
selves together against the wall of Holden Chapel; the
men of the Senior class came last in their grotesque
variety of sweaters and second and third best clothes
for the scramble at the Tree. The regulation cheers
tore from throats that grew hoarser and hoarser, till
every class and every favorite in the faculty had been
cheered. Then the signal-hat was flung into the air,
and the rush at the Tree was made, and the combat
for the flowers that garlanded its burly waist began.

Jeff's size and shape forbade him to try for the
flowers from the shoulders of others. He was one of
a group of jays who set their backs to the Tree, and
fought away all comers except their own; they pulled
down every man not of their sort, and put up a jay
who stripped the Tree of its flowers and flung them
to his fellows below. As he was let drop to the
ground, Jeff snatched a handful of his spoil from him,
and made off with it towards the place where he had
seen Bessie Lynde and her party. But when he
reached the place, shouldering and elbowing his way
through the press, she was no longer there. He saw
her hat at a distance through the crowd, where he did
not choose to follow, and he stuffed the flowers into
his breast to give her later. He expected to meet her
somewhere in the evening; if not, he would try to
find her at her aunt's house in town; failing that, he
could send her the flowers, and trust her for some sort
of leading acknowledgment.

He went and had a bath and dressed himself
freshly, and then he went for a walk in the still even-

"SUDDENLY HE FELT A FIERY STING ON HIS FOREHEAD"

ing air.   He was very hot from the battle which had
been fought over him, and which he had shared with
all his strength, and it seemed to him as if he could
not get cool.   He strolled far out along Concord Avenue, beyond the expanses and ice-houses of Fresh
Pond, into the country towards Belmont, with his hat
off and his head down.   He was very well satisfied,
and he was smiling to himself at the ease of his return
to Bessie, and securely speculating upon the outcome
of their renewed understanding.

He heard a vehicle behind him, rapidly driven, and
he turned out for it without looking around.   Then
suddenly he felt a fiery sting on his forehead, and
then a shower of stings swiftly following each other
over his head and face.   He remembered stumbling,
when he was a boy, into a nest of yellow-jackets, that
swarmed up around him and pierced him like sparks
of fire at every uncovered point.   But he knew at the
same time that it was some one in the vehicle beside
him who was lashing him over the head with a whip.
He bowed his head with his eyes shut and lunged
blindly out towards his assailant, hoping to seize him.

But the horse sprang aside, and tore past him down
the road.   Jeff opened his eyes, and through the
blood that dripped from the cuts above them he saw
the wicked face of Alan Lynde looking back at him
from the dog-cart where he sat with his man beside
him.   He brandished his broken whip in the air, and
flung it into the bushes.   Jeff walked on, and picked
it up, before he turned aside to the pools of the marsh
stretching on either hand, and tried to stanch his

hurts, and get himself into shape for returning to town and stealing back to his lodging. He had to wait till after dark, and watch his chance to get into the house unnoticed.

XLVIII.

The chum to whom Jeff confided the story of his encounter with a man he left nameless inwardly thanked fortune that he was not that man; for he knew him destined sooner or later to make such reparation for the injuries he had inflicted as Jeff chose to exact. He tended him carefully, and respected the reticence Jeff guarded concerning the whole matter, even with the young doctor whom his friend called, and who kept to himself his impressions of the nature of Jeff's injuries.

Jeff lay in his darkened room, and burned with them, and with the thoughts, guesses, purposes which flamed through his mind. Had she, that girl, known what her brother meant to do? Had she wished him to think of her in the moment of his punishment, and had she spoken of her brother so that he might recall her, or had she had some ineffective impulse to warn him against her brother when she spoke of him?

He lay and raged in vain with his conjectures, and he did a thousand imagined murders upon Lynde in revenge of his shame.

Towards the end of the week, while his hurts were

still too evident to allow him to go out-of-doors before
dark, he had a note from Westover asking him to
come in at once to see him.

"Your brother Jackson," Westover wrote, "reached
Boston by the New York train this morning, and is
with me here. I must tell you I think he is not at
all well, but he does not know how sick he is, and so
I forewarn you. He wants to get on home, but I do
not feel easy about letting him make the rest of the
journey alone. Some one ought to go with him. I
write not knowing whether you are still in Cambridge
or not; or whether, if you are, you can get away at
this time. But I think you ought, and I wish, at any
rate, that you would come in at once and see Jackson.
Then we can settle what had best be done."

Jeff wrote back that he had been suffering with a
severe attack of erysipelas—he decided upon erysipelas for the time being, but he meant to let Westover
know later that he had been in a row—and the doctor
would not let him go out yet. He promised to come
in as soon as he possibly could. If Westover thought
Jackson ought to be got home at once, and was not fit
to travel alone, he asked him to send a hospital nurse
with him.

Westover replied by Jeff's messenger that it would
worry and alarm Jackson to be put in charge of a
nurse; but that he would go home with him, and they
would start the next day. He urged Jeff to come and
see his brother if it was at all safe for him to do so.
But if he could not, Westover would give his mother
a reassuring reason for his failure.

Mrs. Durgin did not waste any anxiety for the sickness which prevented Jeff from coming home with his brother. She said ironically that it must be very bad, and she gave all her thought and care to Jackson. The sick man rallied, as he prophesied he should, in his native air, and celebrated the sense and science of the last doctor he had seen in Europe, who told him that he had made a great gain, but he had better hurry home as fast as he could, for he had got all the advantage he could expect to have from his stay abroad, and now home air was the best thing for him.

It could not be known how much of this he believed; he had, at any rate, the pathetic hopefulness of his malady; but his mother believed it all, and she nursed him with a faith in his recovery which Whitwell confided to Westover was about as much as he wanted to see, for *one* while. She seemed to grow younger in the care of him, and to get back to herself, more and more, from the facts of Jeff's behavior, which had aged and broken her. She had to tell Jackson about it all, but he took it with that indifference to the things of this world which the approach of death sometimes brings, and in the light of his passivity it no longer seemed to her so very bad. It was a relief to have Jackson say, Well, perhaps it was for the best; and it was a comfort to see how he and Cynthia took to each other; it was almost as if that dreadful trouble had not been. She told Jackson what hard work she had had to make Cynthia stay with her, and how the girl had consented to stay only until Jeff came home; but she guessed, now that Jack-

son had got back, he could make Cynthia see it all in
another light, and perhaps it would all come right
again.   She consulted him about Jeff's plan of going
abroad, and Jackson said it might be about as well;
he should soon be around, and he thought if Jeff
went it would give Cynthia more of a chance to get
reconciled.   After all, his mother suggested, a good
many fellows behaved worse than Jeff had done and
still had made it up with the girls they were engaged
to; and Jackson gently assented.

He did not talk with Cynthia about Jeff, out of
that delicacy, or that coldness, common to them both.
Perhaps it was not necessary for them to speak of
him; perhaps they understood him aright in their understanding of each other.

Westover stayed on, day after day, thinking somehow that he ought to wait till Jeff came.   There were
only a few other people in the hotel, and these were
of a quiet sort; they were not saddened by the presence of a doomed man under the same roof, as gayer
summer-folks might have been, and they were themselves no disturbance to him.

He sat about with them on the veranda, and he made
friends among them, and they did what they could
to encourage and console him in his impatience to
take up his old cares in the management of the hotel.
The Whitwells easily looked after the welfare of the
guests, and Jackson was so much better to every one's
perception that Westover could honestly write Jeff a
good report of him.

The report may have been so good that Jeff took

the affair too easily. It was a fortnight after Jackson's return to Lion's Head when he began to fail so suddenly and alarmingly that Westover decided upon his own responsibility to telegraph Jeff of his condition. But he had the satisfaction of Whitwell's approval when he told him what he had done.

"Of course, Jackson a'n't long for this world. Anybody but him and his mother could see that; and now he's just melting away, as you might say. I ha'n't liked his not carin' to work plantchette since he got back; looked to me from the start that he kind of knowed that it wa'n't worth while for him to trouble about a world that he'll know all about so soon, anyways; and d' you notice he don't seem to care about Mars, either? I've tried to wake him up on it two-three times, but you can't git him to take an interest. I guess Jeff can't git here any too soon on Jackson's account; but as far forth as I go, he couldn't git here too late. I should like to take the top of his head off."

Westover had been in Whitwell's confidence since their first chance of speech together. He now said, "I know it will be rather painful to you to have him here for some reasons, but—"

"You mean Cynthy? Well! I guess when Cynthy can't get along with the sight of Jeff Durgin, she'll be a different girl from what she's ever been before. If she's *got* to see that skunk ag'in, I guess this is about the best time to do it."

It was Westover who drove to meet Jeff at the station, when he got his dispatch, naming the train he

would take, and he found him looking very well, and
perhaps stouter than he had been.

They left the station in silence, after their greeting
and Jeff's inquiries about Jackson.   Jeff had taken
the reins, and now he put them with the whip in one
hand, and pushed up his hat with the other, and
turned his face full upon Westover.   " Notice anything in particular ? " he demanded.

" No ; yes—some slight marks."

" I guess that fellow fixed me up pretty well : paints
black eyes, and that kind of thing.   I got to scrapping with a man, Class Day ; we wanted to settle a
little business we, began at the Tree, and he left his
marks on me.   I meant to tell you the truth as soon
as I could get at you ; but I had to say erysipelas in
my letter.   I guess, if you don't mind, we'll let erysipelas stand, with the rest."

" I shouldn't have cared," Westover said, " if you'd
let it stand with me."

" Oh, thank you," Jeff returned.

There could have been no show of affection at his
meeting with Jackson even if there had been any fact
of it ; that was not the law of their life.   But Jeff had
always been a turbulent, rebellious younger brother,
resentful of Jackson's control, too much his junior to
have the associations of an equal companionship in the
past, and yet too near him in age to have anything
like a filial regard for him.   They shook hands, and
each asked the other how he was, and then they
seemed to have done with each other.   Jeff's mother
kissed him in addition to the handshaking, but made

him feel her preoccupation with Jackson; she asked him if he had hurried home on Jackson's account, and he promptly lied her out of this anxiety.

He shook hands with Cynthia, too, but it was across the barrier which had not been lowered between them since they parted. He spoke to Jackson about her, the day after he came home, when Jackson said he was feeling unusually strong and well, and the two brothers had strolled out through the orchard together. Now and then he gave the sick man his arm, and when he wanted to sit down in a sunny place, he spread the shawl he carried for him.

"I suppose mother's told you about Cynthy and me, Jackson?" he began.

Jackson answered, with lack-lustre eyes, "Yes." Presently he asked, "What's become of the other girl?"

"Damn her! I don't *know* what's become of her, and I don't care!" Jeff exploded, furiously.

"Then you don't care for her any more?" Jackson pursued, with the same languid calm.

"I *never* cared for her."

Jackson was silent, and the matter seemed to have faded out of his mind. But it was keenly alive in Jeff's mind, and he was in the strange necessity which men in the flush of life and health often feel of seeking counsel of those who stand in the presence of death, as if their words should have something of the mystical authority of the unknown wisdom they are about to penetrate.

"What *I* want to know is, what I am going to do about Cynthy?"

" I don't know," Jackson answered, vaguely, and he
expressed by his indirection the sense he must sometimes have had of his impending fate—" I don't know
what she's going to do, her or mother, either."

"Yes," Jeff assented, "that's what I think of.
And I'd do anything that I could—that you thought
was right."

Jackson apparently concentrated his mind upon the
question by an effort. "Do you care as much for
Cynthy as you used to ? "

"Yes," said Jeff, after a moment, "as much as I
ever did; and more. But I've been thinking, since
the thing happened, that, if I'd cared for her the way
she did for me, it wouldn't have happened. Look
here, Jackson! You know I've never pretended to
be like some men—like Mr. Westover, for example—
always looking out for the right and the wrong, and
all that. I didn't make myself, and I guess if the
Almighty don't make me go right it's because he
don't want me to. But I *have* got a conscience about
Cynthy, and I'd be willing to help out a little if I
knew how, about her. The devil of it is, I've got to
being afraid. I don't mean that I'm not fit for her;
any man's fit for any woman if he wants her bad
enough; but I'm afraid I sha'n't ever care for her in
the right way. That's the point. I've cared for just
one woman in this world, and it a'n't Cynthy, as far
as I can make out. But she's gone, and I guess I
could coax Cynthy round again, and I could be what
she wants me to be, after this."

Jackson lay upon his shawl, looking up at the sky

full of islands of warm clouds in its sea of blue; he
was silent so long that Jeff began to think he had not
been listening; he could not hear him breathe, and he
came forward to him quickly from the shadow of the
tree where he sat.

"Well?" Jackson whispered, turning his eyes upon
him.

"Well?" Jeff returned.

"I guess you'd better let it alone," said Jackson.

"All right.   That's what I think, too."

XLIX.

JACKSON died a week later, and they buried him in the old family lot in the farthest corner of the orchard. His mother and Cynthia put on mourning for him, and they stood together by his open grave, Mrs. Durgin leaning upon her son's arm and the girl upon her father's. The woman wept quietly, but Jeff's eyes were dry, though his face was discharged of all its prepotent impudence. Westover, standing across the grave from him, noticed the marks on his forehead that he said were from his scrapping, and wondered what really made them. He recognized the spot where they were standing as that where the boy had obeyed the law of his nature and revenged the stress put upon him for righteousness. Over the stone of the nearest grave Jeff had shown a face of triumphant derision when he pelted Westover with apples. The painter's mind fell into a chaos of conjecture and misgiving, so that he scarcely took in the words of the composite service which the minister from the Union Chapel at the Huddle read over the dead.

Some of the guests from the hotel came to the fu-

"THEY BURIED HIM IN THE OLD FAMILY LOT"

neral, but others who were not in good health remained away, and there was a general sense among
them, which imparted itself to Westover, that Jackson's dying so, at the beginning of the season, was
not a fortunate incident.   As he sat talking with
Jeff at a corner of the piazza late in the afternoon,
Frank Whitwell came up to them and said there were
some people in the office who had driven over from
another hotel to see about board, but they had heard
there was sickness in the house, and wished to talk
with him.

"I won't come," said Jeff.

"They're not satisfied with what I've said," the
boy urged.   "What shall I tell them?"

"Tell them to—go to the devil," said Jeff, and
when Frank Whitwell made off with this message for
delivery in such decent terms as he could imagine for
it, Jeff said, rather to himself than to Westover, "I
don't see how we're going to run this hotel with that
old family lot down there in the orchard, much
longer."

He assumed the air of full authority at Lion's
Head; and Westover felt the stress of a painful conjecture in regard to the Whitwells intensified upon
him from the moment he turned away from Jackson's
grave.

Cynthia and her father had gone back to their own
house as soon as Jeff returned, and though the girl
came home with Mrs. Durgin after the funeral, and
helped her in their common duties through the afternoon and evening, Westover saw her taking her way

down the hill with her brother when the long day's work was over. Jeff saw her too; he was sitting with Westover at the office door smoking, and he was talking of the Whitwells.

"I suppose they won't stay," he said, "and I can't expect it; but I don't know what mother will do, exactly."

At the same moment Whitwell came round the corner of the hotel from the barn, and approached them. "Jeff, I guess I better tell you straight off that we're goin', the children and me."

"All right, Mr. Whitwell," said Jeff, with respectful gravity, "I was afraid of it."

Westover made a motion to rise, but Whitwell laid a detaining hand upon his knee. "There ain't anything so private about it, so far as I know."

"Don't go, Mr. Westover," said Jeff, and Westover remained.

"We a'n't a-goin' to leave you in the lurch, and we want you should take your time, especially Mis' Durgin. But the sooner the better. Heigh?"

"Yes, I understand *that*, Mr. Whitwell; I guess mother will miss you, but if you must go, you must." The two men remained silent a moment, and then Jeff broke out passionately, rising and flinging his cigar away: "I wish *I* could go, instead! That would be the *right* way, and I guess mother would like it full as well. Do you see any way to manage it?" He put his foot up in his chair, and dropped his elbow on his knee, with his chin propped in his hand. Westover could see that he meant what he was saying.

"If there was *any* way, I'd do it. I know what you think of me, and I should be just like you, in your place. I don't feel right to turn you out here, I don't, Mr. Whitwell, and yet if I stay, I've got to do it. What's the reason I can't go?"

"You can't," said Whitwell, "and that's all about it. We shouldn't let you, if you could. But I a'n't surprised you feel the way you do," he added, unsparingly. "As you say, I should feel just so myself if I was in your place. Well, good-night, Mr. Westover."

Whitwell turned and slouched down the hill, leaving the painter to the most painful moment he had known with Jeff Durgin, and nearer sympathy. "That's all right, Mr. Westover," Jeff said, "I don't blame him."

He remained in a constraint from which he presently broke with mocking hilarity when Jombateeste came round the corner of the house, as if he had been waiting for Whitwell to be gone, and told Jeff he must get somebody else to look after the horses.

"Why don't you wait and take the horses with you, Jombateeste?" he inquired. "They'll be handing in their resignation, the next thing. Why not go altogether?"

The little Canuck paused, as if uncertain whether he was made the object of unfriendly derision or not, and looked at Westover for help. Apparently he decided to chance it in as bitter an answer as he could invent. "The 'oss can't 'elp 'imself, Mr. Durgin. 'E stay. But you don' hown *everybody.*"

"That's so, Jombateeste," said Jeff. "That's a
good hit. It makes me feel awfully. Have a cigar?"
The Canuck declined with a dignified bow, and Jeff
said: "You don't smoke any more? Oh, I see! It's
my tobacco you're down on. What's the matter,
Jombateeste? What are you going away for?" Jeff
lighted for himself the cigar the Canuck had refused,
and smoked down upon the little man.

"Mr. W'itwell goin'," Jombateeste said, a little
confused and daunted.

"What's Mr. Whitwell going for?"

"You hask Mr. W'itwell."

"All right. And if I can get him to stay will you
stay too, Jombateeste? I don't like to see a rat leaving a ship; the ship's sure to sink, if he does. How
do you suppose I'm going to run Lion's Head without
you to throw down hay to the horses? It will be ruin
to me, sure, Jombateeste. All the guests know how
you play on the pitchfork out there, and they'll leave
in a body if they hear you've quit. Do say you'll
stay, and I'll reduce your wages one half on the spot."

Jombateeste waited to hear no more injuries. He
said, "You'll don' got money enough, Mr. Durgin, by
gosh! to reduce my wages," and he started down the
hill towards Whitwell's house with as great loftiness as
could comport with a downhill gait and his stature.

"Well, I seem to be getting it all round, Mr. West-
over," said Jeff. "This must make *you* feel good.
I don't know but I begin to believe there's a God in
Israel, myself."

He walked away without saying good-night, and

Westover went to bed without the chance of setting himself right. In the morning, when he came down to breakfast, and stopped at the desk to engage a conveyance for the station from Frank Whitwell, the boy forestalled him with a grave face. " You don't know about Mrs. Durgin ? "

" No ; what about her ? "

" Well, we can't tell exactly. Father thinks it's a shock ; Jombateeste's gone over to Lovewell for the doctor. Cynthia's with her. It seemed to come on in the night."

He spoke softly, that no one else might hear ; but by noon the fact that Mrs. Durgin had been stricken with paralysis was all over the place. The gloom cast upon the opening season by Jackson's death was deepened among the guests. Some who had talked of staying through July went away that day. But under Cynthia's management the housekeeping was really unaffected by Mrs. Durgin's calamity, and the people who stayed found themselves as comfortable as ever. Jeff came fully into the hotel management, and in their business relation Cynthia and he were continually together ; there was no longer a question of the Whitwells leaving him ; even Jombateeste persuaded himself to stay, and Westover felt obliged to remain at least till the present danger in Mrs. Durgin's case was past.

With the first return of physical strength, Mrs. Durgin was impatient to be seen about the house, and to retrieve the season that her affliction had made so largely a loss. The people who had become accus-

tomed to it stayed on, and the house filled up as she
grew better, but even the sight of her in a wheeled
chair did not bring back the prosperity of other years.
She lamented over it with a keen and full perception
of the fact, but in a cloudy association of it with the
joint future of Jeff and Cynthia.

One day, after Mrs. Durgin had declared that she
did not know what they were to do, if things kept
on as they were going, Whitwell asked his daughter,
" Do you suppose she thinks you and Jeff have made
it up again ? "

" I don't know," said the girl, with a troubled voice,
" and I don't know what to do about it. It don't seem
as if I could tell her, and yet it's wrong to let her go
on."

" Why didn't *he* tell her ? " demanded her father.
" 'Ta'n't fair his leavin' it to you. But it's *like* him ! "

The sick woman's hold upon the fact weakened
most when she was tired. When she was better, she
knew how it was with them. Commonly it was when
Cynthia had got her to bed for the night that she sent
for Jeff, and wished to ask him what he was going to
do. " You can't expect Cynthy to stay here another
winter helpin' you, with Jackson away. You've got
to either take her with you, or else come here yourself. Give up your last year in college, why don't
you ? *I* don't want you should stay, and I don't know
who does. If I was in Cynthia's place, I'd let you
work off your own conditions now, you've give up the
law. She'll kill herself, tryin' to keep you along."

Sometimes her speech became so indistinct that no

one but Cynthia could make it out; and Jeff, listening
with a face as nearly discharged as might be of its
laughing irony, had to turn to Cynthia for the word
which no one else could catch, and which the stricken
woman remained distressfully waiting for her to repeat to him, with her anxious eyes upon the girl's face.
He was dutifully patient with all his mother's whims.
He came whenever she sent for him, and sat quiet
under the severities with which she visited all his past
unworthiness.   "Who you been hectorin' now, I
should like to know," she began on him one evening when he came at her summons.   "Between you
and Fox, I got no peace of my life.   Where *is* the
dog ? "

"Fox is all right, mother," Jeff responded. "You're
feeling a little better to-night, a'n't you ? "

"I don't know; I can't tell," she returned, with a
gleam of intelligence in her eye.   Then she said, "I
don't see why I'm left to strangers all the time."

"You don't call Cynthia a stranger, do you, mother ? " he asked, coaxingly.

"Oh,—Cynthy ! " said Mrs. Durgin, with a glance
as of surprise at seeing her.   "No, Cynthy's all right.
But where's Jackson and your father ?   If I've told
them not to be out in the dew once, I've told 'em a
hundred times.   Cynthy'd better look after her house-
keepin' if she don't want the whole place to run behind, and not a soul left in the house.   What time
o' year is it now ? " she suddenly asked, after a little
weary pause.

"It's the last of August, mother."

"Oh," she sighed, "I thought it was the beginnin' of May. Didn't you come up here in May?"

"Yes."

"Well, then— Or, mebbe that's one o' them tormentin' dreams; they do pester so! What did you come for?"

Jeff was sitting on one side of her bed and Cynthia on the other. She was looking at the sufferer's face, and she did not meet the glance of amusement which Jeff turned upon her at being so fairly cornered. "Well, I don't know," he said. "I thought you might like to see me."

"What'd he come for?"—the sick woman turned to Cynthia.

"You'd better tell her," said the girl, coldly, to Jeff. "She won't be satisfied till you do. She'll keep coming back to it."

"Well, mother," said Jeff, still with something of his hardy amusement, "I hadn't been acting just right, and I thought I'd better tell Cynthy."

"You better let the child alone. If I ever catch you teasin' them children again, I'll make Jackson shoot Fox."

"All right, mother," said Jeff.

She moved herself restively in bed. "What's this," she demanded of her son, "that Whit'ell's tellin' about you and Cynthy breakin' it off?"

"Well, there was talk of that," said Jeff, passing his hand over his lips to keep back the smile that was stealing to them.

"Who done it?"

Cynthia kept her eyes on Jeff, who dropped his to his mother's face. "Cynthy did it; but I guess I gave her good enough reason!"

"About that hussy in Boston? She was full more to blame than what you was. I don't see what Cynthy wanted to do it for on her account."

"I guess Cynthy was right."

Mrs. Durgin's speech had been thickening more and more. She now said something that Jeff could not understand. He looked involuntarily at Cynthia.

"She says she thinks I was hasty with you," the girl interpreted.

Jeff kept his eyes on hers, but he answered to his mother: "Not any more than I deserved. I hadn't any right to expect that she would stand it."

Again the sick woman tried to say something. Jeff made out a few syllables, and after his mother had repeated her words, he had to look to Cynthia for help.

"She wants to know if it's all right now."

"What shall I say?" asked Jeff, huskily.

"Tell her the truth."

"What is the truth?"

"That we haven't made it up."

Jeff hesitated, and then said: "Well, not yet, mother," and he bent an entreating look upon Cynthia which she could not feel was wholly for himself. "I —I guess we can fix it, somehow. I behaved very badly to Cynthia."

"No, not to me!" the girl protested in an indignant burst.

"Not to that little scalawag, then!" cried Jeff. "If the wrong wasn't to you, there wasn't any wrong."

"It was to *you!*" Cynthia retorted.

"Oh, I guess *I* can stand it," said Jeff, and his smile now came to his lips and eyes.

His mother had followed their quick parley with eager looks, as if she were trying to keep her intelligence to its work concerning them. The effort seemed to exhaust her, and when she spoke again her words were so indistinct that even Cynthia could not understand them till she had repeated them several times.

Then the girl was silent, while the invalid kept an eager look upon her. She seemed to understand that Cynthia did not mean to speak; and the tears came into her eyes.

"Do you want me to know what she said?" asked Jeff, respectfully, reverently almost.

Cynthia said, gently, "She says that then you must show you didn't mean any harm to me, and that you cared for me, all through, and you didn't care for anybody else."

"Thank you," said Jeff, and he turned to his mother. "I'll do everything I can to make Cynthy believe that, mother."

The girl broke into tears and went out of the room. She sent in the night-watcher, and then Jeff took leave of his mother with an unwonted kiss.

Into the shadow of a starlit night he saw the figure he had been waiting for glide out of the glitter of the hotel lights. He followed it down the road.

"Cynthia," he called; and when he came up with

her he asked, "What's the reason we can't make it true? Why can't you believe what mother wants me to make you?"

Cynthia stopped, as her wont was when she wished to speak seriously. "Do you ask that for my sake or hers?"

"For both your sakes."

"I thought so. You ought to have asked it for your own sake, Jeff, and then I might have been fool enough to believe you. But now!"

She started swiftly down the hill again, and this time he did not try to follow her.

L.

MRS. DURGIN'S speech never regained the measure of clearness it had before; no one but Cynthia could understand her, and often she could not. The doctor from Lovewell surmised that she had sustained another stroke, lighter, more obscure than the first, and it was that which had rendered her almost inarticulate. The paralysis might have also affected her brain, and silenced her thoughts as well as her words. Either she believed that the reconciliation between Jeff and Cynthia had taken place, or else she could no longer care. She did not question them again, but peacefully weakened more and more. Near the end of September she had a third stroke, and from this she died.

The day after the funeral Jeff had a talk with Whitwell, and opened his mind to him.

"I'm going over to the other side, and I sha'n't be back before spring, or about time to start the season here. What I want to know is whether, if I'm out of the house, and not likely to come back, you'll stay here, and look after the place through the winter. It hasn't been a good season, but I guess I can afford to make it worth your while if you look at it as a matter of business."

Whitwell leaned forward and took a straw into his mouth from the golden wall of oat sheaves in the barn where they were talking. A soft rustling in the mow overhead marked the remote presence of Jombateeste, who was getting forward the hay for the horses, pushing it towards the holes where it should fall into their racks.

"I should want to think about it," said Whitwell. "I do' know as Cynthy' d care much about stayin'; or Frank."

"How long do you want to think about it?" Jeff demanded, ignoring the possible wishes of Cynthia and Frank.

"I guess I could let you know by night."

"All right," said Jeff.

He was turning away, when Whitwell remarked: "I don't know as I should want to stay without I could have somebody I could depend on, with me, to look after the hosses. Frank wouldn't want to."

"Who'd you like?"

"Well,—Jombateeste."

"Ask him."

Whitwell called to the Canuck, and he came forward to the edge of the mow, and stood, fork in hand, looking down.

"Want to stay here this winter and look after the hosses, Jombateeste?" Whitwell asked.

"Nosseh!" said the Canuck, with a misliking eye on Jeff.

"I mean, along with me," Whitwell explained. "If I conclude to stay, will you? Jeff's goin' abroad."

"I guess I stay," said Jombateeste.

"Don't strain yourself, Jombateeste," said Jeff, with malevolent derision.

"Not for you, Jeff Dorrgin," returned the Canuck. "I strain myself till I bust, if I want."

Jeff sneered to Whitwell: "Well, then, the most important point is settled. Let me know about the minor details as soon as you can."

"All right."

Whitwell talked the matter over with his children at supper that evening. Jeff had made him a good offer, and he had the winter before him to provide for.

"*I* don't know what deviltry he's up to," he said in conclusion.

Frank looked to his sister for their common decision. "I am going to try for a school," she said, quietly. "It's pretty late, but I guess I can get something. You and Frank had better stay."

"And you don't feel as if it was kind of meechin', our takin' up with his offer, after what's— ?" Whitwell delicately forbore to fill out his sentence.

"*You* are doing the favor, father," said the girl. "He knows that, and I guess he wouldn't know where to look if you refused. And, after all, what's happened now is as much my doing as his."

"I guess that's something so," said Whitwell, with a long sigh of relief. "Well, I'm glad you can look at it in that light, Cynthy. It's the way the feller's built, I presume, as much as anything."

His daughter waived the point. " I shouldn't feel just right if none of us stayed in the old place. I should feel as if we had turned our backs on Mrs. Durgin."

Her eyes shone, and her father said : " Well, I guess that's so, come to think of it. She's been like a mother to you, this past year, ha'n't she? And it must have come pootty hard for her, sidin' agin Jeff. But she done it."

The girl turned her head away. They were sitting in the little low keeping-room of Whitwell's house, and her father had his hat on provisionally. Through the window they could see the light of the lantern at the office door of the hotel, whose mass was lost in the dark above and behind the lamp. It was all very still outside.

" I declare," Whitwell went on, musingly, " I wisht Mr. Westover was here."

Cynthia started, but it was to ask : " Do you want I should help you with your Latin, Frank ? "

Whitwell came back an hour later and found them still at their books. He told them it was all arranged; Durgin was to give up the place to him in a week, and he was to surrender it again when Jeff came back in the spring. In the meantime things were to remain as they were ; after he was gone, they could all go and live at Lion's Head if they chose.

" We'll see," said Cynthia. " I've been thinking that might be the best way, after all. I might not get a school, it's so late."

" That's so," her father assented. " I declare," he

added, after a moment's muse, " I felt sorry for the
feller settin' up there alone, with nobody to do for
him but that old thing he's got in. She can't cook
any more than—" He desisted for want of a comparison, and said, " Such a *lookin'* table, too."

"Do you think I better go and look after things
a little ?" Cynthia asked.

"Well, you no *need* to," said her father. He got
down the planchette, and labored with it, while his
children returned to Frank's lessons.

" Dumn 'f *I* can make the thing work," he said to
himself at last. " *I* can't git *any* of 'em up. If Jackson was here, now ! "

Thrice a day Cynthia went up to the hotel, and
oversaw the preparation of Jeff's meals, and kept taut
the slack housekeeping of the old Irish woman who
had remained as a favor, after the hotel closed, and
professed to have lost the chance of a place for the
winter by her complaisance. She submitted to Cynthia's authority, and tried to make interest for an indefinite stay by sudden zeal and industry, and the last
days of Jeff in the hotel were more comfortable than
he openly recognized. He left the care of the building wholly to Whitwell, and shut himself up in the
old farm parlor with the plans for a new hotel which
he said he meant to put up some day, if he could ever
get rid of the old one. He went once to Lovewell,
where he renewed the insurance, and somewhat increased it ; and he put a small mortgage on the
property. He forestalled the slow progress of the
knowledge of other's affairs, which, in the country, is

as sure as it is slow, and told Whitwell what he had done. He said he wanted the mortgage money for his journey, and the insurance money, if he could have the luck to cash up by a good fire, to rebuild with.

Cynthia seldom met him in her comings and goings, but if they met they spoke on the terms of their boy and girl associations, and with no approach through resentment or tenderness to the relation that was ended between them. She saw him oftener than at any other time setting off on the long tramps he took through the woods in the afternoons. He was always alone, and, so far as any one knew, his wanderings had no object but to kill the time which hung heavy on his hands during the fortnight after his mother's death, before he sailed. It might have seemed strange that he should prefer to pass the days at Lion's Head after he had arranged for the care of the place with Whitwell, and Whitwell always believed that he stayed in the hope of somehow making up with Cynthia.

One day, towards the very last, Durgin found himself pretty well fagged in the old pulp-mill clearing on the side of Lion's Head, which still belonged to Whitwell, and he sat down on a mouldering log there to rest. It had always been a favorite picnic ground, but the season just past had known few picnics, and it was those of former years that had left their traces in rusty sardine-cans and broken glass and crockery on the border of the clearing, which was now almost covered with white moss. Jeff thought of the day when he lurked in the hollow below with Fox, while Westover remained talking with Whitwell. He

thought of the picnic that Mrs. Marven had embittered
for him, and he thought of the last time that he had
been there with Westover, when they talked of the
Vostrands.

Life had, so far, not been what he meant it, and
just now it occurred to him that he might not have
wholly made it what it had been.   It seemed to him
that a good many other people had come in and taken
a hand in making his own life what it had been; and
if he had meddled with theirs more than he was
wanted, it was about an even thing.   As far as he
could make out, he was a sort of ingredient in the
general mixture.   He had probably done his share of
the flavoring, but he had had very little to do with
the mixing.   There were different ways of looking at
the thing.   Westover had his way, but it struck Jeff
that it put too much responsibility on the ingredient,
and too little on the power that chose it.   He believed
that he could prove a clear case in his own favor, as
far as the question of final justice was concerned, but
he had no complaints to make.   Things had fallen
out very much to his mind.   He was the Landlord at
Lion's Head, at last, with the full right to do what he
pleased with the place, and with half a year's leisure
before him to think it over.   He did not mean to
waste the time while he was abroad; if there was anything to be learned anywhere about keeping a summer
hotel, he was going to learn it; and he thought the
summer hotel could be advantageously studied in its
winter phases in the mild climates of Southern Europe.
He meant to strike for the class of Americans who

resorted to those climates; to divine their characters
and to please their tastes.

He unconsciously included Cynthia in his scheme
of inquiry; he had been used so long to trust to her
instincts and opinions, and to rely upon her help, and
he realized that she was no longer in his life with
something like the shock a man experiences when the
loss of a limb, which continues a part of his inveterate
consciousness, is brought to his sense by some mechanical attempt to use it.   But even in this pang he
did not regret that all was over between them.   He
knew now that he had never cared for her as he had
once thought, and on her account, if not his own, he
was glad their engagement was broken.   A soft melancholy for his own disappointment imparted itself to
his thoughts of Cynthia.   He felt truly sorry for her,
and he truly admired and respected her.   He was in
a very lenient mood towards every one, and he went
so far in thought towards forgiving his enemies that
he was willing at least to pardon all those whom he
had injured.   A little rustling in the underbrush
across the clearing caught his quick ear, and he looked
up to see Jombateeste parting the boughs of the young
pines on its edge, and advancing into the open with a
gun on his shoulder.   He called to him cheerily:
"Hello, John!   Any luck?"

Jombateeste shook his head.   "Nawthing."   He
hesitated.

"What are you after?"

"Partridge," Jombateeste ventured back.

Jeff could not resist the desire to scoff which always

came upon him at sight of the Canuck. " Oh, pshaw !
Why don't you go for woodchucks? They fly low,
and you can hit them on the wing, if you can't sneak
on 'em sitting."

Jombateeste received his raillery in dignified silence,
and turned back into the woods again. He left Durgin in heightened good-humor with himself and with
the world, which had finally so well adapted itself to
his desires and designs.

Jeff watched his resentful going with a grin, and
then threw himself back on the thick bed of dry moss
where he had been sitting, and watched the clouds
drifting across the space of blue which the clearing
opened overhead. His own action reminded him of
Jackson, lying in the orchard, and looking up at the
sky. He felt strangely at one with him, and he experienced a tenderness for his memory which he had
not known before. Jackson had been a good man ;
he realized that with a curious sense of novelty in the
reflection ; he wondered what the incentives and the
objects of such men as Jackson and Westover were,
anyway. Something like grief for his brother came
upon him; not such grief as he had felt passionately
enough, though tacitly, for his mother; but a regret
for not having shown Jackson during his life that he
could appreciate his unselfishness, though he could
not see the reason or the meaning of it. He said to
himself, in their safe remoteness from each other, that
he wished he could do something for Jackson. He
wondered if in the course of time he should get to be
something like him. He imagined trying.

He heard sounds again in the edge of the clearing, but he decided that it was that fool Jombateeste coming back; and when steps approached softly and hesitantly across the moss, he did not trouble himself to take his eyes from the clouds. He was only vexed to have his reverie broken in upon.

A voice that was not Jombateeste's spoke: "I say! Can you tell me the way to the Brooker Institute, or to the road down the mountain?"

Jeff sat suddenly bolt-upright; in another moment he jumped to his feet. The Brooker Institute was a branch of the Keeley Cure recently established near the Huddle, and this must be a patient who had wandered from it, on one of the excursions the inmates made with their guardians, and lost his way. This was the fact that Jeff realized at the first glance he gave the man. The next he recognized that the man was Alan Lynde.

"Oh, it's you," he said, quite simply. He felt so cruelly the hardship of his one unforgiven enemy's coming upon him just when he had resolved to be good, that the tears came into his eyes. Then his rage seemed to swell up in him like the rise of a volcanic flood. "I'm going to kill you!" he roared, and he launched himself upon Lynde, who stood dazed.

But the murder which Jeff meant was not to be so easily done. Lynde had not grown up in dissolute idleness without acquiring some of the arts of self-defence which are called manly. He met Jeff's onset with remembered skill, and with the strength which he had gained in three months of the wholesome regi-

men of the Brooker Institute.   He had been sent
there, not by Dr. Lacy's judgment, but by his despair,
and so far the Cure had cured.   He felt strong and
fresh, and the hate which filled Jeff at sight of him
steeled his shaken nerves, and re-enforced his feebler
muscles too.

He made a desperate fight where he could not hope
for mercy, and kept himself free of his powerful foe,
whom he fought round and foiled, if he could not hurt
him.   Jeff never knew of the blows Lynde got in upon
him; he had his own science too, but he would not
employ it.   He wanted to crash through Lynde's defence, and lay hold of him, and crush the life out of
him.

The contest could not have lasted long at the best;
but before Lynde was worn out he caught his heel in
an old laurel root, and while he whirled to recover his
footing Jeff closed in upon him, caught him by the
middle, flung him down upon the moss, and was
kneeling on his breast with both hands at his throat.

He glared down into his enemy's face, and suddenly it looked pitifully little and weak, like a girl's
face, a child's.

Sometimes, afterwards, it seemed to him that he
forbore because at that instant he saw Jombateeste
appear at the edge of the clearing and come running
upon them.   At other times he had the fancy that his
action was purely voluntary, and that, against the logic
of his hate and the habit of his life, he had mercy
upon his enemy.   He did not pride himself upon it;
he rather humbled himself before the fact, which was

"KNEELING ON HIS BREAST, WITH BOTH HANDS ON HIS THROAT"

accomplished through his will, and not by it, and remained a mystery he did not try to solve.

He took his hands from Lynde's throat and his
knees off his breast. "Get up," he said; and when
Lynde stood trembling on his feet, he said to Jombateeste: "Show this man the way to the Brooker Institute. I'll take your gun home for you," and it was
easy for him to detach the piece from the bewildered
Canuck's grasp. "Go! And if you stop, or even let
him look back, I'll shoot him. Quick!"

LI.

THE day after Thanksgiving, when Westover was trying to feel well after the turkey and cranberry and cider which a lady had given him at a consciously old-fashioned Thanksgiving dinner, but not making it out sufficiently to be able to work, he was astonished to receive a visit from Whitwell.

"Well, sir," said the philosopher, without giving himself pause for the exchange of reflections upon his presence in Boston, which might have been agreeable to him on a less momentous occasion, "it's all up with Lion's Head."

"What do you mean?" demanded Westover, with his mind upon the mountain, which he electrically figured in an incredible destruction.

"She's burnt. Burnt down day before yist'd'y aft'noon. A'n't hardly a stick of her left. Ketched Lord knows how, from the kitchen chimney, and a high northwest wind blowin', that ca'd the sparks to the barn, and set fire to that too. Hosses gone; couldn't get round to 'em; only three of us there, and mixed up so about the house till it was so late the critters wouldn't *come* out. Folks from over Huddle

way see the blaze, and helped all they could; but it
wa'n't no use. I guess all we saved, about, was the
flag-pole."

"But you're all right yourselves? Cynthia—"

"Well, there was our misfortune," said Whitwell,
while Westover's heart stopped in a mere wantonness
of apprehension. "If she'd be'n there, it might ha'
be'n diff'ent. We might ha' had more sense; or *she*
would, anyway. But she was over to Lovewell stock-
in' up for Thanksgivin', and I had to make out the
best I could, with Frank and Jombateeste. Why, that
Canuck didn't seem to have no more head on him than
a hen. I was disgusted; but Cynthy wouldn't let me
say anything to him, and I d' know as 't 'ould done
any good, myself. We've talked it all over in every
light, ever since; guess we've set up most the time
talkin', and nothin' would do her but I should come
down and see you before I took a single step about
it."

"How—step about what?" asked Westover, with
a remote sense of hardship at being brought in, tempered by the fact that it was Cynthia who had brought
him in.

"Why, that devil," said Whitwell, and Westover
knew that he meant Jeff, "went and piled on all the
insurance he could pile on, before he left; and I don't
know what to do about it."

"I should think the best thing was to collect the
insurance," Westover suggested, distractedly.

"It a'n't so easy as what that comes to," said
Whitwell. "I couldn't collect the insurance; and

here's the point, anyway. When a hotel's made a bad season, and she's fully insured, she's pootty certain to burn up some time in the winter. Everybody knows that comical devil wanted Lion's Head to burn up so' t he could build new, and I presume there a'n't a man, woman, or child anywhere round but what believes I set her on fire. Hired to do it. Now, see? Jeff off in Europe; daytime; no lives lost; prop'ty *total* loss. 'S a clear case. Heigh? I tell you, I'm afraid I've got trouble ahead."

Westover tried to protest, to say something in derision or defiance; but he was shaken himself, and he ended by getting his hat and coat; Whitwell had kept his own on, in the excitement. "We'll go out and see a lawyer. A friend of mine; it won't cost you anything." He added this assurance at a certain look of reluctance that came into Whitwell's face, and that left it as soon as he had spoken. Whitwell glanced round the studio even cheerily. "Who'd ha' thought," he said, fastening upon the study which Westover had made of Lion's Head the winter before, "that the old place would 'a' gone so soon?" He did not mean the mountain which he was looking at, but the hotel that was present to his mind's eye; and Westover perceived as he had not before that to Whitwell the hotel and not the mountain was Lion's Head.

He remembered to ask now where Whitwell had left his family, and Whitwell said that Frank and Cynthia were at home in his own house with Jombateeste; but he presumed he could not get back to them now before the next day. He refused to be

interested in any of the aspects of Boston which
Westover casually pointed out, but when they had
seen the lawyer he came forth a new man, vividly interested in everything.   The lawyer had been able to
tell them that though the insurance companies would
look sharply into the cause of the fire, there was no
probability, hardly a possibility, that they would inculpate him, and he need give himself no anxiety
about the affair.

"There's one thing, though," Whitwell said to
Westover when they got out upon the street. "Hadn't
I ought to let Jeff know?"

"Yes, at once.   You'd better cable him.   Have
you got his address?"

Whitwell had it, and he tasted all the dramatic
quality of sending word to Jeff, which he would receive
in Florence an hour after it left Boston.   "I did hope
I could ha' cabled once to Jackson, while he was gone,"
he said, regretfully, "but unless we can fix up a wire
with the other world, I guess I sha'n't ever do it now.
I suppose Jackson's still hangin' round Mars, some-
'res."

He had a sectarian pride in the beauty of the Spiritual Temple which Westover walked him by on his
way to see Trinity Church and the Fine Arts Museum,
and he sorrowed that he could not attend a service
there.   But he was consoled by the lunch which he
had with Westover at a restaurant where it was served
in courses.   "I presume this is what Jeff's goin' to
give 'em at Lion's Head when he gits it goin' again."

"How is it he's in Florence?" it occurred to Westover to ask. "I thought he was going to Nice for the winter."

"I don't know. That's the address he give in his last letter," said Whitwell. "I'll be glad when I've done with him for good and all. He's all kinds of a devil."

It was in Westover's mind to say that he wished the Whitwells had never had anything to do with Durgin after his mother's death. He had felt it a want of delicacy in them that they had been willing to stay on in his employ, and his ideal of Cynthia had suffered a kind of wound from what must have been her decision in the matter. He would have expected something altogether different from her pride, her self-respect. But he now merely said: "Yes, I shall be glad, too. I'm afraid he's a bad fellow."

His words seemed to appeal to Whitwell's impartiality. "Well, I d' know as I should say *bad*, exactly. He's a mixture."

"He's a bad *mixture*," said Westover.

"Well, I guess you're partly right there," Whitwell admitted with a laugh. After a dreamy moment he asked, "Ever hear anything more about that girl here in Boston?"

Westover knew that he meant Bessie Lynde. "She's abroad somewhere, with her aunt"

Whitwell had not taken any wine; apparently he was afraid of forming instantly the habit of drink if he touched it; but he tolerated Westover's pint of Zinfandel, and he seemed to warm sympathetically to a greater confidence as the painter made away with it.

"There's one thing I never told Cynthy yet; well, Jombateeste didn't tell me himself till after Jeff was gone; and then, thinks I, what's the use? But I guess *you* had better know."

He leaned forward across the table, and gave Jombateeste's story of the encounter between Jeff and Alan Lynde in the clearing. "Now what do you suppose was the reason Jeff let up on the feller? Of course, he meant to choke the life out of him, and his just ketchin' sight of Jombateeste, do you believe that was enough to stop him, when he'd started in for a thing like that? Or what was it done it?"

Westover listened with less thought of the fact itself than of another fact that it threw light upon. It was clear to him now that the Class-Day scrapping which had left its marks upon Jeff's face was with Lynde, and that when Jeff got him in his power he was in such a fury for revenge, that no mere motive of prudence could have arrested him. In both events, it must have been Bessie Lynde that was the moving cause; but what was it that stayed Jeff in his vengeance?

"Let him up, and let him walk away, you say?" he demanded of Whitwell.

Whitwell nodded. "That's what Jombateeste said. Said Jeff said if he let the feller look back he'd shoot him. But he didn't haf to."

"I can't make it out," Westover sighed.

"It's been too much for me," Whitwell said. "I told Jombateeste he'd better keep it to himself, and I guess he done so. S'pose Jeff still had a sneakin' fondness for the girl?"

"I don't know ; perhaps," Westover asserted.

Whitwell threw his head back in a sudden laugh that showed all the work of his dentist. "Well, wouldn't it be a joke if he was there in Florence after her? Be just like Jeff."

"It would be like Jeff; I don't know whether it would be a joke or not. I hope he won't find it a joke, if it's so," said Westover, gloomily. A fantastic apprehension seized him, which made him wish for the moment that it might be so, and which then passed, leaving him simply sorry for any chance that might bring Bessie Lynde into the fellow's way again.

For the evening Whitwell's preference would have been a lecture of some sort, but there was none adver- tised, and he consented to go with Westover to the theatre. He came back to the painter at dinner-time, after a wary exploration of the city, which had resulted not only in a personal acquaintance with its monu- ments, but an immunity from its dangers and tempta- tions which he prided himself hardly less upon. He had seen Faneuil Hall, the old State House, Bunker Hill, the Public Library, and the Old South Church, and he had not been sand-bagged, or buncoed, or led astray from the paths of propriety. He was disposed, in the comfortable sense of escape, to moralize upon the civilization of great cities, which he now witnessed at first hand for the first time; and throughout the evening, between the acts of the Old Homestead, which he found a play of some merit, but of not so much novelty in its characters as he had somehow led himself to expect, he recurred to the difficulties and dangers that must beset a young man in coming to a place like Boston.   Westover found him less amusing than he had on his own ground at Lion's Head, and tasted a quality of commonplace in his deliverances which made him question whether he had not, perhaps, always owed more to this environment than he had suspected.   But they parted upon terms of mutual respect, and in the common hope of meeting again. Whitwell promised to let Westover know what he heard of Jeff, but when the painter had walked the philosopher home to his hotel, he found a message awaiting him at his studio, from Jeff direct.

" Whitwell's despatch received.   Wait letter.
"DURGIN."

Westover raged at the intelligent thrift of this telegram, and at the implication that he not only knew all about the business of Whitwell's despatch, but that he was in communication with him, and would be sufficiently interested to convey Jeff's message to him. Of course, Durgin had at once divined that Whitwell must have come to him for advice, and that he would hear from him, whether he was still in Boston or not. By cabling to Westover, Jeff saved the cost of an elaborate address to Whitwell at Lion's Head, and had brought the painter in for further consultation and assistance in his affairs.   What vexed him still more was his own consciousness that he could not defeat this impudent expectation.   He had indeed some difficulty with himself to keep from going to Whitwell's hotel with the despatch at once, and he slept badly, in his fear that he might not get it to him in the morning before he left town.

The sum of Jeff's letter when it came, and it came to Westover and not to Whitwell, was to request the painter to see a lawyer in his behalf, and put his insurance policies in his hands, with full authority to guard his interests in the matter. He told Westover where his policies would be found, and enclosed the key of his box in the Safety Vaults, with a due demand for Westover's admission to it. He registered his letter, and he jocosely promised Westover to do as much for him some day, in pleading that there was really no one else he could turn to. He put the whole business upon him, and Westover discharged himself of it as briefly as he could by delivering the papers to the lawyer he had already consulted for Whitwell.

" Is this another charity patient ? " asked his friend, with a grin.

" No," replied Westover. "You can charge this fellow along the whole line."

Before he parted with the lawyer he had his misgivings, and he said, " I shouldn't want the blackguard to think I had got a friend a fat job out of him."

The lawyer laughed intelligently. "I shall only make the usual charge. Then he *is* a blackguard."

" There ought to be a more blistering word."

" One that would imply that he was capable of setting fire to his property ? "

" I don't say that. But I'm glad he was away when it took fire," said Westover.

" You give him the benefit of the doubt."

" Yes, of every kind of doubt."

LII.

WESTOVER once more promised himself to have
nothing to do with Jeff Durgin or his affairs. But he
did not promise this so confidently as upon former
occasions, and he instinctively waited for a new com-
plication. He could not understand why Jeff should
not have come home to look after his insurance, unless
it was because he had become interested in some
woman even beyond his concern for his own advantage. He believed him capable of throwing away
advantages for disadvantages in a thing of that kind,
but he thought it more probable that he had fallen in
love with one whom he would lose nothing by winning.
It did not seem at all impossible that he should have
again met Bessie Lynde, and that they should have
made up their quarrel, or whatever it was. Jeff would
consider that he had done his whole duty by Cynthia,
and that he was free to renew his suit with Bessie;
and there was nothing in Bessie's character, as Westover understood it, to prevent her taking him back
upon a very small show of repentance if the needed
emotions were in prospect. He had decided pretty
finally that it would be Bessie rather than another

when he received a letter from Mrs. Vostrand. It was dated at Florence, and after some pretty palaver about their old friendship, which she only hoped he remembered half as fondly as she did, the letter ran:

"I am turning to you now in a very *strange difficulty*, but I do not know that I should turn to you even now, and knowing all I do of your *goodness*, if I were not asked to do so by another.

"I believe we have not heard from each other since the first days of my poor Genevieve's *marriage*, when everything looked so bright and fair, and we little realized the *clouds* that were to overcast her happiness. It is a long story, and I will not go into it fully. The truth is that poor Gigi did not treat her very kindly, and that she has not lived with him since the birth of their little girl, now nearly two years old, and the *sweetest little creature* in the world; I wish you could see her; I am sure it would inspire your pencil with the idea of an *angel-child*. At first I hoped that the separation would be only temporary, and that when Genevieve had regained her strength she would be willing to go back to her husband; but nothing would induce her to do so. In fact, poor Gigi had spent all her money, and they would have had nothing to live upon but his pay, and you know that the pay of the Italian officers is *very small*.

"Gigi made several attempts to see her, and he threatened to take the child from her, but he was always willing to compromise for money. I am afraid that he never really loved her, and that we were

both deceived by his fervent *protestations*. We managed to get away from Florence without his knowing
it, and we have spent the last two years in Lausanne,
very *happily*, though very quietly.   Our dear Checco
is in the University there, his father having given up
the plan of sending him to Harvard, and we had him
with us, while we were taking measures to secure the
divorce.   Even in the simple way we lived Genevieve
attracted a great deal of attention, as she always has
done, and she would have had several very *eligible offers*,
if she had been divorced, or if her affections had not
already been engaged, as I did not know at the time.

"We were in this state of uncertainty up to the
middle of last summer, when the news of poor Gigi's
sudden death came.   I am sorry to say that his habits
in some respects were not good, and that probably hastened it some; it had obliged him to leave the army.
Genevieve did not feel that she could consistently put
on black for him, and I did not urge her, under the *peculiar circumstances;* there is so much mere formality in
those kind of things at the best; but we immediately
returned to Florence to try and see if we could not
get back some of her effects which his family had
seized.   I am opposed to *lawsuits* if they can possibly
be avoided, and we arranged with poor Gigi's family
by agreeing to let them have Genevieve's furniture if
they would promise never to molest her with the child,
and I must say they have *behaved very well*.   We are
on the best of terms with them, and they have let us
have some of the things back which were endeared to
her by old associations, at a very reasonble rate.

" This brings me to the *romantic part* of my letter,
and I will say at once that we found your friend Mr.
Durgin in Florence, in the very hotel we went to. We
all met in the dining-room, at the *table d'hôte* one
evening, and Genevieve and he *took to each other* at
once. He spent the evening with us in our private
drawing-room, and she said to me, after he went, that
for the first time in years she felt *rested.* It seems
that she had always secretly *fancied* him, and that she
gave up to me in the matter of marrying poor Gigi,
because she knew I had my heart set upon it, and she
was not very certain of her own feelings when Mr.
D. offered himself in Boston; but the conviction that
she had made a mistake *grew upon her* more and more
after she had married Gigi.

" Well, now, Mr. Westover, I suppose you have
guessed by this time that Mr. Durgin has *renewed his
offer,* and Genevieve has conditionally accepted him;
we do not feel that she is like an *ordinary widow,* and
that she has to fill up a certain season of mourning;
she and Gigi have been *dead to each other* for years;
and Mr. Durgin is as fond of our dear little Bice as
her own father could be, and they are together *all
the time.* Her name is Beatrice de' Popolani Grassi.
Isn't it *lovely ?* She has poor Gigi's black eyes, with
the most beautiful golden hair, which she gets from
our side. You remember Genevieve's hair back in the
dear old days, before any trouble had come, and we
were all so happy together. And this brings me to
what I wanted to say. You are the *oldest friend* we
have, and by a singular coincidence you are the oldest

friend of Mr. Durgin, too. I cannot bear to risk my child's happiness a second time, and though Mr. Vostrand fully approves of the match, and has cabled his consent from Seattle, Washington, still, you know, a mother's heart cannot be at rest without some *positive assurance.* I told Mr. Durgin quite frankly how I felt, and he agreed with me that after our *experience* with poor Gigi we could not be too careful, and he authorized me to write to you, and find out *all you knew* about him. He said you had known him ever since he was a boy, and that if there was anything *bad* in his record you could tell it, and he did not want you to *spare the truth.* He knows you will be just, and he wants you to write out the *facts* as they struck you at the time.

" I shall be on *pins and needles*, as the saying is, till we hear from you, and you know how Genevieve and Mr. D. must be feeling. She is fully resolved not to have him without your *endorsement*, and he is quite willing to abide by what you say. I could almost wish you to cable me just *Good* or *Bad*, but I know that this will not be wise, and I am going to *wait for your letter*, and get your opinion in full.

" We all join in the *kindest regards.* Mr. D. is talking with Genevieve while I write, and has our darling Bice on his knees. You cannot imagine what a *picture* it makes, her childish delicacy contrasted with his stalwart strength. She says to send you a *baciettino*, and I wish you were here to receive it from her *angel lips.* Yours faithfully,

" MEDORA VOSTRAND.

" P. S.—Mr. D. says that he fell in love with Genevieve *across the barrier* between the first and second cabin when he came over with us on the *Acquitaine* four years ago, and that he has never *ceased to love* her, though at one time he persuaded himself that he cared for another because he felt that she was *lost* to him forever, and it was no use.   He really did care for the lady he was engaged to, and had a true affection for her, which he mistook for a *warmer feeling.* He says that she was worthy of any man's love, and of the *highest respect.*   I tell Genevieve that she ought to honor him for it, and that she must never be jealous of a *memory.*   We are very happy in Mr. Vostrand's cordial approval of the match.   He is so glad to think that Mr. D. is a *business man.*   His cable from Seattle was most enthusiastic.   M. D."

Westover did not know whether to laugh or cry when he read this letter, which covered several sheets of paper in lines that traversed each other in different directions.   His old, youthful ideal of Mrs. Vostrand finally perished in its presence, though still he could not blame her for wishing to see her daughter well married after having seen her married so ill.   He asked himself, without getting any very definite response, whether Mrs. Vostrand had always been this kind of a woman, or had grown into it by the use of arts which her peculiar plan of life had rendered necessary to her.   He remembered the intelligent toleration of Cynthia in speaking of her, and his indignation in behalf of the girl was also a thrill of joy for her escape from the fate which Mrs. Vostrand was so eagerly invoking for her daughter. But he thought of Genevieve with something of the same tenderness, and with a compassion that was for her alone. She seemed to him a victim who was to be sacrificed a second time, and he had clearly a duty to her which he must not evade. The only question could be how best to discharge it, and Westover took some hours from his work to turn the question over in his mind. In the end, when he was about to give the whole affair up for the present, and lose a night's sleep over it later, he had an inspiration, and he acted upon it at once. He perceived that he owed no formal response to the sentimental insincerities of Mrs. Vostrand's letter, and he decided to write to Durgin himself, and to put the case altogether in his hands. If Durgin chose to show the Vostrands what he should write, very well ; if he chose not to show it, then Westover's apparent silence would be a sufficient reply to Mrs. Vostrand's appeal.

" I prefer to address you," he began, " because I do not choose to let you think that I have any feeling to indulge against you, and because I do not think I have the right to take you out of your own keeping in any way. You would be in my keeping if I did, and I do not wish that, not only because it would be a bother to me, but because it would be a wrong to you.

" Mrs. Vostrand, whose letter to me I will leave you to answer by showing her this, or in any other manner you choose, tells me you do not want me to spare the truth concerning you. I have never been quite certain what the truth was concerning you ; you know that better than I do; and I do not propose to write your biography here.   But I will remind you of a few things.

"The first day I saw you, I caught you amusing yourself with the terror of two little children, and I had the pleasure of cuffing you for it.   But you were only a boy then, and afterwards you behaved so well that I decided you were not so much cruel as thoughtlessly mischievous.   When you had done all you could to lead me to this favorable conclusion, you suddenly turned and avenged yourself on me, so far as you could, for the help I had given the little ones against you.   I never greatly blamed you for that, for I decided that you had a vindictive temperament, and that you were not responsible for your temperament, but only for your character.

"In your first year at Harvard your associations were bad, and your conduct generally was so bad that you were suspended.   You were arrested with other rowdy students, and passed the night in a police station.   I believe you were justly acquitted of any specific offence, and I always believed that if you had experienced greater kindness socially during your first year in college you would have been a better man.

"You seem to have told Mrs. Vostrand of your engagement, and I will not speak of that.   It was creditable to you that so wise and good a girl as your betrothed should have trusted you, and I do not know that it was against you that another girl who was neither wise nor good should have trusted you at the same time.   You broke with the last, because you had to choose between the two; and, so far as I know, you accepted with a due sense of your faithlessness your dismissal by the first.   In this connection I must remind you that while you were doing your best to make the party to your second engagement believe that you were in love with her, you got her brother, an habitual inebriate, drunk, and were, so far, instrumental in breaking down the weak will with which he was struggling against his propensity.   It is only fair to you that I should add that you persuaded me you got him only a little drunker than he had already got himself, and that you meant to have looked after him, but forgot him in your preoccupation with his sister.

"I do not know what took place between you and these people after you broke your engagement with the sister, until your encounter with the brother in Whitwell's Clearing, and I know of this only at second hand.   I can well believe that you had some real or fancied injury to pay off; and I give you all the credit you may wish to claim for sparing him at last. For one of your vindictive temperament it must have been difficult.

"I have told you the worst things I know of you, and I do not pretend to know them more than superficially.   I am not asked to judge you, and I will not. You must be your own judge.   You are to decide whether these and other acts of yours are the acts of a man good enough to be intrusted with the happiness of a woman who has already been very unhappy.

"You have sometimes, however—oftener than I wished—come to me for advice, and I now offer you

some advice voluntarily. Do not suppose that because
you love this woman, as you believe, you are fit to be
the keeper of her future. Ask yourself how you have
dealt hitherto with those who have loved you, and
whom in a sort you loved, and do not go further unless the answer is such as you can fully and faithfully
report to the woman you wish to marry. What you
have made yourself you will be to the end. You once
called me an idealist, and perhaps you will call this
idealism. I will only add, and I will give the last
word in your defence, you alone know what you are."

LIII.

As soon as Westover had posted his letter he began to blame himself for it. He saw that the right and manly thing would have been to write to Mrs. Vostrand, and tell her frankly what he thought of Durgin. Her folly, her insincerity, her vulgarity, had nothing to do with the affair, so far as he was concerned. If she had once been so kind to him as to bind him to her in grateful friendship, she certainly had a claim upon his best offices. His duty was to her, and not at all to Durgin. He need not have said anything against him because it was against him, but because it was true; and if he had written he must not have said anything less than the truth.

He could have chosen not to write at all. He could have said that her mawkish hypocrisy was a little too much; that she was really wanting him to whitewash Durgin for her, and she had no right to put upon him the responsibility for the step she clearly wished to take. He could have made either of these decisions, and defended them to himself; but in what he had done he had altogether shirked. While he was writing to Durgin, and pretending that he could justly leave this affair to him, he was simply indulging a bit of sentimental pose, far worse than anything in Mrs. Vostrand's sham appeal for his help.

He felt, as the time went by, that she had not written of her own impulse, but at her daughter's urgence, and that it was this poor creature whose trust he had paltered with. He believed that Durgin would not fail to make her unhappy, yet he had not done what he might to deliver her out of his hand. He had satisfied a wretched pseudo-magnanimity towards a faithless scoundrel, as he thought Durgin, at the cost of a woman whose anxious hope of his aid had probably forced her mother's hand.

At first he thought his action irrevocable, and he bitterly upbraided himself for not taking council with Cynthia upon Mrs. Vostrand's letter. He had thought of doing that, and then he had dismissed the thought as involving pain that he had no right to inflict; but now he perceived that the pain was such as she must suffer in the event, and that he had stupidly refused himself the only means of finding out the right thing to do. Her true heart and her clear mind would have been infallible in the affair, and he had trusted to his own muddled impulse.

He began to write other letters: to Durgin, to Mrs. Vostrand, to Genevieve; but none of them satisfied him, and he let the days go by without doing anything to retrieve his error or fulfil his duty. At last he did what he ought to have done at first: he enclosed Mrs. Vostrand's letter to Cynthia, and asked her what she thought he ought to have done. While he was waiting Cynthia's answer to his letter, a cable message reached him from Florence :

"*Kind letter received. Married to-day. Written.*
                                        " Vostrand."

The next mail brought Cynthia's reply, which was very brief :

" I am sorry you had to write at all; nothing could have prevented it. Perhaps if he cares for her he will be good to her."

Since the matter was now irremediable, Westover crept less miserably through the days than he could have believed he should, until the letter which Mrs. Vostrand's cable promised came to hand.

" Dear friend," she wrote, " your generous and *satisfactory* answer came yesterday. It was so delicate and *high-minded*, and so like you, to write to Mr. Durgin, and leave the *whole affair* to him ; and he did not *lose a moment* in showing us your beautiful letter. He said you were a man after his own heart, and I wish you could have heard how he *praised* you. It made Genevieve quite *jealous*, or would have, if it had been *any one else*. But she is *so* happy in your approval of her marriage, which is to take place before the *sindaco to-morrow*. We shall only have the *civil rite ;* she feels that it is more American, and we are all coming home to Lion's Head in the spring to live and die true Americans. I wish you could spend the

summer with us there, but until Lion's Head is re-
built, we can't ask you.   I don't know exactly how
we shall do *ourselves*, but Mr. Durgin is *full of plans*,
and we leave everything *to him*.   He is here, making
Genevieve laugh so that I can *hardly write*.   He joins
us in love and thanks, and our darling Bice sends you
a little kiss.   MEDORA VOSTRAND.

" P. S.—Mr. D. has told us *all about* the affairs you
alluded to.   With Miss L. we cannot feel that he was
to *blame ;* but he blames *himself* in regard to Miss W.
He says his *only excuse* is that he was always in love
with Genevieve; and I think that is quite *excuse
enough.*   M. V."

From time to time during the winter Westover
wrote to Cynthia, and had letters from her in which
he pleased himself fancying almost a personal effect
of that shyness which he thought a charming thing in
her.   But no doubt this was something he read into
them ; on their face they were plain, straightforward
accounts of the life she led in the little old house at
Lion's Head, under the shadow of the black ruin on
the hill.   Westover had taken to sending her books
and magazines, and in thanking him for these she
would sometimes speak of things she had read in them.
Her criticism related to the spirit rather than the
manner of the things she spoke of, and it pleased him
that she seemed, with all her insight, to have very
little artistic sense of any kind; in the world where
he lived there were so many women with an artistic
sense in every kind that he was rather weary of it.

There never was anything about Durgin in the letters, and Westover was both troubled and consoled by
this silence.   It might be from consciousness, and it
probably was; it might be from indifference.   In the
worst event, it hid any pain she might have felt with
a dignity from which no intimation of his moved her.
The nearest she came to speaking of Jeff was when
she said that Jombateeste was going to work at the
Brick-yards in Cambridge as soon as the spring
opened, and was not going to stay any longer at Lion's
Head.   Her brother Frank, she reported, had got a
place with part work in the drug-and-book store at
Lovewell, where he could keep on more easily with his
studies; he had now fully decided to study for the
ministry; he had always wanted to be an Episcopalian.

One day towards the end of April, when several
weeks had passed without bringing Westover any word
from Cynthia, her father presented himself, and enjoyed in the painter's surprise the sensation of having
dropped upon him from the clouds.   He gave due
accounts of the health of each of his household, end-
ing with Jombateeste.   "You know he's out at the
Brick, as he calls it, in Cambridge."

"Cynthia said he was coming.   I didn't know he
had come yet," said Westover.   "I must go out and
look him up, if you think I could find him among all
those Canucks."

"Well, I don't know but you'd better look *us* up at
the same time," said Whitwell, with additional pleasure in the painter's additional surprise.   "I guess
we're out in Cambridge, too," he added, at Westover's

start of question. "We're out there, visitin' one of
our summer folks, as you might say. Remember Mis'
Fredericks?"

"Why, what the deuce kept you from telling me so
at once?" Westover demanded, indignantly.

"Guess I hadn't got round to it," said Whitwell,
with dry relish.

"Do you mean that Cynthia's there?"

"Well, I guess they wouldn't cared much for a visit
from *me*."

Whitwell took advantage of Westover's moment of
mystification to explain that Jeff had written over to
him from Italy, offering him a pretty good rent for
his house, which he wanted to occupy while he was
rebuilding Lion's Head. He was going to push the
work right through in the summer, and be ready for
the season the year after. That was what Whitwell
understood, and he understood that Jeff's family was
going to stay in Lovewell, but Jeff himself wanted to
be on the ground day and night.

"So that's kind of turned us out of doors, as you
may say, and Cynthia's always had this idee of comin'
down Boston way; and she didn't know anybody that
could advise with her as well as Mis' Fredericks, and
she wrote to her, and Mis' Fredericks answered her to
come right down and talk it over." Westover felt a
pang of resentment that Cynthia had not turned to
him for counsel, but he said nothing, and Whitwell
went on: "She said she was ashamed to bother you,
you'd had the whole neighborhood on your hands so
much, and so she wrote to Mis' Fredericks."

Westover had a vague discomfort in it all, which ultimately defined itself as a discontent with the willingness of the Whitwells to let Durgin occupy their house upon any terms, for any purpose, and a lingering grudge that Cynthia should have asked help of any one but himself, even from a motive of delicacy.

In the evening he went out to see the girl at the house of Mrs. Fredericks, whom he found living in the Port. They had a first moment of intolerable shyness on her part. He had been afraid to see her, with the jealousy for her dignity he always felt, lest she should look as if she had been unhappy about Durgin. But he found her looking, not only very well, but very happy and full of peace, as soon as that moment of shyness passed. It seemed to Westover as if she had begun to live on new terms, and that a harassing element, which had always been in it, had gone out of her life, and in its absence she was beginning to rejoice in a lasting repose. He found himself rejoicing with her, and he found himself on simpler and franker terms with her than ever before. Neither of them spoke of Jeff, or made any approach to mention him, and Westover believed that this was not from a morbid feeling in her, but from a final and enduring indifference.

He saw her alone, for Mrs. Fredericks and her daughter had gone into town to a concert, which he made her confess she would have gone to herself if it had not been that her father said he was coming out to see her. She would not let him joke about the sacrifice he pretended she had made; he had a certain pain in fancying that his visit was the highest and finest favor that life could do her. She told him of the ambition she had that she might get a school somewhere in the neighborhood of Boston, and then find something for her brother to do, while he began his studies in the Theological school at Harvard. Frank was still at Lovewell, it seemed.

At the end of the long call he made, he said, abruptly, when he had risen to go, " I should like to paint you."

" Who? *Me?* " she cried, as if it were the most incredible thing, while a glad color rushed over her face.

" Yes. While you're waiting to get your school, couldn't you come in with your father, now and then, and sit for me ? "

" What's he want *me* to come fer? " Whitwell demanded, when the plan was laid before him. He was giving his unlimited leisure to the exploration of Boston, and his tone expressed something of the injury which he also put into words, as a sole objection to the proposed interruption. " Can't you go alone, Cynthy ? "

Cynthia said she did not know, but when the point was referred to Mrs. Fredericks, she was sure Cynthia could not go alone, and she acquainted them both, as far as she could, with that mystery of chaperonage which had never touched their lives before. Whitwell seemed to think that his daughter would give the matter up ; and perhaps she might have done so, though she seemed reluctant, if Mrs. Fredericks had not farther instructed them that it was the highest possible honor Mr. Westover was offering them, and that if he

" ' IT MAKES ME THINK, WELL, OF A BIRD YOU'VE COME ON SUDDEN ' "

had proposed to paint her daughter, she would simply
have gone and lived with him while he was doing it.

Whitwell found some compensation for the time
lost to his study of Boston in the conversation of the
painter, which he said was worth a hundred cents on
the dollar every time, though it dealt less with the
metaphysical aspect of the latest facts of science than
the philosopher could have wished. He did not, to
be sure, take very much stock in the picture as it advanced, somewhat fitfully, with a good many reversions
to its original state of sketch. It appeared to him
always a slight and feeble representation of Cynthia,
though, of course, a native politeness forbade him to
express his disappointment. He avowed a faith in
Westover's ability to get it right in the end, and always bade him go on, and take as much time to it as
he wanted.

He felt less uneasy than at first, because he had now
found a little furnished house in the woodenest out-
skirts of North Cambridge, which he hired cheap from
the recently widowed owner, and they were keeping
house there. Jombateeste lived with them, and
worked in the Brick-yards. Out of hours he helped
Cynthia, and kept the ugly little place looking trim
and neat, and left Whitwell free for the tramps home
to nature, which he began to take over the Belmont
uplands as soon as the spring opened. He was not
homesick, as Cynthia was afraid he might be ; his mind
was fully occupied by the vast and varied interests
opened to it by the intellectual and material activities
of the neighboring city ; and he found ample scope

for his physical energies in doing Cynthia's errands, as well as studying the strange flora of the region. He apparently thought that he had made a distinct rise and advance in the world. Sometimes, in the first days of his satisfaction with his establishment, he expressed the wish that Jackson could only have seen how he was fixed, once. In his preoccupation with other things, he no longer attempted to explore the eternal mysteries with the help of planchette; the ungrateful instrument gathered as much dust as Cynthia would suffer on the what-not in the corner of the solemn parlor; and after two or three visits to the First Spiritual Temple in Boston, he lapsed altogether from an interest in the other world, which had, perhaps, mainly flourished in the absence of pressing subjects of inquiry in this.

When at last Westover confessed that he had carried his picture of Cynthia as far as he could, Whitwell did his best to hide his disappointment. " Well, sir," he said, tolerantly and even cheeringly, " I presume we're every one of us a different person to whoever looks at us. They say that no two men see the same star."

" You mean that she doesn't look so to you," suggested the painter, who seemed not at all abashed.

" Well, you might say— Why here ! It's like her; photograph couldn't get it any better; but it makes me think, well, of a bird that you've come on sudden, and it stoops as if it was goin' to fly—"

" Ah," said Westover, " does it make you think of that ? "

LIV.

THE painter could not make out at first whether the girl herself was pleased with the picture or not, and in his uncertainty he could not give it her at once, as he had hoped and meant to do. It was by a kind of accident he found afterwards that she had always been passionately proud of his having painted her. This was when he returned from the last sojourn he had made in Paris, whither he went soon after the Whitwells settled in North Cambridge. He left the picture behind him to be framed and then sent to her with a letter he had written, begging her to give it house-room while he was gone. He got a short, stiff note in reply after he reached Paris, and he had not tried to continue the correspondence. But as soon as he returned he went out to see the Whitwells in North Cambridge. They were still in their little house there; the young widower had married again; but neither he nor his new wife had cared to take up their joint life in his first home, and he had found Whitwell such a good tenant that he had not tried to put up the rent on him. Frank was at home, now, with an employment that gave him part of his time

for his theological studies; Cynthia had been teaching school ever since the fall after Westover went
away, and they were all, as Whitwell said, in clover.
He was the only member of the family at home when
Westover called on the afternoon of a warm summer
day, and he entertained him with a full account of a
visit he had paid Lion's Head earlier in the season.

"Yes, sir," he said, as if he had already stated the
fact, "I've sold my old place there to that devil."
He said devil without the least rancor; with even a
smile of goodwill, and he enjoyed the astonishment
Westover expressed in his demand:

"Sold Durgin your house?"

"Yes, I see we never wanted to go back there to
live, any of us, and I went up to pass the papers and
close the thing out. Well I *did* have an offer for it
from a feller that wanted to open a boa'din'-house
there, and get the advantage of Jeff's improvements,
and I couldn't seem to make up my mind till I'd
looked the ground over. Fust off, you know, I
thought I'd sell to the other feller, because I could
see in a minute what a thorn it'd be in Jeff's flesh.
But dumn it all! When I met the comical devil I
couldn't seem to want to pester him. Why, here,
thinks I, if we've made an escape from him—and I
guess we have, about the *biggest* escape—what have I
got agin him, anyway? I'd ought to feel *good* to him;
and I guess that's the way I *did* feel, come to boil it
down. He's got a way with him, you know, when
you're with him, that makes you *like* him. He may
have a knife in your ribs the whole while, but so long's

he don't turn it, you don't seem to know it, and you
can't help likin' him. Why, I hadn't been with Jeff five
minutes before I made up my mind to sell to him.   I
told him about the other offer—felt bound to do it—
and he was all on fire. 'I want that place, Mr. Whitwell,' s'd he. 'Name your price.' Well, I wa'n't
goin' to take an advantage of the feller, and I guess
he see it. 'You've offered me three thousand,' s'd I,
' 'n' I don't want to be no ways mean about it.   Five
thousand buys the place.' 'It's mine,' s'd he; just
like that.   I guess he see he had a gentleman to deal
with, and we didn't say a word more.   Don't you
think I done right to sell to him?   I couldn't 'a' got
more'n thirty-five hundred out the other feller, to
save me, and before Jeff begun his improvements I
couldn't 'a realized a thousand dollars on the prop'ty."

"I think you did right to sell to him," said Westover, saddened somewhat by the proof Whitwell al-
leged of his magnanimity.

"Well, sir, I'm glad you do.   I don't believe in
crowdin' a man because you got him in a corner, an' I
don't believe in bearin' malice. *Never* did.   All I wanted was what the place was wo'th—to *him*.   'Twa'n't
wo'th nothin' to me!   He's got the house and the
ten acres around it, and he's got the house on Lion's
Head, includin' the Clearin', that makes the poottiest
picnic-ground in the mountains.   Think of goin' up
there this summer?"

"No," said Westover, briefly.

"Well, I some wish you did.   I sh'd like to know
how Jeff's improvements struck you.   Of course, I

can't judge of 'em so well, but I guess he's made a
pootty sightly thing of it.   He told me he'd had one
of the leadin' Boston architects to plan the thing out
for him, and I tell you he's got something nice.
'Tain't so big as old Lion's Head, and Jeff wants to
cater to a different style of custom, anyway.   The
buildin's longer'n what she is deep, and she spreads
in front so's to give as many rooms a view of the
mountain as she can.   Know what 'runnaysonce' is?
Well, that's the style Jeff said it was; it's all pillars
and pilasters; and you ride up to the office through
a double row of colyums, under a kind of a portico.
It's all painted like them old Colonial houses down on
Brattle Street, buff and white.   Well, it made *me*
think of one of them old pagan temples.   He's got
her shoved along to the south'ard, and he's widened
out a piece of level for her to stand on, so 't that piece
o' wood up the hill there is just behind her, and I tell
you she looks nice, backin' up ag'inst the trees.   I
tell you, Jeff's got a head on him!   I wish you could
see that dinin'-room o' his: all white colyums, and
frontin' on the view.   Why, that devil's got a regular
little theaytre back o' the dinin'-room for the young
folks to act ammyture plays in, and the shows that
come along, and he's got a dance-hall besides; the
parlors ain't much—folks like to set in the office; and
a good many of the rooms are done off into soots,
and got their own parlors.   I tell you, it's *swell*, as
they say.   You can order what you please for breakfast, but for lunch and dinner you got to take what
Jeff gives you; but he *treats* you well.   He's a Dur-

gin, when it comes to that.   Served in cou'ses, and
dinner at seven o'clock.   I don't know where he got
his money for 't all, but I guess he put in his insurance first, and then he put a mortgage on the buildin'; he as much as owned it; said he'd had a splendid season last year, and if he done as well for a couple of seasons more he'd have the whole prop'ty free
o' debt."

Westover could see that the prosperity of the unjust man had corrupted the imagination and con-
founded the conscience of this simple witness, and he
asked, in the hope of giving his praises pause, "What
has he done about the old family burying-ground in
the orchard?"

"Well, there!" said Whitwell. "That *got* me more
than any other one thing.   I naturally expected that
Jeff'd had 'em moved, for *you* know and *I* know, Mr.
Westover, that a place like that couldn't be very pop'-
la' with summer folks; they don't want to have anything to kind of make 'em serious, as you may say.
But that devil got his architect to *treat* the place, as
he calls it, and he put a high stone wall around it, and
planted it to bushes and evergreens so 't looks like a
piece of old garden, down there in the corner of the
orchard, and if you didn't hunt for it you wouldn't
know it was there.   Jeff said 't when folks *did* happen
to find it out, he believed they liked it; they think
it's picturesque and ancient.   Why, some on 'em
wanted him to put up a little chapel alongside and
have services there; and Jeff said he didn't know but
he'd do it yet.   He's got dark-colored stones up for

Mis' Durgin and Jackson, so 't they look as old as any
of 'em. I tell you, he knows how to do things."

"It seems so," said Westover, with a bitterness
apparently lost upon the optimistic philosopher.

"Yes, sir. I guess it's all worked out for the best.
So long's he didn't marry Cynthy, I don't care who
he married, and I guess he's made out first-rate, and
he treats his wife well, and his mother-in-law too.
You wouldn't hardly know they was in the house,
they're so kind of quiet; and if a guest wants to see
Jeff, he's got to send and ask for him; clerk does
everything, but I guess Jeff keeps an eye out, and
knows what's goin' on. He's got an elegant soot of
appartments, and he lives as private as if he was in
his own house, him and his wife. But when there's
anything goin' on that needs a head, they're both
right on deck.

"He don't let his wife worry about things a great
deal; he's got a first-rate of a housekeeper, but I
guess old Mis' Vostrand keeps the housekeeper, as
you may say. I hear some of the boa'ders talkin' up
there, and one of 'em said 't the great thing about
Lion's Head was 't you could feel everywheres in it
that it was a lady's house. I guess Jeff has a pootty
good time, and a time 't suits *him*. He shows up on
the coachin' parties, and he's got himself a reg'lar
English coachman's rig, with boots outside his trou-
se's, and a long coat, and a fuzzy plug-hat: I tell you
he looks *gay !* He don't spend his winters at Lion's
Head: he is off to Europe about as soon as the house
closes in the fall, and he keeps bringin' home new

dodges. Guess you couldn't get no boa'd there for
no $7 a week *now!* I tell you, Jeff's the gentleman
now, and his wife's about the nicest lady *I* ever saw.
Do' know as I care so much about her mother; do'
know as I got anything ag'inst her either, very much.
But that little girl, Beechy, as they call her, she's a
beauty! And round with Jeff all the while! He seems
full as fond of her as her own mother does, and that
devil, that couldn't seem to get enough of tormentin'
little children when he was a boy, is as good and gentle with that little thing as—pie!"

Whitwell seemed to have come to an end of his
celebration of Jeff's success, and Westover asked:
"And what do you make now, of planchette's broken-
shaft business? Or don't you believe in planchette
any more?"

Whitwell's beaming face clouded. "Well, sir,
that's a thing that's always puzzled me. If it wa'n't
that it was Jackson workin' plantchette that night, I
shouldn't placed much dependence on what she said;
but Jackson could get the truth out of her, if anybody could. Sence I b'en up there I b'en figurin' it
out like this: the broken shaft is the old Jeff that
he's left off bein'—"

Whitwell stopped midway in his suggestion, with
an inquiring eye on the painter, who asked, "You
think he's left off being the old Jeff?"

"Well, sir, you got me there," the philosopher confessed. "I didn't see anything to the contrary, but
come to think of it—"

"Why couldn't the broken shaft be his unfulfilled

destiny on the old lines? What reason is there to
believe he isn't what he's always been?"

"Well, come to think of it—"

"People don't change in a day, or a year," Westover went on, "or two or three years, even. Sometimes I doubt if they *ever* change."

"Well, all that I thought," Whitwell urged faintly
against the hard scepticism of a man ordinarily so
yielding, "is 't there must be a moral government of
the universe *somewheres*, and if a bad feller is to get
along and prosper hand over hand, that way, don't it
look kind of as if—"

"There wasn't any moral government of the universe? Not the way I see it," said Westover. "A
tree brings forth of its kind. As a man sows he
reaps. It's dead sure, pitilessly sure. Jeff Durgin
sowed success, in a certain way, and he's reaping it.
He once said to me, when I tried to waken his conscience, that he should get where he was trying to go
if he was strong enough, and being good had nothing
to do with it. I believe now he was right. But he
was wrong too, as such a man always is. That kind
of tree bears Dead Sea apples, after all. He sowed
evil and he must reap evil. He may never know it,
but he will reap what he has sown. The dreadful
thing is that others must share in his harvest. What
do you think?"

Whitwell scratched his head. "Well, sir, there's
something in what you say, I *guess*. But *here!*
What's the use of thinkin' a man can't change?
Wa'n't there ever anything in that old idee of a

change of heart? What do you s'pose made Jeff let up
on that feller that Jombateeste see him have down, that
day, in my Clearin'? What Jeff would natch'ly done
would b'en to shake the life out of him; but he didn't;
he let him up, and he let him go. What's the reason
that wa'n't the beginnin' of a new life for him?"

"We don't know all the ins and outs of that business," said Westover after a moment. "I've puzzled
over it a good deal. The man was the brother of that
girl that Jeff had jilted in Boston. I've found out
that much. I don't know just the size and shape of
the trouble between them, but Jeff may have felt that
he had got even with his enemy before that day. Or
he may have felt that if he was going in for full satisfaction, there was Jombateeste looking on—"

"That's true," said Whitwell, greatly daunted.
After a while he took refuge in the reflection, "Well,
he's a comical devil."

Westover said, in a sort of absence: "Perhaps we're
all broken shafts, here. Perhaps that old hypothesis
of another life, a world where there is room enough
and time enough for all the beginnings of this to complete themselves—"

"Well, now you're shoutin'," said Whitwell. "And
if plantchette—" Westover rose. "Why, a'n't you
goin' to wait and see Cynthy? I'm expectin' her along
every minute now; she's just gone down to Harvard
Square. She'll be awfully put out when she knows
you've be'n here."

"I'll come out again soon," said Westover. "Tell
her—"

"Well, you must see your picture, anyway. We've got it in the parlor. I don't know what she'll say to me, keepin' you here in the settin'-room all the time."

Whitwell led him into the little dark front hall, and into the parlor, less dim than it should have been because the afternoon sun was burning full upon its shutters. The portrait hung over the mantel, in a bad light, but the painter could feel everything in it that he could not see.

"Yes, it has that look in it."

"Well, she ha'n't took wing yet, I'm thankful to think," said Whitwell, and he spoke from his own large mind to the sympathy of an old friend who he felt could almost share his feelings as a father.

LV.

WHEN Westover turned out of the baking little
street where the Whitwells lived into an elm-shaded
stretch of North Avenue, he took off his hat and
strolled bareheaded along in the cooler air. He was
disappointed not to have seen Cynthia, and yet he
found himself hurrying away after his failure, with a
sense of escape, or at least of respite.

What he had come to say, to do, was the effect of
long experience and much meditation. The time had
arrived when he could no longer feign to himself that
his feelings towards the girl were not those of a lov-
er, but he had his modest fears that she could never
imagine him in that character, and that if he should
ask her to do so he should shock and grieve her, and
inflict upon himself an incurable wound.

During this last absence of his he had let his fancy
dwell constantly upon her, until life seemed worth
having only if she would share it with him. He was
an artist, and he had always been a bohemian, but at
heart he was philistine and bourgeois. His ideal was
a settlement, a fixed habitation, a stated existence, a
home where he could work constantly in an air of af-

fection, and unselfishly do his part to make his home happy. It was a very simple-hearted ambition, and I do not quite know how to keep it from appearing commonplace and almost sordid; but such as it was, I must confess that it was his. He had not married his model, because he was mainly a landscapist, perhaps; and he had not married any of his pupils, because he had not been in love with them, charming and good and lovely as he had thought some of them; and of late he had realized more and more why his fancy had not turned in their direction. He perceived that it was already fixed, and possibly had long been fixed.

He did not blink the fact that there were many disparities, and that there would be certain disadvantages which could never be quite overcome. The fact had been brought rather strenuously home to him by his interview with Cynthia's father. He perceived, as indeed he had always known, that with a certain imaginative lift in his thinking and feeling, Whitwell was irreparably rustic, that he was and always must be practically Yankee. Westover was not a Yankee, and he did not love or honor the type, though its struggles against itself touched and amused him. It made him a little sick to hear how Whitwell had profited by Durgin's necessity, and had taken advantage of him with conscientious and self-applausive rapacity, while he admired his prosperity, and tried to account for it by doubt of its injustice. For a moment this seemed to him worse than Durgin's conscientious toughness, which was the antithesis of Whitwell's re-

morseless self-interest. For the moment this claimed
Cynthia of its kind, and Westover beheld her rustic
and Yankee of her father's type. If she was not that
now, she would grow into that through the lapse from
the personal to the ancestral which we all undergo in
the process of the years.

The sight of her face as he had pictured it, and of
the soul which he had imagined for it, restored him to
a better sense of her, but he felt the need of escaping
from the suggestion of her father's presence, and taking further thought. Perhaps he should never again
reach the point that he was aware of deflecting from
now; he filled his lungs with long breaths, which he
exhaled in sighs of relief. It might have been a mistake on the spiritual as well as the worldly side; it
would certainly not have promoted his career; it might
have impeded it. These misgivings flitted over the
surface of thought that more profoundly was occupied
with a question of other things. In the time since he
had seen her last it might very well be that a young
and pretty girl had met some one who had taken her
fancy; and he could not be sure that her fancy had
ever been his, even if this had not happened. He had
no proof at all that she had ever cared or could care
for him except gratefully, respectfully, almost reverently, with that mingling of filial and maternal anxiety which had hitherto been the warmest expression
of her regard. He tried to reason it out, and could
not. He suddenly found himself bitterly disappointed
that he had missed seeing her, for if they had met, he
would have known by this time what to think, what to

hope. He felt old—he felt fully thirty-six years old—
as he passed his hand over his crown, whose gossamer
growth opposed so little resistance to his touch. He
had begun to lose his hair early, but till then he had
not much regretted his baldness. He entered into a
little question of their comparative ages, which led him
to the conclusion that Cynthia must now be about
twenty-five.

Almost at the same moment he saw her coming up
the walk towards him from far down the avenue. For
a reason, or rather a motive, of his own he pretended
to himself that it was not she, but he knew instantly
that it was, and he put on his hat. He could see that
she did not know him, and it was a pretty thing to
witness the recognition dawn on her. When it had
its full effect, he was aware of a flutter, a pause in her
whole figure before she came on towards him, and he
hurried his steps for the charm of her blushing, beautiful face.

It was the spiritual effect of figure and face that he
had carried in his thought ever since he had arrived at
that one-sided intimacy through his study of her for
the picture he had just seen. He had often had to
ask himself whether he had really perceived or only
imagined the character he had translated into it; but
here, for the moment at least, was what he had seen.
He hurried forward and joyfully took the hand she
gave him. He thought he should speak of that at
once, but it was not possible, of course. There had
to come first the unheeded questions and answers about
each other's health, and many other commonplaces.

"HE HURRIED FORWARD AND JOYFULLY TOOK THE HAND SHE
GAVE HIM"

He turned and walked home with her, and at the gate
of the little ugly house she asked him if he would not
come in and take tea with them.

Her father talked with him while she got the tea,
and when it was ready her brother came in from his
walk home out of Old Cambridge and helped her put
it on the table.   He had grown much taller than Westover, and he was very ecclesiastical in his manner;
more so than he would be, probably, if he ever became a bishop, Westover decided.   Jombateeste, in
an interval of suspended work at the Brick-yard, was
paying a visit to his people in Canada, and Westover
did not see him.

All the time while they sat at table and talked together Westover realized more and more that for him,
at least, the separation of the last two years had put
that space between them which alone made it possible
for them to approach each other on new ground.   A
kind of horror, of repulsion, for her engagement to
Jeff Durgin had ceased from his sense of her; it was
as if she had been unhappily married, and the man,
who had been unworthy and unkind, was like a ghost
who could never come to trouble his joy.   He was
more her contemporary, he found, than formerly; she
had grown a great deal in the past two years, and a
certain affliction which her father's fixity had given
him concerning her passed in the assurance of change
which she herself gave him.

She had changed her world, and grown to it, but
her nature had not changed.   Even her look had not
changed, and he told her how he had seen his picture

in her at the moment of their meeting in the street. They all went in to verify his impression from the painting. "Yes, that is the way you looked."

"It seems to me that is the way I felt," she asserted.

Frank went about the house-work, and left her to their guest. When Whitwell came back from the post-office, where he said he would only be gone a minute, he did not rejoin Westover and Cynthia in the parlor.

The parlor door was shut; he had risked his fate, and they were talking it over. Cynthia was not sure; she was sure of nothing but that there was no one in the world she cared for so much; but she was not sure that was enough. She did not pretend that she was surprised; she owned that she had sometimes expected it; she blamed herself for not expecting it then.

Westover said that he did not blame her for not knowing her mind; he had been fifteen years learning his own fully. He asked her to take all the time she wished. If she could not make sure after all, he should always be sure that she was wise and good. She told him everything there was to tell of her breaking with Jeff, and he thought the last episode a supreme proof of her wisdom and goodness.

After a certain time they went for a walk in the warm summer moonlight under the elms, where they had met on the avenue.

"I suppose," she said, as they drew near her door again, "that people don't often talk it over as we've done."

"We only know from the novels," he answered.

" Perhaps people do, oftener than is ever known.   I
don't see why they shouldn't."

" No."

" I've never wished to be sure of you so much as
since you've wished to be sure of yourself."

" And I've never been so sure as since you were
willing to let me," said Cynthia.

" I am glad of that.   Try to think of me, if that
will help my cause, as some one you might have always
known in this way.   We don't really know each other yet.   I'm a great deal older that you, but still I'm
not so very old."

" Oh, I don't care for that.   All I want to be certain of is that the feeling I have is really—the feeling."

" I know, dear," said Westover, and his heart
surged towards her in his tenderness for her simple
conscience, her wise question.   " Take time.   Don't
hurry.   Forget what I've said—or no; that's absurd !
Think of it; but don't let anything but the truth per-
suade you.   Now, good-night, Cynthia."

" Good-night—Mr. Westover."

" Mr. Westover !" he reproached her.

She stood thinking, as if the question were crucial.
Then she said, firmly, " I should always have to call
you Mr. Westover."

" Oh, well," he returned, " if that's all ! "

THE END

A CATALOGUE OF
SELECTED DOVER BOOKS
IN ALL FIELDS OF INTEREST

A CATALOGUE OF SELECTED DOVER
BOOKS IN ALL FIELDS OF INTEREST

RACKHAM'S COLOR ILLUSTRATIONS FOR WAGNER'S RING. Rackham's finest mature work—all 64 full-color watercolors in a faithful and lush interpretation of the *Ring*. Full-sized plates on coated stock of the paintings used by opera companies for authentic staging of Wagner. Captions aid in following complete Ring cycle. Introduction. 64 illustrations plus vignettes. 72pp. 8⅝ x 11¼. 23779-6 Pa. $6.00

CONTEMPORARY POLISH POSTERS IN FULL COLOR, edited by Joseph Czestochowski. 46 full-color examples of brilliant school of Polish graphic design, selected from world's first museum (near Warsaw) dedicated to poster art. Posters on circuses, films, plays, concerts all show cosmopolitan influences, free imagination. Introduction. 48pp. 9⅜ x 12¼. 23780-X Pa. $6.00

GRAPHIC WORKS OF EDVARD MUNCH, Edvard Munch. 90 haunting, evocative prints by first major Expressionist artist and one of the greatest graphic artists of his time: *The Scream, Anxiety, Death Chamber, The Kiss, Madonna,* etc. Introduction by Alfred Werner. 90pp. 9 x 12. 23765-6 Pa. $5.00

THE GOLDEN AGE OF THE POSTER, Hayward and Blanche Cirker. 70 extraordinary posters in full colors, from Maitres de l'Affiche, Mucha, Lautrec, Bradley, Cheret, Beardsley, many others. Total of 78pp. 9⅜ x 12¼. 22753-7 Pa. $5.95

THE NOTEBOOKS OF LEONARDO DA VINCI, edited by J. P. Richter. Extracts from manuscripts reveal great genius; on painting, sculpture, anatomy, sciences, geography, etc. Both Italian and English. 186 ms. pages reproduced, plus 500 additional drawings, including studies for *Last Supper*, Sforza monument, etc. 860pp. 7⅞ x 10¾. (Available in U.S. only) 22572-0, 22573-9 Pa., Two-vol. set $15.90

THE CODEX NUTTALL, as first edited by Zelia Nuttall. Only inexpensive edition, in full color, of a pre-Columbian Mexican (Mixtec) book. 88 color plates show kings, gods, heroes, temples, sacrifices. New explanatory, historical introduction by Arthur G. Miller. 96pp. 11⅜ x 8½. (Available in U.S. only) 23168-2 Pa. $7.95

UNE SEMAINE DE BONTÉ, A SURREALISTIC NOVEL IN COLLAGE, Max Ernst. Masterpiece created out of 19th-century periodical illustrations, explores worlds of terror and surprise. Some consider this Ernst's greatest work. 208pp. 8⅛ x 11. 23252-2 Pa. $6.00

DRAWINGS OF WILLIAM BLAKE, William Blake. 92 plates from Book of Job, *Divine Comedy, Paradise Lost,* visionary heads, mythological figures, Laocoon, etc. Selection, introduction, commentary by Sir Geoffrey Keynes. 178pp. 8⅛ x 11. 22303-5 Pa. $4.00

ENGRAVINGS OF HOGARTH, William Hogarth. 101 of Hogarth's greatest works: *Rake's Progress, Harlot's Progress, Illustrations for Hudibras, Before and After, Beer Street and Gin Lane,* many more. Full commentary. 256pp. 11 x 13¾. 22479-1 Pa. $12.95

DAUMIER: 120 GREAT LITHOGRAPHS, Honore Daumier. Wide-ranging collection of lithographs by the greatest caricaturist of the 19th century. Concentrates on eternally popular series on lawyers, on married life, on liberated women, etc. Selection, introduction, and notes on plates by Charles F. Ramus. Total of 158pp. 9⅜ x 12¼. 23512-2 Pa. $6.00

DRAWINGS OF MUCHA, Alphonse Maria Mucha. Work reveals draftsman of highest caliber: studies for famous posters and paintings, renderings for book illustrations and ads, etc. 70 works, 9 in color; including 6 items not drawings. Introduction. List of illustrations. 72pp. 9⅜ x 12¼. (Available in U.S. only) 23672-2 Pa. $4.00

GIOVANNI BATTISTA PIRANESI: DRAWINGS IN THE PIERPONT MORGAN LIBRARY, Giovanni Battista Piranesi. For first time ever all of Morgan Library's collection, world's largest. 167 illustrations of rare Piranesi drawings—archeological, architectural, decorative and visionary. Essay, detailed list of drawings, chronology, captions. Edited by Felice Stampfle. 144pp. 9⅜ x 12¼. 23714-1 Pa. $7.50

NEW YORK ETCHINGS (1905-1949), John Sloan. All of important American artist's N.Y. life etchings. 67 works include some of his best art; also lively historical record—Greenwich Village, tenement scenes. Edited by Sloan's widow. Introduction and captions. 79pp. 8⅜ x 11¼. 23651-X Pa. $4.00

CHINESE PAINTING AND CALLIGRAPHY: A PICTORIAL SURVEY, Wan-go Weng. 69 fine examples from John M. Crawford's matchless private collection: landscapes, birds, flowers, human figures, etc., plus calligraphy. Every basic form included: hanging scrolls, handscrolls, album leaves, fans, etc. 109 illustrations. Introduction. Captions. 192pp. 8⅞ x 11¾. 23707-9 Pa. $7.95

DRAWINGS OF REMBRANDT, edited by Seymour Slive. Updated Lippmann, Hofstede de Groot edition, with definitive scholarly apparatus. All portraits, biblical sketches, landscapes, nudes, Oriental figures, classical studies, together with selection of work by followers. 550 illustrations. Total of 630pp. 9⅛ x 12¼. 21485-0, 21486-9 Pa., Two-vol. set $15.00

THE DISASTERS OF WAR, Francisco Goya. 83 etchings record horrors of Napoleonic wars in Spain and war in general. Reprint of 1st edition, plus 3 additional plates. Introduction by Philip Hofer. 97pp. 9⅜ x 8¼. 21872-4 Pa. $4.00

THE EARLY WORK OF AUBREY BEARDSLEY, Aubrey Beardsley. 157 plates, 2 in color: *Manon Lescaut, Madame Bovary, Morte Darthur, Salome,* other. Introduction by H. Marillier. 182pp. 8⅛ x 11. 21816-3 Pa. $4.50

THE LATER WORK OF AUBREY BEARDSLEY, Aubrey Beardsley. Exotic masterpieces of full maturity: *Venus and Tannhauser, Lysistrata, Rape of the Lock, Volpone,* Savoy material, etc. 174 plates, 2 in color. 186pp. 8⅛ x 11. 21817-1 Pa. $5.95

THOMAS NAST'S CHRISTMAS DRAWINGS, Thomas Nast. Almost all Christmas drawings by creator of image of Santa Claus as we know it, and one of America's foremost illustrators and political cartoonists. 66 illustrations. 3 illustrations in color on covers. 96pp. 8⅜ x 11¼. 23660-9 Pa. $3.50

THE DORÉ ILLUSTRATIONS FOR DANTE'S DIVINE COMEDY, Gustave Doré. All 135 plates from Inferno, Purgatory, Paradise; fantastic tortures, infernal landscapes, celestial wonders. Each plate with appropriate (translated) verses. 141pp. 9 x 12. 23231-X Pa. $4.50

DORÉ'S ILLUSTRATIONS FOR RABELAIS, Gustave Doré. 252 striking illustrations of *Gargantua and Pantagruel* books by foremost 19th-century illustrator. Including 60 plates, 192 delightful smaller illustrations. 153pp. 9 x 12. 23656-0 Pa. $5.00

LONDON: A PILGRIMAGE, Gustave Doré, Blanchard Jerrold. Squalor, riches, misery, beauty of mid-Victorian metropolis; 55 wonderful plates, 125 other illustrations, full social, cultural text by Jerrold. 191pp. of text. 9⅜ x 12¼. 22306-X Pa. $7.00

THE RIME OF THE ANCIENT MARINER, Gustave Doré, S. T. Coleridge. Dore's finest work, 34 plates capture moods, subtleties of poem. Full text. Introduction by Millicent Rose. 77pp. 9¼ x 12. 22305-1 Pa. $3.50

THE DORE BIBLE ILLUSTRATIONS, Gustave Doré. All wonderful, detailed plates: Adam and Eve, Flood, Babylon, Life of Jesus, etc. Brief King James text with each plate. Introduction by Millicent Rose. 241 plates. 241pp. 9 x 12. 23004-X Pa. $6.00

THE COMPLETE ENGRAVINGS, ETCHINGS AND DRYPOINTS OF ALBRECHT DURER. "Knight, Death and Devil"; "Melencolia," and more—all Dürer's known works in all three media, including 6 works formerly attributed to him. 120 plates. 235pp. 8⅜ x 11¼. 22851-7 Pa. $6.50

MECHANICK EXERCISES ON THE WHOLE ART OF PRINTING, Joseph Moxon. First complete book (1683-4) ever written about typography, a compendium of everything known about printing at the latter part of 17th century. Reprint of 2nd (1962) Oxford Univ. Press edition. 74 illustrations. Total of 550pp. 6⅛ x 9¼. 23617-X Pa. $7.95

THE COMPLETE WOODCUTS OF ALBRECHT DURER, edited by Dr. W. Kurth. 346 in all: "Old Testament," "St. Jerome," "Passion," "Life of Virgin," Apocalypse," many others. Introduction by Campbell Dodgson. 285pp. 8½ x 12¼. 21097-9 Pa. $7.50

DRAWINGS OF ALBRECHT DURER, edited by Heinrich Wolfflin. 81 plates show development from youth to full style. Many favorites; many new. Introduction by Alfred Werner. 96pp. 8⅛ x 11. 22352-3 Pa. $5.00

THE HUMAN FIGURE, Albrecht Dürer. Experiments in various techniques—stereometric, progressive proportional, and others. Also life studies that rank among finest ever done. Complete reprinting of *Dresden Sketchbook*. 170 plates. 355pp. 8⅜ x 11¼. 21042-1 Pa. $7.95

OF THE JUST SHAPING OF LETTERS, Albrecht Dürer. Renaissance artist explains design of Roman majuscules by geometry, also Gothic lower and capitals. Grolier Club edition. 43pp. 7⅞ x 10¾ 21306-4 Pa. $3.00

TEN BOOKS ON ARCHITECTURE, Vitruvius. The most important book ever written on architecture. Early Roman aesthetics, technology, classical orders, site selection, all other aspects. Stands behind everything since. Morgan translation. 331pp. 5⅜ x 8½. 20645-9 Pa. $4.50

THE FOUR BOOKS OF ARCHITECTURE, Andrea Palladio. 16th-century classic responsible for Palladian movement and style. Covers classical architectural remains, Renaissance revivals, classical orders, etc. 1738 Ware English edition. Introduction by A. Placzek. 216 plates. 110pp. of text. 9½ x 12¾. 21308-0 Pa. $10.00

HORIZONS, Norman Bel Geddes. Great industrialist stage designer, "father of streamlining," on application of aesthetics to transportation, amusement, architecture, etc. 1932 prophetic account; function, theory, specific projects. 222 illustrations. 312pp. 7⅞ x 10¾. 23514-9 Pa. $6.95

FRANK LLOYD WRIGHT'S FALLINGWATER, Donald Hoffmann. Full, illustrated story of conception and building of Wright's masterwork at Bear Run, Pa. 100 photographs of site, construction, and details of completed structure. 112pp. 9¼ x 10. 23671-4 Pa. $5.50

THE ELEMENTS OF DRAWING, John Ruskin. Timeless classic by great Viltorian; starts with basic ideas, works through more difficult. Many practical exercises. 48 illustrations. Introduction by Lawrence Campbell. 228pp. 5⅜ x 8½. 22730-8 Pa. $3.75

GIST OF ART, John Sloan. Greatest modern American teacher, Art Students League, offers innumerable hints, instructions, guided comments to help you in painting. Not a formal course. 46 illustrations. Introduction by Helen Sloan. 200pp. 5⅜ x 8½. 23435-5 Pa. $4.00

THE ANATOMY OF THE HORSE, George Stubbs. Often considered the great masterpiece of animal anatomy. Full reproduction of 1766 edition, plus prospectus; original text and modernized text. 36 plates. Introduction by Eleanor Garvey. 121pp. 11 x 14¾. 23402-9 Pa. $6.00

BRIDGMAN'S LIFE DRAWING, George B. Bridgman. More than 500 illustrative drawings and text teach you to abstract the body into its major masses, use light and shade, proportion; as well as specific areas of anatomy, of which Bridgman is master. 192pp. 6½ x 9¼. (Available in U.S. only) 22710-3 Pa. $3.50

ART NOUVEAU DESIGNS IN COLOR, Alphonse Mucha, Maurice Verneuil, Georges Auriol. Full-color reproduction of *Combinaisons ornementales* (c. 1900) by Art Nouveau masters. Floral, animal, geometric, interlacings, swashes—borders, frames, spots—all incredibly beautiful. 60 plates, hundreds of designs. 9⅜ x 8-1/16. 22885-1 Pa. $4.00

FULL-COLOR FLORAL DESIGNS IN THE ART NOUVEAU STYLE, E. A. Seguy. 166 motifs, on 40 plates, from *Les fleurs et leurs applications decoratives* (1902): borders, circular designs, repeats, allovers, "spots." All in authentic Art Nouveau colors. 48pp. 9⅜ x 12¼.
23439-8 Pa. $5.00

A DIDEROT PICTORIAL ENCYCLOPEDIA OF TRADES AND IN-DUSTRY, edited by Charles C. Gillispie. 485 most interesting plates from the great French Encyclopedia of the 18th century show hundreds of working figures, artifacts, process, land and cityscapes; glassmaking, paper-making, metal extraction, construction, weaving, making furniture, clothing, wigs, dozens of other activities. Plates fully explained. 920pp. 9 x 12.
22284-5, 22285-3 Clothbd., Two-vol. set $40.00

HANDBOOK OF EARLY ADVERTISING ART, Clarence P. Hornung. Largest collection of copyright-free early and antique advertising art ever compiled. Over 6,000 illustrations, from Franklin's time to the 1890's for special effects, novelty. Valuable source, almost inexhaustible.
Pictorial Volume. Agriculture, the zodiac, animals, autos, birds, Christmas, fire engines, flowers, trees, musical instruments, ships, games and sports, much more. Arranged by subject matter and use. 237 plates. 288pp. 9 x 12.
20122-8 Clothbd. $14.50

Typographical Volume. Roman and Gothic faces ranging from 10 point to 300 point, "Barnum," German and Old English faces, script, logotypes, scrolls and flourishes, 1115 ornamental initials, 67 complete alphabets, more. 310 plates. 320pp. 9 x 12. 20123-6 Clothbd. $15.00

CALLIGRAPHY (CALLIGRAPHIA LATINA), J. G. Schwandner. High point of 18th-century ornamental calligraphy. Very ornate initials, scrolls, borders, cherubs, birds, lettered examples. 172pp. 9 x 13.
20475-8 Pa. $7.00

ART FORMS IN NATURE, Ernst Haeckel. Multitude of strangely beautiful natural forms: Radiolaria, Foraminifera, jellyfishes, fungi, turtles, bats, etc. All 100 plates of the 19th-century evolutionist's *Kunstformen der Natur* (1904). 100pp. 9⅜ x 12¼.   22987-4 Pa. $5.00

CHILDREN: A PICTORIAL ARCHIVE FROM NINETEENTH-CENTURY SOURCES, edited by Carol Belanger Grafton. 242 rare, copyright-free wood engravings for artists and designers. Widest such selection available. All illustrations in line. 119pp. 8⅜ x 11¼.
23694-3 Pa. $4.00

WOMEN: A PICTORIAL ARCHIVE FROM NINETEENTH-CENTURY SOURCES, edited by Jim Harter. 391 copyright-free wood engravings for artists and designers selected from rare periodicals. Most extensive such collection available. All illustrations in line. 128pp. 9 x 12.
23703-6 Pa. $4.50

ARABIC ART IN COLOR, Prisse d'Avennes. From the greatest ornamentalists of all time—50 plates in color, rarely seen outside the Near East, rich in suggestion and stimulus. Includes 4 plates on covers. 46pp. 9⅜ x 12¼.   23658-7 Pa. $6.00

AUTHENTIC ALGERIAN CARPET DESIGNS AND MOTIFS, edited by June Beveridge. Algerian carpets are world famous. Dozens of geometrical motifs are charted on grids, color-coded, for weavers, needleworkers, craftsmen, designers. 53 illustrations plus 4 in color. 48pp. 8¼ x 11. (Available in U.S. only)   23650-1 Pa. $1.75

DICTIONARY OF AMERICAN PORTRAITS, edited by Hayward and Blanche Cirker. 4000 important Americans, earliest times to 1905, mostly in clear line. Politicians, writers, soldiers, scientists, inventors, industrialists, Indians, Blacks, women, outlaws, etc. Identificatory information. 756pp. 9¼ x 12¾.   21823-6 Clothbd. $40.00

HOW THE OTHER HALF LIVES, Jacob A. Riis. Journalistic record of filth, degradation, upward drive in New York immigrant slums, shops, around 1900. New edition includes 100 original Riis photos, monuments of early photography. 233pp. 10 x 7⅞.   22012-5 Pa. $7.00

NEW YORK IN THE THIRTIES, Berenice Abbott. Noted photographer's fascinating study of city shows new buildings that have become famous and old sights that have disappeared forever. Insightful commentary. 97 photographs. 97pp. 11⅜ x 10.   22967-X Pa. $5.00

MEN AT WORK, Lewis W. Hine. Famous photographic studies of construction workers, railroad men, factory workers and coal miners. New supplement of 18 photos on Empire State building construction. New introduction by Jonathan L. Doherty. Total of 69 photos. 63pp. 8 x 10¾.
23475-4 Pa. $3.00

THE DEPRESSION YEARS AS PHOTOGRAPHED BY ARTHUR ROTH-STEIN, Arthur Rothstein. First collection devoted entirely to the work of outstanding 1930s photographer: famous dust storm photo, ragged children, unemployed, etc. 120 photographs. Captions. 119pp. 9¼ x 10¾.
23590-4 Pa. $5.00

CAMERA WORK: A PICTORIAL GUIDE, Alfred Stieglitz. All 559 illustrations and plates from the most important periodical in the history of art photography, Camera Work (1903-17). Presented four to a page, reduced in size but still clear, in strict chronological order, with complete captions. Three indexes. Glossary. Bibliography. 176pp. 8⅜ x 11¼.
23591-2 Pa. $6.95

ALVIN LANGDON COBURN, PHOTOGRAPHER, Alvin L. Coburn. Revealing autobiography by one of greatest photographers of 20th century gives insider's version of Photo-Secession, plus comments on his own work. 77 photographs by Coburn. Edited by Helmut and Alison Gernsheim. 160pp. 8⅛ x 11.
23685-4 Pa. $6.00

NEW YORK IN THE FORTIES, Andreas Feininger. 162 brilliant photographs by the well-known photographer, formerly with Life magazine, show commuters, shoppers, Times Square at night, Harlem nightclub, Lower East Side, etc. Introduction and full captions by John von Hartz. 181pp. 9¼ x 10¾.
23585-8 Pa. $6.95

GREAT NEWS PHOTOS AND THE STORIES BEHIND THEM, John Faber. Dramatic volume of 140 great news photos, 1855 through 1976, and revealing stories behind them, with both historical and technical information. Hindenburg disaster, shooting of Oswald, nomination of Jimmy Carter, etc. 160pp. 8¼ x 11.
23667-6 Pa. $5.00

THE ART OF THE CINEMATOGRAPHER, Leonard Maltin. Survey of American cinematography history and anecdotal interviews with 5 masters—Arthur Miller, Hal Mohr, Hal Rosson, Lucien Ballard, and Conrad Hall. Very large selection of behind-the-scenes production photos. 105 photographs. Filmographies. Index. Originally Behind the Camera. 144pp. 8¼ x 11.
23686-2 Pa. $5.00

DESIGNS FOR THE THREE-CORNERED HAT (LE TRICORNE), Pablo Picasso. 32 fabulously rare drawings—including 31 color illustrations of costumes and accessories—for 1919 production of famous ballet. Edited by Parmenia Migel, who has written new introduction. 48pp. 9⅜ x 12¼. (Available in U.S. only)
23709-5 Pa. $5.00

NOTES OF A FILM DIRECTOR, Sergei Eisenstein. Greatest Russian filmmaker explains montage, making of Alexander Nevsky, aesthetics; comments on self, associates, great rivals (Chaplin), similar material. 78 illustrations. 240pp. 5⅜ x 8½.
22392-2 Pa. $4.50

HOLLYWOOD GLAMOUR PORTRAITS, edited by John Kobal. 145 photos capture the stars from 1926-49, the high point in portrait photography. Gable, Harlow, Bogart, Bacall, Hedy Lamarr, Marlene Dietrich, Robert Montgomery, Marlon Brando, Veronica Lake; 94 stars in all. Full background on photographers, technical aspects, much more. Total of 160pp. 8⅜ x 11¼. 23352-9 Pa. $6.00

THE NEW YORK STAGE: FAMOUS PRODUCTIONS IN PHOTO-GRAPHS, edited by Stanley Appelbaum. 148 photographs from Museum of City of New York show 142 plays, 1883-1939. *Peter Pan, The Front Page, Dead End, Our Town,* O'Neill, hundreds of actors and actresses, etc. Full indexes. 154pp. 9½ x 10. 23241-7 Pa. $6.00

DIALOGUES CONCERNING TWO NEW SCIENCES, Galileo Galilei. Encompassing 30 years of experiment and thought, these dialogues deal with geometric demonstrations of fracture of solid bodies, cohesion, leverage, speed of light and sound, pendulums, falling bodies, accelerated motion, etc. 300pp. 5⅜ x 8½. 60099-8 Pa. $4.00

THE GREAT OPERA STARS IN HISTORIC PHOTOGRAPHS, edited by James Camner. 343 portraits from the 1850s to the 1940s: Tamburini, Mario, Caliapin, Jeritza, Melchior, Melba, Patti, Pinza, Schipa, Caruso, Farrar, Steber, Gobbi, and many more—270 performers in all. Index. 199pp. 8⅜ x 11¼. 23575-0 Pa. $7.50

J. S. BACH, Albert Schweitzer. Great full-length study of Bach, life, background to music, music, by foremost modern scholar. Ernest Newman translation. 650 musical examples. Total of 928pp. 5⅜ x 8½. (Available in U.S. only) 21631-4, 21632-2 Pa., Two-vol. set $11.00

COMPLETE PIANO SONATAS, Ludwig van Beethoven. All sonatas in the fine Schenker edition, with fingering, analytical material. One of best modern editions. Total of 615pp. 9 x 12. (Available in U.S. only) 23134-8, 23135-6 Pa., Two-vol. set $15.50

KEYBOARD MUSIC, J. S. Bach. Bach-Gesellschaft edition. For harpsichord, piano, other keyboard instruments. English Suites, French Suites, Six Partitas, Goldberg Variations, Two-Part Inventions, Three-Part Sinfonias. 312pp. 8⅛ x 11. (Available in U.S. only) 22360-4 Pa. $6.95

FOUR SYMPHONIES IN FULL SCORE, Franz Schubert. Schubert's four most popular symphonies: No. 4 in C Minor ("Tragic"); No. 5 in B-flat Major; No. 8 in B Minor ("Unfinished"); No. 9 in C Major ("Great"). Breitkopf & Hartel edition. Study score. 261pp. 9⅜ x 12¼. 23681-1 Pa. $6.50

THE AUTHENTIC GILBERT & SULLIVAN SONGBOOK, W. S. Gilbert, A. S. Sullivan. Largest selection available; 92 songs, uncut, original keys, in piano rendering approved by Sullivan. Favorites and lesser-known fine numbers. Edited with plot synopses by James Spero. 3 illustrations. 399pp. 9 x 12. 23482-7 Pa. $9.95

PRINCIPLES OF ORCHESTRATION, Nikolay Rimsky-Korsakov. Great classical orchestrator provides fundamentals of tonal resonance, progression of parts, voice and orchestra, tutti effects, much else in major document. 330pp. of musical excerpts. 489pp. 6½ x 9¼.   21266-1 Pa. $7.50

TRISTAN UND ISOLDE, Richard Wagner. Full orchestral score with complete instrumentation. Do not confuse with piano reduction. Commentary by Felix Mottl, great Wagnerian conductor and scholar. Study score. 655pp. 8⅛ x 11.   22915-7 Pa. $13.95

REQUIEM IN FULL SCORE, Giuseppe Verdi. Immensely popular with choral groups and music lovers. Republication of edition published by C. F. Peters, Leipzig, n. d. German frontmaker in English translation. Glossary. Text in Latin. Study score. 204pp. 9⅜ x 12¼.
23682-X Pa. $6.00

COMPLETE CHAMBER MUSIC FOR STRINGS, Felix Mendelssohn. All of Mendelssohn's chamber music: Octet, 2 Quintets, 6 Quartets, and Four Pieces for String Quartet. (Nothing with piano is included). Complete works edition (1874-7). Study score. 283 pp. 9⅜ x 12¼.
23679-X Pa. $7.50

POPULAR SONGS OF NINETEENTH-CENTURY AMERICA, edited by Richard Jackson. 64 most important songs: "Old Oaken Bucket," "Arkansas Traveler," "Yellow Rose of Texas," etc. Authentic original sheet music, full introduction and commentaries. 290pp. 9 x 12.   23270-0 Pa. $7.95

COLLECTED PIANO WORKS, Scott Joplin. Edited by Vera Brodsky Lawrence. Practically all of Joplin's piano works—rags, two-steps, marches, waltzes, etc., 51 works in all. Extensive introduction by Rudi Blesh. Total of 345pp. 9 x 12.   23106-2 Pa. $14.95

BASIC PRINCIPLES OF CLASSICAL BALLET, Agrippina Vaganova. Great Russian theoretician, teacher explains methods for teaching classical ballet; incorporates best from French, Italian, Russian schools. 118 illustrations. 175pp. 5⅜ x 8½.   22036-2 Pa. $2.50

CHINESE CHARACTERS, L. Wieger. Rich analysis of 2300 characters according to traditional systems into primitives. Historical-semantic analysis to phonetics (Classical Mandarin) and radicals. 820pp. 6⅛ x 9¼.
21321-8 Pa. $10.00

EGYPTIAN LANGUAGE: EASY LESSONS IN EGYPTIAN HIERO-GLYPHICS, E. A. Wallis Budge. Foremost Egyptologist offers Egyptian grammar, explanation of hieroglyphics, many reading texts, dictionary of symbols. 246pp. 5 x 7½. (Available in U.S. only)
21394-3 Clothbd. $7.50

AN ETYMOLOGICAL DICTIONARY OF MODERN ENGLISH, Ernest Weekley. Richest, fullest work, by foremost British lexicographer. Detailed word histories. Inexhaustible. Do not confuse this with Concise Etymological Dictionary, which is abridged. Total of 856pp. 6½ x 9¼.
21873-2, 21874-0 Pa., Two-vol. set $12.00

A MAYA GRAMMAR, Alfred M. Tozzer. Practical, useful English-language grammar by the Harvard anthropologist who was one of the three greatest American scholars in the area of Maya culture. Phonetics, grammatical processes, syntax, more. 301pp. 5⅜ x 8½.   23465-7 Pa. $4.00

THE JOURNAL OF HENRY D. THOREAU, edited by Bradford Torrey, F. H. Allen. Complete reprinting of 14 volumes, 1837-61, over two million words; the sourcebooks for *Walden*, etc. Definitive. All original sketches, plus 75 photographs. Introduction by Walter Harding. Total of 1804pp. 8½ x 12¼.   20312-3, 20313-1 Clothbd., Two-vol. set $70.00

CLASSIC GHOST STORIES, Charles Dickens and others. 18 wonderful stories you've wanted to reread: "The Monkey's Paw," "The House and the Brain," "The Upper Berth," "The Signalman," "Dracula's Guest," "The Tapestried Chamber," etc. Dickens, Scott, Mary Shelley, Stoker, etc. 330pp. 5⅜ x 8½.   20735-8 Pa. $4.50

SEVEN SCIENCE FICTION NOVELS, H. G. Wells. Full novels. *First Men in the Moon, Island of Dr. Moreau, War of the Worlds, Food of the Gods, Invisible Man, Time Machine, In the Days of the Comet.* A basic science-fiction library. 1015pp. 5⅜ x 8½. (Available in U.S. only)
20264-X Clothbd. $8.95

ARMADALE, Wilkie Collins. Third great mystery novel by the author of *The Woman in White* and *The Moonstone*. Ingeniously plotted narrative shows an exceptional command of character, incident and mood. Original magazine version with 40 illustrations. 597pp. 5⅜ x 8½.
23429-0 Pa. $6.00

MASTERS OF MYSTERY, H. Douglas Thomson. The first book in English (1931) devoted to history and aesthetics of detective story. Poe, Doyle, LeFanu, Dickens, many others, up to 1930. New introduction and notes by E. F. Bleiler. 288pp. 5⅜ x 8½. (Available in U.S. only)
23606-4 Pa. $4.00

FLATLAND, E. A. Abbott. Science-fiction classic explores life of 2-D being in 3-D world. Read also as introduction to thought about hyperspace. Introduction by Banesh Hoffmann. 16 illustrations. 103pp. 5⅜ x 8½.
20001-9 Pa. $2.00

THREE SUPERNATURAL NOVELS OF THE VICTORIAN PERIOD, edited, with an introduction, by E. F. Bleiler. Reprinted complete and unabridged, three great classics of the supernatural: *The Haunted Hotel* by Wilkie Collins, *The Haunted House at Latchford* by Mrs. J. H. Riddell, and *The Lost Stradivarius* by J. Meade Falkner. 325pp. 5⅜ x 8½.
22571-2 Pa. $4.00

AYESHA: THE RETURN OF "SHE," H. Rider Haggard. Virtuoso sequel featuring the great mythic creation, Ayesha, in an adventure that is fully as good as the first book, *She*. Original magazine version, with 47 original illustrations by Maurice Greiffenhagen. 189pp. 6½ x 9¼.
23649-8 Pa. $3.50

UNCLE SILAS, J. Sheridan LeFanu. Victorian Gothic mystery novel, considered by many best of period, even better than Collins or Dickens. Wonderful psychological terror. Introduction by Frederick Shroyer. 436pp. 5⅜ x 8½. 21715-9 Pa. $6.00

JURGEN, James Branch Cabell. The great erotic fantasy of the 1920's that delighted thousands, shocked thousands more. Full final text, Lane edition with 13 plates by Frank Pape. 346pp. 5⅜ x 8½. 23507-6 Pa. $4.50

THE CLAVERINGS, Anthony Trollope. Major novel, chronicling aspects of British Victorian society, personalities. Reprint of Cornhill serialization, 16 plates by M. Edwards; first reprint of full text. Introduction by Norman Donaldson. 412pp. 5⅜ x 8½. 23464-9 Pa. $5.00

KEPT IN THE DARK, Anthony Trollope. Unusual short novel about Victorian morality and abnormal psychology by the great English author. Probably the first American publication. Frontispiece by Sir John Millais. 92pp. 6½ x 9¼. 23609-9 Pa. $2.50

RALPH THE HEIR, Anthony Trollope. Forgotten tale of illegitimacy, inheritance. Master novel of Trollope's later years. Victorian country estates, clubs, Parliament, fox hunting, world of fully realized characters. Reprint of 1871 edition. 12 illustrations by F. A. Faser. 434pp. of text. 5⅜ x 8½. 23642-0 Pa. $5.00

YEKL and THE IMPORTED BRIDEGROOM AND OTHER STORIES OF THE NEW YORK GHETTO, Abraham Cahan. Film *Hester Street* based on *Yekl* (1896). Novel, other stories among first about Jewish immigrants of N.Y.'s East Side. Highly praised by W. D. Howells—Cahan "a new star of realism." New introduction by Bernard G. Richards. 240pp. 5⅜ x 8½. 22427-9 Pa. $3.50

THE HIGH PLACE, James Branch Cabell. Great fantasy writer's enchanting comedy of disenchantment set in 18th-century France. Considered by some critics to be even better than his famous *Jurgen*. 10 illustrations and numerous vignettes by noted fantasy artist Frank C. Pape. 320pp. 5⅜ x 8½. 23670-6 Pa. $4.00

ALICE'S ADVENTURES UNDER GROUND, Lewis Carroll. Facsimile of ms. Carroll gave Alice Liddell in 1864. Different in many ways from final Alice. Handlettered, illustrated by Carroll. Introduction by Martin Gardner. 128pp. 5⅜ x 8½. 21482-6 Pa. $2.50

FAVORITE ANDREW LANG FAIRY TALE BOOKS IN MANY COLORS, Andrew Lang. The four Lang favorites in a boxed set—the complete *Red, Green, Yellow* and *Blue* Fairy Books. 164 stories; 439 illustrations by Lancelot Speed, Henry Ford and G. P. Jacob Hood. Total of about 1500pp. 5⅜ x 8½. 23407-X Boxed set, Pa. $15.95

HOUSEHOLD STORIES BY THE BROTHERS GRIMM. All the great Grimm stories: "Rumpelstiltskin," "Snow White," "Hansel and Gretel," etc., with 114 illustrations by Walter Crane. 269pp. 5⅜ x 8½.
21080-4 Pa. $3.50

SLEEPING BEAUTY, illustrated by Arthur Rackham. Perhaps the fullest, most delightful version ever, told by C. S. Evans. Rackham's best work. 49 illustrations. 110pp. 7⅞ x 10¾.
22756-1 Pa. $2.50

AMERICAN FAIRY TALES, L. Frank Baum. Young cowboy lassoes Father Time; dummy in Mr. Floman's department store window comes to life; and 10 other fairy tales. 41 illustrations by N. P. Hall, Harry Kennedy, Ike Morgan, and Ralph Gardner. 209pp. 5⅜ x 8½.
23643-9 Pa. $3.00

THE WONDERFUL WIZARD OF OZ, L. Frank Baum. Facsimile in full color of America's finest children's classic. Introduction by Martin Gardner. 143 illustrations by W. W. Denslow. 267pp. 5⅜ x 8½.
20691-2 Pa. $3.50

THE TALE OF PETER RABBIT, Beatrix Potter. The inimitable Peter's terrifying adventure in Mr. McGregor's garden, with all 27 wonderful, full-color Potter illustrations. 55pp. 4¼ x 5½. (Available in U.S. only)
22827-4 Pa. $1.25

THE STORY OF KING ARTHUR AND HIS KNIGHTS, Howard Pyle. Finest children's version of life of King Arthur. 48 illustrations by Pyle. 131pp. 6⅛ x 9¼.
21445-1 Pa. $4.95

CARUSO'S CARICATURES, Enrico Caruso. Great tenor's remarkable caricatures of self, fellow musicians, composers, others. Toscanini, Puccini, Farrar, etc. Impish, cutting, insightful. 473 illustrations. Preface by M. Sisca. 217pp. 8⅜ x 11¼.
23528-9 Pa. $6.95

PERSONAL NARRATIVE OF A PILGRIMAGE TO ALMADINAH AND MECCAH, Richard Burton. Great travel classic by remarkably colorful personality. Burton, disguised as a Moroccan, visited sacred shrines of Islam, narrowly escaping death. Wonderful observations of Islamic life, customs, personalities. 47 illustrations. Total of 959pp. 5⅜ x 8½.
21217-3, 21218-1 Pa., Two-vol. set $12.00

INCIDENTS OF TRAVEL IN YUCATAN, John L. Stephens. Classic (1843) exploration of jungles of Yucatan, looking for evidences of Maya civilization. Travel adventures, Mexican and Indian culture, etc. Total of 669pp. 5⅜ x 8½.
20926-1, 20927-X Pa., Two-vol. set $7.90

AMERICAN LITERARY AUTOGRAPHS FROM WASHINGTON IRVING TO HENRY JAMES, Herbert Cahoon, et al. Letters, poems, manuscripts of Hawthorne, Thoreau, Twain, Alcott, Whitman, 67 other prominent American authors. Reproductions, full transcripts and commentary. Plus checklist of all American Literary Autographs in The Pierpont Morgan Library. Printed on exceptionally high-quality paper. 136 illustrations. 212pp. 9⅛ x 12¼.
23548-3 Pa. $12.50

AN AUTOBIOGRAPHY, Margaret Sanger. Exciting personal account of hard-fought battle for woman's right to birth control, against prejudice, church, law. Foremost feminist document. 504pp. 5⅜ x 8½.
20470-7 Pa. $5.50

MY BONDAGE AND MY FREEDOM, Frederick Douglass. Born as a slave, Douglass became outspoken force in antislavery movement. The best of Douglass's autobiographies. Graphic description of slave life. Introduction by P. Foner. 464pp. 5⅜ x 8½.
22457-0 Pa. $5.50

LIVING MY LIFE, Emma Goldman. Candid, no holds barred account by foremost American anarchist: her own life, anarchist movement, famous contemporaries, ideas and their impact. Struggles and confrontations in America, plus deportation to U.S.S.R. Shocking inside account of persecution of anarchists under Lenin. 13 plates. Total of 944pp. 5⅜ x 8½.
22543-7, 22544-5 Pa., Two-vol. set $12.00

LETTERS AND NOTES ON THE MANNERS, CUSTOMS AND CONDITIONS OF THE NORTH AMERICAN INDIANS, George Catlin. Classic account of life among Plains Indians: ceremonies, hunt, warfare, etc. Dover edition reproduces for first time all original paintings. 312 plates. 572pp. of text. 6⅛ x 9¼.
22118-0, 22119-9 Pa.. Two-vol. set $12.00

THE MAYA AND THEIR NEIGHBORS, edited by Clarence L. Hay, others. Synoptic view of Maya civilization in broadest sense, together with Northern, Southern neighbors. Integrates much background, valuable detail not elsewhere. Prepared by greatest scholars: Kroeber, Morley, Thompson, Spinden, Vaillant, many others. Sometimes called Tozzer Memorial Volume. 60 illustrations, linguistic map. 634pp. 5⅜ x 8½.
23510-6 Pa. $10.00

HANDBOOK OF THE INDIANS OF CALIFORNIA, A. L. Kroeber. Foremost American anthropologist offers complete ethnographic study of each group. Monumental classic. 459 illustrations, maps. 995pp. 5⅜ x 8½.
23368-5 Pa. $13.00

SHAKTI AND SHAKTA, Arthur Avalon. First book to give clear, cohesive analysis of Shakta doctrine, Shakta ritual and Kundalini Shakti (yoga). Important work by one of world's foremost students of Shaktic and Tantric thought. 732pp. 5⅜ x 8½. (Available in U.S. only)
23645-5 Pa. $7.95

AN INTRODUCTION TO THE STUDY OF THE MAYA HIEROGLYPHS, Syvanus Griswold Morley. Classic study by one of the truly great figures in hieroglyph research. Still the best introduction for the student for reading Maya hieroglyphs. New introduction by J. Eric S. Thompson. 117 illustrations. 284pp. 5⅜ x 8½.
23108-9 Pa. $4.00

A STUDY OF MAYA ART, Herbert J. Spinden. Landmark classic interprets Maya symbolism, estimates styles, covers ceramics, architecture, murals, stone carvings as artforms. Still a basic book in area. New introduction by J. Eric Thompson. Over 750 illustrations. 341pp. 8⅜ x 11¼.
21235-1 Pa. $6.95

GEOMETRY, RELATIVITY AND THE FOURTH DIMENSION, Rudolf Rucker. Exposition of fourth dimension, means of visualization, concepts of relativity as Flatland characters continue adventures. Popular, easily followed yet accurate, profound. 141 illustrations. 133pp. 5⅜ x 8½.
23400-2 Pa. $2.75

THE ORIGIN OF LIFE, A. I. Oparin. Modern classic in biochemistry, the first rigorous examination of possible evolution of life from nitrocarbon compounds. Non-technical, easily followed. Total of 295pp. 5⅜ x 8½.
60213-3 Pa. $4.00

PLANETS, STARS AND GALAXIES, A. E. Fanning. Comprehensive introductory survey: the sun, solar system, stars, galaxies, universe, cosmology; quasars, radio stars, etc. 24pp. of photographs. 189pp. 5⅜ x 8½. (Available in U.S. only)
21680-2 Pa. $3.75

THE THIRTEEN BOOKS OF EUCLID'S ELEMENTS, translated with introduction and commentary by Sir Thomas L. Heath. Definitive edition. Textual and linguistic notes, mathematical analysis, 2500 years of critical commentary. Do not confuse with abridged school editions. Total of 1414pp. 5⅜ x 8½. 60088-2, 60089-0, 60090-4 Pa., Three-vol. set $18.50

Prices subject to change without notice.

Available at your book dealer or write for free catalogue to Dept. GI, Dover Publications, Inc., 180 Varick St., N.Y., N.Y. 10014. Dover publishes more than 175 books each year on science, elementary and advanced mathematics, biology, music, art, literary history, social sciences and other areas.